WORLDS
AWAY

Valmore Daniels

WORLDS AWAY

The Interstellar Age Book 3

Valmore Daniels

THE INTERSTELLAR AGE

Forbidden the Stars

Music of the Spheres

Worlds Away

The Complete Trilogy

For a complete list of available books, visit:

ValmoreDaniels.com

1

CHRYSALIS

Quiriguá :
Guatemala :

Long Count: 9.19.19.17.9

It had been seven days since I began my warrior's trial, and I feared I would not succeed in my quest. I would either be captured by the Q'eqchi', the northern tribe, or I would spend the remaining days of my life shamed by my failure. I would not be Subo Ak, the warrior; I would be Subo Ak, the unworthy.

The only way I could return to my people, the Ch'orti', with any dignity was to bring back a trophy.

For the past two days, I had been scouting the forests south of Quiriguá, waiting to catch one of their warriors out alone. I would kill him and take something of his to prove my victory. My hope was to find a warrior who had many kills of his own. He would have tattoos showing his conquests; his skin would be a suitable prize, and might gain me enough status to obtain a wife. I had seen Ysalane smiling at me whenever I passed near...

The Q'eqchi' warriors, however, only went out on patrol in numbers, and they never strayed from their party. They were very disciplined; it was no wonder their tribe had grown so large over the past generation.

They had invaded our lands many times in the past, killed our men or captured them for sacrifice, stolen our women, and burned our crops. My brother, Atal Ak, died from a spear wound during one such raid a year ago. Since then, I have been dreaming of joining the warrior caste and avenging my brother.

We have many story stones that tell of a time when the Q'eqchi' paid tribute to the kings of Copán, when we had been their overlords. That had ended many generations ago when the king of Quiriguá captured our last great king, Uaxaclajuun Ub'aah K'awiil, and took his head. The Q'eqchi' have harassed us for more than a hundred years since then.

Now, Copán is but a shadow of its former glory, and we struggle for our very survival. My village, east of Copán city, has seen our numbers dwindle more every year. We have suffered from poor harvests, sparse hunting, and raids from the Q'eqchi'.

One day, the Ch'orti' will become powerful again, and all tribes in the world will make the pilgrimage to Copán to offer their tribute.

It was my desire.

Before I could help restore power to my people, I had to achieve honor for myself. At this point, I would have attempted an attack on two, or even three of their warriors. I was desperate.

I decided to head east where the forest thickened. Perhaps I needed a better spot to wait for my prey. As I stood to go, I heard the snap of a branch behind me.

Spear in my hand, I turned, ready for combat. Had a warrior crept up behind me? Had I turned from the hunter into the hunted?

A laugh escaped my lips when I saw a dark-feathered turkey a distance away. It was walking through the brush, its head bobbing and jerking while it foraged.

My stomach rumbled. I had not hunted game since I arrived at Quiriguá, and I was down to the last bit of meat in my pack. If I were weakened from hunger, I would never last in a match against a single Q'eqchi' warrior, let alone two or three.

The turkey did not see me. It was my lucky day.

Silently, I lowered my spear to the ground, picked up my atlatl, and placed a long dart in the shaft.

Stepping carefully to avoid any fallen branches that would alert the turkey to my presence, I got as close as I could to the bird. Taking aim, I flung the dart at my prey, and cursed as the tip hit the dirt in front of the turkey.

It immediately took flight. In the confines of the forest, however, it didn't have enough room to get any height. Several times, it was forced to land after swerving to avoid the trunk of a tree.

I gave chase, picking up my spear and my pack as I ran after the bird. If I got close enough, I could try to throw another dart at it.

We were nearing the edge of the wooded area. I knew that once the turkey reached the plain, it could fly faster than I could run. When I saw it hit a tree with a wing, and lose balance, I knew it was my best and last opportunity.

Dropping everything except my atlatl, I quickly loaded another dart and let it fly.

This time my aim was true, and the dart hit the turkey through the upper part of its wing. It would not be able to fly from me now. Though it tried to run, the dart in its wing unbalanced it, and slowed it down.

Drawing my knife from my belt, I ran to the bird and jumped on it. My first strike missed its throat, slicing instead into the meat of its breast. My second cut found its mark, and I held the bird down as it died.

The turkey made a terrible noise in its death throes, however. Several Q'eqchi' warriors, who had been following a path through the woods, heard the sounds and ran to investigate.

I saw them and felt a moment of panic. If I stayed to fight them, they would overwhelm me. They would either kill me or drag me back to Quiriguá for sacrifice.

If I ran, I would only prove that I was a coward, and unfit to be a warrior of the Ch'orti'.

A plan came to me, and I only had a moment in which to act.

Leaving the dead turkey where it was, and the dart still sticking through its wing, I picked up my spear, hurried a distance away, and crouched behind a thick copse of bush.

The warriors would know the turkey had been killed by a hunter; they would most likely be able to identify the dart as one of Ch'orti' design. Their first thought would be that their enemy had decided to flee.

With any luck, they would split up in their search for me. I would then follow one of them. When I saw my chance, I would ambush him.

I waited, daring to raise my head above the top of the bush to see what the warriors were doing.

A few more moments passed, and I still had not heard the sounds of their pursuit. Clutching my spear in both hands, I crept out from behind the bush and searched for them. They were nowhere to be seen.

Puzzled, I returned to the spot where I had killed the turkey, careful to remain as silent as I could. The bird remained undisturbed, and I chanced to move through the woods to the path.

I could not believe my eyes when I finally spotted the four warriors. They were running back to their city. *Cowards!*

Still trying to figure out what had caused them to flee, I turned around, intending to return to the turkey and claim my dinner.

A shadow crept across the path in front of me, and I looked skyward, expecting to see an eagle or some other bird of prey circling as if it had sensed my earlier kill.

It was not a bird, however. I felt cold fear grip my bowels.

One of the story stones at Copán foretold a time when the sun would fall from the sky and burn the world.

For the span of a heartbeat, I believed it was happening right then. Then I realized it was not the sun, but an impossibly bright ball of light streaking across the afternoon sky.

I remembered one of our elders, Yax Kuk, who spoke often of the gods of the sky. On clear nights, sometimes you could see them as they traveled on the backs of firebirds. Once in my lifetime, I witnessed such an event. A thin line of light cut its way across the evening sky, as if one of the stars tried to slice through the blanket of night.

Now, however, the ball of light was much larger than the one I had seen in my youth. Instead of long tendrils of fire and smoke, there was only a faint sparkling, like cooling embers in a campfire.

Unlike the Q'eqchi' warriors, who fled in fear of the strange occurrence, I became emboldened when I realized that the object was not passing through the sky; it was going to land in the mountains to the northwest.

If it were indeed a god in his flying boat, then the first human he encountered would be assured a place of honor.

That person would become a prophet.

I had to be that person.

With the blessings of a god, I could lead the Ch'orti', and regain our rightful place as the overlords of all the tribes. I would become king. Subo Ak, savior of all the People.

Thoughts of the turkey and my empty stomach left me as I broke into a run, following the path to the god who had returned to Earth.

Patrol Ship :
Sol System :

Alex came out of the photonic state to a scene of chaos. Ah
Tabai's Sentinel ship was shaking, and an immense roaring
sound filled the passenger compartment.

A klaxon sounded from somewhere, and Alex heard a cry
from the other side of the chamber. Michael was on the floor
on his side, holding his knee. His face was contorted into a
grimace of pain. Kenny and Yaxche were still in their molded
seats, hands gripping the sides to keep from being thrown off.

The ship rocked again, and a moment later, the door melted
away. Ah Tabai stumbled inside.

"What's happening?" Kenny asked, his voice desperate.

"We ran into something that exploded and breached our
hull, perhaps a mine." Ah Tabai motioned his hand,
encompassing all of them in the room. "We have to get you to
the escape pod."

"Aren't we back in Sol System?" Alex asked as he carefully
got out of the molded chair, keeping one hand on the edge for
support.

Nodding, Ah Tabai said, "Yes. Someone was expecting
your return. The moment we arrived, we entered a minefield
of some kind. We hit one, and it disrupted our computers long

enough to prevent us from jumping back into Aetherspace."

"Kinemetic?" Michael asked. He was still on the floor, gritting his teeth, but it looked as if the pain from his fall was subsiding. He was in a sitting position.

"I don't think so," Ah Tabai said. "We have defenses against that. The explosion has damaged our hull. Our Aether Engine is offline. There is a ship approaching, and they will be on us in minutes, well before we can make repairs." He turned to Alex. "It's against protocol for us to be here; but to let an un-Emerged society have access to our technology is one of our most serious crimes. We will have to self-destruct. Our escape pod is made with very basic technology; it is your only option. You must hurry."

Kenny got completely up from his seat, went to assist Michael, and got him to his feet. "Did you try to contact the ship? They could be one of ours."

"No," Ah Tabai said. "I ran their signature through your ship's database. It is not in your records."

Alex helped Yaxche up. "It could be the same ship—or same people—who came after us four years ago." It was odd thinking about the span of time. From Alex's perspective, it had only been a day.

"If so, how did they know we'd be back?" Kenny asked.

Michael, on his feet, though favoring his hurt leg as he let himself be led out of the passenger compartment, said, "Probably doesn't matter to them. Whoever it was who attacked us before didn't want our technology; they were already developing their own. I'd guess they've been stationed out here all along with orders to intercept any ship that came out of quantum space."

"Or destroy them. Best way to have a monopoly is to eliminate the competition," Kenny said, his lips pressing together in a sour expression.

Ah Tabai showed them the way to the belly of the ship, and opened a portal to a small, cramped escape pod. It was a circular chamber, with four seats set into the outer wall facing inward.

"You aren't coming with us?" Kenny asked.

"No." Ah Tabai shook his head. "Aliah and I will attempt to return to our system in the command pod—it has a portable Aether engine similar to the one we used for Alex before. We'll try to come back with another ship—and this time, we'll be ready for an attack."

Before heading inside, Alex said, "Won't they fire on our escape pod?"

"We've programmed a trajectory into the pod to take you to the star beacon. The energy field around it should mask you from their sensors. The pod has enough air and liquid nutrients to keep you all alive for several weeks. Alex, you may begin to feel adverse effects by being on Pluto, but you aren't as sensitive as full Aethers. It won't be pleasant, but it's your best chance until we can come back for you. When our ship self-destructs, the Aether shock should disrupt the attacker's sensors for some time."

"Ah Tabai," Alex said, "thank you."

"No thanks are necessary," he said. "Just keep yourself alive until we can get back to you."

With that, Alex crawled into the escape pod and squished himself between Yaxche and Kenny, opposite Michael. Ah Tabai closed the portal behind him as they strapped themselves in.

The four men shared uneasy glances at each other in the dim light from a monitor display that showed life support levels. There weren't many controls on the pod—obviously, it wasn't designed as a navigable spacecraft.

"Who do you think it is?" Kenny asked. "The attacker, I

mean."

Michael, looking as if he were still in pain from his fall, said, "Figuring out who chased us out of Sol System four years ago is less important than the fact that they're still out here, waiting for us."

"How is that more important?" Kenny asked.

"It means things on Earth have changed. Even though NASA funding had been cut back at the time we left, they would have—at the very least—maintained an unmanned alert station out here on Pluto. The star beacon is the most significant discovery we've ever made. It's hard to believe they'd leave it abandoned. If USA, Inc. maintained a presence here, they wouldn't adopt a 'shoot first' policy. The only reason I can think of that they weren't here is that some foreign power has taken control of Plutonian space. Perhaps more than that."

"Foreign power? Wasn't it an Arab Conglomerates signal that came from that ship that chased us?" Kenny said.

"Signals can be disguised. The truth is, we have no idea who it is. All I can say is the situation on Earth must be dire."

All through the evacuation to the escape pod, and the discussion while they waited to be launched, Yaxche had remained silent.

"Are you all right?" Alex asked him.

"Ahyah," the old man said, and offered Alex a reassuring smile. "I am not used to so much excitement."

"We'll be fine." Alex hoped his words would prove true.

A small chime sounded, and they heard Ah Tabai's voice. "We're going to launch the command pod first, to distract the attackers. Once your escape pod is ejected, our ship will begin a one-minute countdown. We'll wait until the pod is near the star beacon before we enter Aetherflight."

"We're all set, here," Alex said.

A sharp rumbling sound came a few moments later, and

Alex assumed that was the command pod with Ah Tabai and Aliah.

Ah Tabai confirmed this when his voice came through the escape pod. "We're away. They're firing missiles at us, but they're far too slow. Our countermeasures have disabled them."

The four in the escape pod waited anxiously for what seemed like ages, but was more like ten seconds.

"Prepare for launch," Ah Tabai said, and the entire pod began to shake as the engines propelled them out of the ship.

The pressure suddenly increased, and Alex found himself unable to breath for a few moments until the acceleration leveled out.

"You're on your way," Ah Tabai said over the speaker. "Countdown to self-destruct has started."

As the escape pod's velocity leveled out, they lost gravity, and Alex saw Kenny go pale—many people became disoriented and nauseated in a weightless environment.

"Thirty seconds," Ah Tabai said. "There will most likely be an aftershock. You should grab on to something."

"How are you doing?" Alex asked, and then remembered that he could use his ability to find out for himself. Closing his eyes, he pushed his *sight* out.

The escape pod was hurtling toward Pluto and the *Dis Pater*—Sol System's star beacon. At their current rate, they should arrive in less than five minutes.

In the space around Pluto, the attacking ship was pursuing the command pod. Behind them, Ah Tabai and Aliah's scout ship drifted slowly away from them.

"Twenty seconds," Ah Tabai said, then his voice changed pitch. "They've fired a torpedo at us. It's not Aether-based. Their aim is off the mark. But the concussion wave has caused the main Gliesan ship to change direction."

"What?" Michael asked.

"I'm not sure..." Alex started to say. Then he saw that the attacking ship had changed course.

The Gliesan vessel drifted into another mine.

The explosion sent out enough of a shock wave to crush the command pod's hull.

"Ah Tabai!" Alex called out, but there was no answer.

In the escape pod, Alex didn't feel the aftershock of the blast, since they were already far enough away to escape the effects. When the Gliesan scout ship exploded ten seconds later, however, the concussion wave slammed against them so hard that, even in their restraints, the occupants were knocked around.

The monitor of the escape pod blinked on and off, and Alex had to turn his head as an electric spark shot out of the console.

He could feel the pod tumbling, but the only thing he could do was hold on. There was no way to control its spin.

A low moaning sound filled the chamber, but Alex couldn't tell who it was.

He tried to push his *sight* out again, but before he could focus, the escape pod struck something hard and unyielding. The impact knocked him unconscious.

3

Escape Pod :
Sol System :

Michael was the first to return to consciousness.

It took a long time for him to orient himself. There were no interior lights inside the escape pod, but he could still breathe air. He moved his leg, and pain from his bruised knee coursed up through his body. He tried to bite back a cry, but it came out anyway.

Grimacing until the pain subsided, Michael took a deep breath and reached out beside him. His hand touched Kenny's shoulder, and he gently shook the physicist.

"Kenny, are you all right?"

A low-pitched moan came out of the younger man, and when Kenny spoke, it was with obvious effort. "It's hard to breathe."

"Hold still. Don't move. If you've broken a rib, the last you want is for it to puncture your lung."

He reached out in the other direction and felt Yaxche's hair. Moving his hand down to the older man's neck, he felt for a pulse. It was there, but faint. "Yaxche?" he asked. "Are you hurt?"

Gently, he tapped the side of Yaxche's face, and then repeated his question when he felt the older man flinch.

Yaxche said, "Ahyah. I'm fine, except I think I might be blind."

"The lights are out," Michael said. He was still secured by the restraints and fumbled for the safety latch. "I can't reach Alex. Is he still unconscious?"

Michael couldn't see whether Yaxche nudged Alex or not, but a moment later, the young man groaned.

"What happened?"

Michael said, "I was going to ask you the same question."

"My head hurts. I think I banged it on something."

"Can you use your *sight* to *see* where we are?" Michael asked.

"Yeah," Alex said. "Give me a minute." A moment later, he let out a sound of despair.

"What is it?" Kenny asked.

"I can see the remains of the scout ship, and … I can't tell for sure, but it looks like the command pod is destroyed."

"Ah Tabai." Michael's voice was hoarse. "Aliah."

"I can't feel their Kinemetic signatures. I think they're dead." Alex made a moaning sound. "They risked everything to help us, and they paid with their lives."

Michael felt a deep anger at the news. More lives lost needlessly. Who were these maniacs who had attacked them without warning?

Kenny said, "So that means we're stranded here?"

"We're not that lucky," Alex replied.

"What do you mean by that?"

"We landed on Pluto. The bad news is we didn't land close enough to the star beacon for it to mask us. Our attackers are heading in this direction."

∞

They sat in silence as the long minutes stretched out.

Michael knew that even if none of them were claustrophobic by nature, being in the dark in an enclosed space could work on anyone's psyche.

"What are they doing now?" he asked, keeping his voice as calm as he could.

Alex cleared his throat. "I'm not sure. They've established an orbit, but they haven't sent a shuttle or anything. Maybe they're waiting for instructions."

"From where?" Michael asked. "If they're contacting Earth, it could be over eight hours before they get a reply. It seems like a long time to wait."

"Maybe they can't see us," Kenny said, his voice filled with hope.

Alex said, "Our sensors and lights are offline. It's possible that's enough to hide us. They might know the general area where we landed, but can't tell our exact location."

Michael let out a short, hollow laugh. "If that's the case, then maybe we should let them know we're here."

"Are you crazy?" Kenny's voice was strained. "They'll kill us."

"Maybe," Michael said, "but if we don't take that chance, we're dead, anyway."

"What do you mean?"

Instead of answering the question directly, Michael asked Alex, "Is there any way you can be sure that Ah Tabai and Aliah are dead? Maybe they just quantized themselves, like you did."

"I can still sense traces of the Kinemetic radiation around where their command pod exploded. If they quantized themselves, I should be able to detect them the same way. I'm sorry to say it: I don't think they survived."

"Then no one knows we're out here," Michael said. "It looks as if the life-support systems are working fine. We've just lost communications and lights. If we can jump-start the systems, we can send out a distress call."

"Wait a minute," Kenny said. "Don't you think we should vote on this?"

"If you have any better suggestions," Michael said, "now's the time…"

After a moment, Kenny huffed. "Fine. How do we get communications back up?"

"When we were setting up the quantum drive on the *Ultio*, Justine mentioned that she was the spark to engage the damping field and kick-start the main engines. Alex, can you use your electropathic ability to do that here?"

"I can try," Alex said. "Give me a minute. The systems here are completely unfamiliar."

They all waited in silence for a short eternity. Without warning, the cabin lights turned on, and all of them cried out in surprise. Michael, feeling like he'd been blinded, covered his eyes with his hand until he adjusted to the light.

Alex said, "I think I can trace the communications array … ah, yes, here we go."

The display on the wall lit up, showing life support.

"Oh. That was the diagnostics array," Alex said. "Still looking for communications."

While Alex continued to use his abilities to try to repair the communications system, Michael looked over at Kenny. The young physicist wasn't looking very good.

"Are you all right?" he asked.

Kenny, his face drained of color, forced a smile. "It only hurts when I breathe—at least that means I'm still alive, right?"

Alex said, "Got it. We have communications again." He glanced at Michael. "I'm broadcasting on several frequencies."

Nodding at Alex, Michael spoke in a louder voice. "Attention unidentified vessel orbiting Pluto. This is Michael

Sanderson, a Canada Corp. citizen. There are three others aboard our pod—Alex Manez and Kenny Harriman, who are also Canadians, and a Honduran translator named Yaxche. We offer our surrender."

The four men looked at one another uneasily until the speaker crackled.

"This is Lieutenant Gao of the Solan Empire. You have arrived in imperial space on a vessel of unfamiliar manufacture. According to our records, the four people you named have all been declared traitors by your respective governments. Furthermore, they have been missing for over four years and presumed dead. We must conclude you are spies for a foreign government, or you are fugitives attempting to disguise yourselves with false identities. In either case, the penalty for espionage is clear."

"We're not fugitives," Michael said. "And we're not spies. We are who we say we are. If our governments have warrants out for us, I'm sure they would appreciate it if you arrested us and turned us over. It's all a big misunderstanding. Please, we have an injured man here. He may have broken some ribs and will require medical attention."

The radio went silent for a moment. With a note of apprehension, Kenny asked, "Why aren't they replying? Does that mean they're just going to fire on us?"

Michael looked at Alex. "Can you *see* what they're doing?"

Alex closed his eyes in concentration. "They're approaching our geosynchronous position. I can't tell if they are arming weapons or not."

"They're going to blast us," Kenny said in misery.

Lieutenant Gao's voice came over the speaker. "Occupants of the escape pod. Stand by. We are sending a shuttle down to investigate. Should you not be who you said you are, you will be destroyed on the spot."

"Thank you, Lieutenant," Michael said.

The lieutenant did not reply, but a moment later, Alex told them a shuttle had been launched from the patrol ship.

Before it arrived, Michael said, "I suggest none of us say anything about Ah Tabai, Aliah, or the Kulsat."

"What do we tell them, then?" Kenny asked. "How do we explain the alien ship, or this escape pod?"

"Play dumb. Tell them we have no knowledge of what happened to us after we left Sol System."

Alex, his voice dry, added, "It worked for me last time."

∞

After latching onto the escape pod with a magnetic clasp, the shuttle lifted off Pluto and headed back to the patrol ship.

Once they were safely in the docking bay, and Alex told them that the soldiers were approaching to surround the pod, Michael said, "See if you can open the hatch."

Alex did so, and a hiss of cool air flowed into their compartment.

A voice from outside called out an order. It sounded like Lieutenant Gao. "Step out of the pod one at a time, slowly, and with your hands on top of your heads."

"Coming out," Michael called back, and got out first, walking gingerly. His knee still throbbed.

Six armed soldiers aimed their pulse rifles at Michael. As if seeing that he was, indeed, human, they all relaxed to a small degree—at least as far as Michael could tell by the expressions on their faces. They still trained their guns on him as they would a dangerous criminal.

Next out was Alex, followed by Yaxche.

Lieutenant Gao stepped forward. Though there was writing on the patch on his chest, it was in Chinese, as was the patch on the epaulet. He was clearly oriental, but he spoke English with no accent. His tone held no humor. "Where is the last one?"

Nodding toward the pod, Michael said, "He'll need help."

"Very well. You three will follow the guards to the detention area. If you do not follow instructions precisely, you will be shot without hesitation." The lieutenant pointed to two of his soldiers. "You two, retrieve the injured prisoner and bring him to the infirmary. Ensure he is fully secured."

"Thank you, Lieutenant Gao," Michael said. "We have been out of the picture for some time. Can you tell me what the Solan Empire is?"

"Be silent," the lieutenant said. "Until we receive further instructions, you will be held incommunicado. You will not speak to your guards, nor will you be given any information."

Michael wanted to watch as the two soldiers reached into the escape pod to help Kenny get out, but one of his guards pressed the barrel of his pulse rifle between his shoulder blades. The three of them headed out of the docking bay, none of them saying anything, as they'd been instructed.

Just before they exited the main doors, Michael swiveled his head around and got a brief look at Kenny. The young physicist hung limply between the two soldiers, and was possibly even unconscious. Michael wanted to race back to help, but he knew anything he did might jeopardize the cooperation of the Solan Empire soldiers—whoever they were.

∞

It was nearly nine hours later before anyone came to their cell. Michael was growing more and more worried that they hadn't heard anything about Kenny, nor had they had any indication from the stoic soldier standing guard as to what their fate would be.

Michael stood up from the long bench set into the wall of the cell when he recognized Lieutenant Gao, who was followed by two other soldiers holding handguns.

"How is he?" Michael asked, glancing nervously at the guns. "Is Kenny all right?"

"That should be the last of your concerns, Mr. Sanderson," the lieutenant said, an ominous tone in his voice.

Alex got up and stood next to Michael while Yaxche remained sitting.

Michael asked, "What do you mean by that?"

"We've received instructions from Central Command. They were explicit." With that, he made a motion with his hand to the two soldiers. Both raised their guns and pointed them at Michael and Alex.

"What are you doing?" Michael cried out. The only response he got from Lieutenant Gao was an amused smile.

The lieutenant nodded at his men.

Alex yelled, "No!"

The soldiers opened fire.

4

Kulsat Ship :
Centauri System :

When Justine had quantized herself in the past, she'd been completely aware of her surroundings.

Not so this time.

Her consciousness only returned to her when she materialized out of the quantized state—through no action of her own. It took her several seconds to remember what had happened to her.

The *Ultio*.

Someone, or something, on the Kulsat ship had scanned her with the *sight* and then, against her will, transformed her into quanta.

… And then what?

Her thoughts were thick; she had trouble concentrating. Where was she?

She opened her eyes to an all-encompassing blanket of darkness. There was no Kinemetic radiation left in her body; she could not use its influence to sense her surroundings.

Panic surged through her, and she fought back a scream. She had to keep her head.

Though she was blind, she had other senses.

She could breathe; therefore, there was oxygen. It smelled

musky and a little stale. It reminded her of being in a large industrial complex with climate control.

Straining her ears, she could hear the echo of her breathing; that meant there were walls, and she was in an enclosed space. A prison?

Under her back was a hard floor, cold to the touch. Tapping it with a fingernail produced a high-pitched metallic sound.

Extending her arms around in a fan-like motion, her hands did not come in contact with any walls or other objects in her immediate vicinity. She reached above her and felt no resistance in that direction.

Carefully, she rolled to her stomach, drew her legs under her, and raised herself to her knees. Though her muscles were stiff and sore, she didn't need much effort to push herself up. The gravity level was about half of Earth normal.

She moved her arms around in a circular motion, searching for a wall or ceiling.

"Hello?" she said. Her voice came back to her sounding small and frightened, but there was no reply.

Stretching one hand out in front of her, Justine crawled forward on her knees. She needed to know the limitations of her prison cell, if that were, indeed, where she was.

Her fingers came up against a wall, and she let out a small grunt at the sudden discovery. The surface of the wall was smooth and cool, but unlike the floor, when she tapped her nail against it, the reverberation sounded more like glass than metal.

Rapping on it with her knuckles, she called out. "Hello. Is there anyone there?"

No answer except the echo of her own voice.

She used the glass wall as support and pulled herself to her feet. Reaching up as high as she could, even standing on the tips of her toes, she could not feel a ceiling.

Keeping her hand firmly on the wall, she moved to her left until she came to a corner. The adjoining wall was made of the same glass-like material.

Soon, Justine made a complete circuit of her cell. The room she was in was a cube, each wall at least three meters. She assumed the ceiling was at least a similar height. Although she couldn't reach it, when she was near one corner, she could feel a hiss of oxygen coming from above her.

Was she a prisoner of the Kulsat? Was she on their ship? The hull had been made of Kinemet. She'd sensed that before they abducted her. There had to be some dampening around her, however, because she could not sense any radiation.

Alex, Michael, Kenny, Yaxche! Had they been abducted as well? Killed?

Her military training told her that there was a possibility she would be tortured for information. She remembered the story Alex had told them moments before the alien ship had appeared before them.

The Kulsat wanted to find the legacy left behind by the Grace, which they believed was in a pre-Emerged system. The Sentinel who had left the message for Alex had told them the Kulsat would not hesitate to destroy anything that got in their way.

Justine knew they would question her about her home world: where it was, what level of technology they had, and any other information that would provide them with a tactical advantage. Now that they'd become aware of humanity, it would only be a matter of time before the Kulsat investigated the system.

Earth would not stand a chance against a species who had the level of technology the Kulsat possessed—and for all Justine knew, what she'd seen might only be a small portion of their capabilities.

During her four-year journey to the Centauri system, Justine had been fully conscious in her quantized state. Something during the Kinemetic conversion had altered her body's chemistry in a permanent way.

One of the other major side effects was that she retained information. She could recall the text of every book she'd ever read. Her mind was a storehouse of knowledge that an enemy would be eager to pillage.

Again, she felt her heart rate increase. It wasn't the thought of torture that frightened her; it was the thought that she wouldn't be able to withstand their interrogation techniques. If they broke her, she would essentially be giving up her entire world to the enemy. She didn't know if she could live with that … if she survived.

She couldn't let her imagination get the better of her. Her isolation and the fear of the future were playing with her emotions. Willing herself to be calm, she took a deep breath, and then another. With her back against one of the walls, she sat down and waited.

Although she'd been conscious for only a few minutes, she had no idea how long it had been since she'd been abducted from the *Ultio*. Hours? Days? For all she knew, they could have kept her in the quantized state for years, and there would be no physical evidence to prove otherwise.

She also did not know how long they planned to keep her in the cell. Certainly, it was not set up for long-term confinement. Though she was not looking forward to it, she knew whatever the Kulsat planned to do her, she had to keep all the information stored in her mind from them.

∞

She didn't have to wait very long.

Twelve minutes after she'd regained consciousness, she became aware of another Kinemetic presence nearby.

With her *sight*, she realized that the damping field was not around her cell, which was in a very large room. There was a barrier dividing the room itself from the rest of the ship.

Alex? was her first thought. Had they captured him as well? He was the only other human who had been through the Kinemetic process—though his transformation had not been complete.

When she'd been on Lucis Observatory, she'd been able to recharge herself just by being close to dormant Kinemet. The new presence gave off enough radiation that some of it leaked into her. It wasn't enough for her to quantize herself, but she regained some of her ability to *see*, though in a severely diminished capacity.

It was as if someone had turned on a very dim spotlight. Outside the confines of her cell, at least twenty feet away, a form took shape in her mind's eye.

Just as her hopes started to rise, they plummeted as the presence came closer.

What she *saw* made her stomach clench.

It was not human.

The creature had a large, bulbous head that bore the rough shape of a spade. Two protuberances on either side of its head held large eyes. Instead of a torso, eight long tentacle-like arms, connected at their base by a membranous web, extended out. The alien resembled a cephalopod.

From the top of its head to the end of its arms, it was less than half the height of an average human. She had no way of figuring out what gender the Kulsat was, or even if it had a gender, but in her mind, she thought of it as male.

So this is a Kulsat...

At first, she thought the creature was hovering, or floating somehow. Then his arms expanded and contracted, propelling the alien closer to her prison cell, and she realized he was swimming.

The Kulsat must have a water-based physiology. Was the inside of the alien ship completely filled with water?

That meant that if she were to break the glass of her terrarium, water would pour in and drown her.

In her mind, she'd been preparing for a bipedal alien species, but the realization of how different the Kulsat were from humans came as a shock.

The alien swam closer to Justine's tank, and as he did so, her *sight* grew marginally stronger. While her prison was a perfect cube, the room in which it was situated was far more complicated.

It looked like a complex laboratory, with dozens of open-faced cupboards on the walls. She couldn't identify several large constructs. Tubes extended from them into the ceiling.

There were three long tables. Various objects that could have been tools, containers, or other scientific apparatuses were strewn over their surfaces. Short vertical walls lined the edges, and Justine realized that they were there to prevent anything on the table from falling off—when the alien moved past, his motion created a wake in the water. A number of items shifted position.

When the alien reached Justine's prison, he extended one tentacle to what looked like a control panel attached to the outside wall of the cell.

Though Justine had not absorbed enough Kinemetic radiation to quantize herself, or manipulate any electric current in the area, her *sight* was enough for her to start making out details, rather than seeing rough shapes.

At the end of the Kulsat's tentacle were several wormlike fingers. With these, he touched the control panel in a pattern.

A moment later, a mechanical voice spoke, the sound coming through the glass muted and partially distorted.

"Hello."

Justine flinched, then got hold of herself. She looked at the Kulsat.

"What do you mean, 'hello'?" She slapped her hand against the glass wall, all the anger and fear she'd been suppressing coming out. "Who the hell are you? Why did you kidnap me? What have you done with my friends?" When the alien did not respond, she asked, "What are you going to do to me?"

The alien extended his arm to the control panel again, as if typing.

"What do you mean hello who the hell are you why did you kidnap me what have you done with my friends what are you going to do to me."

Justine took a step back. The alien had mimicked her words.

She asked, "How do you know my language?"

The alien typed. "My do not have language. My have to *do* language."

He motioned to a spot between his eye and one of his arms, and Justine put her hand on her neck near the corresponding area. Her fingers felt a small rectangular piece of metal attached to her collar. A transmitter? The control panel attached to her tank must be a linguistic computer. Everything she'd said must have gone into it and been analyzed. The computer had already interpreted basic grammatical structure based on the few sentences she'd spoken.

While Justine did not want to give the Kulsat any information, she understood the need for communication. Perhaps she would be able to negotiate a treaty between the Kulsat and Earth. Then there would be no need for an invasion.

She started small. With her enhanced memory, she could

recall the very first books she'd read as a child. Even without corresponding images to associate with the words or phrases, the alien's computer should be able to build a rudimentary language database.

Taking a deep breath to focus, Justine spoke, beginning with a number of the simpler titles, and moving up to some of her favorite children's books, including *Peter Pan.* By the time was she was on the fifth chapter of that classic, the alien interrupted her.

"You are able."

"Able?" Justine asked. "To do what?"

The Kulsat typed on his console. "You are able to be well."

"Am I hurt?" Justine asked. "No. I am not hurt."

"You are to be not expired? To be continuous?"

Justine struggled to understand the alien's meaning. "Yes, I'll live." She took a breath to illustrate. "Who are you? What is your name?"

"I am being the science leader."

Justine asked, "What do you want from me? What are you going to do to me?"

The alien did not type a reply immediately. It seemed to consider her question. Finally, it reached out to the computer again.

"You are to be cooperating. You are to be giving your knowledge to us. Then you are to be expiring."

5

Sierra de las Minas :
Guatemala :

Long Count: 9.19.19.17.9

With thoughts of glory, both for myself and for my people, I watched as the god completed his journey across the sky and toward the mountains. I fixed the spot where he landed in my mind, and then gathered my packs and my weapons and broke into a slow jog.

I was aware that I was going further into enemy territory the nearer I got to the mountains. To the north, on the other side of the mountains, was Lake Izabal, where many Q'eqchi' villages made their homes. Copán was two days' south through the highlands. If I got into trouble, there would be no help for me.

It would take me the better part of the day to get to the area where the god had come down. I knew, once I had left the relative safety of the forested areas south of Quiriguá, any patrol could spot me easily as I traveled across the river valley toward the mountains.

If anyone else had seen the god, then they might come to investigate. However, they would have to discuss the venture with their leaders before they could organize. For the time being, I had an advantage, if I could get there first.

Halfway there, I stopped beside a stream to drink and to eat the last of my rations, then continued across the valley.

I reached the base of the mountains just as the sun started to dip below the horizon.

I knew I was close. The god had landed about a quarter of the way up from the base of the mountain. It was slower going, picking my way up the face. A few times I stopped to catch my breath and see if any of the Q'eqchi' were following. From where I was, I could see the entire plain to the east. If I strained, I imagined I could see clear to the great ocean.

Night was falling, and if I didn't hurry, I might lose my sense of direction in the dark. Pushing myself, I climbed the rest of the way.

I expected something grand when I arrived. In my imagination, I pictured a tall and imposing god sitting on a glowing throne of jade, wearing a feathered headdress that would put anything I had ever seen to shame. Jaguars would lie at his feet, and a great eagle would perch on one shoulder— or perhaps it would be a firebird, flexing its blazing wings.

Instead, what I saw confused me.

There was no throne, no jaguars, no eagles, and no firebirds.

There was a short boat before me, and it was tilted on its side. A canopy covered the top of it, and it was open. The vessel was made from a material unlike anything I had ever seen. The shell seemed to be in motion, like the running water of a stream. Across the surface, it was as if an artist had created a living painting of bright and glowing colors. I found myself captivated by it.

I heard a faint sound and stepped around the mysterious boat.

A god did not wait there for me. Instead, I saw what looked

like a plump young boy. He lay on his side, curled up, arms wrapped around him, with his back to a tree.

Once I got close enough to him, I froze.

His body had no hair, and his pale white skin was leathery, and mottled with blue patches.

His face was unlike any I had ever seen before. The top of his head was shorter than normal, and he had a thick, bony ridge starting where his eyebrows should have been, and wrapped around the sides of his bald head and to the back of his neck. I couldn't see any earlobes, but there was a small bump where his ears should have been. His eyes were large and spaced wide apart over high cheekbones. Although his nose was extremely small, his mouth and jaw were long and beaklike. Overall, he bore a slight resemblance to a turtle without a shell.

"You must help me," the creature said, and he spoke as if he were native to my village.

Overcoming my shock at his strange appearance, I rushed forward to see what was wrong.

He opened his slatted eyes and looked at me. "How are you called?" From this distance, I noticed that the words he mouthed did not match the sounds that came out.

"I am Subo Ak of the Ch'orti'," I said. "Who are you? *What* are you?"

"You may call me Ekahua. The people of the sky call us the Grace, though my people call ourselves Xtôti."

"Are you a god?" I asked.

He shook his head. "I am not. My people once came from a world much like this one."

I saw that he was having trouble breathing, and asked, "Are you injured?"

"I am dying," Ekahua said. "I will not live long on the surface of your planet; it is destroying me. My ship is too damaged to take me back to the sky."

"Will anyone from your tribe come to help you?"

He said, "There are only a few of my people left, and they are very far away. There will be no help from them. No one knows I am here.

"But there are other star tribes who might come. They cannot be allowed to find my sky boat or me. It is too dangerous for them. You must help me."

I glanced at his ship. "How?"

"Inside my boat there is a—" He said something then that sounded like stones grinding together. "It is a box with many square shapes, with many drawings on them."

Leaving Ekahua where he was, I strode back to the vessel. I felt the hairs of my arms stand up when I leaned close to look inside. I didn't want to touch the surface. I feared it would burn me, or that it would suck me into its swirling current.

There was a long, curved seat built into the ship. In front of the seat was a flat box with many smaller boxes outlined within, some larger than others. In the center of the box was a square that contained glowing, moving shapes.

"Touch the shape that has a picture of a circle with a line through the bottom edge."

I looked over the boxes until I saw one that fit the description. Once again, I hesitated. This could be a test or a trap. I didn't know what would happen if I did as Ekahua instructed. He said he was not a god; therefore, I could disobey him without risking any divine wrath. However, he was obviously very powerful; he could sail through the sky in this flying boat.

I remembered my people and how we were being slowly overrun by the Q'eqchi'.

"If I help you, will you help me? Will you help us defeat our enemies, who kill our men and steal our women? My village is near Copán. It was once a great and beautiful city, but our

34

numbers grow smaller every season. We need help, as you do."

He said, "My very presence here is a danger to the future of this world, much greater than the conflict with your neighboring tribes. Having knowledge of me, your entire world is at risk."

I didn't understand what he was talking about, and it seemed he grew sadder.

"I have no weapons to give you," he said. "But I can give you a gift, Subo Ak."

"What gift?"

"I will teach you the Song of the Stars. Perhaps you will pass it on to your children and grandchildren."

"A song?" I asked.

"There is great power to be had in the song."

I was doubtful, but at the very least, I would have something to bring back to my village. A new song would not bring me as much honor as the skin of a Q'eqchi' warrior, but perhaps the song would gain me a level of respect with the elders. It was always good to be in their graces.

I nodded. "I will accept that bargain."

"Press the shape marked with the circle and line," Ekahua said.

I did so, and jumped back when a plate on the back of the boat opened. I stepped over to the opening and looked in. The inside of the boat resembled a mass of roots wrapped around a solid block of dark polished stone.

"There are twelve cords on the top of the—" He said another word I did not understand. I pointed to the top of the block, and when Ekahua nodded, I touched one of the root-like cords.

"It will be difficult, but you must pull them all out, and then put them back in different spots. You will need to work quickly. The ship will—" When I glanced at him, he said, "The ship will become like fire and burn. Within moments, it will turn to light and disappear."

Shocked, I pulled my fingers away from the cords. Suddenly, I became uncertain. The task sounded dangerous, and I did not want to be hurt or killed for a song.

"No harm will come to you, Subo Ak, if you are fast, and so long as the canopy keeps the cords shadowed from the sun. Once you have finished, return to me here where you will be safe."

I considered the device once more. There must be great power inside those roots if they could destroy such a wondrous boat so quickly.

Taking a deep breath, I plucked the first root out of the block. I felt an odd sensation in my hand, as if a small insect were crawling across my palm. A quick look showed me that my hand was empty. I peered into the hole left by the root and saw a small glowing object, no bigger than a grain of sand, resting in the gap.

Mindful that I had to work quickly, I yanked the remainder of the roots out.

"Hurry," Ekahua said, and feeling the urgency in his words, I replaced the roots into the openings in a random order.

"Good, now run back here."

Just as I started to turn, I noticed that one of the glowing grains of sand was resting in a nook partway down the polished block of stone. It must have fallen out when I pulled the roots.

I snatched the pebble up between my finger and thumb, and raced back to Ekahua as quickly as I could.

He was watching the boat, not me, and did not see when I slid the grain of sand inside one of the loose beads on my belt.

I turned to see what was becoming of the boat. At first, there was no change in the vessel.

A high-pitched sound came from it, soft at first, then

louder. The swirls on the surface of the boat became frantic, and the vessel began to vibrate. The canopy snapped closed with a loud bark, and the plate on the back dropped back into place.

The ship began to shine bright like the sun.

"Shield your eyes," Ekahua said, and I put my hand over my face, looking at the vessel between the cracks of my fingers.

The sound became louder, and just when I thought I couldn't handle it any longer, the boat burst into thousands of flecks of light. Each of those flecks burnt out within moments.

When I took my hand away from my face, I saw that the boat had completely disappeared. I cautiously approached the spot where it had rested, and could not see any sign that it had ever existed.

"Thank you, Subo Ak," Ekahua said.

I felt a raindrop fall on my cheek and looked up into the evening sky. Clouds had gathered, and we would soon be caught in a downpour.

"We need to find shelter," I said.

"I do not have the strength to rise; you must carry me."

I picked Ekahua up, and he was far lighter than I had expected.

When I had climbed the side of the mountain earlier, I had passed a cliff where I had seen a small crevice. I didn't know how deep the crevice went, but I hoped it would be large enough for us to fit inside.

At the very least, it would keep the rain off Ekahua, and we would be hidden in case the Q'eqchi' warriors sent a scouting party this way.

6

Unknown Station :
Sol System :

To Alex's complete surprise, he woke up.

The last memory he had was of the Solan Empire soldiers firing at them. In retrospect, he realized they'd been shot with tranquilizers rather than bullets or ion pulses.

Opening his eyes, he looked around. He was in an infirmary, along with the other three. They were all hooked up to medical equipment and life support. An oxygen mask pressed against his mouth, and he felt the pinch of an IV needle in his arm feeding him nutrients.

Michael and Yaxche were still unconscious, but Alex saw that Kenny was coming to. A soft moan escaped the physicist's lips, muffled by his own mask, and he moved his head in quick, jerky motions.

Alex recognized the signs of bio stasis. Some people did not come out of it as well as others. NASA had experimented with the technique in the past, inducing a state similar to a medical coma in their astronauts on deep-space missions, but had discontinued the practice after determining the long-term effects were potentially harmful, ranging from muscle atrophy to dementia.

How long has they been in stasis? It was apparent the Solan

Empire soldiers had decided it would be easier to put their prisoners to sleep for the trip, rather than deal with them. Depending on how bad Kenny's injuries were, he might have actually benefited from the long sleep, giving his bones time to knit.

Alex had a gnawing feeling deep in his stomach. He hadn't eaten solid food in who knew how long; he was suddenly famished. Quelling the hunger for the time being, he closed his eyes and concentrated. Where were they?

Pushing his *sight* out, he was shocked to discover that they were no longer on the patrol ship that had attacked them.

He surveyed their immediate surroundings. They were in a large station, the design of which was not familiar to him. In passing, he sensed there were more than a thousand people on the station. It wasn't until he looked beyond the edges of the complex that he realized they were nowhere near Pluto.

From the moment Alex had been exposed to Kinemet on Macklin's Rock, he'd been able to hear the planets—the Music of the Spheres, as Yaxche called it. Every celestial body had a unique combination of forces—radiation, gravity, spin, mineral composition, and chemical makeup. Over the past several years, Alex had been able to identify the planets by their individual frequencies. With an odd feeling, he realized they were in orbit between the inner asteroid belt and Mars.

Based on ion pulse engine technology, it would have taken them four months to traverse the distance. That didn't seem plausible to Alex; he should have suffered far worse aftereffects from the medical stasis in that case. At the very least, he would have had significant weight loss in that time, and though he was acutely hungry, he didn't feel much slimmer than before.

Waking up must have triggered a sensor. He pulled his *sight* back as he heard a door open in the infirmary, and footsteps approaching.

Turning his head, he saw an unfamiliar man in a white lab coat coming toward him. Middle-aged, with a pronounced aquiline nose and a balding pate, the doctor smiled at Alex.

"Ah, I see our patients are starting to wake up."

Alex tried to rise, but couldn't even prop himself up on his elbows. Thick restraints around his arms and ankles held him to the bed.

"Oh, you mustn't try to move around until we can be sure you haven't suffered any muscle damage from your trip." The doctor removed the oxygen mask.

Alex tried to speak. With his dry throat, the words came out as a croak. He moved his tongue around to moisten his mouth, and tried again. "How long have we been in stasis?"

The doctor waited patiently for Alex to finish the question before answering. "Two weeks, my boy."

"Two...?"

The doctor smiled wider as he went to the other three patients and removed their masks as well. "Yes. We've made a few advances since you were last among us."

Kenny had come fully awake, and seemed to have overcome his reaction to the stasis. "Who are you?" the physicist asked.

"Pardon my manners. I am Doctor Naysmith." He went over to the diagnostic computer beside Kenny and looked over the readout. "Ah, good. It looks as if you are making a full recovery. Your ribs will still feel tender for a while, but give it another week or two, and you'll be right as rain."

"I think he meant, who are all of you?" came the question from Michael. "Who are you people? Where are we?"

"As I said," the doctor replied, a cheery note to his voice, "quite a bit has changed in the past four years, and my job is *not* to bring you up to speed. I'm just here to make sure you will be fit for an audience."

"An audience?" Alex asked. "With who?"

"With the Emperor, of course."

"Emperor?" Alex realized he was simply repeating everything as a question, and felt completely in the dark.

"Rest assured," Doctor Naysmith said, "all your questions will be answered in time. For now, if you'll permit me, I will go over your diagnostics and ensure you are all healthy. Do not stress about things which are beyond your control."

As if by unspoken consensus, the four of them pressed the doctor no further, and let him go about his business, reading scans and interpreting the output from the diagnostic computers. When he was finished, the doctor offered a bright smile to all of them, as if he'd accomplished a great feat.

"I will inform His Majesty of your full recovery. Have a pleasant day."

With that, the doctor left the four of them alone in the room. The overhead lights dimmed, leaving them in semi-darkness.

"What the hell is going on?" Kenny asked.

Michael said, "We've obviously stumbled into the middle of something big. We need more information. Alex, do you know where we are?"

Alex nodded, then realized that the others might not be able to see him. "Yes. We're on an asteroid mining and processing station. I'm not sure which station, though—it could be Chinese; I don't know their characters. It's in a solar orbit inside the inner belt."

Michael asked, "In line with Mars' orbit?"

"Yes."

"It's the Qin Station, named after the first Emperor of China, the one who initiated construction of the Great Wall."

Kenny said, "Emperors! Do you think there's been a civil

war in China? Did they overthrow the communist party and resurrect the imperial dynasties?"

"It's a possibility," Michael said. "What concerns me is that they've apparently managed to supplant USA, Inc.'s presence on Pluto. I know, when we left, things were dicey back home, but how bad could it have gotten?"

"So what's the plan?"

"For the moment," Michael said, "it looks as if we have to take the doctor's advice. It's out of our hands. Once we've met this Emperor, whoever he is, then we'll know more." He added in a lower voice, "I would suggest that we all continue to be extremely discreet. When we meet this Emperor, let me do the talking."

Alex said, "Fine by me."

"Me, too," Kenny said. He turned his head to the other bed. "Yaxche. You haven't said much. Are you all right?"

"Ahyah," the old man said. "My stomach is upset. I'm a little dizzy."

"That's probably because of the bio stasis," Michael said. "It will most likely pass in a few hours. It looks like we all have to play the waiting game, anyway."

Alex couldn't just lie there and do nothing. He still had enough Kinemetic radiation flowing through him to continue to use his *sight,* so he began to search Qin Station.

For the most part, the station was much like any other mining station, populated with engineers, miners, pilots, administrators, supervisors, and technicians of all the disciplines required to keep the operation going. Expecting a mostly Chinese population, Alex was a little surprised to find an even representation from all Earth cultures.

The question remained: whoever this Emperor was, would he be in a position to defend Sol against the Kulsat? However much power he'd accumulated, it wouldn't matter if the Kulsat wiped them all out.

While he searched, Alex became aware of an area of the station where his senses could not penetrate. The moment he got close, it was as if he hit a wall.

A Kinemetic damper surrounded the large area, which could have been rooms, offices, or labs, for all Alex knew.

After all his effort, Alex didn't have much more information than when he started. It looked as if they would have to follow the doctor's advice after all, and wait.

∞

It was nearly twelve hours later when a squad of armed soldiers entered the infirmary, accompanying the doctor.

"Good news," Doctor Naysmith said, "the Emperor will see you now. First, however, we need to get you all cleaned up. Once I remove the stasis equipment, you'll have one hour to acclimate yourselves. We've kept gravity at two-thirds on the station, so it should be easier for you to get your feet. No doubt, you all are feeling hunger pains. It's been a while since you've had solid food, so we'll provide you with a nutrient paste for today. Your stomachs should be back to normal by tomorrow. Now, I hope you will all give me your complete cooperation."

Alex frowned. Having spent two weeks lying on a bed, he wasn't sure he could offer any resistance if he wanted to. Though the bio stasis kept muscle tone up with electrotherapy, all four of them would have the physical responsiveness of newborns for at least a while.

Without waiting for a reply, the doctor began to shut down the remaining bio machines. He unhooked Yaxche from his IV first, and unlatched his restraints. With the help of one of the soldiers, he assisted him into a sitting position.

"How are you feeling?" the doctor asked.

Yaxche nodded. "Like an old man."

With a short, polite laugh, Doctor Naysmith said, "Private Lund will help you to do some stretching exercises."

The doctor signaled one of the other soldiers to assist him with Kenny, following the same procedures. He got Michael up next, and Alex last.

When all four of them could walk around unassisted, the doctor motioned toward a door on the other side of the infirmary. They followed him into the next room.

"There are showers here," the doctor said, "as well as toiletries and clothing. I will return in half an hour to check on your progress. If you require assistance, any of the guards will be more than happy to help." The soldiers entered the room behind them. It looked like they weren't going to have any privacy.

Turning on his heel, the doctor hurried out of the infirmary, and left the four prisoners to put themselves together.

In silence, Alex and the others cleaned up, showering, shaving and getting dressed. The clothes were simple jumpsuits with black leather boots. The epaulets had the sigil of the Solan Empire on them.

When the doctor finally returned, he gave them all a conciliatory nod of approval.

"Gentlemen, my purpose has been served. Thank you for your time. Please follow these soldiers; they will take you to your audience. Have a nice day."

Alex automatically said, "Thank you." Kenny looked at him and lifted an eyebrow as if asking why he was being polite to their captor.

They all exited the infirmary. The doctor went down the hall in one direction, and the rest of them headed in the other.

As they went, several of the station's residents looked at

them curiously, but no one spoke.

Reaching the end of the hall, they stopped at an elevator, and got in once the doors opened. One soldier tapped a button for the top floor, and Alex remembered that the area surrounded by the Kinemetic damper was there.

He felt the growing anticipation as they approached the barrier his senses could not penetrate.

The moment the elevator went past the damping field, Alex's senses were overwhelmed by the sheer quantity of Kinemet stored on that level. There was enough to power hundreds of quantum ships. It was more Kinemet than USA, Inc. and Canada Corp. had mined in ten years.

The overwhelming radiation made him reel. He was so distracted by the sensation that he hadn't thought to use his senses to see if there were any people there.

It was only when the elevator doors opened that he realized there was a large welcoming party waiting for them.

He hung his mouth open in shock when the Emperor of Sol System, surrounded by a dozen armed soldiers, spoke to him.

"It's been a long time, Alex."

7

PRC Penal Station :
Earth-Sun Lagrange Three :

During the latter third of the last century, several observational stations had been put into orbit in the Lagrange Three point, on the opposite side of the Sun from the Earth. These stations were designed to forecast sunspots, flares and coronal ejections, giving advance warning of solar disturbances.

At one time, quite a few of the stations had been populated, but as it turned out, it was such an unpopular assignment—there was a psychological effect of never being in a direct line of communication with Earth, since the Sun interfered with most radio signals—that the world's governments had abandoned their efforts there, and only maintained the unmanned stations. All except one.

That orbital, built by the People's Republic of China, had been converted to a penal station for those criminals the government decided could not be rehabilitated: serial killers, traitors, drug lords, terrorists, human traffickers, and war criminals. Since the Chinese government had abolished capital punishment, they decided this was the next-best thing.

There were no guards, and the inmates themselves were charged with the maintenance and operation of the station as part of their sentence. Should the convicts fail to organize, it would be their own undoing.

The only contact the penal station had with Earth was the monthly transport—a military PRC warship—which brought supplies, equipment, and new prisoners. Sensors all over the outside of the station would broadcast an EPS alert to the government of China via relay satellites should any unauthorized vessel approach the station.

This station was where Chow Yin, convicted of nearly every capital crime in the Chinese justice system, was sentenced to spend the rest of his days.

Chow Yin wasted no time, and began to plot his escape from the moment he embarked on the military transport to the penal colony. On Luna Station, he'd built a criminal empire in a very simple, but effective manner, and now applied the technique in his current situation.

The first day on the military transport, he sized up the four other prisoners. There was Tza, a heavily muscled opium smuggler; Huan, convicted of espionage; Sang, who—if the newsvids could be believed—was a serial killer who had murdered more than forty women over the past twelve years; and Sian, a frail young man who had somehow managed to hack into China's largest bank, where he'd worked, and embezzle close to a half-billion yuans.

The cargo bay of the transport was magnetically sealed, and that's where the five of them would spend the fourteen-day journey to the penal station. There was no need for guards, since there was no possible way any of the prisoners could breach the hold's security system.

Four long tables made from metal were set up along one wall of the bay, on the opposite side from the six sleeping cots, which were little more than sheets of canvas wrapped around a plastic frame. Those were the only furnishings in the area, except for the one lavatory set into the farthest corner of the hold.

At mealtimes, a dumbwaiter opened in one wall to reveal trays of food on paper plates. They were not provided with utensils, so the prisoners were only able to use their fingers to feed themselves.

Even in the low gravity, Chow Yin's legs were all but useless. Having spent months on Earth during the trial, his condition had worsened until the point when he required the constant use of a molded plastic wheelchair.

He expected to become the first and obvious target of one of the other prisoners, but to his surprise, Sian was the focus of Tza's first attempt at extortion.

At the first meal, Chow Yin held back and observed. Sian got up before anyone else and headed over to the dumbwaiter. Without hesitation, he grabbed a plate and made his way to the tables.

Tza, instead of going to the dumbwaiter to get his meal, approached Sian.

"You're the runt of the litter," he said. "You don't need as much as the rest of us."

With that, he backhanded Sian, knocking the smaller man to the ground, and picked up the plate.

"You can have my scraps, if there are any left," he said in a snarl, heading to the dumbwaiter and grabbing another plate.

The big drug lord paused a moment, glancing at Chow Yin. "You got something to say, cripple?"

Shaking his head slowly, Chow Yin remained where he was, still waiting. Moments later, Sang and Huan decided to split Chow Yin's plate before he even approached to get it. Both smirked at him as they divided their spoils.

Only after Tza, Sang, and Huan had eaten did Chow Yin approach Sian.

Shaking and looking miserable, the young computer hacker glanced up at Chow Yin. His eye was already swelling up. "He would have killed me if I fought back."

"Of course he would have," Chow Yin said.

"Next time I'll be smart like you, and let them go first."

Shaking his head, Chow Yin said, "No, next time you will go first again, except you will get a plate for me as well."

With a look of horror at the thought, Sian said, "That's suicide."

"Trust me," Chow Yin said, and wheeled himself away to the farthest table, positioning himself at it as if waiting to be served.

It was several hours later, when the dumbwaiter once again sounded that a meal was being delivered, that Sian glanced at Chow Yin, who nodded confidently.

Tza, seeing Sian get up and approach the panel first, laughed and said to the others, "Do you believe this? Some people never learn."

Chow Yin, still at the farthest table, waited for Sian to bring him his meal.

Sian, sweating and shaking in fear, grabbed two plates the moment the door panel opened, and hurried over to Chow Yin's table.

Tza guffawed at the action, and slowly stood up. He put his fist in his hand and cracked his knuckles.

"Watch this," he said, and lumbered over to Chow Yin and Sian. He stood over the two, as if deciding which of them to punish first.

Chow Yin pushed his plate a centimeter toward Tza. "We were foolish to try to take what is rightfully yours," he said, his words obviously surprising both Sian and Tza. "Please accept our apologies."

"Damn right, it's mine," Tza said, and reached down to grab

the plate.

Tza's eyes bulged when Chow Yin casually flicked his hand out and stabbed the smuggler in the neck with a short shiv, slicing into the carotid artery.

Both the body and the wheels of Chow Yin's wheelchair were made of plastic. For the past few hours, Chow Yin had loosened one plastic axle a few centimeters, and snapped it off. He had spent the rest of the time rubbing the shiv against the bottom of the metal table, sharpening the point.

It was obvious Tza could not figure out what had happened. As the opium smuggler fell to the deck, clutching at his neck and trying to stem the flow of blood, Chow Yin casually took his plate back and began to eat.

A biosensor detected Tza's condition, and an alarm sounded. By the time the soldiers entered the hold to assess the situation, Tza was dead.

Though the guards did not seem to express any outrage at the death of a known criminal, they had to follow protocol, and the remaining prisoners were secured to their cots for the remainder of the trip. From that point on, they were only released one at a time for meals and biological needs.

The restrictions did not matter to Chow Yin; he'd already achieved his goal. By the time the military transport arrived at the penal station, the remaining prisoners had sworn complete allegiance to him.

∞

For the next twelve years, Chow Yin did not simply rule the cadre of criminals in the penal station. He enforced a strict regimen of education on them. Doing what the justice system could not, he turned these criminals into productive soldiers in his burgeoning empire. He found out what each inmate's unique talents were, and schooled them on how to use those abilities more effectively. Whenever a transport came, he would sort through the newly arriving prisoners and indoctrinate them to his cause.

No matter how much control he had, however, he could not tip his hand to the outside world. Whenever the military inspectors arrived, they found what they'd always come to expect: a typical prison environment, the station maintained to its minimum standards, and the occasional dead body—if the soldiers reported back that everything was perfect, that would arouse suspicion.

Though there were grumblings from his subordinates that their escape was taking too long, Chow Yin knew that any premature action would result in their recapture. Freeing himself of the penal colony was a secondary consideration; before he could make any move, he had to be certain that his escape was permanent. His ultimate goal was not simply freedom; the only way he could ensure his future was a complete reversal of the game he played on Luna Station. He would not skulk in the shadows. It was time for him to seize control of his future, and nothing less than the complete domination of Sol System would do.

All electronic communications were monitored by the government satellites throughout the Lagrange Point, so Chow Yin had no way to communicate with the rest of the solar system. Before he left Earth, he'd managed to send out a short message to a trusted subordinate through one of his lawyers, but he had no way of knowing if it was received, or if the man would be successful.

Finally, his patience was rewarded.

When the monthly military transport arrived, the entire population of the station gathered in front of the docking bay doors, as they always did.

This time was different. When the ship opened its cargo doors, instead of prisoners disembarking, seven soldiers marched out onto the dock and formed a line in front of the gate.

To the inmates' complete surprise, the pilot of the ship, a grizzled officer, opened the gate and took a step forward. He stood at attention in front of Chow Yin and, with a salute, said, "We are at your service, Emperor Yin."

"It took you long enough, Mr. Leong." Chow Yin's words were only half-reproachful.

It would have taken Captain Leong years to get himself assigned to the penal station duty, and to get the military transport staffed with those who were loyal to the movement.

During the months of his trial, Chow Yin had spent a considerable amount of time listening to the news. He realized that there were people from all areas of China who had become disillusioned with the policies that had turned the PRC from one of the most powerful nations in the world to its current state as nothing more than a puppet for the Earth Council. The military, becoming less of a necessity as China slowly moved away from communism and toward democracy, had particularly suffered in the interim. Many officers and enlisted, who had dedicated their lives to the defense of the country they loved, believed it was time to restore the old system of divine leadership. The Emperors of China had always relied heavily on their military to enforce their rule.

Before he'd been captured on Luna Station, one of Chow Yin's hobbies had been genealogy. He had been able to trace his lineage back to the Qing, the last imperial dynasty of China two centuries before. With a legitimate claim through bloodlines, all he had to do was to get a message to imperialist sympathizers of his incarceration.

Before his exile from Earth, Chow Yin had managed to

convince the imperialists, through Leong—who had never managed to make a rank higher than captain in the PRC Space Force—that they should set their sights higher than simply retaking China. With Chow Yin as a figurehead, it was only a matter of time before the disillusioned officers managed to organize and put their plan into effect.

Captain Leong said, "My apologies for the delay, Sire."

"You are here now," Chow Yin said, then added, *"General* Leong."

Though the newly promoted general's expression did not change, Chow Yin saw that he stood a little straighter.

Chow Yin gestured to the inmates of the penal station. "I'd like to introduce you to our newest recruits."

General Leong took a step forward and surveyed the growing crowd of convicts.

He spoke in a booming voice for all to hear. "We don't have much time before the false Chinese government realizes we've commandeered their ship, so I'll be brief. We need to ensure no one suspects that we have liberated you from the station. Your cooperation is mandatory." He made a gesture, and four of his men came out of the ship, carrying two heavy crates between them. They set the crates down beside the general and pulled the lid off.

General Leong continued his speech. "I need everyone to grab an incendiary canister and bring it to your quarters. Place it in the center of your cell. They're connected with a remote, which we will activate once we have left dock."

One of the inmates, the serial killer named Sang, spoke up. "What about our stuff?"

"You must leave all your personal possessions behind. Inspectors will come. If you've packed all your things, they will know the escape was planned. We want them to investigate all possibilities; this will delay their efforts."

Chow Yin cleared his throat and gave the general a furtive look.

General Leong opened his holoslate and said, "Would the following prisoners please step forward." He read off a list of eleven names, including Sian, the hacker.

As the eleven men separated themselves from the main group, four more soldiers jogged out of the transport ship, pulse rifles in their hands, and circled them.

Sang said, "What's this all about?"

Holding up a hand, General Leong gave the man a conciliatory nod. "Not to worry. There are some who do not deserve to be part of the new Empire. We will ensure the purity of our cause."

Giving the eleven another assessment, Sang nodded. "I see what you mean." The separated men shared common traits: they were all considered the weakest of the inmates. Over the past few years, Chow Yin had had to intervene several times to spare them a beating from one of the other more violent inmates. "Besides, you probably want to leave a few bodies behind to throw off the scent." A number of the other prisoners chuckled.

Sian gave Chow Yin a look of panic. Chow Yin did not even glance in his direction.

General Leong spoke in an authoritative voice. "Gentlemen, we are embarking on a new chapter in the history of Sol System. Today marks the first day in the rule of the First Empire of Sol. Please do as I instructed."

With alacrity, the seventy-one remaining inmates rushed to the crates and picked up an incendiary canister. As they filed out of the docking area and back to the main compound, Chow Yin looked up at General Leong.

"Tell me she is safe."

Nodding, the general said, "It wasn't easy, Sire, but we've

secured her for you. You were correct; she was integral in developing the weaponized Kinemet."

"Good."

After a moment's hesitation, General Leong said, "I have other news, Emperor. Klaus has been located. He has made himself a hidden base on Venus. We believe he has made a breakthrough in the process—"

Chow Yin waved an impertinent hand at him. "That will be our first destination, then. I trust we have enough resources to accomplish our objective."

"Yes, Sire. More than enough. General Zhang has given us his full support, and he controls over a hundred-thousand troops. We also have four colonels, six members of the state council, and several private sector CEOs who have chafed under PRC rule. We have people in every level of government. As you suspected, all seven nations we reached out to have informally offered support and a willingness to sign fealty to an imperial charter—it seems the USA, Inc. stranglehold on future technologies is a sore point with them; they'd like nothing more than to see the giant fall."

"Excellent," Chow Yin said.

Once the last inmate to grab an incendiary left the bay, General Leong signaled his men surrounding the eleven who had been held back. The soldiers all raised their pulse rifles.

"Quickly now," the general said to the eleven in a low voice, "board the ship. Not a word."

Confused, the men stared at him.

"Would you rather be shot?" the general asked. "Move it!"

The men, glancing at the soldiers nervously, did as they were told, and hurried aboard the ship. Sian tried to catch Chow Yin's eye, but the self-styled Emperor was wheeling his chair to a control center at the main bay doors of the prison.

As he tapped out a few commands, one of the prisoners,

Sang, was returning to the dock area from his task. The bay doors began to close.

"Hey!" he called out, and broke into a run. A soldier who had been standing watch over his Emperor raised his pulse rifle, leveled it at Sang, and fired. The electric whir of the rifle was followed by a meaty thud as Sang's dead body fell to the cement floor. A few other prisoners noticed the closing doors and the body, and within a few moments, they stampeded for the docking bay.

The soldier only had to fire two more shots to put down the lead prisoners before the door closed, locking electromagnetically.

Shouldering the rifle strap, the soldier quickly raced behind Chow Yin's wheelchair, grasped the handles, and wheeled his Emperor onto the ship, which immediately lifted off.

Once Chow Yin was on the bridge, General Leong issued a command to one of the other officers. "Detonate the incendiaries."

Chow Yin could not observe the dozens of small explosions within the prison compound, but he knew the fire would quickly spread throughout the station and gut the colony.

If there was one thing that serial killer Sang was right about, there would be plenty of bodies for the Chinese investigators to find.

∞

Sitting in his wheelchair on the bridge of the ship six weeks after breaking out of the penal station, Chow Yin forced himself to keep his temper in check.

General Leong carefully watched the monitors at his station and did not turn around to face his Emperor. If he knew how angry Chow Yin was, he didn't give any indication.

First, they'd arrived at Lucis Observatory too late: Klaus was already dead; his research destroyed. After questioning Klaus's uncle, Gruber, they'd learned two things before the man had succumbed to the wounds sustained during questioning. The first was the general process Klaus had used to develop the Kinemetic conversion—the Kinemet had to be 'primed' somehow. Secondly, Gruber told them that Major Justine Turner had been converted to a Kinemat and was on the way to Canada Station Three, where Alex Manez was kept under military protection.

Chow Yin glanced at Sian, who sat at the main computer terminal. The programmer had been able to monitor the communications between the Earth Council and Canada Station Three, and learned about the injunction against Kinemetic research. He'd also picked up a message that the Arab Conglomerates were sending a team of observers to CS3—Chow Yin, knowing Alex and Justine's history, made a guess that they wouldn't just sit idly by and wait to be put under a microscope. "We need to be ready to intercept them," he told his crew, and General Leong put in a course for CS3.

His hunch had proved correct: Alex and Justine were trying to get away from CS3 before the observers arrived, and Chow Yin ordered General Leong to pursue them.

"How many of the Kinemetic torpedoes do you have on board?" he asked.

"Three," the general responded. "If we use them, we'll destroy their ship."

"That's the idea," Chow Yin said. "According to Captain Gruber, no one knows Klaus's process; the secret died with him. The last thing we need is for someone to leak the information; we cannot have competition. In order for us to control space, we need to have a monopoly on the technology; anyone who is undertaking research must be eliminated."

"Understood, Sire," General Leong said, but their efforts to destroy the *Ultio* and its passengers fell short when, to everyone's surprise, their first Kinemetic torpedo detonated before it impacted. When the general ordered the launch of the remaining two torpedoes, the *Ultio* quantized and disappeared from normal space.

The silence on the bridge stretched out for several minutes before Chow Yin finally spoke.

"Well, there is no help for it." He turned to General Leong. "We must return to our original plan."

The general nodded, and gave the order to his pilot. "Lay in a course to Qin Station."

Chow Yin swore under his breath, "It's time I took back what is rightfully mine."

∞

Over the following four years, Chow Yin wrested control of all space operations in Sol System through a combination of force and misdirection.

His greatest asset was to use the paranoia of Earth's nations against them. Before he launched his first strike against Luna Station, he arranged for the detonation of a Nepali nuclear warhead on Bhutan soil. Key members of the PRC Parliament, as directed by Chow Yin, called for immediate sanctions against Nepal.

India, a long-time ally of Nepal, called for sanctions against China, who then declared war on India. Within months, nearly every nation on Earth was taking sides, and military conflict was at an all-time high.

Once the superpowers withdrew the bulk of their military forces back to Earth, Luna Station was Chow Yin's for the taking. The most tenuous moment in his plans for empire came when the United States Space Force launched a major offensive to retake their four mining stations near the asteroid belt—which was important to the war effort, since asteroid mining was the only way to replenish their stocks of metals. Earth had been depleted the majority of their resources long ago.

Instead of protecting those mining stations, Chow Yin ordered their complete destruction—which served as a warning to any other nation that attempted a similar action.

In a public relations move, he relocated all the personnel on those stations to the Qin Station. He made it a point to have the news feeds report that there had not been any loss of life in the action. The reality was that Chow Yin valued those engineers and scientists more than the stations they worked on.

At the same time, Chow Yin informed every news agency about the catastrophic losses of Chinese military in the conflict, most of whom had died at the hands of American soldiers. With world sentiment rising against the USA, Inc., Chow Yin instructed the members of the PRC state council who were loyal to him to declare war on USA, Inc.

The declaration went through, and China launched its first strike—Chinese troops managed to get a foothold on the pacific coast before finally being repelled from American soil.

The conflict proved an effective distraction, and kept the news focused on the terrestrial conflict, and away from events in space, which was what Chow Yin wanted in the first place.

Any vessel—whether military or civilian—launched from Earth was intercepted, the crew given the choice to swear fealty to the new Emperor of Sol System, or be ejected into space.

His military strategy, however, was considerably more successful than his scientific ones. After four years, his team of scientists was no closer to figuring out the key to Kinemetic conversion. Not that they hadn't tried. Chow Yin had no problem coming up with hundreds of 'volunteers' for the experiments, none of whom survived.

The furthest they'd been able to push his technology agenda was to convert Kinemet to a super fuel, giving their ships the ability to fly at ten times the velocity of ion pulse engines. The first Orca mission to Pluto had taken nearly six months; Chow Yin's engineers had developed engines that would propel their ships from Luna to Pluto in two-and-a-half weeks.

It was not nearly fast enough for Chow Yin. When he received the communication from the patrol ship he had placed in Plutonian orbit that an alien vessel had materialized in Sol System space, he longed for near-light-speed travel.

The captain of the patrol ship reported that the alien vessel had been destroyed by the minefield they'd placed there.

Grimacing as he listened to the message, knowing the events described had already occurred four hours previous, Chow Yin breathed a sigh only when he heard the last sentence:

"…and we have recovered four passengers who used an escape pod—all humans. We have identified them, and have them in custody. Alex Manez, Michael Sanderson, Kenny Harriman, and the Mayan historian, Yaxche.

"Sire, your instructions were to destroy anything that entered Sol's space, but we wanted to confirm those instructions, considering the identities of the prisoners."

This was one time Chow Yin was happy his subordinates did not completely obey his instructions. With the difficulties he had in replicating Klaus's research, having access to those four might give his team of researchers a catalyst to perfecting the Kinemetic process. The only person who would have been more beneficial to him was Major Turner. He wondered what had become of her.

Chow Yin encoded a return message to the patrol ship.

"Excellent work, Lieutenant Gao. You are to return to Qin Station immediately with the prisoners. We'll send a relief patrol ship to replace you."

Once he sent the message, he contacted the lab facility and informed them to prepare for the impending arrival of their 'guests'.

8

Qin Station :
Sol System :

"Chow Yin?" **Michael** blurted out.

The criminal who had once secretly controlled Luna Station from the shadows stood in front of them, beaming as if pleased that he had suitably surprised his guests.

When he'd been arrested on Luna, Chow Yin had barely been able to get around the station with the aid of a cane. During his trial in China, the stress of the planet's gravity had done considerable damage to his already weakened legs, Michael recalled. At the time of his incarceration, Chow Yin had been confined to a wheelchair.

Now, Michael saw, he'd been fitted with a full set of biomechatronic legs, similar to the braces Alex had used on Canada Station Three. The prosthetics were bulky, making him look disproportionate, but it gave him the ability to walk around under his own power.

Chow Yin did so, stepping forward amid the mechanical hum of the electronic pistons, and nodded to Michael. "Mr. Sanderson, welcome back to Sol System. I see you've noticed my new legs. My engineers just fitted me with them. Tell me, do they make me look too tall?"

Michael ignored the question. "Why have you kidnapped

us?"

The Emperor only widened his smile. He turned to the others. "Kenneth Harriman, Yaxche, pleased to have you join us."

A thousand thoughts raced through Michael's mind. The last he'd heard, Chow Yin had been sent to a penal station on the L3 point on the opposite side of the Sun. In the span of four years, Chow Yin went from prisoner to Emperor. Michael wondered at the events that had led to this development.

Alex took a step back. "I won't do it."

"Now, now," said Chow Yin. "I had hoped we could be civil."

At first, Michael didn't know what they were talking about, but a moment later, it came to him. Assuming it was Chow Yin's engineers who had advanced Kinemet technology to the point where they could fly a ship from Pluto to the asteroid belt in two weeks, they still hadn't mastered the element's superluminal aspect. As powerful as Chow Yin had become, carving out his own empire, it was obvious he still had not been able to develop a Kinemat.

That's why he'd captured them, instead of killing them. Alex was the only living Kinemat in Sol System, though he was not fully converted. They would need him for study. Kenneth had been working with Alex, and was one of the brightest quantum physicists in the community. Though Quantum Resources had made recordings of Yaxche's recitation of the Song of the Stars in Mayan, it was more than likely they had not allowed those to get into Chow Yin's hands. Without the musical recipe, they could spend a century trying to get the frequencies correct to prime Kinemet for a transformation.

The Emperor needed Alex, Kenny, and Yaxche.

He did not need Michael, and proved it a moment later when he nodded to one of the soldiers near him. The man raised his rifle, aiming directly at Michael's head.

Chow Yin said, "I had a banquet planned, where we could have something to eat while we negotiated our partnership. It's disappointing that you've brought us to the ultimatum stage so quickly. You're taking all the fun out of it, Alex." With a look of forced patience, he spoke slowly. "You will help us, or your friend will die. There. Is that simple enough for you?"

Michael gritted his teeth. "Don't do it, Alex. Don't give this madman anything."

"Ah, I see you think I am bluffing. I assure you. I am not." The Emperor's expression turned grave. "A demonstration is in order." To the soldier, he said, "Kill Mr. Sanderson, if you would be so kind."

"No!" Alex shouted, and instinctively tried to push Michael out of the line of fire.

Kenny was a second faster, and hit Michael with his body. The ion pulse that was meant for the older man seared through Kenny's chest, instantly killing the physicist.

Alex changed direction, reaching out to catch Kenny's falling body. A cry of outrage and despair escaped him.

"You murdered him!" he yelled, though the words came out incoherently.

Michael, who had recovered his balance, slowly stood up straight. He couldn't believe Kenny was dead. A primal savagery began to grow inside him. Thought did not control his actions. On pure instinct, he launched himself at Chow Yin with only the image of his hands wrapped around the self-styled Emperor's neck to fuel him. He had no care that he would most likely be shot dead by a soldier before he got more than half way to their leader. Kenny had never hurt anyone. He didn't deserve to be cut down like an animal.

Instead of shooting Michael, the soldier who had killed Kenny reversed his rifle and hit him with the butt square in the head. Michael fell to the floor in a heap. His head exploded with pain, but the blow hadn't knocked him unconscious.

"I see you continue to test my resolve," Chow Yin said. "Perhaps we need to repeat the lesson."

Michael slowly looked up; any action sent waves of agony through him, and a sickening nausea gripped his guts.

"Leave him alone," Alex said. "I'll cooperate." A moment later, he added, "On one condition."

"Yes?" Chow Yin asked.

"Send them all home." Alex, who had knelt beside Michael to check on his friend, stood up. "Send them back to Earth. I'll give you what you want."

It took Michael a moment to understand the words. "No," he said in protest, his voice weak. "Don't give the bastard the satisfaction. I'd rather die than give him that kind of power."

"What you fail to realize, my dear Mr. Sanderson, is that the power has always been mine. Alex's decision was inevitable." Chow Yin turned around on his biomechatronic legs and walked away.

∞

Michael was brought back to the infirmary, two soldiers on either side of him grasping him by the arms. The blow to the head had been hard enough that he didn't have any fight left in him now, even if he'd wanted to do anything.

The soldiers led Alex and Yaxche in a different direction, while several other guards brought in a gurney on which they loaded Kenny's body.

The suddenness of the young man's death was almost too much for Michael to process. He'd only known Kenny for a short time, but the two of them had worked very well together. The younger man was extremely intelligent, and as far as

Michael was concerned, he would have had a brilliant career ahead of him.

Grief and regret edged into Michael's consciousness as he realized he didn't even know whether Kenny had any family. He should have taken the time to get to know the other man better.

Chow Yin. Michael couldn't wrap his mind around it. How had he escaped the penal station? How had he enlisted so many to his mad cause? How had he managed to wrest control of space from the nations of Earth? There were a hundred other questions he had. Ignorance was as big an enemy to Michael as Chow Yin. Without more information, Michael was at a complete disadvantage; he was at their mercy.

After strapping Michael onto the infirmary bed by the forearms and ankles, the soldiers stood guard until Doctor Naysmith returned.

"Back so soon?" the doctor asked, with that same innocent smile on his face. "Oh, it looks as if you've had an accident."

"How can you work for these animals?" Michael asked. "They murdered Kenny right in front of me."

"Sad to hear it." The doctor pulled out a tray from one of the rolling cabinets and extracted a few sheets of medical absorbent cloths. He stood over Michael and examined the head wound.

His voice low in a growl, Michael said, "Chow Yin is a madman who wants more than to rule the world; he wants to rule the entire universe. If you work for him, you're just another traitor."

While he gently placed the cloth on the injured spot to soak up the excess blood, Doctor Naysmith leaned in and said, "My life is medicine. It's all that matters." He continued to work on Michael, maintaining his smile. "I took an oath: 'I will not permit considerations of religion, nationality, race, gender, politics, socioeconomic standing, or sexual orientation to intervene between my duty and my patient.' Everyone has a right to medical treatment, Mr. Sanderson, even madmen."

Doctor Naysmith reached into the tray again and retrieved a laser suture gun. He pointed it at the gash on Michael's head and pressed the trigger.

There was an uncomfortable pulling sensation that grew more painful as the skin on his forehead mended. Just when Michael thought he couldn't handle it anymore, the doctor finished the procedure.

"There," Doctor Naysmith said, giving Michael a pat on the shoulder, "good as new."

∞

It was a few hours later when the soldiers came for him. With ruthless efficiency, they unstrapped him from the gurney. Michael hadn't seen Doctor Naysmith since he'd tended his head wound, and there was no sign of him now.

The soldiers didn't give him time to get his balance. When his pace proved too slow for them, two of them grabbed his arms and dragged him out of the infirmary.

"You're ripping my arms out of their sockets," Michael said, not expecting his words to have any effect.

"We're almost there," the squad leader said, as if to reassure him that the discomfort was temporary.

They led him through the halls and back to the elevator, though this time they descended to the lower levels. When the doors opened, Michael saw that they were in the main docking bay area.

Yaxche was there, standing beside a metal casket. The moment Michael's guards let his arms go, he hurried over to the old man. The soldiers fanned out, rifles at the ready, but they didn't stop him.

"Are you all right?" he asked, and felt a surge of relief when Yaxche nodded.

"Ahyah. They only wanted me to tell them my story."

Lowering his voice, Michael asked, "The Song of the Stars?"

Nodding, Yaxche said, "Alex said to go ahead and do so; that it would make no difference."

That puzzled Michael, and he gave Yaxche a quizzical look. The Mayan shrugged one shoulder. "Alex could have sung it from memory, but I think he wanted a chance to say goodbye to me."

Michael put his hand on the casket. "I feel bad for Kenny."

"He makes the final journey. I do not worry; his is a wise spirit."

The sound of boot steps got Michael's attention, and he looked around to see Lieutenant Gao approach.

"Mr. Sanderson, I've been assigned to transport the three of you to Luna Station, where you will then be put on a rapid transit capsule, which we will send to the Nova Scotia Space Port. I trust you will not resist, or cause any trouble during the flight. I would rather not put you into bio stasis again."

Michael took a deep breath, then nodded. "You have my word." He glanced at Yaxche, who gave the lieutenant a toothy smile.

"Good," Lieutenant Gao said. He took one measured step back, and gestured toward where his ship was docked. "If you will follow me, we'll get you situated in secure quarters. The flight will last approximately three days, and the capsule trip should take less than twelve hours."

They trailed behind Lieutenant Gao as he led them to his ship, while the Solan soldiers followed, watchful for any transgression.

In the ship, one of the officer's quarters had been converted to a temporary detention area. It was cramped for two people, but at least they had some privacy.

Michael wanted to share his theories on what had happened in Sol System, but Yaxche didn't seem very interested in conversation or company.

At one point, Michael asked if there was anything wrong with him, to which Yaxche shook his head. "I have not had much time for meditation," he told him. "I am a simple man; I am not used to all this excitement. I only wish to go home."

Once they reached orbit around the Moon, they were given an hour to stretch their legs before they were taken to the capsule area of the ship.

Lieutenant Gao was there to see them off. "I can't promise you it will be a smooth ride," he said. "It will only get rougher when you hit the atmosphere. If you make it through that without any serious damage, you should be fine. We're aiming for a splashdown off the coast of Nova Scotia. I've been authorized to notify your government of your return; they should be waiting for you."

Michael's diplomatic side compelled him to say something. "Unlike certain others, you've treated us decently, Lieutenant."

"Of course," the lieutenant said with a slight nod.

"It's not too late to change your ship's course. Come with us. Turn yourself in. I will speak on your behalf."

"I'm sorry. I'm afraid my loyalty is unwavering."

Michael said, "I understand."

With that, he and Yaxche got into the rapid transit capsule and waited as two soldiers strapped them in securely. A moment later, they sealed the hatch, and darkness surrounded the two passengers.

The power of the sudden thrust as they were launched into space toward Earth was surprising to Michael, even though he was expecting the terrific forces pounding his body.

It was nothing compared to the shock he got twelve hours later, after landing in the Atlantic Ocean. When his rescuers opened the hatch of the capsule and pulled him and Yaxche out, a military police officer slapped handcuffs on the two of them.

"Michael Sanderson," the officer said, "you are under arrest for the crime of treason against Canada Corp."

9

Kulsat Ship :
Centauri System :

Justine couldn't think straight. A cold chill ran through her entire body.

You are to be expiring.

They were going to extract information from her and then kill her.

"No," she said. "I'm not going to cooperate."

The alien typed. "Where is your kind to be living? How many are they being? How many are Risen? Describe your discovery of the Gift."

Instead of answering, Justine shook her head, though she wasn't certain the Kulsat could interpret the gesture.

"We have biology information. Your kind does not see. Why do you motion respond?"

He thought all humans were blind, based on Justine's condition. She wasn't about to correct his wrong assumption.

The alien typed. "Why does your kind have eyes, if you do not see? Are you unit-defective?"

The Kulsat were obviously an intelligent species, and Justine assumed this one would eventually figure it out, but she wasn't about to speed up the process.

"Biology information," the machine voice said. "Your kind

is to be communicating with sound. We require testing."

A low humming sound filled Justine's tank, growing louder and louder until she felt the vibrations go through her body. The intensity increased. Her muscles began to ache, as if she'd just run a marathon. Unsteady on her feet, she had to lie down.

The sound waves pounded through her, and she started feeling nauseated. Her heart beat erratically, as if trying to match the pulse of the vibrations.

She let out a groan, and held her stomach as every nerve in her body ignited in pain.

The low hum changed, rising in pitch. The sound waves no longer affected her body, but her hearing. She clapped her hands over her ears. It felt as if her eardrums were going to burst. If the torture continued, she would lose her hearing, and she would be deaf and blind.

The agony grew, and as much as she tried to hold it in, she couldn't bear it anymore.

"Stop!" she screamed. "Enough!"

The sound abruptly stopped, but there was a persistent ringing in Justine's ears. She rubbed around her lobes and moved her jaw to increase blood and air flow.

"Sound communication able to be causing discomfort," the machine voice said. "You are to be cooperating, or there is to be additional discomfort."

The alien was going to torture her with sound waves. Justine didn't know how much of that she could take before he broke her, or before he went too far and ruptured either her eardrums or another internal organ. Sonics could be used as a very powerful weapon.

The science leader had just proven to Justine that he had no compassion or concern for her well-being outside of what information she could provide him. If he were representative of his kind, then a species like that would not hesitate to bring destruction to any world that got in their way. The story Alex had told them was proving true.

Justine had a choice.

She could cooperate and avoid torture; but the alien had already told her he would kill her once he was done with her. The Kulsat would then, most likely, plan their invasion of Earth.

Alternatively, she could defy him. That would mean torture until he decided she was of no use to him. Then he would 'expire' her, and still plan the invasion ... but her resistance might delay those plans. Space was big; without more information, the Kulsat could conceivably spend years trying to find Sol System.

If Alex and the others had managed to escape the Kulsat attack, they might be able to return to Earth and warn them about the invasion. Justine had no idea how they would accomplish that, since Alex was not a fully transformed Kinemat; but any chance she could afford them, she would take.

She got to her feet. Though she was still unsteady from the sonic attack, she stepped closer to the glass wall and put both hands on it.

"Do your worst," she said, and braced for another blast.

The alien twitched, and his entire body rippled. Justine had no basis on which to interpret Kulsat body language, but she thought she'd managed to annoy the creature.

It typed something on the computer, and the machine voice spoke. "Comprehension difficulty. Risen being is superior to others. You chose discomfort to protect unGifted and Deficients. You are unit-defective in your eyes. Are you unit-defective in comprehension?"

"I'm not crazy," Justine said. "I value the lives of all of my kind, even if they aren't 'Risen'."

The alien typed. "Units not Risen do not contain true value. Demonstration."

Turning fluidly, the Kulsat made a rippling gesture with one of his arms. At the other end of the room, another Kulsat, smaller than the first, swam into the area of Justine's *sight*. The newcomer, she sensed, was irradiated with Kinemet.

The scientist made several motions with his arms, and after a few moments, Justine realized he was using a form of sign language to communicate with the other Kulsat. That made sense. If they were physiologically comparable to cephalopods, then they had limited hearing capabilities, and most likely had not developed vocal cords.

When the leader finished signing, the smaller alien swam over to a table and retrieved a long, thin object. On one end, there was a loop, which the alien wrapped a tentacle around to carry it. The other end of the device came to a point, like a needle.

The smaller alien gave the tool to the science leader, who typed for quite some time on his computer.

He waited while the mechanical voice spoke to Justine.

"This unit was offered the Gift, but failed to become Risen. He is of limited use. This Deficient serves me, but should he expire, there are millions of Deficients to replace him."

Then, to Justine's horror, the science leader plunged the spike directly into the other alien's head.

"No!" Justine cried, but it was too late. The smaller Kulsat's body twitched, his arms flailing about for several seconds. Then he went still, floating away with the spike lodged in his head.

The science leader made another motion toward the entranceway, and three other small aliens swam in quickly. They grabbed the dead Kulsat and dragged him away.

"Without the Gift of Light, that unit would be expired soon.

Deficients are having little value. There is no loss."

Justine couldn't believe what she was seeing and hearing. The Kulsat had been the favored of the Grace? From what she'd taken from Alex's story, the Grace was a benevolent race. Either someone had been sorely mistaken about the Kulsat, or the cephalopod race had undergone a radical societal change in the past thousand years.

Justine knew she couldn't impose her own system of values on another culture, but she couldn't condone murder under any circumstance.

The Kulsat typed. "If you are unit-defective, then you are to be expiring. There are several more of your kind in this system. They are not Risen, but they are possible to be not unit-defective. We will retrieve them now and increase knowledge of your kind."

"No," Justine said.

She was aware the Kulsat had given her vital information. Alex, Kenny, Michael and Yaxche had not been captured. Some of them, if not all, were still alive.

She had to give them as much time to escape as she could. If she didn't cooperate, the Kulsat would simply kill her and go after the others.

While the Kulsat possessed advanced technology, she suspected that they might not be a superior race. Perhaps she could distract them.

She said, "I am not unit-defective. I will cooperate. But I need something from you."

"What are requirements of cooperation?"

Justine noted that the linguistic computer had improved its capability for translation. She would have to choose her words carefully in the future.

"I need time to recover from your sonic attack, and I need to eat." She took a breath before adding, "I also require more

Kinemet—the Gift of Light. With it, I am able to see."

"Ability to see is not required for cooperation," the alien typed back. "You will be allowed sustenance and rest. Cooperation will resume after a delay of time."

With that, the alien swam to one wall and tapped a sequence on another control panel.

Above Justine, near where the oxygen flowed, there was a scraping sound, and when she looked up, she saw a cylindrical container, the size of a kitchen pail, descending from the ceiling on a cord. A few drops of water, smelling like brine, fell from it and splashed on her cheek.

Once the container reached the floor, the cord separated from it, and retracted into the ceiling again. Justine put her hands on the cylinder. The sides of it felt as if it were made from the shells of clams or mussels. Instead of a solid lid, there was a membranous skin covering the top. When she put her fingers against it and applied pressure, the skin broke away.

Inside the container, there were two compartments. One half held a clear liquid. When Justine dipped a finger in and brought it to her lips, she was relieved that it was fresh water.

In the bottom of the other half of the container was some kind of gelatinous substance.

Justine tentatively stuck her finger in. It was slimy, cold, and thick. When she pulled her finger out, the gelatin stuck to her skin, and she used her thumb to scrape most of it off. Her stomach rolled at the thought of eating whatever it was they'd served her, but she was mindful that the Kulsat was observing her. If she did not eat, as she'd requested, it might arouse suspicion.

Steeling herself, she lifted her finger to her mouth. Before tasting the food, she sniffed. It smelled fishy, but not overpowering.

It took every bit of her willpower to stick her tongue out to taste the viscous gelatin on her finger. To her relief, it had a rather bland flavor. The problem was that it had the consistency of nasal mucus.

Trying not to think about what she was eating, Justine scooped up a small amount with her fingers and stuffed it in her mouth. She gagged, but stopped herself from vomiting it out. With an act of sheer stubbornness, she forced herself to swallow it.

It felt disgusting going down, and tears sprung to Justine's eyes. She had a task to undertake, and an act to play out. She lifted the container and angled the water half toward her, careful not to let any of the gelatin pour out on her. Tilting the container to her lips, she drank to wash the gelatin down, and that helped.

To take her mind off the food, she thought back to what her captor had said when he killed the other alien, that the smaller Kulsat had failed to become Risen, and that there were many others who had undergone the process unsuccessfully.

On Earth, there had been several volunteers during the early days of the quanta experiments. Even when Klaus had discovered the formula hidden in the Song of the Stars, he still had more failures than successes. The thought that made her blood run cold at that moment was that there might not be a single, guaranteed process. Even if Klaus had gotten every factor right, there was a chance that Justine might not have survived the experiment.

It was an important piece of information, one she needed to bring back with her—if she managed to convince the Kulsat that she was more valuable alive than dead.

Just as she finished the last of the slop, Justine noticed another small Kulsat enter the room. He approached the leader and signed for more than half a minute. The leader made a few signs in reply, and the smaller one swam away quickly.

Approaching the control panel, the leader typed. "Time delay is increased. You will rest now. Cooperation will resume after one sleep cycle."

He turned around to one of the machines behind him, tapped something on the pad on the front of the machine. Then he swam away toward the exit.

Justine heard a whirring sound from above her, where the oxygen was pumping into her tank. She smelled something gaseous a moment before she realized she was being tranquilized.

She reached her hands out to break her fall, but before she hit the floor, she was already deep into a dreamless sleep.

10

Sierra de las Minas :
Guatemala :

Long Count: 9.19.19.17.9

The opening in the crevice was barely wide enough for me to
crawl through, but I was able to pull Ekahua inside after me.
As I went deeper, the gap became much wider, and the cave
floor was big enough that we could both lie down, if we had to
spend the night there.

There was a small crack in the ceiling that allowed a thin
stream of moonlight into the cave. It was barely enough light
to let me make out the shape of my own hand when I held it
up in front of my face.

"Are you hungry?" I asked Ekahua. "I could go hunt
something for us, though I don't think we should risk making
a fire."

Ekahua said, "No, thank you. By the time you returned, I
would be gone."

I shifted, uncomfortable at how casually he spoke about his
own death. It did not seem like a glorious death to me. Fading
away in a cave was not how I wanted to die. If I were to meet
my end in battle or on a hunt, then my tribe would sing of my

heroism.

"I didn't see any wounds," I said to Ekahua. "What is killing you?"

He seemed to think about how to explain himself to me. "It has been eons since our world, Xtôtix, was destroyed. I, like all of my people, have spent my life among the stars; I am one of the last of my kind.

"It is because of the Grace—which gives us power to travel the stars—that we cannot survive on a planet. We become like fish on dry land."

"Then why did you not stay in the sky?" I asked, trying to understand what he was telling me.

"I have been visiting your system for quite some time, watching your world from the sky. You have grasped the nature of the universe much quicker in your evolution than other races. It is very interesting to follow your progress.

"This time, there was a flare in your sun that hit my sky boat. By the time I got control, it was too late." He made a sound, which I decided was a laugh.

Not understanding half of what he said, I asked, "You said there are only a few of you left. Did they also come to the world and die?"

"No." He closed his eyes. "The Grace—what we call the power of light—that lets us travel the stars also gives us very long lives, Subo Ak. I have lived for thousands and thousands of your years. But everything has a cost. You see, there was an accident on our world. Only a few of us survived, and we were changed. Unfortunately, though we have great power, we are not able to have children. Once, there were many Xtôti; now, there are only a few. It has been a long time since I have seen another of my kind. For all I know, I may even be the last."

I felt him reach out to me and rest his trembling hand on mine. It must have been a terrible effort on his part; it was a moment before he spoke again.

"That is why it was important to destroy my ship, and why none of the other tribes can find me. If they learned how to use the full power, as we did, their people would also begin to die out. We cannot allow that to happen."

There was a pleading look in his eyes. "You must promise me that when I die, you will build a fire. Make it as hot as you can, and burn my body so that not even ashes remain. Make sure you get very far away, so that you will not be harmed. Will you do this for me, Subo Ak?"

I was so stunned by his story and request, I didn't realize I had been holding my breath. I let it out and said, "You will not have any path to the Underworld. Let me bury you. This cave is a sure way to the spirit world. I will bring you many gifts for your journey."

"No," Ekahua said. "I know it is not your tradition to do as I ask, but you must promise to do so."

For a time, I thought about his story. The power he talked about was mighty, and I dreamed about what I could do if I lived for thousands of years. Then I felt a moment of doubt. It would be an offense against the gods if we never had children. The Ch'orti' were already dying out because of our wars with the northern tribes. We needed to increase our numbers, not lose them.

I thought I understood what Ekahua was trying to tell me, and I nodded. "Yes, I will do as you ask."

"Thank you, Subo Ak." He closed his eyes. "There are many cultures in your world, but I believe yours is the most promising. Already you look to the stars to guide your lives." Ekahua smiled.

"Of course," I said. "We all await our rebirth among the heavens."

"It is for that reason I have left a message for your people, once you begin to explore beyond the shores of your world."

"What message?"

"It is more of a marker to point the way." He opened his eyes and gave me an odd look. "Though I am not certain I have managed to write it correctly; your symbols and glyphs don't always bear the same meaning as your spoken words."

I waved a hand. "We leave the writing to the priests and elders. I prefer *hearing* the stories."

"And so, now you must listen carefully to my story. I will teach you the Song of the Stars. It is very important to learn it exactly, and pass it along to your children. The knowledge will give your people power in the generations to come."

Ekahua sang a song to me in a language that I could not understand. Respectfully, I did not interrupt him, but listened as carefully as I could.

"I do not know what those words mean," I said to him when he'd finished.

"The words are not important." He turned his head toward me. "The meaning is in the song itself. You must be able to sing the melody as I have. I will sing it again, and then you can try."

"What is this song?" I asked. "How will it give my children power?"

Some time passed before Ekahua said, "It is the song that we hear when we become one with the Grace. One day, that Song will allow your people to travel across the stars."

We practiced throughout the evening, until Ekahua finally told me that I had learned the song correctly. When I sang the song, I could feel something powerful in the music. It was as if it were a reminder of an event in my life I had never experienced.

Ekahua said, "Come closer, Subo Ak, and I will give you a final gift. You have heard the song from me; now you will hear the song from the stars themselves."

When I moved over to him, he raised one hand and placed it on my forehead. My first reaction when his body began to glow and light up the cave was to pull away, but though he was weak, his grip was strong, and he held me there.

It was as if he became light itself. A quick thought came to me that maybe Ekahua was a god, and had only led me to believe otherwise. What person could become light?

A soft ringing in my ears caught my attention. That sound grew louder in my head until it fully consumed my thoughts. I detected the faint melody of the song, and once I did so, it was all I could hear.

The Song enveloped me, took me away from my mortal self. It was stronger than any dream I'd ever had, more powerful than any spirit vision I'd ever heard of. Soon, my entire being became that Song, and there was nothing else in the universe.

∞

When I woke up, it was morning, and faint light streamed through the crevice into the cave.

I reached out to shake Ekahua, but pulled my hand back when there was no resistance. He made no sound. I held my fingers at his mouth and felt no breath.

Ekahua was dead. The effort of that last gift to me must have been too much for him.

Though I had only known him for a short time, I felt a heavy sadness in my heart and a great loss. I wanted nothing more than to hear that Song again and for the rest of my life. Now, I only had the memory.

Slowly, I made my way out of the cave. Squeezing through the small opening in the cliff face, I blinked at the sudden brightness of the morning sun.

Ekahua's last request was for me to make an offering of his body through fire. I thought, perhaps it was so that the smoke would carry his spirit back to the sky to join his people. It was important to honor the dead, and I intended to do as I was asked.

Before I gathered dried wood to build the fire, though, I went in search of food, taking my atlatl and two darts. I had gone too long without eating, and I needed to keep my strength up if I were to make the long journey home and tell my strange tale to the other villagers.

I was in luck, and found a bird's nest with three eggs. My hunger got the better of me, and I quickly cracked the shells open and sucked the eggs down.

After finishing the third one, I heard a sound from a distance behind me. Dropping down to a knee, I searched through the woods. Soon, I saw the forms of three Q'eqchi' warriors. They were walking in the direction of the crevice where Ekahua's body rested.

I could not let them find him. They would be certain to take his remains back to Quiriguá. I would not be able to honor Ekahua's final wishes, and would risk angering his dead spirit.

Desperate to lead them away, I stood and loaded a dart in my atlatl. Immediately, I threw it toward the three warriors. I had no thought to hit any of them. My plan was simply to get their attention. My dart struck home, however, running right through the neck of one of the warriors. He made a gurgling scream as he fell to the ground.

As one, the other two warriors spun on their heels, crouching defensively until they could spot their attacker.

Turning, I broke into a run. In the back of my mind, I congratulated myself. I had accomplished my original mission to either capture or kill an enemy, though I didn't know whether I would be able to take a trophy of my victory.

The two warriors spotted me. One of them threw his spear at me, but it went wide. The other warrior broke into a run, chasing after me through the forest.

I had to lead them as far away from the crevice as I could, but I could not let them catch me. If they did not kill me, they would bring me to Quiriguá to become a slave, or a sacrifice.

I scrambled as fast I could down the mountain. If I could reach the valley floor, I might be able to outrun them.

My foot caught on a root sticking out of the ground, and I lost my balance. I fell hard on my stomach, and pain lanced through my body as the breath rushed out of me.

Cursing, I fought to suck air back in and get to my feet.

The lead warrior was almost upon me, and he drew back his spear and aimed at me. I grabbed a handful of dirt and flung it in his face. He yelled as he turned his head away and threw his hand up to protect himself.

Taking the opportunity, I picked up my atlatl, which had fallen from my grip, and swung it like a club at the warrior's head. The end connected with his temple, and he fell to the ground in a heap.

The second warrior was only a few paces behind his companion, and caught up during the fight. Still at a run, he jumped at me, swinging a long knife at my throat.

I batted at the knife with my atlatl and knocked it out of his hand. At the same time, I tried to duck under the warrior's flying body, but he hit me with his entire weight. Both of us crashed backward into a tree trunk. I felt a snap, a surge of pain, and knew that one of my ribs was broken.

The agony made my head swim. My breath came in painful gasps.

Having bounced off me and landed a few steps away, the enemy warrior jumped back to his feet. He let out an animal roar and rushed at me.

I threw myself to my back and, in one motion, reached out to grab the first warrior's spear and bring the point up.

The second warrior tried to turn away at the last moment, but he was running at me too quickly. The spear caught him in the chest and went straight through him.

He gave me a puzzled look, and then the life went out of his eyes as he toppled over onto his side.

I could not believe it. I'd defeated three of the Q'eqchi' warriors by myself.

The pride I felt was short-lived. I could barely breathe, and I knew if I did not find help, I would not survive. With my rib broken, I would not be able to hunt for food. If more warriors came, I would not be able to outrun them.

With great effort, I drew myself to my feet. Picking up my atlatl, I slowly picked my way back to the crevice where I had left my pack.

Even if I managed to build a fire to burn Ekahua's body and send his spirit to the sky, I did not have the strength to pull his body out of the cave. As it was, I didn't know if I had the strength to make it back to my village outside Copán, which was a two-day march away.

As I hefted my pack, grimacing at the pain and holding one arm close to protect my broken rib, I vowed to return. If I had to, I would bring more warriors with me to complete the ritual and honor the sky traveler.

11

Qin Station :
Sol System :

Alex was taken deeper into the laboratory section of the station without being given the opportunity to say goodbye to his friends. His thoughts were clouded with outrage over Kenny's murder, and he was barely aware of his surroundings when they arrived at the destination.

The lab was similar to the one Klaus had set up on the station orbiting Venus—Alex recognized it from the description Michael and Justine had given him. There were two sections: the main lab area, and the room where the subjects underwent Kinemetic process trials.

He took a hard look around, and it was only then that he saw there was another person in the lab besides his guards and himself.

An oriental woman, who looked to be in her mid-thirties, her long jet-black hair tied back in a ponytail, and wearing a white lab coat, glared at him as he entered.

Three of the guards, having completed their escort mission, stepped back out of the lab without a word and sealed the door behind him. One guard remained inside the lab, standing in a relaxed but attentive position, with his rifle cradled in his arms across his chest.

Alex, feeling decidedly uncomfortable, cleared his throat. "My name is—"

"I know who you are," the woman said. "And I don't need you here. I told him that. I can do this myself."

"Do what?" Alex asked. "And who are you?"

She gave him an inscrutable look. "Do you know nothing? This is a waste of my time." Storming to a communications console in the wall, she tapped something on the control, and a voice came through.

"Yes, Your Highness?"

"I told you, Dr. Yin will suffice. Get my father."

Dr. Yin! Alex reeled from shock. This young woman was Chow Yin's daughter?

He glanced at the guard in the room, as if he could give Alex some kind of confirmation. The guard did not so much as react.

The monitor lit up, and Chow Yin appeared on-screen. "What is the problem, Alice?"

"I told you I didn't need this boy to help me. I am perfectly capable of discovering the process on my own."

"You've had four years to do so," the Emperor said.

Alice Yin's face flushed visibly. She protested, "Now that we have the Mayan's story recorded, it's only a matter of time."

"Time is a luxury we can no longer afford. After all, the Americans had the story for over a decade, and they never solved the problem. There is obviously a missing element. Alex Manez knows the secret; he has been in close contact with the involved parties all along. He has agreed to cooperate."

"I can figure it out myself," Alice said, though her words were not as vehement as before.

"Of course you could," Emperor Yin said, giving her a patient smile. "I have every confidence in your abilities. We are on a timetable, however, and so I ask you to set aside your pride and work with the Westerner. Make me proud." He cut the communications link before his daughter could say anything more.

Alice Yin stared at the blank monitor for several seconds before turning around. Alex got the impression she was trying to compose herself.

Her efforts, apparently, were not enough. She gave Alex a hateful glare and stormed out of the lab through a door on the opposite wall.

When Alex glanced at the solitary guard, the only reaction the man made was a very slight relaxing of his shoulders. It seemed high drama ran in the Yin family.

∞

Much had happened in so short a time, and Alex felt more than a little disoriented. Kenny's death hadn't fully hit home yet; his initial outrage at the killing had settled into a strange, disconnected numbness. When he'd first met the young physicist, he and Kenny had done nothing but butt heads. Their friction had turned to friendship. Alex didn't want to think about it, didn't want to process the finality of the other's death.

Alone with the uncommunicative guard, Alex felt helpless. As a distraction, he took it upon himself to take a tour of the lab.

On a hunch, he tried to initialize one of the computers, and it prompted him for a password. He tried a few others but could not get access. The lab had a Kinemetic damper, so Alex could not use his electropathy to circumvent the computer's security protocols.

From his quick investigation, he concluded that they had all the necessary equipment to perform the Kinemetic process. All they were missing was Kinemet and a subject.

He gravitated toward the experimentation room, and his thoughts drifted back to Klaus, who had killed several American soldiers in his attempt to refine the process before succeeding with Justine.

The last time Alex had seen Klaus was at his uncle's base several hundred kilometers from Luna Station. He'd spent a few years in the company of the young man. Though they'd never indulged in conversation, and had been barely polite to each other during Alex's stay, he always felt Klaus could have matured past his abusive childhood.

Initially angry and bitter, Klaus had become quiet and introspective over the first few years, and had spent his time focusing his studies on physics and chemistry, rather than on computer technology. At one point, Alex thought he might take Klaus into his confidence, and see if either of them could understand Alex's condition.

That was never to be. Word reached Klaus through his uncle that his estranged father had died from liver failure, a legacy from his alcoholism. His mother, who had left them years before, refused to acknowledge Klaus and rebuffed all attempts at communication. Klaus became increasingly agitated and violent. He went on several raids with his uncle, and Alex came to understand the young man had taken someone's life unnecessarily.

It was then that Alex realized he could no longer depend on Klaus or his uncle to harbor him. With his deteriorating health, Alex knew the clock on his life was ticking, and made the plan to hijack the *Quanta*. Though he'd tricked Captain Gruber into helping him, Alex had not thought about what his deception would have done to Klaus. It was only years later that the repercussions became evident, when Klaus enlisted the Cruzados to aid him in his experiments.

Now, Klaus was dead, but his mad pursuit had been picked up by Emperor Yin and his daughter.

Alex was, once again, right in the thick of it. He had promised his cooperation to save his friends, and couldn't think of any way to back out. Even if they told him Michael and the others had been returned to safety, there was no way for Alex to know whether it was the truth or a lie.

If he refused to cooperate now, it would only be a matter of time before they rediscovered the formula for the Kinemetic process. Alex had to do his best to delay their progress by any means necessary.

The Kulsat were on the hunt for Sol System. They would eventually find it. Humanity needed Kinemats to defend themselves against the threat; but someone like Emperor Yin would never use the technology to save Sol System. He would use the knowledge for his own gain, and sacrifice the masses.

Alex started and let out a gasp when he realized someone had come back into the lab. Alice Yin studied him with cold, dark eyes.

"I didn't see you there," Alex said, struggling to even out his breathing.

"It seems we must work together," Alice said. Her voice was even, but Alex could sense the hostile undertones. She was struggling to keep her anger in check.

"That was the arrangement." If she was going to play it cold, so would Alex.

"Then tell me the big secret. Tell me what I've been missing all this time."

Alex shook his head. "Not until I am satisfied my friends have arrived on Earth alive."

"You doubt my father's word? He is the Emperor of Sol System. Argh," she said, throwing up her hands in frustration. "Do you not understand? Once your 'friends' are in the custody of your government, they will tell them the secret. We must succeed before they do."

"That would be too bad," Alex said, unable to keep the sarcasm from his voice.

She pointed a finger at him. "You gave your word you would cooperate. If you do not, then we have no reason to ensure their safety. So long as you are helping me, your friends will safely continue their journey to Earth. Once we have developed the Kinemetic process, it won't matter that they also know it," she said. "We have amassed more Kinemet than they have. We can create hundreds of Kinemats before they have their first one."

"You're mad," Alex said, the accusation coming out before he could stop himself.

Alice's face turned a bright shade of red, and for a moment, Alex thought she would attack him.

He couldn't help himself. He asked, "Don't you care that you're killing innocent people in your experiments? If you do succeed, you surely know the Emperor will use the power to kill thousands—perhaps millions—of others. How can you be a part of that?"

"Why should I care?" Alice said in a hiss. "Humanity turned its back on me a long time ago. Anyone who opposes us will get what they deserve."

She glanced at the guard, and then back at Alex.

"You will cooperate now, or I will give the guard the order to shoot you on the spot."

12

Department of Defense HQ :
Ottawa, Canada :

Michael had never felt so despondent in his life.

After three days in a holding cell in the military detention center, he thought he would never see a friendly face again. They had not even let him contact his family to let them know he was still alive. Until they could assess the national security risk he posed, he was kept incommunicado.

They gave him access to a computer for the purposes of filing a statement, but he'd been supervised for the duration. Though he'd submitted the report a day ago, no one had come back to let him know what his status was, or whether they would simply leave him in his cell indefinitely.

From the moment Michael and the others had re-entered Sol System, he'd been imprisoned in one form or another, and he'd had his fill of the experience. All he wanted was to speak to someone in authority and plead his case. Even if they decided to lock him away forever, he wanted someone to take his warning of the Kulsat threat seriously, at the very least.

When one of the two guards outside his cell unlocked the door, Michael first thought it was to bring him a meal, but the man who entered the cell was not a soldier.

"Calbert!" Michael said. "You have no idea how happy I am

to see you." He stood up and took a step forward, but Calbert Loche put up a hand, motioning for Michael to sit down on his cot again.

"You may not be so happy once you hear what I have to say," he said.

"Oh?"

Calbert glanced around the holding cell quickly. There was a small, plain desk with a chair on one wall. He pulled the chair out by the backrest and turned it around. Slowly, he eased himself down on it.

"I'll cut to the chase: they're not going to drop the charges against you," he said, "...yet."

"Yet?" Michael asked. "Then there's a possibility."

"Maybe. Your report made a lot of people unhappy." Calbert took a deep breath. "Billions of dollars were spent on Quantum Resources and Alex Manez. Now, from your statement, we find out he was lying to us from the moment he returned from Centauri—some even doubt he made the initial trip.

"Half the senators on the oversight committee think you were operating in collusion with Chow Yin—after all, how did he manage to figure out how to weaponize Kinemet?"

"That's ridiculous," Michael said. "Why would he ship us back here if we were working with him?"

"I don't know." Calbert shrugged. "Maybe he needs more information, and thinks you can get it for him."

Grimacing, Michael said, "Ludicrous."

Calbert continued. "The rest believe you're not a traitor, but simply guilty of gross incompetence."

"What?" He couldn't keep the shock from his face.

"From the beginning, Quantum Resources faced failure after failure; it was only after your retirement that the company turned itself around. Once you were brought back into the fold, things went sour in a hurry."

"They want a scapegoat? Pin everything that went wrong on me?"

"It wouldn't be the first time something like this happened."

"So either I'm a traitor or an idiot," Michael said.

"Don't forget 'a liar'," Calbert said. "All of them think your report of some super alien species massing an invasion is pure fiction, a legerdemain designed to distract us from your other activities."

"Are you serious? I wouldn't make something like that up." Michael felt the figurative noose tightening around his neck. He looked Calbert in the eye. "What does Alliras think?"

"Alliras is no longer the Minister of Energy, Mines and Resources. He recommended me for the minister's ballot before he left the position. I've been in the seat for a year now."

"You got political?" Michael gaped. "What about Quantum Resources?"

"Dissolved. Since Chow Yin has put an embargo on space operations for all earthbound nations, we lost our mandate. Space Mining Division has been gutted. The country has more important needs, such as fighting the war."

"The war?" He gasped, feeling completely out of touch.

"I have to say, it was a brilliant move on Chow Yin's part. He corrupted a good portion of the PRC government, got them to start trouble in Asia. Within months, everyone was picking sides, and I mean everyone. The rub of it is that World War III is nothing more than a distraction. While we're all busy fighting each other, Chow Yin's been taking advantage and securing control of the rest of Sol System."

"Murderous bastard," Michael said, grinding his teeth.

"Yes, I'm sorry about Kenny Harriman." Calbert bowed his head a moment before continuing. "A month ago, the PRC government regained control of China. They're in the process of rooting out the imperialist sympathizers, and they've initiated a ceasefire. Everyone is in a holding pattern at the moment."

"That's good news," Michael said. "We can turn our attention back to Chow Yin and the Kulsat."

Calbert clicked his tongue. "That might take a bit of time, and might be more problematic than realistic. There were a lot of shots fired by both sides. It'll take years to smooth out ruffled feathers. Worldwide resources are already taxed. We need those space-based production stations controlled by Chow Yin. There's been talk that it would be easier to negotiate a deal rather than commit resources to another fight, especially when the Solan Empire has the high ground."

"I can't believe my ears." Michael's eyes were wide. "They're going to give in?"

Lifting his shoulders in a sign of helplessness, Calbert said, "The economy was tenuous when you left; now, it's reaching a critical point. The war exhausted everyone's reserves. People are tired of fighting."

"Well," Michael said, his voice upset, "people better get un-tired. The Kulsat are going to find us, and when they do, we'll be wiped out."

With a half-smile, Calbert said, "It would be easier to convince the government to swallow the Moon, than to swallow that story."

"And you?" He looked at Calbert through the corner of his eye. "What do you believe?"

Taking a long time to answer, he finally said, "I believe that if your story is true, then we're all in very serious trouble."

"That wasn't what I was asking." Michael held his breath.

Finally, Calbert nodded, "We are all in very serious trouble."

Though Michael felt a surge of relief when he heard that—

at least someone in the entire world didn't think he was either a complete moron or a traitor—he knew his situation was far from optimistic.

"To break it down," he said, pulling at his lip, "we've got two problems: Emperor Chow Yin, and the Kulsat Consortium. I hate to say it, but Yin is the lesser of the two evils. He wants to rule Sol System; the Kulsat want to decimate it."

"What do you suggest?"

Michael scratched an eyebrow. "Do we have the technology to weaponize Kinemet?"

"Before Quantum Resources was shut down, we bandied a few theories about. The first problem is, we don't have any Kinemet stockpile to test the theories. Second, even if we did, those theories can't be tested planet-side. Unfortunately, Chow Yin has all the marbles, and he's not sharing."

"It sounds like you're trying to convince me that making a deal with Chow Yin is the sensible option." He gave Calbert a sharp look.

"The devil you know..."

Shaking his head, Michael sighed. "I can't believe that option is on the table."

Then he noticed Calbert looking at him oddly.

"What?"

A smile crept into Calbert's lips. "You realize that, not once in this conversation did you ask about what's going to happen to you?"

Tilting his head, Michael let out a hollow laugh. "I thought it was a foregone conclusion. I figure I'm the administration's worst nightmare. If they reveal I'm back, the newsvids will investigate. The moment they find out about an alien invasion, there'd be mass panic. If they prosecute me, they'll have to disclose certain facts to the public, and hide others. Anything they hide will come back to bite them later; a cover-up is a sensational scandal."

With a bittersweet smile, he said, "If I were them, I'd keep pushing the paperwork from office to office indefinitely, or just bury it. Put me in a hole somewhere and forget where they hid the key."

Calbert gave him a hard look. "You're not wrong about that. It's taken a lot of fast-talking to keep knowledge of your return limited to the oversight committee. At this point, there are only about twenty people in the world who know you're still alive."

"Well," Michael said, trying to keep the defeat out of his voice, "no matter what happens, I appreciate you taking the time to come down here in person."

"I wanted to come down here," he said, "but not just because I consider you a friend."

"Oh?"

"I wanted to ask you about Yaxche."

"He's a good man." Michael leaned forward. "I hope you realize that he had nothing to do with anything. He just came along to help save Alex."

Calbert put up his hands. "There are no worries on that part. We've actually contacted the Honduran Departmental and arranged for his return to his village."

Letting out a sigh of relief, Michael said, "That's good."

Slowly, Calbert said, "I'm glad you vouched for him."

Michael narrowed his eyes. "I never knew you for someone to beat around the bush."

Calbert laughed. "Normally, I'm not. I guess this last year of glad-handing politicians and captains of industry has made me more circumspect."

"Just you and I here," Michael said. "Spit it out."

"All right." The minister took a moment, as if to sort out

what he was going to say. "I spoke with Yaxche in private yesterday. He remembers me from when we met at Quantum Resources—just a few weeks ago from his perspective, but over four years ago for me." He held Michael's eye. "At first, he didn't want to talk to me, but when I reassured him I only wanted the best for you, and I believed your story about what happened in Centauri, he relented and said something I wasn't sure how to take.

"He said the Kulsat were once the favored of the Grace, and that they're trying to find the legacy of the Grace."

Nodding, Michael said, "That's what the Gliesans told Alex. I have no idea what it really means. We didn't really have a lot of time to talk about it before the Kulsat blew up our ship."

"Right." Calbert scratched his jaw. "Yaxche said he believes the Grace could be the gods in the Mayan pantheon."

Michael frowned. "He never mentioned that to anyone."

"And he said he might know how to find the old gods' legacy."

"How to find—?" Michael gaped. "You mean it might actually be here, on Earth?"

Calbert made an uncertain face. "He says it might be somewhere near his village."

"No wonder he didn't want to say anything. Chow Yin's agents could have been listening the whole time." He stood up. "You need to send someone with Yaxche. If you can find this legacy, it might just be the thing we need to deal with the Kulsat."

"It might be a long shot—no, it's definitely a long shot— but I agree it's worth exploring," Calbert said. "But, since we don't want to leak anything to the public about this, we need to send someone with Yaxche who we can trust, and who can get the job done."

Michael searched his memory for someone who would fit

the bill. Then he noticed Calbert looking at him oddly again, but this time with a playful smile on his face.

"What?"

"How'd you like to go back to Honduras?"

Stunned, Michael opened and closed his mouth without saying anything. When he finally recovered his senses, he asked, "Me? How?"

"First of all," Calbert said, pulling a folded letter out from inside the breast of his jacket, "I need you to sign this affidavit stating that you have been operating undercover as an agent of the Canadian government for the past four years under direct authority of the Prime Minister."

Signing that would immediately exonerate Michael of any charges the Department of Defense had on him.

"As long as you agree to a full retraction of your earlier statement, we've prepared a replacement statement detailing how you've spent the last four years infiltrating Chow Yin's empire."

Michael couldn't believe it. "How did you get Prime Minister Dolbeau to agree to that?"

Calbert's smile widened. "I didn't. I got Prime Minister Rainier to agree to it."

"Alliras? But I thought you said—?"

"I just said he was no longer the Minister of Energy, Mines and Resources."

Michael pointed a finger at him. "You damned trickster."

Laughing out loud, Calbert said, "Just sign the affidavit so we can get you on a skybus to Honduras."

13

Kulsat Ship :
Centauri System :

A pounding headache woke Justine. After she regained consciousness, she decided it was most likely an aftereffect of the sleep agent the Kulsat had introduced into her tank.

She pushed herself up on one arm, but the motion made her stomach heave, and she let herself lie back down until the queasiness faded.

Darkness filled her awareness. The minute amount of Kinemetic radiation she'd absorbed from the presence of the Kulsat science leader was gone and her *sight* with it.

Two conflicting emotions warred inside her: if the Kulsat returned, she would absorb enough of the radiation to *see* again; but that meant the interrogation would resume. Justine was running out of tricks to delay the science leader.

Her situation was looking more and more hopeless.

"Is it true?"

Justine jerked at the sound of the mechanical voice. She couldn't *see* anyone—or anything—but someone had obviously used the linguistic computer to communicate with her.

She made a guess. "You're not the science leader."

"He is undertaking other tasks, and will not return for some time."

"Who are you?" Justine asked.

There was a long pause, and for a moment, she thought the newcomer might have gone away.

The mechanical voice said, "I am being the cleaner of floors and walls."

"What is your name?" Justine asked, but only a long silence answered her. "Do you have a name?"

"I have an identifier. There is no corresponding sound."

Perhaps the computer needed a frame of reference. "My name is Justine."

A moment later, the mechanical voice replied, "The computer does not have a corresponding motion for that word."

"It means 'just' or 'fair'. What does your name mean?" she asked the newcomer.

"I have a circle-shaped red spot above my left eye."

"Is that how you identify each other," Justine asked, "by distinguishing marks?"

"Yes, you have knowledge now."

"May I call you 'Red Spot' for short?"

"The computer is using the correct motion for my name, Justine. What is your station?"

"I'm…" For a moment, Justine was going to say she was a retired major, but she didn't know whether the language computer could interpret rank. "I am the pilot of our ship."

"You are the transportation leader?"

"I guess you could call it that." A moment later, she asked, "Does your science leader have a name?"

"He has a pattern of three dark crescents on the webbing of one limb."

"Three Crescents?" Justine said.

"Yes. He is one of the oldest Risen in the Consortium."

Justine felt a kernel of hope growing inside her. The newcomer seemed curious, and was much more communicative than the science leader. Then a thought hit her: maybe the Kulsat were employing a psychological trick. The science leader was the bad cop; Red Spot was the good cop.

"Are you a Risen?" Justine asked, testing to see if the alien would lie. "Or a Deficient?"

"I have not been offered the Gift," Red Spot said. "I am not of suitable station yet to attempt to Rise."

"Are you not supposed to be here?"

The mechanical voice spoke. "The science laboratory is for the science leader and his servants. This room is restricted from Potentials. It is an offense to disobey rules. You will report my offense?"

"I won't say anything." Justine shook her head. "If it is against the rules, why did you take the risk to talk to me?"

The mechanical voice spoke. "I need to know if it is true."

"If what is true?"

"We were told you are a scout for a barbarian army that wishes the expiration of our kind."

"That's not true," Justine said. "For the most part, our people are explorers."

"Then you practice deception?"

Shocked at the accusation, Justine asked, "What makes you say that?"

"You related a history of your conduct. There is violence. There is atrocity. There is abduction. You are no different than the other races."

Gasping, Justine realized that the Kulsat must have analyzed the story she'd recited for the translation computer, *Peter Pan,* and thought she was talking about something that had happened in her past. Without a cultural reference, the story must have sounded terrible to an alien species.

"That was a fantasy," she said. "For entertainment."

"You do not practice atrocity? You do not cut off the limbs of your enemies and feed them to animals?"

Justine let out a huff. "Not as a rule, no." Then she thought that if she told Red Spot a truth, she might engender trust. "It is true that there are some individuals from our world who break our laws, but we have a system in place to punish the offenders and to protect the innocent, and to protect those who do not have power."

"Your system protects those with no value?"

"Red Spot," she said, "our kind believes all beings have value."

There was a long silence, and for a moment, Justine thought Red Spot might have left, but then the mechanical voice came through.

"Green Stripe Over One Eye shared time with me. He was assisting me to increase my station so that one day I may attempt to Rise. He provided companionship. He had value ... to me. Now he is expired."

At first, Justine didn't know what Red Spot was trying to tell her, but then she understood. Green Stripe must have been the Deficient who the science leader had killed. She guessed the two of them had some kind of intimate relationship—though Justine really didn't have a basis to understand what that would entail. In her mind, she began to think of Red Spot as female.

"I must go," Red Spot said via the mechanical voice. "I will be discovered."

"No, wait!" Justine cried out, but then she smelled the familiar scent of the tranquilizer agent, and before she had a chance to protest, she fell back to the floor, unconscious.

∞

The headache was worse the next time she woke. At least some of her *sight* had been restored. Of course, that meant one thing: Three Crescents was back.

Justine struggled to a sitting position and used her *sight* to look around. The science leader was not alone. There was another Kulsat in the room, floating a few meters away from Three Crescents. The Kinemetic radiation in him was much stronger than that in the science leader.

Three Crescents typed. "You have completed your sleep cycle. Cooperation will resume now."

"Good morning," Justine said, and watched as the two Kulsat signed to each other.

Three Crescents turned back to the computer. "Irrelevant information. We require specifications of your home system. Population. Location. Technology level. Describe your understanding of the Gift. Do you possess the final component?"

When Justine didn't reply right away, the Kulsat typed again. "Cooperation was assured."

"You didn't even introduce me to your new friend." She got to her feet and gave the other Kulsat a nod. "My name is Justine," she said.

All eight of Three Crescents' tentacles twitched. "Your name is a deception."

"It's just a name," she said. "Something to call each other. Certainly, no harm will come from sharing our names."

Three Crescents turned to the other Kulsat. Whatever it was they were discussing, it seemed to be a heated debate. By the end of the conversation, Three Crescents was quivering. Justine guessed it was in frustration.

He moved away from the control panel, and the other Kulsat approached.

"I am Ship Leader Long Fingers On Two Of His Limbs.

We have analyzed your confession. You are the shadow form. You are to be using stealth techniques to capture our spawn. We are familiar with this purpose. You wish to examine our biology, and develop a means to destroy us."

"You've got it all wrong," Justine said, wishing she'd never picked *Peter Pan* to recite. "I had no intention of kidnapping anyone. It was you who abducted me, remember?"

"All aliens that encroach on our territory wish to destroy us. Your confession has confirmed this fact. We are validated to collect you."

"It wasn't a confession." Justine had to restrain herself from slapping the glass; that would only demonstrate that she was capable of violence, and it was imperative that she be as diplomatic and politic as she could. "It was a story. If you'll let me explain, I'm sure we can come to an understanding—"

Long Fingers typed. "It is apparent your kind practice deception. Any information you provide may be false. You attempt to conceal the final component of the Gift. We will attempt to search for other specimens of your kind, should they exist in this system, and extract biological information."

The ship leader turned from the computer and signed something to Three Crescents. Justine didn't need a translation program to interpret its meaning.

As Long Fingers swam out of the room, and Three Crescents turned to one of his other computers, Justine's frustration boiled over.

"I said I would cooperate. I'm not lying. I'll talk to you, if you'll just listen to me. This is all a big misunderstanding."

When the science leader continued working on his machine, ignoring Justine, she slapped the glass to get his attention, not caring how it looked to them.

"Three Crescents," she said. "I'm talking to you."

He turned around, and a ripple went through his body as he

stared at Justine with those large eyes of his. Finally, he propelled himself to the translation control panel and typed.

"I have never offered my identifier. How did you acquire this knowledge?"

Cursing herself for the slip, Justine said, "It was a guess. I see the three dark crescents on the web between your tentacles. You name yourself after distinguishing marks, don't you?"

Three Crescents seemed to consider her answer. "You are practicing additional deception." He went to another computer station and typed on the control panel. For the first time, Justine could see one of their displays, but the information on it was meaningless to her. It looked like a series of squiggles and dashes—obviously their written language—but there was no way she could interpret them.

Turning back to the translation computer, Three Crescents typed to her. "There has been unauthorized access to this laboratory. We have a traitor. Did you promise information of final component to gain assistance from the defector? Reveal the conspirator, and there will be no discomfort in your expiry. Refuse cooperation and I will apply continuous discomfort."

Backing away from the glass, Justine felt the terror growing in her. She had no idea how much torture she could endure, and didn't know if the sonic attack was the limit of what they could do to her.

She wasn't about to give up Red Spot to them. Even though she was a Kulsat, she'd demonstrated that not all of their kind had the same disregard for life as Three Crescents or Long Fingers. Red Spot had grieved for the death of Green Stripe, even though their society had labeled him a Deficient. She had also put her trust in Justine not to betray her.

Three Crescents typed something. "Discomfort will begin now."

The familiar hum of the sonic attack filled the tank, and

before Justine could yell out a curse at Three Crescents, she doubled over in pain.

The torture went on for some time…

∞

At one point, Justine began to wish her tormentor would just finish her off and put an end to the agony. She was certain the sonic blasts had caused some internal damage. The low-wave attacks made her vomit, and the high-pitched sonics left her dizzy and disoriented.

When she felt a trickle of blood leak out from one ear, she yelled at Three Crescents in frustration. "How can I hear your questions if I'm deaf?"

The sonic blasts ceased, but the ringing in her ears continued. Even through that, she heard Three Crescents' next question.

"You are prepared to cooperate? Please identify the traitor."

She shrugged. "I can't tell. You all look the same to me."

"Describe distinguishing marks."

Justine found it difficult to concentrate, and felt nauseated, but she had to keep delaying Three Crescents. Every minute she stalled him was another minute for Alex and the others to get farther away.

She said, "I don't know. He had a green stripe running down one arm."

"Deception. That Deficient has expired." Three Crescents typed for a few moments. "You have provided verification that your kind are an imminent threat to the Kulsat and must be eliminated. Once you are all removed from existence, we will investigate your world for the final component."

"No, you can't do that," Justine said. "Why won't you listen to reason?"

"Identify the traitor."

Justine shook her head. "There is no traitor."

"You have displayed the willingness to endure discomfort to protect conspirators, though they are not your species. Should conspirators no longer exist, you will have no reason to withhold cooperation."

He turned around and signed to one of the other Kulsat floating just outside the laboratory's entranceway. That Kulsat swam away in a rush.

Within a minute, he returned with what looked like an army of Kulsat. They all tried to fit inside the laboratory, but it soon became too crowded. Three Crescents signed something to them, and the majority of the aliens swam back outside, but remained in waiting.

Justine counted twenty Kulsat still in the laboratory, not including Three Crescents. Of those, three had Kinemetic radiation in them—Deficients—and the rest were normal Kulsat. With her senses, she detected seven other 'Deficients' among those waiting outside the laboratory. Justine had no idea if Red Spot was among the twenty.

Three Crescents typed on the computer.

"All Kulsat who have been in this section since your arrival are displayed here. One of them is the traitor. To be assured, all twenty will be expired. The others will learn the result of betrayal."

Three Crescents swam a short distance to one of the worktables and picked up a device that looked like a soldering iron. It had a long cord that was attached to the nearest wall. With two of his tentacles, he pointed the sharp end of the tool at one of the Kulsat in the line.

A thin stream of something jetted out from the device, detectable only because of the rippling of the water between Three Crescents and his target. Justine heard a deep thrumming sound and felt the vibrations of what must have been some kind of sonic agitator. The Kulsat at the receiving end of the wave began to pulsate, and his arms started to contract and expand in sharp movements. His entire body seemed to go into a rapid series of spasms, and then the water around him turned murky as his flesh burst into a cloud of black and red.

On the wall behind the victim, a large circular opening appeared and, as if it were a giant pump, began to draw water into it. The dead alien's body drifted back to the opening and was sucked out of the room.

The nineteen remaining Kulsat did not make any sign of protest, or attempt to flee.

Justine, unable to fathom the horror she was witnessing, struggled to her feet and pounded on the glass separating her from the others.

"You monster!" she screamed. "Stop killing them. They're innocent!"

Three Crescents gave no indication that he was aware of her protest. He raised the device up at the next Kulsat in line, a small one with orange mottling on his arms, and fired again.

Again, the Kulsat spasmed, the water around him clouded over with his bodily fluids.

"Stop it!" Justine screamed. She punched and kicked the glass as hard as she could but the only damage done was to her fist.

"Name the traitor. The others will be spared."

How could she betray one Kulsat to save the rest of them? How could she watch more sentient beings die horribly to keep her word to an alien being who she barely knew? No matter what she did, Red Spot was going to die.

"All right," Justine said, choking back the tears. "I'll tell you. Just stop killing them."

"Name the traitor."

Pointing to the second murdered Kulsat, Justine said, "That was the one. You got him already."

"Deception has been employed." Three Crescents typed. "These twenty have never been in this section before. It is apparent that your kind cannot be trusted. Your species are an imminent threat, and will contaminate all Kulsat you contact. We will now expire all Deficients and Potentials in this section of the ship. We will report to our superiors and recommend the expiry of all your kind."

The overwhelming futility of it consumed Justine. No matter what she'd done, Three Crescents had been single-minded in his purpose and his conviction that she, and all humankind, was a threat. The story Alex had conveyed was now confirmed in her mind. Paranoia drove the Kulsat to destroy any new alien species they encountered.

Not knowing if any of the other Kulsat could see the translation monitor, Justine nevertheless called out to them. "Save yourselves. Fight him. He's only one. You outnumber him."

Three Crescents made a rippling motion with his arms, similar to when Justine had caused him frustration earlier, and he touched something on the computer. The soft hum on the transmitter on her collar—a sound she hadn't noticed up until that point—disappeared. The Kulsat had shut off the translator.

The alien then raised the energy emitter device in his tentacles and began to fire into the remaining Kulsat in the room.

Justine couldn't understand why the Kulsat simply waited for their death. Had the elite class—those like Three Crescents—so completely conditioned the others to believe they had no value unless they were Risen?

Even knowing in her heart it would make no difference, that none of the Kulsat could understand her, Justine slapped her hands against the glass. "Fight him, damn you. Defend yourselves."

It was as if one of them had heard her. From the entranceway, a small Kulsat flicked all eight of her tentacles and dashed toward Three Crescents. Red Spot? Justine spied the distinctive mark above her eye.

Intent on murdering the non-Risen Kulsat in the lab, Three Crescents didn't see her until she was right next to him.

He twisted around to aim the rod at Red Spot, but her plan wasn't to attack him. Instead, she darted to the wall where the cord of the energy rod was attached. She wrapped three tentacles around it and yanked. It came free before Three Crescents could fire at her.

With a huge ripple of frustration going through his arms, Three Crescents quantized her. In the place where the small Kulsat had been, now there was only a collection of light particles.

The pump in the opposite wall was working overtime, sucking in the remnants of the other dead Kulsat. It was also creating a current in the water, and the quantized bits of the small alien were slowly being drawn across the lab.

Three Crescents, having dealt with the situation, swam over to the wall and went about repairing the connection to the energy rod.

He was going to resume his killing spree.

When Justine had been fully irradiated with Kinemet, she'd been able to quantize herself at will. It had never occurred to her to try to quantize another being. She believed a quantum engine was required to begin the quantization process. It was only after the quantized state existed that Justine had been able to reverse the change of state and return the ship and its passengers to their tangible selves.

With her senses, she could not detect any Kinemet in this section of the ship, whether charged or dormant. How had Three Crescents done that to Red Spot? When she'd been quantized and removed from the *Ultio,* her suspicion had been that the Kulsat had developed some kind of technology they'd used to target her. Now, she wondered if it was another stage in the development of a Kinemat.

Even though Justine barely had any radiation in her system, she had enough to see ... and maybe, if she concentrated, she might have enough to reverse the quantization on Red Spot before the ship's pumps sucked her out of the room and to destinations unknown.

Willing herself to focus, she reached out with every trace of the Kinemetic radiation in her. The strain was incredible, and her entire body shook with the effort.

The effort completely drained her, and panic streaked through her when she suddenly lost her ability to *see.*

14

Copán :
Honduras :

Long Count: 9.19.19.17.11

I had no sense of time. It seemed as if I had been walking for
tens of days. The pain in my chest was worse since I started on
my way back to my village, and with every step I took, it felt as
if I were being struck in the ribs with a heavy club.

I paused to drink whenever there was a stream of water, and
eat whenever I came across a bush ripe with berries.

I could not recall when I stopped to sleep, though I must
have, because I found myself lying on the ground in the
morning, looking up into a cloudless sky.

The thin wisps of a dream floated away as full
consciousness returned. The pain surrounded me like a
blanket, and I wondered if I would ever rise again.

Somehow, I managed to get back on my feet, gather my
pack, and complete the journey to my village.

Papan, one of the hunters who had taught me how to track
prey, was the first to spot me, and he let out a cry to others to
come and help me.

Knowing that I was among family and friends, I let myself

succumb to my weariness, and passed out as several strong men picked me up to bring me to my hut.

∞

I don't know how long I slept, but when I woke, my chest was wrapped with a bandage, and I was covered with several woven blankets.

There were three others in my hut. My father, Tohil Ak, stood over me, his face beaming with pride. Beside him, my mother, Xmucane, clasped her hands together and gave me a look that was a mix of relief and worry.

The third person in the tent was Balam Ix, our priest, who was the oldest person in our village.

"Subo," my father said, "it is good to see you awake. Your mother feared the worst."

I tried to sit up, but it felt as if a boulder pressed down on my chest.

"Don't try to move," the priest said. He put a wrinkled hand on my shoulder. "It will be many days before you are healed."

I relaxed my muscles and lay back. "I have succeeded, father." Smiling up at him, I spoke with pride. "Three Q'eqchi' came upon me. I did not take their skin, but I defeated them."

"That is good, my son." He nodded. "The warriors will welcome you to their ranks once you are able."

Balam said, "There is much more to your story, young Subo, is there not?"

I looked back and forth between the holy man and my father, who said, "You spoke of it in your fever sleep. Is it a dream, or a vision?"

"You must tell me," Balam said, "now, before we bring the story to the council. You had a holy vision. Did a god grant you audience, young one?"

Though it was difficult to do so, I took a deep breath. "He said he was not a god, but he was a sky traveler. I saw his boat flying through the sky while I was waiting for a Q'eqchi' warrior to fight."

I told them Ekahua's story from beginning to end. When I was finished, I could feel myself tiring from the effort.

"Do you remember the Song of the Stars he taught you?" Balam asked. His voice was pitched low, full of wonder. I saw in the way he looked at me that he did not doubt my story.

"Yes," I said, and closed my eyes as I sang the song in Ekahua's strange language.

When I sang the last line of the song, I looked again at our holy man. He nodded.

"It is a powerful Song. It is a great gift he has given you, Subo Ak. It will take you your entire life to understand its meaning. Perhaps you will never understand. We will study the song together."

"Together...?" I asked, wondering at Balam's words.

"Yes." He stood, then. "I have been to Copán and spoken with King Ukit Took about your fever dream. This Ekahua is a spirit who visited you in a vision. It is a sign from the gods. Only a prophet may receive such portents from the Underworld."

My father spoke the words before I could. "Subo is to be a warrior. He has achieved a great victory over our enemies."

Balam smiled and nodded. "Only with the power of a great spirit was he able to defeat three Q'eqchi' warriors. It has been decided, Tohil. Subo will become my apprentice, and one day he will take my place as the high priest of the village. It is prophesied."

He turned to me. "In seven days, you will begin your training." With that, Balam took his leave of us.

I was completely stunned by the news, and I felt a rising

anger at the king's decision.

Me, a holy man? I had never thought about being anything other than a warrior like my father, and to honor the memory of my slain brother.

I could see the disappointment in my father's eyes. From the time I was a child, he'd schooled me in the ways of battle. Now, all that effort was for nothing.

Clenching his jaw, my father turned on his heel and strode from my hut. Only my mother remained, and she would not meet my eyes.

Ysalane! She could not marry me. Holy men did not take wives, and would never have children.

It did not matter to me that the priest was one of the most revered members of our people, that the elders took counsel with him, and that he commanded the respect of all in the village. Right then, I felt I'd been cheated out of my reward, and I cursed the day I had seen Exahua's flying boat.

∞

Over the next few days, I healed, and soon I could get up from my bed and walk on my own. I tired quickly, and could only make short trips at first. Soon, however, I could wander around for long periods of time.

Our village had twenty houses spaced out over a sizeable area. The largest building was in the center of the village, near the common circle, and was used by the elders to hold their meetings. One house was reserved for the priest. The others were for the families of the elders, weavers, toolmakers, traders, and the warrior-hunters.

There were several temporary huts for those of us who were unmarried, but who no longer lived with our families. It was where we stayed until we completed our manhood rituals, and until our parents and elders arranged a marriage for us.

Most of the villagers lived on their own compounds outside of the village, where they tended their fields.

Everywhere I went, the other villagers would watch and stare as I passed. No one would approach or talk to me other than my mother and father. Word had spread that I was going to be apprenticed to our village's priest.

Returning to my hut, I lay on my bed and thought about how miserable my life had become. I would have to learn numbers, stars and the calendar; I would need to learn to write glyphs to record our stories; I would need to learn to help heal the sick with potions and rituals; I would have to advise new families on what to name their children. There would be hundreds of other tasks I had never wanted.

At that moment, I decided I would sneak away from the village once I was healed enough to do so. I would return to Quiriguá and kill as many of our enemies as I could before they captured and sacrificed me. Then, at least, there would be songs sung of my heroic deeds.

The Song. Over the past few days, I had been trying to avoid remembering it, but once I let it enter my thoughts, I couldn't put it out of my mind.

Without being consciously aware that I was doing it, I began to hum the song. Soon, the humming turned into singing, and a sense of peace crept into my troubled heart.

I was angry at my fate, but I could take comfort in the great gift Ekahua had given me.

When I finished singing, I started it again from the beginning.

I was so consumed by the song, I wasn't immediately aware that the ground was shaking underneath me. It only lasted a few seconds, but I knew from experience that small earth tremors often led to larger earthquakes.

Rolling off my bed, I bit my tongue as a sharp pain went through my chest at the sudden movement. It took me a moment before I could get to my feet and step outside my hut.

Several of the women were running across the village common, calling out for their children to come to them and find a safe spot to hide.

A second tremor hit, sending me off-balance. I had to grasp the supports on my hut to keep it from collapsing.

One of the huts on the other side of the village toppled over. The story stone in the center of our common vibrated, sending rock dust down in plumes.

My father, who had been preparing a skin by the fire outside his hut, hurried over to see if anyone was in danger and needed help.

A small child, who had been knocked over by the tremor, screamed in fear, not understanding, even as he threw his arms out for his mother. She raced over and scooped him up in her arms.

My father and I shared a quick glance, but it seemed as if a collapsed hut and a frightened child was the extent of the damage.

"Tohil," Bil'al, a young warrior-in-training who had stayed back from the hunt because of a broken ankle, said to my father, "is everyone all right?"

Nodding, my father surveyed the village, taking a head count of everyone who should be there.

"Everyone seems to be unharmed," he said, but then he changed his expression.

A moment later, I realized there was one person who had not come out of their house at the commotion: the priest, Balam Ix.

As quickly as I could, I headed for the priest's home. It was a larger dwelling than my hut, but not as big as the family houses. My father got there well before I did, and looked inside. Instead of going in, he paused at the doorway, and I could see his shoulders slump.

He backed out just as I arrived.

"What?" I asked, searching his face before I ducked inside the priest's hut to see for myself.

Balam Ix had been the oldest person in our village, and had lived for many more years than most would. Everyone suspected he would not live for much more, but witnessing him lying on his bed without moving, his eyes open but not seeing, lips slightly parted but not breathing, I felt a momentary twinge of disbelief. Balam had been a part of everyday life in our village all my life, and now he was gone.

My father spoke in a muted tone. "The Underworld has called for him."

"It is an omen," I said, though I kept my voice too low for anyone to hear.

My father put his hand on my shoulder. He said, "When the others return from the hunt and patrol tonight, we will prepare him for burial."

One other result I had not immediately considered became alarmingly clear when Bil'al, who had come up behind us, asked, "Is Subo the priest of the village, now?" Widening his eyes, he added, "I hope you can remember all the words to the prayers."

∞

I spent the rest of the day sweating, and not because of the heat. Only a short while ago, I was on the path of the warrior, moving toward the future I desired. Now, the villagers were expecting me, who had not yet seen eighteen summers, and who had not spent a single day in religious study, to be their spiritual leader—at least for the time being.

In cases where the high priest of a village died without an apprentice, the elders would send a request to the High Priest of Copán to provide them with a temporary holy man. The elders had, indeed, charged one of the warriors to travel to the city to deliver the news, and he'd returned at dusk. Because of the earthquake, the Holy Order was too busy aiding the citizens of Copán, where the damage had been more severe than in our village. It could be several days before they sent anyone, perhaps longer.

It was up to me to lead the ritual.

We'd had several burials in the past few years, and I had to admit that I had not given them my full attention. To my relief, my father and the other warriors took charge of preparing the priest's house for the burial. After gathering the priest's story stones and calendars, they tore the building down. All the construction materials were removed from the site except for the floor, which they raised high enough so that several others could dig a grave for the priest.

The three elders, Yax Kuk, Ohtli Ti, and Nentil Mo'Nab, brought me to their house, where they instructed me on how to wear the priest's headdress and costume. It did not fit me very well; I was much taller than the priest had been, and rounder of the shoulder. I endured and followed the elders back to the priest's house.

Balam's body lay on the ground in front of the remains of his home. Ensuring that I assisted throughout the entire process, the elders prepared the priest's body. First, they wrapped him in a cotton shroud and then they filled his mouth with maize. Without thinking about what I was doing, I began the ritual.

"Accept this food to sustain you through your journey through Xibalba."

At the elders' prompting, I placed a jade bead in the priest's mouth on top of the maize.

"The road to rebirth may be long; the jade will give you breath in the Underworld."

The elders wrapped his head with the shroud.

"We wrap you to protect you from the cold of the Underworld."

The slaves picked up the priest's body and carried him to the grave they had dug under where his house once stood. Gently, they placed him in it.

I lifted a ceramic pot full of water and slowly poured it over the priest, starting at his head and moving down to his torso.

"The Underworld is a world of water. You must enter the water to begin your journey."

One of the elders lit sticks of incense and placed them in the ground outside the grave as the others arranged the priest's possessions around his body.

"Accept these gifts. May they help you on your path to rebirth."

I stepped back as other members of the village came forward to make offerings of their own and to speak prayers for the man who had been their priest all their lives.

Catching my father looking at me thoughtfully, I realized that I had spoken the ritual word-for-word. I did not make a single mistake. It was as if I had performed the rites of burial a hundred times before. The thought came to me that, had I never met Ekahua and learned his Song, I would never have been able to remember the words of prayer today. Somehow, when he'd touched me with light, he'd changed me.

The men filled in the grave, and then lowered the platform floor over it.

We would begin building my home on top of the priest's grave tomorrow. His spirit would watch over and guard the new dwelling, and perhaps visit me in my dreams.

15

Qin Station :
Sol System :

Alex knew he couldn't use any more delaying tactics right then, at least, not under direct threat of being shot.

"As long as you can promise to give me periodic updates on my friends' progress home, I will cooperate. I gave Chow Yin my word."

"His Highness," Alice corrected, but it sounded more like an automatic response. "So," she said, "what's the big secret?"

"The big secret is that I don't know what Klaus discovered."

Seeing Alice's eyes widen in outrage, Alex held his hands up. "However, I know the road he took to get there."

"The Song of the Stars. Is the formula hidden in it?"

"Yes, though it's not precisely what you think."

Alice folded her arms across her chest. "I'm waiting."

"The words in the story are unimportant. It's the melody itself. There are certain notes that translate to sound frequencies. These sound frequencies have a corresponding light-wave frequency. Those light-wave frequencies are used to bombard Kinemet before initiating a reaction—in essence, priming it—to achieve the desired effect on a person. The result, of course, is irradiating that person, and attuning them to the radiation signature of Kinemet."

"What notes?"

"I'm not certain. I believe Klaus wrote a computer program that disseminated the most likely possibilities. Unfortunately, that program was destroyed along with the station on Venus."

Alice chewed her lip. "We have many computer programmers with us. I'm sure we can reproduce that algorithm. I assume you have some idea which notes are important and which ones aren't?"

Nodding, Alex said, "I listened to Yaxche recite the song several times. I have some ideas."

"Good." Alice went to her computer and typed something. "Sian is my father's best programmer. We'll get him here to write the code." A moment later, a message came back on-screen, and Alice smiled. "Good. He's currently finishing an assignment, but should be here in a few hours."

She logged off the computer and faced Alex. "I will have some food delivered here for you. If you require rest, there is a cot set up in the storage room over there." She pointed to a door on the other side of the lab.

"Thank you," Alex said. There was no point in being impolite. After all, the more cooperative he seemed, the easier it would be to delay their progress.

"A guard will be posted in this room at all times. He has my permission to shoot you if you do anything to arouse suspicion."

"Understood," Alex said amicably.

Narrowing her eyes at him once more, she strode out of the lab.

∞

Alex presumed Alice was off either to report to her father,

complain about the working arrangement, or have something to eat. No matter which it was, Alex wouldn't have much time.

Confidently, he walked over to the computer Alice had used to contact the programmer. Just as he started toward it, the guard turned his rifle on him.

As casually as he could, Alex took a seat in front of the console and typed in Alice's password—she had not been careful enough to hide it from him. Perhaps she thought he could not see what she typed from across the room, or that he couldn't use a keyboard with Chinese characters on it. Though there was a Kinemetic damper in the room, that only prevented Alex's electropathy and his *sight*. His eidetic memory was intact, and though he didn't know how to interpret the characters on the keyboard, he remembered precisely which keys Alice pressed and in what sequence.

"What are you doing?" The guard took a few steps forward, and pointed his rifle directly at Alex.

Forcing a calmness into his voice that he didn't feel, Alex said, "Cooperating. What did you think I was doing?"

The guard didn't reply, but neither did he lower his weapon.

Affecting a sigh of irritation, Alex turned in the seat to face the suspicious guard. "If you must know, I'm going to access the recording of the Song the Stars and begin logging the sound waves of each note. It could take some time."

Without waiting to see if his explanation satisfied the guard, Alex turned back to the computer and tapped a key to see what it would do. A navigation screen appeared. "After all," he said, "that's what they brought me here to do, isn't it?"

He tapped another key, and then another and another, memorizing each of their functions. Once he had a baseline, deciphering the remaining characters only took a few minutes. By the time he had a working knowledge of the computer's operation, he noticed the guard had retreated to his post, and had adopted his previous watchful position.

What Alex needed was more information, both on how much they knew about Klaus's progress, and about their empire.

The first database Alex accessed prompted him for a password. He entered Alice's and smiled; she was one of those people who used the same password for everything. It occurred to him that he had no idea what that password was, and opened a translator and frowned when it spat out the English letters: qinguangwangfoursevensevenzero.

At first, he thought it might be a random string of characters, but then he had an idea, and did a general search. Qin Guang Wang was the Chinese ruler of the first court of Feng-du, the equivalent of the Western version of hell. He judged the dead and decided whether their souls went to paradise or were sent into hell for punishment.

Using her password, Alex accessed Alice's personnel file and confirmed the date of her birth. 4770 was the Chinese equivalent to 2073 in the Gregorian calendar.

Alice used the Chinese god of retribution and her birthday as her password.

What events had occurred to make Alice Yin the person she was? There was such anger in her.

Quickly, Alex skimmed the rest of her file. It gave some basic details, but not enough to paint a complete picture. Alex didn't know how much access he had, but he did a comprehensive search throughout the entire station's databases for any document that would give him a hint to Alice Yin's background.

With his enhanced memory, he only needed to glance at each document once to retain everything on it. By the time his lunch arrived, Alex had read all the information in the database concerning the Emperor's daughter. Whatever wasn't there, he could fill in himself.

∞

When Chow Yin had started to build his criminal organization in the depths of Luna Station, he'd done so despite his disability. For the kind of man he was, he believed the only women who would be attracted to him were those seeking his money, power, and security. To let himself become romantically involved with someone was a weakness, a vulnerability he could not afford. He was still a man, however, with a man's needs. Those needs were met by those women who provided such services.

To prevent any possibility of such a woman becoming familiar with him or his operation, he never contracted the same person twice, and always ensured they were on Luna temporarily.

Chow Yin took as many precautions as he could, but no safeguard was infallible, as he found out when one of the women contacted him and attempted to extort money: their union had produced a baby girl. Alice.

In an attempt to plug the breach in security, Chow Yin sent a man to eliminate the two. Some paternal weakness in him made him change his orders at the last moment: let the baby live.

Since the woman had no living relatives, Alice ended up in China's orphanage system. Though Chow Yin had no desire to meet or publicly acknowledge his daughter, he nevertheless checked in on her from time to time.

When he received a report that Alice had an affinity for the sciences, he arranged a scholarship to Peking University in their Astrophysics department, and ensured various professors and university officials monitored and encouraged her progress.

After Chow Yin was arrested on Luna Station, the media dug into every aspect of his life.

A reporter from Beijing broke the story, linking Chow Yin to Alice.

It became a media circus for her: daughter of the most infamous criminal of the century. Her scholarship funds were seized by the government. Trying to dispel any suspicion of bribery, the university administration immediately expelled her from their program. She lost her apartment and all her friends.

No legitimate company would hire Alice after that, and—homeless, destitute, and desperate—she ended up working for an arms dealer who was developing biological weapons.

Three years after her father was prosecuted and sent to the penal colony on the other side of the Sun, the organization Alice worked for was raided. Alice was convicted and sentenced to life in Chongqing Prison.

A follow-up piece several years later illustrated how prison life was unkind to Alice. The prison had a reputation for torture by the male guards, severe deprivation, and brutality among the inmates.

The last article Alex read was about an unexplained fire in a poorly maintained section of the prison that killed more than a dozen inmates and guards, including Alice Yin, a month before Chow Yin's own escape from the remote penal station.

Alex guessed Chow Yin had arranged for her escape and brought her to Qin Station to work for him.

She'd been working on the Kinemetic process since then. The only means of testing any Kinemetic theory was to use human subjects; and there had not been any successes in all that time.

With horror, Alex wondered how many people had died in her experiments.

At thirty-six, Alice Yin was as brilliant and insane as her father.

16

Tegucigalpa, Honduras :
Central American Conglomeration :

As much as the radical events that had occurred in the four years he'd been away had alarmed Michael, the overwhelming sameness of the Honduran capital was a sharp contrast. The country had always had a struggling economy, and the war that had ravaged the world since Michael had left hadn't improved the standard of living for the people of Honduras.

The last time Michael had been here was with George, and they'd been on a fact-finding mission. This time, the only difference was that he was accompanied by Yaxche. For the duration of the flight, through the landing at the Toncontin International Airport, and the sluggish wading through the country's customs procedures, neither of them spoke of anything of importance. They kept their conversation light, and off-topic from their mission, just in case any other curious passenger or official overheard them.

Yaxche, as a returning national, had an easier time passing the customs interview, but when Michael offered up his identification, he was flagged. He had to spend an hour in a small room while the officers contacted Canadian officials. Michael's name had been plastered all over the local newsvids after his involvement in the events at the Ruiz plantation four years before, then again after his disappearance from Canada Station Three. Whoever the Honduran officers contacted back home, they managed to convince them that Michael was not only *not* under suspicion for any wrongdoing—any outstanding charges had been rescinded—but he was a fully authorized government agent, whose current mission was to escort Yaxche to his home.

Michael's first task was to check in to the consulate, and then head to the bus terminal to catch the daily shuttle to Santa Rosa de Copán. Customs had taken so long, they only had half an hour to get to the Tegucigalpa bus terminal, which was almost across the city.

It proved harder to find an autotaxi than to get through customs. When Michael, with Yaxche quietly trailing behind, went to the kiosk to get one assigned, there was an attendant there, a young kid who couldn't have been more than fifteen.

Though his Spanish had improved over the past while, Michael was glad he'd remembered to bring his translator with him.

"Sorry, sir," the attendant said. "All the computers are down this morning. The autotaxis are grounded."

"For how long?" Michael asked.

"They're doing some kind of upgrade—it's been needed for a long time. They were supposed to be finished overnight, but it's taking forever."

Michael made a grunt of displeasure and looked around.

"A city bus should arrive in twenty minutes, if you want to wait."

There was no way they would make the terminal in time.

"How far away is a car rental office from here?" Michael asked.

The attendant said, "Oh, the del Angel Vehicle Hire is right over there, near the north end of the terminal. You could walk there in five minutes."

"Thank you." He gave the attendant a tip, and then hefted his luggage. He glanced at Yaxche. "I don't think we're going to make the daily shuttle in time. If we can rent a car, we could drive to Santa Rosa ourselves after we check in with the consulate." Yaxche gave Michael a nod that he agreed with the plan. He had a backpack full of souvenirs he'd bought at the Pearson gift shop, and he slung it over his shoulder before following.

When they entered the rental agency, the harried clerk behind the counter shook his head. "If you're looking to rent, all our cars and trucks are gone. With the autotaxis down, we sold out almost an hour ago."

If they hadn't been so delayed by customs…

Not only would they miss the shuttle out of the capital, but they also seemed to be stranded at the airport.

Michael grimaced, and looked at Yaxche. The older man was looking pale; after spending so long in air-conditioned space craft, and in the cool Canadian climate, it would take a bit of time for them both the acclimatize to the heat of Honduras.

"Maybe I'll call the consulate, and see if they can send a car."

They stepped back out of the rental agency, and Michael scanned up and down the terminal for a comm kiosk. He strode over to it, logged in, and placed the call. A young-sounding female voice answered.

"Thank you for calling the Canadian Consulate of Honduras. Beth speaking. How may I direct your call?"

"This is Michael Sanderson. I'm a special emissary escorting a Honduran national. I believe Allan Perkins was informed of my arrival. It seems we're stuck at the airport without transport, and we've missed the daily shuttle to Santa Rosa de

Copán." A moment later, he remembered to give her his official access code to verify his identity.

The secretary said, "I'm sorry, Mr. Sanderson. Consul Perkins had an all-day conference today. Unfortunately, because of budget cuts, we no longer have any vehicles for official use. We contract with a chauffeur service, but they don't travel outside the capital. I could send one to bring you here. There's a hotel near here where you can stay until tomorrow."

Trying not to sound ungrateful for the offer, Michael said, "We were hoping to make Santa Rosa de Copán today."

"I'm sorry, Mr. Sanderson," the secretary said.

It seemed they didn't have any other choice. "Thank you, Beth. We'll be waiting at the north parking lot."

After disconnecting, Michael said to Yaxche. "We might as well find a shady spot and sit down."

There was an outdoor food vendor, where Michael bought two iced teas. They sat at one of the round patio tables and took refuge in the shadow of its umbrella.

"How does it feel to finally be back home?" Michael asked.

Looking around the busy streets, Yaxche said, "This is not home."

"Well, with luck, we should be in your village tomorrow evening at the latest."

"It has been a long time since I slept in my own bed." He gave Michael a toothy smile. "Your beds are all too soft."

Since his release from the detention center in Ottawa, Michael hadn't pressed Yaxche on specifics, taking the older man at his word that he might know the whereabouts of the alien race Ah Tabai called the Grace. Thinking about it, the information the Mayan had given them was fairly thin—that he *might* know where they'd gone—but then again, everyone had discounted that the ancient Song of the Stars document contained the key to unlocking the photonic properties of Kinemet. Michael was prepared to go on a little faith, but his curiosity got the better of him.

Casually, he asked, "So, what is it we're looking for?" When Yaxche glanced at him questioningly, Michael added, "I mean, is there another ancient scroll or something?"

"I don't know."

"What do you mean, you don't know?"

"It's possible, but I do not think so."

Michael looked at Yaxche pointedly. "If it's not a scroll, then what is it?"

"It is a story."

"What story?"

"I cannot tell you. It is not my story." After a moment, he said, "I already told you *my* story."

Michael cleared his throat. "Now you're just being cryptic."

Yaxche, as if enjoying teasing Michael, smiled wide. Letting out a small laugh, he said, "We need to speak to an old friend of mine. Perhaps, if he likes you, he will tell you his story."

"The story of the Grace?"

Keeping his smile firmly in place, Yaxche shrugged helplessly. "It is best to hear the story from the storyteller."

Michael recalled that the key to the Song of the Stars wasn't the story itself, it was in the telling, and he resigned himself to be patient.

Yaxche patted him on the arm. "Do not worry. I think my friend will like you."

By the time they finished their iced teas, they spotted a long black car pulling into the parking lot. The decal on the door read 'Tegucigalpa Chauffeur Service'. Michael stood and hefted his luggage as the car pulled up.

The driver spoke in English with a heavy Spanish accent. "Mr. Sanderson for the Canadian Consulate?" The man, who was short but quite stocky, wore an odd-fitting black suit. The tie around his neck was loosened, and the top button of the collar was undone. As if realizing the fact, he quickly did the button up and tightened the tie.

"Yes, that's us," Michael said.

Reaching into his vehicle, the driver pressed the trunk release, then hurried over to help Michael and Yaxche with their luggage.

Once Michael and Yaxche climbed into the back seat, the driver engaged the navigation computer and typed in their destination.

They drove along the Bulevard Fuerzas Armadas, weaving in and out of traffic, and Michael looked out of the window at the city. When he glanced over to Yaxche, he saw that the older man seemed not to take any interest in the city.

When they reached the Boulevard Centromerica, instead of turning north toward the Canadian Embassy, they kept going east.

"I think you missed the turnoff," Michael called out to the driver.

"Construction," the driver said. "We'll take a side street around. It'll be faster."

Sitting back uneasily, Michael searched his memory. It had been a few months—his time—since he'd been in Tegucigalpa, and though he didn't have as keen a memory as Alex or Justine, he'd taken the time to look at a street map of the capital more than once. There were no side streets from the turnoff until they crossed the Anillo Periférico. Even in a roundabout way, that would more than double their travel time.

"City's going through a lot of problems this morning," Michael said.

"*Sí.*"

The man didn't seem to be acting suspiciously. Perhaps

Michael was just being paranoid. He decided to wait and see what happened.

When they reached the turnoff to Anillo Periférico, and continued heading east, Michael sat forward.

"Where are you taking us?"

"Please relax, *señor.*" The driver drew a pistol from inside his suit jacket and held it up a moment for Michael to see before putting it back. "It's for your own good."

17

Kulsat Ship :
Centauri System :

Blind both physically and Kinemetically, and trapped inside a small tank surrounded by water on a hostile alien ship was enough to make Justine feel overwhelmed. Knowing there could either be a mass slaughter or a revolution just outside her reach, the outcome of which would directly decide her own fate, Justine fought to keep herself from succumbing to the emotional overload.

Sounds didn't travel very well into her terrarium, but what she could hear, she couldn't interpret. Had her efforts returned Red Spot to physical form? Had Three Crescents repaired his energy rod and blasted her? Was he finishing his insane task of killing every non-Risen on the ship?

The Kinemetic radiation coming from the alien Risen started to seep back into Justine's system, and her *sight* returned to her slowly.

In the span of a few seconds, she saw what had transpired during her blackout. Three Crescents had reconnected his energy rod and was blasting it at the other aliens, but he was doing it out of desperation. As if Red Spot's courage had bolstered them, the other Kulsat charged Three Crescents. They grabbed loose tools and canisters to use as weapons. So far, none of them had gotten close enough to strike Three Crescents, but he'd killed more than half a dozen of them and wounded several others.

Red Spot was still alive, Justine saw, but she was injured. One of her tentacles hung limply from her torso—perhaps a graze from the energy weapon.

Helplessly, Justine watched the army of cephalopods throw themselves at Three Crescents, but he seemed an expert in his aim and kept fending them off.

The sheer numbers were on the rebels' side, though. As if sensing that he couldn't keep up his defense forever, Three Crescents quantized himself. In control of himself in that state, he raced out of the laboratory, leaving the survivors and Justine behind. He was no doubt going to report to Long Fingers.

Justine didn't know how many Risen were on board the alien ship, but one was all that was needed if they decided to quantize the entire vessel. Once everyone was neutralized in a photonic state, the pilot could navigate back to their home system, where the numbers would undoubtedly favor the elite Kulsat rather than the rebels.

Red Spot swam to the terrarium and turned on the translation computer with a flick of one long tentacle. The familiar hum of the link on her collar gave Justine a sense of comfort she hadn't expected.

"Red Spot," Justine said. "Are you all right?"

The little alien typed. "Your concern is unexpected. I will continue. I am not certain our actions were wise, however. We have no power against Long Fingers."

Behind her, dozens of Kulsat waited, as if unsure what to do now that they had succeeded in scaring Three Crescents away.

Justine said, "Is there a shuttle on this ship?"

"Yes, we have six such vessels. They are used to mine the

Gift of the Grace on asteroids. The shuttles do not have the engines to use the Grace."

The Grace. According to Alex's story, that was what Ah Tabai had called the race who created the system of star beacons. Maybe, for the Kulsat and the other Emerged races, the name was homonymous for the power of Kinemet, the photonic state of being, and for the race that had first mastered the technology.

"Do you have any of the Gift on board?" Justine asked. "If we can get some of it to my friends and our ship, we might have a chance."

Red Spot turned to the aliens behind her and signed to the group. Several of them signed in return, and the back and forth went on for what seemed like forever—at least, to Justine.

She waited, barely containing her impatience, as Red Spot spun back to the computer and took a very long time to type the results of the conversation.

"There are several stores of the Gift on board. We can collect a quantity of it and load it on the mining shuttle. The problem we have is how to bring you to the shuttle. Your observation platform is affixed to the hull. Even if we could move it, the loading door to the shuttle is too small for it to fit. There is no provision for one of your kind on the shuttle. Our alien biologist informs us that you are an air-based species and cannot process oxygen under water. It will only be a short duration before Three Crescents and Long Fingers return to destroy us."

A few times, Justine tried to interrupt the message that came in, but since it had been pre-typed, there was no way to stop the translation. She bit her lip until the machine voice finished speaking.

"Bring some of the Gift here, to me. Once I'm recharged, I can turn to light and follow you to the ship. We won't have any way of communicating while I'm in that state, but if we can find my ship and my friends, they will be able to help us."

Red Spot made a unique set of signs to her, which Justine took as acknowledgement. The little alien then turned around and handed out instructions to the small band of revolutionaries. The individual Kulsat swam off to complete their assigned tasks. Only Red Spot remained in the lab.

"Is everyone with us?" Justine asked.

"We are conditioned to obey those in authority. The Kulsat on board regard me as their new sub-commander. I told them Three Crescents is unit-defective and wanted your alien technology for himself. That is the reason they attacked him. They are all still loyal to the Consortium. If they encounter Long Fingers, however, he will be able to counter my instructions."

Justine felt herself grow frustrated with the Kulsat's culture. They were alien to her in every sense of the word.

"Are you still loyal to the Consortium?"

Red Spot replied. "Yes." She continued to type. "Our kind has been persecuted throughout history. When the Grace disappeared from the universe, the other races became jealous of our knowledge and warred against us. They invaded our home world. Only because of our superiority were we able to survive. Now, we are the dominant race in the galaxy, but we are not secure. The other races continue to plot against us. Only with the final component will we assure our continued survival."

If what Red Spot said was true, then the Kulsat had reason to be paranoid of other worlds. Justine asked, "Why did you save me?"

"The Consortium believes all non-Kulsat races are an imminent threat and must be expired to ensure our continuance. The Consortium believes non-Kulsat have no value. The Consortium believes Deficients have no value." She held Justine's eyes as her next statement filtered through the translator. "You believe all beings have value. There is validity in that. Perhaps there is an opportunity to reevaluate some of the polices of the Consortium."

Justine was overwhelmed by what she was hearing. How many other Kulsat felt their culture was overzealous in its xenophobia? Although it was difficult to avoid imposing one's own values on other cultures, Justine didn't know how a society could progress when it completely discarded those who failed to achieve the Kinemetic change.

She would save her philosophizing for later. Right now, time was working against her.

From what she gathered, Three Crescents and Long Fingers were completely ensconced in their status as elites. They believed the rest of the Kulsat were thoroughly subjugated; the ship didn't have much in the way of internal security. That slight advantage would disappear the moment Long Fingers felt the situation was out of his control.

Even if they all managed to get on the shuttle and flee the ship, the moment the two Risen became aware of the exodus, they could easily pull her back, as they did when she was on the *Ultio*. Then they could blast the shuttle to bits at their leisure.

Justine had to increase her chances of escape, somehow, and ensure the other Kulsat weren't killed in the process.

"Red Spot," she said, "are there any other Risen on the ship besides Three Crescents and Long Fingers?"

"No. We are not military. We are a mining vessel. There is only one science leader and one ship leader on board."

"Can you describe the layout to me? Where is the main cabin, engineering, crew quarters, loading dock, everything?"

"Yes. I can explain that." Red Spot typed for a long while.

∞

By the time Justine absorbed all the information Red Spot gave her, she had a very solid idea of the ship's geography.

She sensed one of the non-Risen Kulsat returning to the lab. He was carrying a small quantity of Kinemet—the Gift of the Grace—in a spherical container. The radiation level was minimal, and Justine assumed the enclosure was made of some kind of damping material, like the titanium they had used in Sol System to keep the Kinemet from playing havoc with nearby electronics.

As the alien got closer to Justine's tank, she felt a surge ripple through her. Although she'd been able to absorb second-hand radiation from Three Crescents, that had been little more than a drop of water on the tongue; nowhere near enough to quench her thirst. Even sealed by the damping container, Justine could feel every fiber of her being reaching out for the nourishment of Kinemet.

When Klaus had conducted his experiment on her, he'd used a milligram of the kinetic metal. Justine sensed the Kulsat had brought her at least a full gram. If she never quantized herself, that much would most likely be enough Kinemet to sustain her for the rest of her life. It was being in the photonic state that consumed Kinemet at a rapid rate.

Hungrily, she waited for the Kulsat to get to her tank. With Red Spot's assistance, the two swam up to the top of her glass cage and placed the container in the cylinder that had been used to feed her previously. They placed the cylinder in the delivery mechanism and triggered the winch.

As the Kinemet was lowered within her reach, Justine heard Red Spot's message come through the translator.

"Only a Risen is capable of opening the container."

For a moment, Justine's impatience got the better of her,

and she felt a rush of heat to her cheeks.

Whatever substance the container was made of must be impenetrable by physical means. Since a Risen had the ability to quantize others at will—as they had done to her—then it followed that they had the ability to quantize objects as well. Once the sphere was converted to photons, the Risen had full access to the Grace inside.

The problem was that, even if she were fully irradiated, Justine didn't have any idea how to quantize anything except herself. Radiation still leaked out of the container, but at a rate so slow it would take her an hour or longer to become charged enough to make the change—and even then, she would use up that charge very quickly.

They didn't have that kind of time. It was hard to tell how long it had been since Three Crescents had fled the lab, and she expected him and Long Fingers to show up any moment and take control of the situation. When the Kulsat had quantized her to bring her aboard their ship, Justine had not been conscious in that state, much the same as none of the other passengers on the *Ultio*—Alex included—had been aware during the journey.

Justine didn't know nearly enough about the 'Gift' of light, although she'd spent over four years in that state. Given the chance, she was determined to learn as much as possible.

She held the sphere close to her chest, and sat on the floor of the tank, letting the Kinemetic radiation flow into her. She would hold on as long as she could.

Soon, another alien entered the lab and signed to Red Spot, who conveyed the information to Justine. "We have loaded the shuttle with the Gift. Squiggles Over A Small Circle spotted Long Fingers on the bridge, but did not interact with the ship leader. Perhaps Three Crescents has not reported us to him yet."

That was good news, Justine thought to herself. That would give them more time. It also hinted that Three Crescents may have exceeded his authority, if he was afraid of letting the ship leader know what was happening.

Red Spot typed. "The rest of the crew are on the shuttle waiting for instructions."

Justine said, "I need a little more time with the Grace before I am charged enough to quantize myself. You three get to the shuttle and get off the ship—"

The mechanized voice interrupted her. "The others are helping only to get you away from Three Crescents. If we leave you here, they will see no reason to leave the ship."

"I promise," Justine said, "I will get to the shuttle as soon as I am capable." She didn't know if Red Spot could interpret the sincerity in her words, so she looked through the glass at the cephalopod so that the alien could see it in her eyes.

"You have not employed deception to me in the past. I do not believe you will employ deception in the future. We will be waiting for you on the shuttle. Utilize haste, Justine."

With that, Red Spot and the two others flicked their tentacles and darted out of the lab.

It had only been a few minutes with the Kinemet, but Justine was already feeling the effects of its influence. She wished she knew how the Kulsat Risen were able to quantize others. After decades of experiments, the only method NASA and Quantum Resources' scientists had discovered for quantizing a ship was to use a quantum drive.

Justine had read many of the theoretical papers about the process, and while she sat there waiting to be fully charged, she reviewed all the texts stored in her memory. The crash-course took her several minutes to complete, but by the end, there was nothing in the experiments to suggest the possibility of external quantization. Of course, no one had imagined that it was possible to quantize anything without a quantum drive—which, basically, was a high-powered hydrogen bombardment device.

Something tickled the back of her mind.

What would happen if she was in a quantized state, and bombarded an atom of Kinemet with a photon of her own? Would that, in turn, begin the quantum change in an external object? And if so, could she somehow target that energy?

Justine didn't get the chance to test her theory. With her *sight,* she sensed the arrival of a Kinemetic presence outside the lab.

She stood up, clutching the sphere to her as Three Crescents entered the room, holding what looked like a portable energy rod.

The moment he spotted Justine, he aimed the rod at her tank and fired.

The glass shattered and thousands of liters of water slammed into her.

18

Sierra de las Minas :
Guatemala :

Long Count: 9.19.19.17.18

I spent the following days in my hut, waiting for my new home
to be finished. I felt terrible that I was not able to help.
Although I seemed to be recovering faster than expected, I still
had difficulty with simple tasks. I could walk around, but I
couldn't lift a bucket of water without pain shooting through
my chest.

Though I hated my new chosen role in the village, I owed
it to my people to become the best priest I could. As a warrior,
I'd had some lessons in reading glyphs. It was important to
understand decrees or orders from the king's guard. Until a
priest arrived from Copán to begin my lessons, I decided to try
to teach myself.

The scrolls the priest had left behind were far beyond my
understanding. At first, when I tried to read them, I quickly
became frustrated. Without a teacher to guide me, I might as
well have tried to learn the language of birds. Even still, I kept
trying. After all, I had nothing else to do, and lying down for
hours on end was maddening.

After most of a day trying to figure out the meaning of a certain glyph that was repeated many times in the scrolls, I decided to bring my question to Ohtli Ti, the oldest of our elders.

It was bad form to approach an elder without first requesting an audience, and even worse to ask an elder to lower themselves to the role of teacher. Without another priest to guide me, however, I had no other choice.

I picked Ohtli only because, when I was a child, he'd taken supper with my father and our family several times.

My ribs ached from the effort, and I stood outside the doorway of his house in silence, as much out of respect for his position as to catch my breath.

I was certain he had noticed me right away, but he went about his own tasks for several minutes before lifting one hand for me to enter his house.

Bowing and keeping my head lowered, I said, "Forgive me for being familiar, Elder Ti. I mean no disrespect."

"The king has decreed you are to become the priest of our village, Subo. It is only right that the elders listen to the counsel of our holy men."

I felt a heat rise to my cheeks. "I would not dare to offer my opinions to those who are more learned than I."

"But you will." He nodded to me. "You must become accustomed to your new rank."

"Thank you, Elder Ti. I will do my best."

I looked up, and he smiled at me.

"I'm sure you will," he said. "Now, do we have business today?"

"Please excuse my ignorance, Elder. I am trying to learn to read Balam Ix's scrolls, but I am having difficulty."

"Show me."

I held the scroll out to him and pointed to the glyph that

kept appearing.

He glanced at it and then looked up at me in surprise. "Do you not remember your first lesson? I thought warriors were taught the difference between sound symbols and word symbols."

As he said it, I recalled that there were often two ways to write the same word: it could be written out with a symbol for each sound, or a single symbol that represented the word. Most of Balam's scroll was written with sound symbols, but the one I was not familiar with was a word symbol I had never seen before.

I flushed. "My apologies, Elder. I should have known. If you could, please tell me what that symbol represents."

"Flower," he said. "Or the essence from that flower."

"Thank you, Elder Ti," I said, and bowed as I backed out of his house.

Hoping none of the other villagers had witnessed my embarrassment, I headed back to my hut and worked my way through the first scroll. By the time the sun set, I had a basic understanding of the scroll's meaning: it was a recipe for a paste that would soothe light burns.

I was excited that I had made so much progress. Over the next two days, I went through as many of Balam's writings as I could. By the time my new home was completed, I was able to figure out the meaning behind each of the scrolls I had inherited.

I didn't let the other villagers know how far I had come. If I told them that I had learned in three days what it would take most others three months to understand, they would regard me with suspicion, and might think I had been replaced by a demon.

One other thing happened that was more difficult to hide. My ribs were healing faster than they should. I knew, from others who had broken bones, that it could be as many as two *winals*—forty-days—to recover. At the rate I was healing, I would be fully recovered in a few more days.

I became nervous that the other villagers would realize that I was different. Though I hated to deceive them, I pretended to be worse than I actually was. If someone questioned me about how I was healing so fast, I would tell them that perhaps I hadn't been as injured as we had first thought.

My only explanation was that when Ekahua had put his hand on me and taught me the Song of the Stars, he had somehow changed me. Whether it was a gift or curse, I couldn't say. I knew that my being different from the others would only draw their fear. At the same time, I couldn't help but feel grateful for my ability to learn as fast as I had been, and to heal quickly.

On the fourth morning after we had buried Balam, I woke up and decided to confess everything to my father. He'd heard the story about Ekahua already, and I hoped he would understand that I had not been changed into a demon; that my new abilities were a gift from the sky traveler.

Before I could reveal myself to him, however, a small squad of warriors from Copán arrived. To my disappointment and confusion, they were not accompanied by a priest.

Several villagers came out to greet the newcomers. Our smiles of welcome turned to frowns of concern when we realized it was a war party.

The leader of the squad—a man I had not met before—quickly identified my father, and spoke directly to him. His words were spoken loud enough for the rest of us to hear.

"Tohil Ak, I hope I find you well."

My father greeted him with a hand gesture. "Chaan Xiu, I am well. May we offer you shelter and food?"

"No," Chaan said. "I bring orders from Copán. King Ukit

Took has been in discussion with the holy order and the council of elders. They have all agreed that the earthquake four days ago was a sign from the gods. The time for us to attack Quiriguá is now. It has been long overdue, do you not agree, Tohil?"

"I do." My father glanced around the villagers and spotted me. He pointed to me. "My son has recently come back from his warrior's trial, where he defeated three Q'eqchi' fighters. Our enemies have grown weak and lazy."

Chaan nodded to me. "I have heard of this conquest by young Subo, who is blessed of the gods." Turning back to my father, the war leader said, "We are calling all able men to gather in the ceremony field south of Copán tomorrow morning. We will march to Quiriguá and attack at dawn two days from now. Our victory will be sung to our great-grandchildren's grandchildren."

With that, my father and Chaan clasped hands, and the war leader ordered his men on to the next village to spread the call to arms.

Immediately, my father gathered the eight hunter-warriors in our village and gave them orders to prepare weapons and supplies, and to visit each of the farms in the area to call all men of fighting age to the village. Although they were not dedicated warriors, the farmers had all been trained in basic combat in case of invasion from the Q'eqchi'.

Once his men were set to the task, my father approached me. My expression of hope turned to disappointment when he put his hand on my shoulder and said, "I am saddened that you must remain here in the village. I promise you I will bring home many Q'eqchi' slaves for sacrifice. It will be our honor for you to perform the rituals."

My father must have mistaken the look on my face for one of uncertainty, because he squeezed my arm. "I have seen you with Balam's scrolls. You are already able to read them. One of them will describe the ritual of sacrifice, and you will have time before we return to learn what to do. The only thing that would make me more proud than to have you join us in victory is to have you bless our victory with the holy rites."

"I will do my best," I said to my father, trying to hide my personal disappointment as he left me behind and went off to prepare for war.

∞

I woke up the next morning well before the sun rose, and watched from my hut as all the men of the village gathered in the common area, waiting for my father's order to begin their march to Copán. Their wives and children hovered outside the common area with the few older men who were no longer capable of fighting.

Before the troop left the village, my father spotted me and waved me over. I approached him, and when I stood next to him, he spoke to the crowd of fighters.

"Good warriors," he said, "before we march to battle, I ask that we all pray for a swift and glorious victory. My son, Subo Ak, will lead us in that prayer."

For a moment, I froze under the sudden attention from more than a hundred people.

Somehow, my mind called up the prayer Balam Ix had recited to me before I began my warrior's trial. Using that as a starting point, I spoke.

"Nacon, god of war, give our warriors a great revelation of the spiritual and the natural realms. Let them see the strategies of our enemies, give them the might to drive our enemies from their camp, and grant them the strength to withstand any attack.

"Go with all speed, and return with honor."

The warriors raised their arms and cheered. Out of the corner of my eye, I saw my father smile and nod to me, and his approval filled my heart.

Many of the warriors reached out to touch me for additional blessings as they marched out of the village.

∞

I spent the rest of that day elevated in spirit. I'd performed a service to the village, and offered courage and blessing to the warriors. Perhaps becoming the village priest wasn't the worst thing that could have ever happened to me.

My mother also benefited. With her husband being the village's war chief, and her son soon to be the village's holy leader, her status was greatly raised. Only the elders' wives received more respect.

Several of the women in the village brought me food. One of the weavers, Tepin Cer., offered to make me a new set of priest's clothes. Balam's were ill fitting.

I did not have the skill to make my own costume, and so I said, "Yes, please."

Since I was still not fully healed, and she did not want me to stand while she took measurements, she asked me for some of my other clothes to use for comparison.

I gave her the pack I had used on my warrior's trial, and she picked it up and left my home, promising that she would have something for me to try on the next day.

Having nothing more to do, I spent the rest of the afternoon trying to read Balam's scrolls, proud that I could understand most of what he wrote.

It was less than an hour later when I heard a scream from the other side of the village. My ribs were still tender, and I could not run, but I walked as fast as I could to where a group of people had gathered around Tepin's house. The women were all speaking at once, pointing and asking each other what had happened.

When I arrived, they parted for me. Though I had no skill in healing, I was still their priest. A few of the women looked at me expectantly.

In front of the weaver's house, Tepin was lying on the ground. The skin on her hands and face was blistering and turning black, as if she were being burned by fire. She looked up at me, and made a horrible sound, pleading for help.

Beside her was my pack. Several of the items in it were strewn about on the ground, as if the pack had been upturned.

Neither her body nor my pack was what drew my attention. She had taken the items out of my pack. Near my belt, there was a tiny ball of glowing light on the ground in front of Tepin. Slowly, it grew brighter and brighter.

I remembered the grain of what I had thought was sand, which I had taken from Ekahua's sky boat, and I recalled his warning not to let the sun shine on the stone block, which held those grains.

One of the younger girls, Mizquixaual, who was standing very close to Tepin, cried out and fell over. Her skin began to blister and bubble. I grabbed her and pulled her away from the growing star grain, but the effort of it sent a sharp pain through my chest, and I suddenly felt like throwing up.

Elder Nentil Mo'Nab, who arrived moments after I had, pointed at the glowing ball and said, "It is a tear from Kinich Ahau, the sun god! It is a weapon sent by the Q'eqchi'."

I saw my mother push her way through the gathering crowd. She had a stick in her hand. Before I could yell at her to stop, she swung it at the glowing grain. I was certain her only intention was to send the burning object as far away as possible. I watched with growing dread as the stick connected with the star grain, sending it arcing through the air straight for the fire pit in the common area.

"Run!" I yelled to everyone, and despite the sharp pain in my chest, I grabbed Mizquixaual by her arms and dragged her behind the weaver's house.

The burst of light that washed over the village was brighter than the sun at noon, and hotter than the biggest fire we'd ever built in the common area. The power of it knocked me off my feet, and the breath rushed out of me when I hit the ground.

It seemed like hours before I could focus and look around the village. Most everyone was still lying on the ground. Some were curled up, either moaning in pain, or crying in fear. Others, closer to the common area, were not moving at all, and I feared they might be dead. Everyone I saw had burns on their skin.

Elder Mo'Nab was on the ground beside me. His eyes were open, but unseeing. I saw a trickle of blood coming from under his hairline, and his head lay on a jagged rock. He was dead.

On the other side of me, Mizquixaual was alive, but the burns she'd gotten earlier had begun to peel and bleed.

Groaning with the effort, I pushed myself to my hands and knees.

Where the fire pit had once been, there was now a huge crater. The entire common area was blackened and scorched.

Several of the houses closer to the common area, including mine and the elders', were ablaze. Wincing with every step, I hurried over, but long before I got there, I knew there were no survivors.

Several women, who had been far enough away to have escaped the blast, ran to the stream outside the village, buckets in hand. I knew I would not be capable of helping fight the fire, but I had another job to do. I was the village priest, and it was up to me to help heal the wounded.

My mother was on her feet. Though she'd also suffered burns, the look of shock on her face was not because of her injuries. She was staring in the direction of the common area, as if trying to understand what had happened.

"Mother," I said to her. When she didn't react, I grabbed her arms and gave her a gentle shake. "Mother."

She looked at me, and her mouth opened, but no words came out.

"You must help me," I said. "My house is destroyed, and all the priest's scrolls and medicines are gone. We need to make a salve to ease the burns. I need you to find pots and utensils. I will gather the flowers I need to make the medicine."

When my words sank in, my mother nodded and said, "Yes, of course. I have everything in our house. I will get them ready for you."

I called out to the more able women who were helping the others, and instructed them to bring everyone to my mother's house, where I would try to heal them.

As I made my way out into the fields, searching for the plants and flowers called for in Balam's recipe scroll, there was one thing I realized. Though everyone else who was near me had suffered burns when the fire pit exploded, I'd remained completely untouched and unharmed.

19

Qin Station :
Sol System :

"What do you think you are doing?" Alice asked in a shrill voice when she came into the lab and saw Alex at her computer station.

Forcing a disarming smile, Alex looked up at her. "Like I told the guard, I'm beginning to outline the notes for the Song of the Stars, and convert the sound frequencies to their light-wave counterparts."

"How did you get onto my computer?" Alice demanded, striding forward and looking at the screen. Indeed, Alex had begun to build a comprehensive analysis of the song.

Shrugging, Alex said, "I used your password. I thought I'd take the initiative and get started. After all, the faster we finish this, the sooner you'll let me go, right?"

There was a clouded look on Alice's face that told him not to get his hopes up, no matter whether they promised to release him.

He noticed another person in the room following closely behind Alice. Alex glanced up at him and said, "Hello."

Alice introduced the newcomer. "This is Sian. He's our computer genius."

"Ah," Alex said, and got up from the chair. He gestured to

the seat. "I got it started for you."

Sian, giving Alex an inquisitive look, sat down and went over the work. Letting out a grunt of approval, Sian said, "Good start. If you can finish this analysis, I can begin writing an algorithm to determine the most likely possible combinations for the primer."

Alice, seeming a little out of her depth in this area, gestured to another computer terminal. She said to Alex, "You can use that one." To Sian, she asked, "How long will it take to write the program?"

Sian bobbed his head back and forth, calculating in his mind. "Alex seems to know his way around a computer. With his help, we should have something ready in a week or two."

"A week or two!" Alice looked positively outraged.

Sian seemed to shrink into himself. "If I had a team of programmers—"

"No!" Alice glared at him. "No one else. Can't you do it any faster?"

"Maybe if we had Klaus's notes…"

Alice shook her head. "They were destroyed in the attack."

"I'm sorry, Your Highness," Sian said. "It's a complex algorithm. I'm sure Klaus worked on it for months before getting the raw data. At least we have that advantage."

As if sensing that any further browbeating would not speed up the process any more, Alice said, "I'll hold you to your estimate. I'll prepare samples and ready our subjects. The moment you receive the first possible combination for the bombardment formula, you will inform me, and we'll begin the trials."

∞

For the following two days, Alex worked alongside Sian.

The first afternoon, he finished converting frequencies for the song. After that, he assisted the programmer in coming up with identifiers on which frequencies were most likely part of the priming sequence.

They didn't engage in any conversations of a personal nature; the guard standing in the room was an effective deterrent. When they did talk, they kept it professional, limiting their exchanges to technical aspects of the program and the desired results.

When Sian was done for the day, the only words he spoke to Alex were, "Until tomorrow."

A new guard came in to relieve the other one, and turned off all the computers, giving Alex a look of warning.

With nothing else to do, Alex spent the night thinking about how to delay, or even stop, Alice and Chow Yin. Deep into the night, when his thoughts started to turn to his parents, Kenny Harriman, George Markowitz, Ah Tabai, Aliah, and even Klaus, Alex despaired at the enormous loss of life that had happened from the moment of discovering Kinemet.

To keep despair at bay, Alex distracted himself by offering to play a game of cards with the guard.

"It is not permitted."

"What about solitaire?" Alex asked. "What harm could it do?"

The guard spoke into his communicator, and within five minutes, another solider arrived with a deck of cards for him. Since Alex could not sleep, and he soon tired of the more familiar games, he made up his own versions. It was mind numbing, but it was better than staring at the wall.

∞

The second day unfolded much the same as the first, but at

the end of the third day, Alex knew Sian was stalling. From what he saw of the programming, the coder should have been able to complete that portion of the application in one day. Alex was far from an experienced programmer, and he hadn't spent much time pursuing it since he was a teenager. He saw, however, where Sian included several unnecessary redundancies in the code, as well as dozens of extraneous pages of instructions.

When Alex followed a logic thread and found himself in an infinite loop, he was certain something was up.

He didn't give anything away, and carried on assisting as if everything were progressing as it should have.

To test his theory, Alex, added a small code to the program. When Sian ran that segment, his computer's clock would begin to run in reverse. It was a question, and soon after Sian ran the segment, Alex saw that his code had been deleted, and a new code was in its place.

He didn't need to run it: he recognized it as an 'oxbow code'—a fragment that was once needed, but no longer.

Alex knew that once his efforts were successful, his usefulness would be at an end, and with it, his life. Sian was obviously aware of this, and most likely thought he was in the same situation. He was playing for time, trying to help the both of them.

In response, Alex sent back a code that would produce a false positive, intending to let Sian know how he should proceed.

They did not share any more messages through code after that, or else they might risk alerting anyone monitoring them that they were in collusion.

∞

On the fourth day, Alex had nothing more to contribute to the effort until the algorithm was completed. When Alice came to check on their progress, she ordered him to follow her out of the lab and leave Sian to his work.

She brought him to an adjacent room with a plain table and two chairs. It was obviously someone's office, perhaps even Alice's. Now, it served as an interrogation room. There was one window, but it was covered with a blind.

Gesturing for Alex to take a seat, Alice sat opposite him.

"We held up our end of the bargain," she said, her words hard. "You have not held up your end."

"Michael and Yaxche...?"

"They have been delivered as promised. You, however, have withheld vital information."

"I'm not sure what—"

"Please," Alice said. "Don't insult our intelligence. We were aware you were keeping secrets, but we didn't want to press you until we had proof."

Alex felt his skin grow hot. "Didn't want to press? You killed my friend, held a gun to our heads. I'm surprised we weren't tortured."

Leveling her eyes on him, Alice said, "Don't worry. Unless I get the answers I'm looking for today, I have been authorized to engage in more aggressive interrogation techniques."

Pushing thoughts of torture to the back of his mind, Alex spoke in a calm voice. "What information do you imagine I'm withholding?"

Letting a small smile escape her lips, Alice said, "First of all, we are all aware that a quantum drive can only fly just under the speed of light. Your first adventure to the Centauri System took a little over eight-and-a-half years, round trip. Now, you're back in half that time."

"We were—"

She held up a hand to stop him. "If you're going to come up with some excuse that you turned around halfway there, or that you were hiding just out of range all this time, spare me.

"No," she said, "we are quite confident you traveled to the Centauri System. It would have taken you the four years or so to get there, but the return trip must have been near instantaneous."

Alex pursed his lips.

"That led us to speculate on the means. Up until a few hours ago, we had no evidence, but now we do."

She stood up from the table and drew the blinds from the window.

Alex looked out into the large room beside him. There, being dismantled by a crew of engineers, was the Gliesan escape pod. A sinking feeling in the pit of his stomach, Alex realized there was no way for him to deny it. He'd hoped it would take months, if ever, for someone to return to Pluto and recover the pod near the *Dis Pater*.

"The moment we received word they'd found you, we launched a nearby salvage ship. It arrived here this morning. Oh," Alice said, a smug smile playing over her face, "at first we thought it was just an unfamiliar design ... until we got to the communications computer."

Drawing the blinds once more, Alice sat down and folded her hands in front of her on the table. "Now, please leave out no details. Who are the alien species? What is your relationship with them? What is their level of technology? What are their intentions here?"

A dozen thoughts raced through Alex's mind, then. Every one of them ended with the same conclusion: he couldn't hide the truth from Alice and Chow Yin any longer. If he did so, they would see through it.

Also, he knew the clock was ticking. Sol System was running

out of time, and though he had hoped to play for that time, and give the nations of Earth a chance to gain the upper hand on Chow Yin, he knew he was gambling with the lives of billions of people.

After all, sometimes it was better to side with the devil you knew.

"There are tens of thousands of species out there, but the ones you need to worry about are called the Kulsat. They are like the Huns of the galaxy, but they don't care about conquest; their purpose is the annihilation of any race who stands in their way. They've had millennia to build their armada of warships, and have destroyed thousands of alien cultures."

Alice's eyes slowly grew wider as Alex spoke, but her mouth opened in a silent gasp when he concluded:

"And they're actively hunting for Sol System. For all I know, they could arrive any minute. If they do, we're all dead."

20

Tegucigalpa, Honduras :
Central American Conglomeration :

It wasn't until they were several miles outside Tegucigalpa that the driver pulled off the highway and down a dirt road to a small industrial development.

For the duration of the trip, the driver did not speak to them, not even to respond to Michael's questions. At no time did they slow down enough to let anyone jump out. Even if Michael had attempted such a foolish escape, Yaxche would never be able to follow him. Most likely, neither of them would survive the fall.

It occurred to him at one point that he was an old man in a young man's game. The problem was, there didn't seem to be anyone else to play his role.

At the end of the country road, they turned into a long driveway leading to what looked like a storage facility. There weren't any signs on the property or the building, but Michael spotted several guards wandering around, all armed with hunting rifles.

Shutting off the engine after he parked in front of a bay door, the driver turned in his seat. "Say nothing and follow me."

He got out, and stepped back to open the passenger door

for his two captives. They slid out of the car and looked around. The heat of the morning hit Michael like a wave. Of course, the last time he'd been in Honduras, it had been later in the year. High summer was nearly unbearable.

Holding a finger to his lips to make sure the two kept their silence, the driver headed toward a door off to the side. Without knocking, he stood in front of it and waited. Michael assumed there was some kind of camera or recognition system in play, for a moment later, there was a short beeping sound, and the door swung in.

The driver motioned for them to go in first.

Reluctantly, and with a sidelong glance at the driver as he passed, Michael went in, his imagination running wild. Was he simply a lamb going meekly to his own slaughter?

It was completely dark beyond the door, and Michael hesitated. The driver waved him in again. It seemed there was no other option.

Michael stepped in, Yaxche following, and the door closed behind them, trapping them in darkness and silence.

Holding his breath, waiting for the sharp crack of a rifle shot, or something worse, Michael was startled when he heard the hum of electricity surrounding him. It lasted a few seconds, and then someone turned on a light. He winced against it, but his eyes quickly adjusted.

In sharp contrast to the ragged, worn building outside, the chamber they'd stepped into was high-tech. Michael recognized what it was: a security gate similar to the one at the airport terminal. Providing state-of-the art metal detection, x-ray, and electromagnetic scanning, they didn't come cheap.

The gate was completing its cycle. When it finished, a stocky, olive-skinned man with a thick mustache appeared at the other end of the gate. His short-cropped hair showed streaks of gray at the temples, a change from the last time

Michael had seen him.

Mind racing to figure out what was going on, he blurted, "Humberto?"

"*Sí.*" He had a wide smile on his face. "It is good to see you again." He nodded and focused his eyes behind Michael. "Yaxche, my old friend. You look well."

"As well as can be."

Facing Michael once more, Humberto said, "I must apologize if I alarmed you. We needed to take precautions."

"Against what?"

Pointing to the security gate, Humberto said, "We found several listening devices planted on you. They have been disabled. Unfortunately, your luggage has a GPS tracker in it. We put an EM damper in the trunk of the car to kill the signal. Our driver, Migel, will drive to another location and dump the baggage to throw them off. Don't worry; we'll get you fresh clothes."

"What is going on?" Michael asked.

Humberto motioned for them to step out of the security gate, and he led them down a long hall to an office.

Inside was a sofa against one wall. The back of the office had a boarded-up window, and in front of it was a plain desk and chair. There were a few folders and papers on the surface of the desk, as well as a palm-sized portable holoslate. Humberto sat on the edge of the desk and picked up the slate. He tapped a few commands into it as Michael and Yaxche sat on the sofa, and then handed the slate to him.

Michael looked at the readout. It was written in Spanish. He glanced up at Humberto.

"It's a list of encrypted messages sent from a private commlink of a guard at La Granja Prison."

"A guard?"

Nodding, Humberto said, "The first message, sent an hour

after you left Canada, is to a customs agent at the Toncontin airport, telling him of your arrival this morning, and to delay you as long as possible. The second message is to Servicio Informático Rápido—the computer company subcontracted to the autotaxi service—instructing them to shut down the taxis. A third message was sent to a driver who works for Tegucigalpa Chauffeur Service, with instructions to take you to the Canadian Embassy."

"That doesn't make a lot of sense."

"There are several other messages—twenty, in fact—to various organizations and companies across Honduras. All of them are instructions to follow you and find out what you are doing here. Everything is set up to ensure their people are near you at all times. It's easier to keep track of you if one of their operatives is accompanying you."

"Operatives?" Michael asked. "Whose operatives? Not the Honduran Conglomerate?"

"No." Humberto took the holoslate back and laid it down on the desk. "Though it could easily look that way. We managed to get Migel, who works as a mechanic for the chauffeur service, to pick you up first."

"You?" Michael couldn't believe what he was hearing. "You set this all up?"

"No. Our man in the prison is a double agent. Do you remember Oscar Ruiz?"

Michael blanched. "Yes. I never followed up on what happened here after I left. George and I thought he might have been coerced by the Cruzados."

"As it turned out in the investigation, he was one of their main sympathizers. Though he never condoned the violent aspect of the organization, he did not speak out against it either."

Then Michael made the connection. "Let me guess; he's in

La Granja?"

"Yes. He still has a lot of power, and controls quite a few large companies in Honduras, though not in name."

"What does he want with me?" Michael asked. "Revenge?"

Shaking his head, Humberto said, "I don't think so. No, I believe he is like every other powerful man; he simply wants more power. He suspects you are back in Honduras for a reason other than to escort Yaxche home. Whatever information he can get from you, he could then turn around and sell it to the highest bidder. I understand the Emperor of Sol System is generous in such matters."

Chow Yin! If that madman found out what Michael was doing, he would use every resource available to get that information and keep it for himself. Once again, Michael realized he'd been naïve to think that the Emperor's reach wouldn't extend so far.

He looked up at Humberto. "Where do you come into this?"

"We are what we should have been: the Cruzados. When last we spoke, I told you I believed in their cause. Now, we work to restore ourselves to our rightful place." He smiled widely. "Our mission is to protect the heritage of the Mayan Civilization. For the most part, we lobby for advocacy groups in Honduras, Guatemala, and Mexico. There are many corporations and countries that wish to exploit our culture. We do everything in our power to prevent that."

"Including kidnapping me?"

Humberto shrugged. "I prefer to think we liberated you from covert surveillance."

"Then you are not holding me hostage?"

"Not at all. You are free to go any time you like. We will even take you back to your embassy, if you want—though I must insist that Yaxche remains under our protection. He's one of our own. Without our assistance, he will be vulnerable to Oscar Ruiz and those who are like him."

Michael glanced over at Yaxche, who was listening, but didn't seem very affected by the discussion.

"What do you want with Yaxche?" he asked carefully.

"We'll bring him home, make sure he's safe. Two of our men will remain in his village for protection."

Michael sat back on the sofa. "And that's all you want to do, protect him?"

Humberto nodded, then said, "Unless there is something more to your interest here? Perhaps we can help?"

"You saved my life," Michael said. "For that I owe you, but as you've illustrated, a lot has happened in the past four years."

"I see you do not trust me, *mi amigo,* and you are wise to be cautious." He spread his hands. "However, I do not see how you have any other choice? Your government has little power here. Our government is not suited for subtle operations, and there is corruption everywhere. You need help from someone, or your purpose will have failed before it even started."

Michael still wasn't completely convinced of Humberto's intentions, but he wasn't about to turn tail and go back to Canada with nothing to show for his efforts. Even Calbert would think him either incompetent, or that the entire mission had been a sham all along.

"Let's say I do trust you—" he began.

"That would be nice." Humberto gestured to Yaxche. "But it does not matter that you trust me. Only that *abuelo* trusts me, no?"

Michael gave Yaxche a sharp look, but the older man regarded Humberto with consideration. "Ahyah," he said finally. "I think my friend will like you, too."

21

Kulsat Ship :
Centauri System :

The water was freezing, and the shock of it caused her to gasp. She swallowed a mouthful of the salty liquid and tried to choke it back up.

Panic set in as she realized she was going to drown. In desperation, she tried to quantize herself, but she hadn't charged herself nearly enough to make the transformation. If she didn't do something, she was going to die.

Three Crescents, whether he'd been pulled in by the current or had come closer of his own volition, was almost on top of her. He pointed his energy rod at her, but he seemed to be hesitating before finishing her off. Perhaps he was curious to see an air-breather drown. Whatever the reasons for his delaying the death blow, his proximity had the effect of pumping more radiation into Justine.

It still wasn't enough to let her convert her entire self to protons, but maybe, if she concentrated, she could convert a portion of herself. Knowing she had only seconds before she would pass out from oxygen deprivation, she tried to focus on her hand, wrapped around the sphere containing Kinemet.

All she needed—she hoped—was a single proton to penetrate the outer shell of the container. The quantum drives they had developed at NASA had used hundreds of thousands of free protons to initiate the reaction in charged Kinemet. She had no idea what to expect, if her experiment worked.

A ripple went through Three Crescents' tentacles. He must have seen her clutching the sphere of Kinemet, Justine guessed. Bringing the energy rod up, he fired.

Without consciously thinking about it, Justine willed her hand to convert from the physical to the photonic state. In a microsecond, the change occurred, and her hand passed through the sphere and to the grain of Kinemet within.

Whatever the container was made of dampened the Kinemetic radiation, but wasn't resistant to Justine's photons.

The boost of radiation was enough for her to quantize herself a split-second before the beam of energy would have sliced through her body, and before the water in her lungs would have drowned her.

In the quantized state, she could no longer effectively hold the container, and the sphere fell to the floor of the lab.

Justine instinctively stretched out her essence, one point reaching for the pebble of Kinemet, the other point extending toward Three Crescents. The moment she felt her photonic self come into contact with the Kinemetic atom, she willed a single proton to hit that atom with as much force as she could generate.

A wave of energy coursed through her, coming up from that one point and traveling out of the other point, which had reached Three Crescents.

As the Kulsat had done to her when she was on the *Ultio*, Justine converted Three Crescents into particles of light. She hoped, because he'd been quantized by her, rather than having done it himself, he would not be aware while he was in that condition, as Justine had not been conscious when they'd done it to her.

She waited for a few moments, carefully watching the collection of photons—Three Crescents—to see if the Kulsat would once again flee. The quantized essence continued to float where it was, and Justine's theory was confirmed. The science leader was neutralized.

Though she could manipulate electricity in her quantized state, she had no ability to move solid objects. She couldn't convert back to her human self, or she would drown, and she wasn't about to leave the Kinemet where it was. It was precious.

She had an idea.

Pushing her *sight* out, she saw that the non-Risen Kulsat were all aboard the shuttle, and it had already launched. They were several hundred meters away from the Kulsat mining ship. Changing direction, Justine searched the Kulsat ship. Her exploration confirmed that Long Fingers was the only other Risen on board. He was on the bridge, all eight tentacles working at a rapid pace on a bank of computer consoles.

Justine felt a gravitational shift as the Kulsat ship slowed and banked, obviously coming around to pursue the shuttle. Deep down, she knew Long Fingers would destroy the other aliens.

Extending herself back to the Kinemet on the floor, Justine attempted to quantize the Kulsat ship.

She didn't have nearly enough power. The attempt was like trying to open a magnetically sealed door by ramming it with her body. The ship remained unaffected, and Justine nearly knocked herself unconscious with the effort. If she lost awareness, she would be at Long Finger's mercy.

The Kulsat ship had completed its turn, and it rumbled as the engines went into overdrive. Whatever distance the shuttle had managed to gain would soon be cut short.

There had to be another way to distract Long Fingers.

She formed a plan, but before she tried it, she reached out to the Kinemet and absorbed all of its radiation as quickly as she could, becoming fully charged in a matter of seconds.

With the layout of the ship clear in her mind, Justine raced toward the engine room, which housed both the Kulsat's quantum drive and their normal space engines. She didn't know what kind of propulsion the Kulsat used, but she did know they would use some form of electric power to run the computers. Risen or Kinemats—whatever they were called—could manipulate electrical current. She would shred every conduit and computer in that room.

When she got to the engine room, she headed for the normal space engine first. It was unlike any other engine she'd seen before, but she detected trace elements of plasma. She guessed their engine used a form of ion propulsion, similar to what was equipped on the majority of ships in Sol System.

Justine had to stop the Kulsat ship from accelerating. Reaching out with her senses, she traced the various conductors and capacitors, and forced as much electrical current through them as she could.

Many of the systems were waterproofed, but as the first circuits overloaded and blew, the explosions ruptured the firewalls, and salty water poured into the computer banks. The few brief sparks were extinguished quickly, but the water itself did more damage than Justine. The entire array of computers beside the normal space engine fizzled and died.

The plasma engine cooled, and then ceased to function.

Next up was the quantum drive. Justine intended to cripple the Kulsat ship.

Before she could turn her attention to the computers on the other side of the room, the quantum drive turned on. Long Fingers must have realized his ship was being sabotaged. If the ship were quantized, it would effectively stop any further destruction. Long Fingers could travel at light speed to the beacon, and simply return to his home system. Once there, he could marshal the military, warn them of the threat humanity posed, and return in force.

Also, Justine had no idea what would happen to her if she were on a ship that quantized while she was already in the quantized state. Would she be trapped on the ship? Would she retain her consciousness? She didn't want to find out.

By force of will, she pushed her essence through the water environment toward the quantum engine control computers. Before she got there, however, she ran into something. That fact alone shocked her. She was made of photonic particles; what substance out there was dense enough to stop her?

She realized there was some kind of damping shield around the quantum engines. Perhaps, she speculated, it was there to contain or focus the quantization procedure. The scientists back at Quantum Resources and NASA would kill to study the Kulsat technology. Whatever the reason for the damping field, it prevented her from sabotaging the engines. She could sense they would fire in a matter of seconds.

Directing her energy toward the hull of the ship, she streaked to it, through it, and out into space mere moments before the Kulsat vessel quantized. It raced away at the speed of light.

With her *sight,* she tracked it for the two seconds it took to reach the star beacon, over six-hundred-thousand kilometers away. One instant, the ship existed, and the next, it disappeared from the Centauri System.

∞

Using her ability to visualize the space around her, Justine scanned for the Kulsat shuttle, and soon spied it flying toward a large asteroid in the distance. The shuttle had traveled over a hundred kilometers away in the few minutes since it had left the Kulsat ship. Justine propelled herself toward the small vessel. With her *sight*, she saw that she was closing the gap, though slowly. Although she was made of photonic particles, she did not seem to have the ability to push her essence even a fraction of the speed of light—obviously, another reason for a quantum engine.

Even though she'd been fully irradiated, Justine knew from the experimentation on the Lucis Observatory that she would not be able to maintain her quantized form for more than a few hours without additional exposure to Kinemet. The shuttle, however, carried enough of the metal to fuel her for the rest of her life. With it, she would be able to scan the entire sector of the Centauri System in search of Alex and the others. She just needed to reach the shuttle before her radiation levels dropped to the point where she turned corporeal again.

A nagging thought crept up from the back of her mind as she raced forward. When she'd been on Venus, she'd been able to sense Alex on Canada Station Three, even though his essence had been very faint to her. Now, she did not sense him at all. Although the Kulsat ship had traveled quite a distance away from the space port, it wasn't even a fraction of the distance from Venus to Canada Station Three. Three Crescents had given her no indication that they had killed her friends, and the science leader had said that if she weren't going to cooperate, they would gather the others for questioning.

It made no sense to her, unless something had happened in the last few hours.

After what seemed like an eternity, Justine halved the distance between her and the Kulsat shuttle. She estimated she would reach it before it arrived at the asteroid.

Her *sight* still extended, she sensed the star beacon pulse. A moment later, a ship appeared in the Centauri System. Had the Kulsat returned already?

Justine knew they would be able to sense her, and would head straight toward her. Even if she changed her course, they would eventually find their wayward shuttle and recover the cargo. She also knew there was a good chance they would kill all the Kulsat on board.

With renewed determination, Justine pushed the limits of her powers. Though she had no idea what she was going to do when she got there, she knew she had to get to the shuttle before the Kulsat ship did.

The newly arrived ship quantized, and the streak of light crossed the distance between the beacon and her in a blink.

It rematerialized a few hundred meters away from her. Unlike the Kulsat ship, whose shape resembled a gigantic narwhal, this ship had the contours of an enormous bird. The hull, also made of Kinemet, swirled with reds and golds. *Was this a Kulsat warship?* Justine wondered.

The ship seemed to sense the shuttle beyond them, and changed course, powering toward the helpless vessel. Even going as fast as she could, Justine knew she would never reach the shuttle in time. In a desperate gamble, Justine put herself on an intercept course with the new ship. She would do the same to it as she had to the first Kulsat ship; with the last bits of her Kinemetic power, she would tear it apart from within.

When her essence raced through the hull, and into the belly of the ship, she felt a momentary disorientation. It took her a moment to realize she wasn't floating in water. The inside of the new ship was filled with air. Instead of the dull gray sheen of metal that covered the walls and floors of the mining ship, the inner surfaces of this ship were painted in a mosaic of bright patterns.

This isn't a Kulsat ship, she realized.

Detecting two Kinemetic presences on board, Justine flew in their direction instead of trying to find the engine room.

At the bridge, she froze in momentary shock when she saw two tall, bird-like bipeds sitting at the controls. In front of them was an electronic display showing the Kulsat shuttle. Though Justine could not understand any of the words on the readout, she was very familiar with what a targeting system looked like.

The new aliens were preparing to blast the shuttle, along with Red Spot and all the other Kulsat passengers, out of space.

22

Sierra de las Minas :
Guatemala :

Long Count: 10.0.0.0.0

For the next two days, I treated the burns and did as much as I could to help the survivors recover from the tragedy.

My mother and some of the other women had set blankets around the outside of her house to serve as beds. While they all had burned skin, soon they began to complain of upset stomachs. Some became so weak, they could not even lift themselves up off the blankets. Some soiled themselves where they lay.

Those who were still able helped to bury those who had died, while I tended the sick as best I could.

The three elders were dead, leaving me the only remaining adult male; and I was still not completely healed from my broken ribs.

When one of the women from a nearby farm came to the village, I bade her travel to Copán and ask them to send help. By the time she gathered supplies for the journey there, she'd fallen ill and didn't have the strength to pick up her pack, let alone hike the distance.

Of the fifty-two women and children in our community, seventeen had been in the village itself when the star grain exploded. Four women and one child had been killed in the blast, and two children and an older woman had died from their burns the first night. By all accounts, there should have only been nine wounded left for me to tend, but as I surveyed my patients, I counted fifteen women and four children who needed my aid. Some of the women who had been on their farms were showing the same symptoms.

My mother became ill as well, and had fallen into unconsciousness a number of times.

She died that night, along with the rest of the women and children who had been in the village during the blast.

By morning, every surviving member of our community made their way to me, begging me to help them.

I had no idea how to do that. I had only read a few of Balam's healing scrolls, and those had only told me how to heal physical wounds. Nothing I had read had given me the knowledge to treat inner sickness.

Ysalane, who lived on the farm farthest from the village, was one of the few women left who could still walk around on their own. When she'd come to us with her two younger brothers yesterday, she had not shown any signs that she was burned, but by mid-morning, blisters were appearing on her arms and legs, and both of her brothers had started vomiting.

By that afternoon, she became too weak to stand.

I was completely overwhelmed by the death and pain surrounding me. There was nothing I could do to save them, and I couldn't stand listening to the dozens of pleading voices begging me to ease their suffering.

I ran into the woods east of our village, trying to escape the desperation I felt. When I reached the stream where we got our water, I fell to my knees along the bank and looked at my rippling reflection.

For the first time since I was a child, tears rolled down my cheeks.

Why had I not been affected by the illness and burns? Did it have something to do with Ekahua sharing his gift with me? Had that, somehow, made me immune to the effects of the star grain?

I was so consumed by my own misery, I did not immediately notice that the sky was growing brighter. When I finally looked up, my breath caught in my chest, and I rose to my feet.

It was another sky boat.

Unlike Ekahua's vessel, which had streaked across the sky and crashed into the mountain range, this one was coming to land on the ground near our village in a very slow and controlled manner. It was large, and resembled a massive phoenix. The hull of the ship looked to be made of the same kind of material as Ekahua's.

My first thought was to run for the ship, and call whoever was in there to come out and help save the women and children of our village. Then I remembered Ekahua's warning, that others might come looking for him. I didn't know why he didn't want to be found, but by the way he'd said it, I assumed their intentions might not have been pure.

Were these Ekahua's enemies, then? Or his rivals?

I stopped myself from rushing forward, and hid behind a tree until I could figure out what these newcomers wanted from us.

The ship landed on eight long, thick legs. Some of the women in the village were shouting in alarm, but none of them was strong enough to get up and flee. I felt guilty for not running to their rescue, but I knew I had no power to defend my villagers against the newcomers.

A rectangular opening in the side of the ship appeared, and a platform slid out from inside the vessel. Two impossibly tall people stepped onto it.

I could not believe what I was seeing. They had arms and legs just like any other person, but they wore costumes unlike anything I had seen. Their outfits were made of a shiny material, almost like polished stone, and covered every part of their bodies except their heads. Instead of hair, they had what looked like a headdress of white and yellow feathers. The lower parts of their faces were drawn forward, ending in small mouths and chins. Like Ekahua, they had no ears that I could see.

From where I was, I couldn't make out the words they spoke, but it sounded like the chirping and squawking of a bird.

They carried something in their hands, but it did not look like a weapon to me—it was shaped more like a small box. They pointed it around the village, and there were portions of the box that seemed to light up. It reminded me of the picture boxes in Ekahua's sky boat. The creatures made more chirping sounds, this time quite excited.

My heart skipped a beat as the platform lowered to the ground, and the sky travelers stepped off. Some of the women yelled curses at them; others cried out in fear. They were too weak to get up and fight the invaders.

I felt terrible for not doing anything, but though I was not as weak as the others were, I knew I was powerless to stop the sky travelers.

When they approached Ysalane, however, I stood from my hiding place and had every intention of charging them. I had no idea what I could do to stop them, but I had to do something. When I saw that they were not trying to grab her, I stopped, and moved back behind the tree once again.

They spoke to Ysalane, and though their words came out in

chirps and squawks, a moment later, a secondary voice spoke in our language.

"I am a Sentinel of the Collection; I am a protector," the sky traveler said to Ysalane. "You have been touched by star fire. If you come with us into the sky, we will complete the change in you and your people. Your lives will continue. If you remain here, this world will consume you and you will die."

"You can save us?" she asked, looking at her brother, who was lying on the ground beside her, curled into a ball. "You can save him?"

"Yes, but you will never be able to return here."

Ysalane looked at some of the others, who nodded to her. She said, "We will go with you. Just save my brother."

The leader motioned to the other sky traveler, and they assisted all the villagers off the ground and to the platform. In groups of four, they lifted the women and children up and into their sky ship.

Once all the survivors of the blast were inside, the leader approached one of the dead women—I couldn't see whom. He swept the box over her body. He made a squawking sound, and then gestured to the other. They picked up the woman's body and carried her back to the platform. The sky travelers repeated the process for all the dead.

When all the villagers, both living and dead, were in their ship, the leader took something out of one of the pouches on his costume. It looked like a large ball, similar in size to the ones used at the ball court in Copán. This one, however, was not made of rubber. The surface of the ball was similar to the stone block from Ekahua's sky boat.

The sky traveler stepped over to the blackened crater where the common fire pit once stood, and placed the ball in the center. He returned to his ship, and went inside.

Stepping on the platform, which lifted him up and into the

ship, the sky traveler made a gesture with the box in his hand moments before the rectangular opening in his ship closed.

The ball on the ground began to glow and vibrate.

When I realized what the ball was for, I knew I had to flee.

The sky ship rumbled and lifted off the ground.

I turned away from the village and, trying to ignore the pain in my chest, ran as hard as I could.

By the time I reached the closest farm, a blast of light, many times brighter than the one that had ripped through our village before, covered our entire village.

I turned my head before it blinded me, and dove inside the house on the farm just as an ocean of heat, more intense than I could ever have imagined, washed over me. It burned the very air around me, and I could not breathe.

Certain that I would die, I prayed to the gods. Perhaps they heard me. Just when I thought I could hold my breath no longer, the heat and light faded, and air filled my lungs when I opened my mouth and inhaled.

When I felt strong enough to rise, I made my way back to the village, but it was no longer there. No buildings, no common area, no trees, and no grass; there was nothing but a huge circle of bare earth. It was as if a thousand farmers had come and tilled the soil.

For a very long time, I could only stand there and wonder at what had happened. I knew everything that had occurred over the past week was greater than anything written in any of the story stones at Copán.

The affairs of the gods were beyond me, and though I had been thrown into the center of these events, I could not divine their purpose.

I don't know how long it was before I returned to the farmhouse, but the sun had begun its slow descent from the sky, and the moon had come out from hiding.

Sleep was not something that I thought about, but exhaustion got the better of me, and by the time I woke up, it was morning again. It had been five days since the men of the village had gone to war.

I searched through the house for some basic supplies—a pack, some tools, a knife, and food—and then I set out on the trail for Quiriguá.

∞

By the time I arrived near the area where the Ch'orti' army was encamped, I'd had plenty of time to think about what had happened. Unfortunately, I was just as confused as I had ever been.

The sky travelers had said they would heal the women and children of the village, but the same time, they would never be able to return. Did that make them good or evil? Were they taking them away to become slaves? There was no way I could know.

Ekahua had asked me to burn his body, rather than bury it. I didn't know if he didn't have the desire to journey through the Underworld and be reborn in Heaven. In my mind, I had not felt any remorse that I had left him buried in the cave, and not burned his body as he'd requested. Now, however, I was having doubts.

He'd told me that other sky tribes would arrive and look for him, and I could not let his body be found by them. Without knowing the birdlike sky travelers' intentions, I had to believe that Ekahua had been right all along. After all, he'd given me a gift that had protected me from the star fire.

Instead of continuing on to the warrior camp, I went wide around them, being as stealthy as I could. I decided to find the cave where I had left Ekahua, and burn his body as he'd instructed me to do.

It was several hours before I reached the mountain, and I realized that my chest no longer hurt. My ribs had healed, and my breathing was once again strong and sure.

With a little searching, I finally found the cliff where the crevice was, but to my dismay, the entire area was covered in rocks, boulders, and gravel. The earthquake must have caused the cliff wall to crumble.

Even with a team of twenty men, it would take a hundred days to dig through to the cave, and there was every chance the cave itself had collapsed in on itself. For a single man, it could take years.

The cave-in had hidden Ekahua's body from the bird-like sky travelers. They would never find him. After all, who would think this enormous pile of rubble was a grave for a sky traveler?

I had one duty left: to find my father and the other Ch'orti' warriors and tell them what had become of our village. It was a task I did not want to undertake, and I sat down among the ruins of the cliff and thought long and hard about how I was going to tell them their wives and children were either dead, or taken by invaders from the sky tribes.

They would never understand about the star fire, or about sky ships. The elders of my village, and the King of Copán, believed Ekahua was a god, no matter what I'd said. If I told my people exactly what had happened, they would doubt my words. I had to tell them the story in a way they would understand.

A thought came to me, then. The Song of the Stars. The words Ekahua had used for the song were gibberish to me, and he'd said the words didn't matter—it was the melody that was important for our descendants.

I would use the Song of the Stars, replace Ekahua's words

with my own, and tell the story of our downfall. I had to make certain the story was powerful. I might have been protected from the star fire at the village, but I knew I would pass on to the Underworld one day. Combining the story of my village with the song was the best way to ensure that both would survive me.

Over the next few hours, I created the story, and composed the words to match the melody of the Song of the Stars.

The bird-like sky traveler who had spoken to Ysalane was Kinich Ahua, the firebird god and messenger of Hanab Ku, creator of the People. The other sky traveler was Kukulcan, the feathered serpent.

Kinich Ahua must have been angry with us because of the war with the northern tribes, and this was his punishment.

I did not sleep that night. Instead, I worked on the story, and completed it as the sun rose in the morning.

I headed down the mountain and across the valley to look for my father and the other warriors, and found them before the sun set that night.

Though more tired than I had ever been in my life, I told them the story, and I felt their grief as they listened.

After hearing the tale, my father spoke to the King of Copán. The war council agreed that the gods did not approve of the war with the Q'eqchi', and we would return home.

My father and the other men of our village decided to erect a monument to the memory of our lost ones where we were, to remind any Ch'orti who came north not to engage in war with the northern tribes.

In the following months, I carved the story into the stone of four mighty columns, and vowed to return every year to recite the story and honor my people.

23

Qin Station :
Sol System :

Alice stood straight up, her face reddening with anger. "You idiot!" she screamed at Alex.

Taken aback by her reaction, he sat there as still as he could.

"This is exactly the reason the nations of Earth have driven themselves to the brink of destruction," Alice said through gritted teeth. "They didn't need any alien enemy; they're doing a good enough job all on their own. They've been on a downward spiral for a century. Corruption and apathy in the government, greed and avarice in the economy, cruelty and malice in the people."

She swung an accusatory finger toward Alex. "And you kept this information from the one person in the system who has the resources and the strength of will to save it. My father was right; you are a petty, selfish little child."

The words stung, and Alex felt they were unfair. He had a brief urge to refute her claim. After all, Alex had sacrificed everything from the moment his parents had died on Macklin's Rock.

He shot back at her. "All those words you used—corruption, apathy, greed, avarice, cruelty, malice—those are all good words to describe your father. He may have fooled you, as he fooled so many others; as he tried to fool me. He plays on your weaknesses, preys on your feelings of abandonment. When he sees someone who he can use for his own purposes, he befriends them, tells them they are important and powerful. But once he has what he wants from you, he chews you up and spits you out."

Alice shook her head. "You lie!"

"Why do you think he ended up in prison? Because of me?" Alex let out a hollow laugh. "It was Klaus, if you must know. Your father underestimated him. When I was kidnapped, your father thought he no longer needed him. Klaus figured out where he stood pretty quick, and took steps to take down your father first." He swung a hand around as if to encompass everyone on the station. "Look around. Why do you think your father surrounds himself with people who have run afoul of the law, or are repressed, or who've been ostracized by society? Not out of the goodness of his heart, I can tell you. It's because they let their anger and desperation rule them, and because of that, they're easy to fool."

Alice looked ready to burst. "I'm not a fool," she said, but her voice was low.

"You've been deeply hurt. Betrayed and shamed by society for something that wasn't your fault—I'm sorry; I know about your history: your mother, the newspapers in Beijing. It wasn't fair, but your life was still ruined. Now, you want to make someone pay." He shook his head at her. "But just because they did this to you, it doesn't give you the right to conquer them or kill them."

Looking suddenly like a little girl, Alice lowered her head.

Alex said, "I know you're angry, but you don't want to watch the world burn. If you did, you would simply do nothing and let the Kulsat do your dirty work for you. No, you got angry at me because, deep down, you care."

There were tears streaking down her cheeks. "I don't care."

"Yes, you do," Alex said, his voice taking on a soothing tone. "And so do I. The Kulsat will destroy us. It will be quick. Emperor Yin is going to take his time about it, but he'll end up doing the same thing. I won't trade one doomsday scenario for another. But you—"

Alice looked up. "What about me?"

"You have the power to make a difference. There is a chance to stop the Kulsat. I've been told there is a way, but in order to get to that point, we need to work together."

Narrowing her eyes, Alice said, "Against my father...?"

Alex nodded. "Yes." Seeing her teetering on the brink of a decision, he added, "He was directly responsible for the murder of my friend, Kenny, and he's given the order for many others all in the name of power. You've watched the newsvids; surely not everyone is telling the exact same lie about him."

Alice wiped the tears from her cheeks. "Say I believe you," she said. "Say I want to help you. What do we do?"

Alex lifted one shoulder in a half-shrug. "We continue our work."

Looking up sharply, Alice spoke in a breathy rush. "What?"

"The goal is the same. We need Kinemats. Only then can we learn how to defend ourselves. I told the truth: I have no idea how long it will take the Kulsat to find us. It could be minutes; it could be a millennium. When they do find us, we need to be prepared. Other systems have been able to defend themselves. It's possible."

"Then you will tell Sian to stop delaying and complete his algorithm?" Alice asked, and gave him a sly smile. "I told you: I'm not a fool. Don't worry, my father is occupied with other matters; I need not concern him with every little detail."

"Thank you," Alex said.

"If we do solve the formula for priming the Kinemet, we're

going to have to test it."

Alex shook his head. "We're not going to sacrifice any more innocent lives."

"Then how will we know if it works?"

"I have a thought about that," Alex said. "As someone who is attuned to Kinemet and its radiation, I may be able to tell if the formula is correct or not."

Alice stood up. "What are we waiting for?"

24

Copán Departmental :
Honduras :

Yaxche insisted that they return to his village, and would not give anyone a hint of his friend's location until they agreed. Five of them piled into a hydrogen-powered crew cab. Yaxche sat up front with Migel, who continued his role as the driver. Michael sat in the back with another Cruzado named Diego, and Humberto, who squeezed between them. After the five-hour drive, Michael was thankful to get out and stretch his legs.

Little had changed in Pueblo de Santa Brio since Michael had been there last. Even the older woman selling handcrafted trinkets sat on the same wooden chair in the same spot as before. She smiled at him, as if recognizing him. He nodded to her, returning the smile, though he didn't stop to peruse her wares.

There was a young tourist couple in town, recording their journey on a digital recorder. Humberto gave them no more than a cursory glance before dismissing their presence.

The house that was once Yaxche's now belonged to another family. Four years was too long to remain vacant, and without news, the village would have assumed he wasn't alive.

Yaxche headed straight for a different house, and before he reached it, a middle-aged woman ran out, tears streaking down her face and a cry on her lips. Michael recognized her as Yaxche's daughter.

The two embraced, and it was a long time before the woman stopped crying.

Michael, not wanting to intrude on the reunion, turned to Humberto. "We might be here a while."

"Oh?"

"I feel like an ass," Michael said. "I was so wrapped up in everything else that's happened in the past while, it completely slipped my mind. Four years ago, Yaxche's grandson, Terry, was killed on Venus." The sharp memory of Kenny's recent murder cut through his mind. He intended to contact the young physicist's family and extend his condolences, and vowed to do so the first chance he got.

"Ah." Humberto nodded. "Te'irjiil. Another victim of Jose's madness. I regret my part in involving him in that mess."

When Michael looked up, he noticed Yaxche waving him over. Humberto followed a few steps behind.

Yaxche said, "My daughter wants to thank you for bringing me back to her. She wishes us to spend the evening to hear the story of my grandson's sacrifice. There is plenty of room on the floor, and she has spare blankets for the night. In the morning, we will go."

"Of course," Michael said.

Humberto turned to his two men and instructed them to park the truck on the outskirts of the village. "The three of us will set up rotating patrols."

Michael followed Yaxche and his daughter into the house, where they waited for her husband to return from work before they ate supper. Yaxche's two granddaughters, Rosalia and Maria, clung to their grandfather and would not let him do anything for himself.

Michael's translator had been disabled by Humberto, in case

it had a tracker, and he fervently wished he'd had time to pick up another one. He had some difficulty following the conversation among the Hernandez family, and had to rely on Humberto to translate.

They spent the evening listening to stories of Terry's youth, and his love for Itzel. When it came time for Michael to share what he knew of Terry's fate, he told his mother that he was sorry that he'd never had the chance to meet the young man.

To his surprise, Humberto told of his experiences with Terry, and didn't gloss over his role in inducting the youth into the Cruzados.

"He had the heart of a crusader," Humberto said in conclusion. "And it is because of his true spirit, and those like him, that we continue our fight."

Michael expected Yaxche's daughter to be outraged at Humberto, but instead, she held her husband's hand and said, *"Te'irjül le habría perdonado, estoy segura. No podemos hacer menos."*

"Gracias," Humberto said, his voice solemn.

∞

The next morning, the five of them piled back in the truck and headed out. Yaxche would not tell them their destination. He merely indicated which turns to take.

As they headed west toward Copán Ruinas, Migel gave Humberto a concerned look.

Humberto, checking his holoslate, leaned forward and spoke to Yaxche. "It looks as if you are taking us to the border crossing of Guatemala. If that's our destination, we need to stop. We can't get past the border patrol."

Having read up on the region, Michael knew that under ordinary circumstances, crossing into Guatemala wouldn't be a problem. The custom's office was more of a prolonged toll operation and casual check stop. If Michael gave them his passport, however, it would register on the national-security grid, flagging him to Ruiz and his operation.

"Head north at the ruins," Yaxche said to Migel, and Humberto let out a sigh of relief.

"We've only got a few more hours' hydrogen in the tank," Migel said. "How far north is your friend?"

"We will be fine," Yaxche said.

Sensing everyone else's discomfort, Michael asked, "Can you show us on a map?"

Turning in his seat, Yaxche said, "I have not seen my friend since I was a young man, but I will remember how to get there."

Realizing that, for a great number of cultures, landmark navigation was the primary means of travel, Michael sat back in the seat and looked out the window, watching the farms and forests fly past.

After a little over an hour, turning one direction and then another on dirt roads, they arrived at a small plantation. Michael glanced at Humberto's holoslate.

"We're here," he said, pointing to a spot on the small map on the holoslate display. "Right near the border."

There weren't any signs telling them what plantation it was, and Michael fervently hoped they had nothing to do with Oscar Ruiz.

A horse and rider plodding along the edge of the main entranceway spotted them, and turned toward them.

Migel spoke to the man in Spanish, and Michael wished he had a translator with him. He didn't want to ask Humberto what was being said every time.

The rider looked across the seat to Yaxche, who spoke rapidly. A moment later, the rider replied, and pointed farther north along the road.

"Gracias," Migel said, putting the truck into gear.

Yaxche, sounding excited, said, "My friend has retired from the plantation, and has a villa down the road."

The road, little better than a goat trail, cut left and right several times before leading to a small clearing. A modest house stood there. A dozen chickens walked freely around the property. There was a small barn with a pen holding a few pigs.

As Migel pulled up, a man who could only be described as ancient stepped out from the doorway, a wide grin on his face as he waved to his visitors.

Stepping out of the truck, Yaxche hurried over to his friend, shook his hand and gave him a heartfelt slap on the arm.

They spoke in Spanish, and Michael didn't need Humberto to figure out they were re-acquainting themselves with one another.

If they hadn't seen each other in over half a century, there would be a lot of catching up to do.

Michael noticed that Migel and Diego automatically migrated to either end of the property, trying to look casual as they set up watch posts. The paranoia might not be necessary, this far away from any major population, but then again, if something happened, help was a long way off. He decided to be thankful the men were on guard.

Humberto patiently waited until the two older men finished saying hello to each other.

Yaxche turned and said, "Michael, Humberto, I am pleased to introduce my oldest friend to you. This is Patli, who is also the grandnephew to my grandfather's brother. He does not speak English, but he has agreed to talk to you for a time. Perhaps he will share his story with you. Come, sit."

They followed Yaxche and Patli to a small area on the side of the house opposite the pen, where several wooden chairs were set out around a barrel.

"Patli does not often get visitors, but he always has a few spare chairs just in case."

The four of them arranged themselves around the barrel, and Patli spoke, looking at Michael with a kindly smile.

"He says he wonders if this is the first time you have stepped out into the sun." Yaxche grinned. "He's never seen a person so pale before."

With a nod, Michael said, "I come from a land far to the north, where it snows half of the year. The sun is much colder there than here."

Yaxche translated, and then said, "He has never seen snow, but he heard a story about a man made of snow once, and thought someone was pulling a trick on him."

Michael laughed. "It's true. I've made a few myself, when I was younger."

They spoke casually like that for an hour, allowing Patli to get to know them.

Just as the noon sun peaked, Patli spoke at length to Yaxche.

Humberto narrowed his eyes at what he heard, and Michael's anticipation grew.

Turning to Michael, Yaxche spoke. "I have told my friend that you and George were the first ones, besides my grandson, who understood the Song of the Stars, and that you needed to hear the rest of the story. Patli says he has not told the story in many years—no one is interested in the ramblings of us old men—but he is happy that you have shown patience today. If you have a little more patience, he will tell you the story that was passed down from his grandfather's grandfather many generations back.

"It is the story of the dying god, and of the young hunter who discovered him, and who was the first to hear the divine Song of the Stars. He was my and Patli's ancestor, who wrote the Song of the Stars as told to him by the dying god. His name was Subo Ak."

25

Gliesan Ship :
Centauri System :

"Stop," Justine said the moment after she returned to her corporeal self on the bridge of the alien ship. "Don't kill them."

To her surprise, the two bird-like bipeds stopped their attack. A power indicator on the display of the control array leveled down.

Both aliens, sitting on chairs that floated a meter off the floor, turned to face her. Their faces were vaguely human in shape, except that the lower halves were drawn forward and came to a point, like a soft beak. Neither had hair; instead, their heads were covered with a feather-like down. One of them had predominately blue and green coloring, while the other was yellow and orange.

Both regarded her with cocked heads.

It was only under their scrutiny that Justine realized she was completely naked. When she'd quantized herself, she had not converted her clothing, since she'd only just developed the theory on how to quantize other beings or objects. Her attention had been focused on Three Crescents' attack, and defending herself by changing him into photons. She realized that, from this point on, she should be able to quantize her clothing and spare herself further embarrassment when she returned to her physical form.

Self-consciously, she threw one arm over her breasts and used her other hand to cover her lower regions. As hard as she could, she willed herself not to let her face flush red with embarrassment.

Justine's discomfort was forgotten when the blue-and-green-colored alien spoke, and she heard the translation a split-second later. The voice was male and soft-spoken; a complete contrast to the impersonal machine voice of the Kulsat translator computer.

"Apologies. You must be Major Justine Turner. We sensed your Aetherform." He pointed to the ship on his display console. "We believed you were trying to destroy the Kulsat shuttle, and we were attempting to assist."

Justine, stunned that they knew her name, said, "The Kulsat on the shuttle helped me escape the mining ship where I was taken prisoner by two of their 'Risen'."

Although she'd been one of the first to discover the evidence that the universe was home to thousands of different species of sentient beings, and had just spent the last few days interacting with a race of cephalopods, it still took her some time to adjust to meeting a new life form. She wished the circumstances were less dramatic and proper introductions could be made.

"It is amusing," the alien said, and Justine wasn't immediately certain the translator was working correctly. "We came to the Centauri System to attempt to rescue you from the Kulsat. Now, you are rescuing the Kulsat from us."

"Rescue me?" Justine asked. "Who are you? How do you know who I am?"

The pilot got up from the floating chair. A moment later, the chair slowly sank down and seemed to melt into the floor, as if being absorbed into the superstructure.

Standing well over three meters in height, the alien made a bowing motion and fluttered two wing-like hands.

"Forgive our impoliteness. Our names are not completely pronounceable in your language, but a reasonable representation of mine is 'Naila'. I am the Primary Sentinel of the *Fainne*, our ship. This is 'Fairamai'. She is the navigator and copilot. We are from the system you call Gliese."

The other alien stood up and made a bowing gesture of her own. Her translation voice was feminine with dulcet tones. "Pleased to meet you, Solan being."

"I'm Justine," she said. The two Gliesans made a funny little cock of their heads, and Justine flushed when she remembered that they already knew who she was. "Uhm. Is it possible to borrow some clothing?"

The two aliens conferred, and Fairamai nodded to Justine. "We have some nesting fabric that may be long enough for you to use as an outer wrap, if that is suitable."

"Thank you," Justine said, and offered a grateful smile as the tall alien exited the bridge, presumably to retrieve the clothing.

Naila resumed his story. "We received a report from one of our patrol vessels detailing your arrival in this system, followed by the Kulsat attack and your abduction. They requested we come to this system to investigate and should you still be here, retrieve you."

"Patrol?" Justine asked. "Did they find my friends, our ship?"

"According to our readings, the remains of your vessel are on a disused port several hundred-thousand kilometers from here. Your ship is no longer serviceable. It was severed with a mining energy beam. Your friends are no longer in this system."

His last sentence had a reproachful tone to it.

"Where are they?" She looked up as Fairamai returned with a long, multicolored sheet of thin fabric. It was very soft and bore a faint floral scent. Justine wrapped it around herself in a makeshift toga, and immediately felt less vulnerable.

Naila made a clucking sound. "Our colleagues have escorted your friends to your home system after transmitting their report to us."

"That's a relief," Justine said. "Can you take me to my system as well?"

The alien made a vibrating motion with his head, which Justine interpreted as a negative. "I'm afraid travel to your system is forbidden to us by law. Aliah and Ah Tabai have broken protocol. When they return, they will certainly face criminal charges for their transgression."

Justine felt herself grow more frustrated. New obstacles seemed to develop at every step.

"Why is it forbidden?"

"Yours is not an Emerged system. The ancient law of the Grace forbids interference with non-Emerged cultures. I will be happy to explain this all to you, but for now, it is vital we leave Centauri and return to Gliese System."

"Will the Kulsat return?" Justine guessed.

Naila nodded. "Centauri is barren of a native population. The Kulsat frequent this system, looking for Aetherock to mine—I believe you refer to it as 'Kinemet'. They obviously detected your presence."

"What will they do now?" Justine asked.

Naila said, "They will report your presence here, and the Kulsat will return in force. We must leave this system."

Justine's mind was awhirl with all the information. Her immediate concern was the safety of her friends and Earth. "Won't the Kulsat be able to follow us to Gliese?"

"No. Emerged systems have some defense against attack.

Our star beacons are masked. Only when a star beacon is active can an Aetherbeing detect it."

"So the Kulsat won't be able to follow the other patrol ship to my home system, either?"

Naila shook his head. "Only if they were close enough to the star beacon to sense the activation. If that were the case, they would be in your solar system now. We do not have any indication that is the case."

"Why wouldn't they just go to the nearest solar system in this area of space?" she asked, aware that Centauri and Sol were close neighbors.

Naila crooked his head in what Justine assumed was a sign of amusement. "There are billions of systems in the galaxy, and spacial proximity is not a factor when traveling by the star beacons. You could have arrived here from anywhere. The star beacon in your system is unknown to the Kulsat or the galactic network. The Gliesans are the only ones who know its location, and we have guarded the secret for a very long time."

"How will they find us, then?"

Naila said, "The Kulsat will most likely set up a permanent post in Centauri at first. Should anyone from Sol System travel here again, the Kulsat will be able to track them."

It took a moment for Justine to absorb it all. The next ship to use the star beacon to travel to Centauri would be flying into a trap. She felt overwhelmed. "So what can I do?"

"Return to our home system with us. You will be safe until our Council can make a determination."

"Determination?"

"On whether yours is to be considered an Emerged system or not."

"And what will that accomplish?"

"If you are invited to join the Collection of Worlds, we may offer your system the technology to defend yourselves." Naila paused before he added, "If you are not granted status as an Emerged system, we cannot interfere, even if the Kulsat invade you."

Justine took that all in. She knew she was a guest aboard the Gliesan patrol ship. Though she didn't want to seem ungrateful, she couldn't accept or understand their policy.

"If you can't interfere, then why are you helping me?"

"Simply put," Naila said, "there is an ambiguity in the galactic law. You, individually, are physically outside your pre-Emerged system. We may assist you, personally, without actually interfering in the pre-Emerged progress of your world. Though we can offer you amnesty and protection, we are not permitted to offer you technological advances. You will be remanded to a holding station at the outer edge of our system until a decision can be made, and you will not have access to any restricted information or material."

"What happens if you break the law and interfere?" Justine asked.

"The other member systems of the Collection would turn against our world. This is the reason we are at war with the Kulsat; they broke the law of the Grace."

"And you've been at war for how long?" Justine asked.

"The equivalent of over one-thousand Solan years." Naila seemed to be growing impatient with all the questions. "Though there are more than twenty-thousand member systems in the Collection, the Kulsat outnumber us. They have colonized thousands of non-populated systems."

"Twenty-thousand?" Justine remembered the writing on the *Dis Pater,* the monument housing the star beacon on Pluto. "I thought there were over thirty-thousand races out there?"

Naila dropped his head. "At one time," he said, "there were. Many systems were destroyed in the early days of the war, before we developed technology to restrict how many

Aetherbeings can enter our system at the same time." He made a gesture to the display showing the Kulsat shuttle. "We cannot delay anymore. Once we are in Gliesan space, I will grant you limited access to our history files, though I must warn you, many of our records will be off-limits."

"I understand," Justine said. "Thank you for taking the time to explain what you have. I look forward to meeting with your government."

Naila nodded to Fairamai, who used her feathery fingers to tap instructions into their control computer. The targeting system went back online, and the power level indicator rose.

"What are you doing?" Justine barked out.

"We must destroy the shuttle," Naila said. "If they report our presence here to their masters, the Kulsat will focus their aggression on Gliese. Even with our technology, they may eventually be able to swarm us."

Justine took a few steps forward. "You can't kill them. They're innocent. Red Spot risked her life to save me."

"Red Spot?"

"She's a Potential." Justine hoped the Gliesans were familiar with the Kulsat social structure, and understood what she was trying to tell them. "The science leader on the ship, Three Crescents, killed her friend, Green Stripe, just to scare me into talking. Then he went on a rampage, and was going to kill all the crew. Red Spot saved the other Kulsat from destruction, and she saved me."

Naila continued to regard Justine as if her words weren't translating properly.

Exasperated, Justine said, "Not all Kulsat have a complete disregard for life."

The two Gliesans exchanged glances with one another, but made no comment.

Justine took a deep breath. "From what I've experienced, it

seems the Risen are the aggressive caste in Kulsat society. The others are subservient, almost like peasants."

"Kulsat hierarchy is familiar to us," Naila said. "Though the non-Risen on the shuttle pose little direct threat, they would reveal knowledge of our system should they ever escape and return to the Consortium. Bringing them with us to Gliese is a security risk, as is leaving them here."

"Red Spot said there are other non-Risen who don't agree with the Consortium's policies," she added. "She could prove to be a valuable ally."

"The Solan may be right," Fairamai said to Naila. "Perhaps the Potential will give us tactical information on their fleet movements."

That wasn't what Justine had in mind. She didn't think Red Spot would betray the Consortium, but as long as the Gliesans didn't destroy the shuttle, she would go along with them.

Naila nodded. "Very well. I will leave the decision to our commander." He turned back to his console. A blob of Kinemetic material rose out of the floor and formed into a seat that floated up behind the Gliesan. Automatically, he sat and began to flick his feathery fingers over the computer controls. "We will take them with us as prisoners of war." He glanced back at Justine.

Justine nodded. However the Gliesans chose to consider the Kulsat on that shuttle, she thought of them as political refugees, not soldiers.

26

Qin Station :
Sol System :

After his conversation with Alice, Alex gave her a brief rundown of the events that occurred from the moment he first entered the Centauri system over more than fourteen years ago, to the point when they were captured by Chow Yin's patrol.

He left out a few choice tidbits, such as the fact that Ah Tabai was human, and that Justine had been captured by the Kulsat. Instead, he told her that his friend had died when the alien ship was destroyed by the mines around Pluto.

When he'd finished his story, the two of them returned to the larger lab and approached Sian. The programmer gave him an inquisitive look.

"How is it coming along?" Alex asked. He kept his voice even.

Sian blinked. "Slow going. There are a lot of variables."

"Is there anything I can do to help?" Alex asked. "We need to speed up the timetable."

Glancing at Alice, Sian took on a look of concern.

Alice turned to the guard. "Leave us." At first, the soldier didn't budge, but under her continued glare, he finally nodded.

"Your Highness," he said, and stepped outside.

Alice closed the door behind him and faced Sian. "I am aware that you and Alex have been dragging your feet on this project." She held up a hand. "Not to worry. I will report that you were merely being meticulous in your calculations. There are new developments that require the utmost efficiency."

Sian said, "There's a lot of work to do, in that case."

Stepping over to the other computer, Alex opened the program code. "Just tell me what you need. It's been a while, but I catch on quickly."

∞

Over the next two days, Sian and Alex worked through the program to create the algorithm to disseminate the frequencies hidden in the Song of the Stars. While they wrote code, Alex wondered at how Klaus had managed to create his program so accurately: according to Justine's report, he ended up with six possible combinations of the code.

At one point, Alex couldn't follow Sian's work anymore, and he was just getting in the way.

Every few hours, Alice came in to check on their progress. Whenever she was there, she ordered the guard to leave them alone.

One such time, as the code was nearing completion, she motioned for Alex to join her on the other side of the lab.

"Yes?"

She turned on a holoslate and called up several astrophysics charts.

"I don't know how much you learned from your alien friends, or how much you've theorized on your own, but I have a few thoughts I'd like to run past you."

"Of course."

"It has to do with the nature of the star beacons. When you

traveled to the Centauri System, you did so just under the speed of light—though you were not conscious for the duration. However, once the Gliesans returned you here, the trip was near instantaneous."

"Yes," Alex said. "They said the star beacons exist at the same point in space."

Alice's face clouded over. "That would imply some kind of quantum entanglement, but that's not what you said earlier. You said, 'outside light, the star beacons all occupy the same space.' "

"Right."

She shook her head. "That's not the same thing."

"I don't understand."

"For centuries, physicists have been toying with the concepts of faster-than-light travel. For example, Einstein-Rosen bridges, or wormholes. They've toyed with the concepts of quantum tunneling based on the Casimir effect. There's the slipstream theory, which you might know as hyperspace. Now, one might assume 'outside light' is a reference to this. After all, how can light exist if you are traveling faster than it? But something doesn't add up. I don't think that's the answer."

"Then what?"

"Well, how can two or more objects occupy the same space? It's a physical impossibility."

"What about decoherence?" Alex asked. "Some kind of a quantum immortality and quantum suicide relationship?"

Alice nodded. "That's what I was thinking. But I think there's something more to it."

"Go on."

"Well, that's where I run into a wall. I can't help but think that many of these concepts have roots in ancient religions. It's almost as if our ancestors from thousands of years ago had a better grasp of the metaphysical aspects of the universe, and weren't encumbered by our need to quantify it in scientific terms."

"You think this all might have something to do with religion?"

"Well," Alice said, "a great deal of your Mayan mysticism is based on your ancestors' contact with these 'luminous' beings. The Grace, as you called them. Is it such a stretch that other religions and cultures may have had some kind of contact, and developed their own explanations for it?"

Not certain where the conversation was going, Alex asked, "So you think the ancient religions had a better understanding of the universe than we do?"

"Maybe not in a scientific way, but their lack of hard astrophysical knowledge didn't hinder them from coming up with theories." Alice raised a finger. "Now, if we examine your alien friend's use of the phrase, 'outside light' again, we must admit the possibility of dimensional transference."

"You think the star beacons can send a ship to another dimension—"

"Where there might exist a corresponding star beacon at a fixed point in their space."

"—and then send the ship back into our dimension in a different point in space."

"That would explain it, wouldn't it?"

Alex nodded. "I guess it would."

For the first time since meeting Alice, Alex saw that her expression was one of pure wonder. Gone was the angry and bitter young woman. Astrophysics was her calling, and he could tell it was what made her the happiest. Deep inside, he wished the events that had led her here had never happened, and that they'd met in other circumstances.

Alex was aware that, though he was over thirty-years old chronologically—only a few years younger than Alice—

because of the time he'd spent in photonic travel, he was biologically an eighteen-year-old. There were too many differences between the two of them besides age.

A sharp pang of regret ran through him over how the course of his life had affected him. Suddenly, Alex felt more alone than he ever had.

"Done!" Sian said, shocking him out of his reverie.

Practically jumping out of her seat, Alice hurried over to look at the completed code. Alex followed at a slower pace.

"It's compiling," the programmer said. "Give it a minute, and then we can run the algorithm."

Together, the three of them watched, as if that very act could speed up the process.

When the program was ready, Sian looked up at them. "Shall I run it?"

Alice nodded, her face revealing that she was too excited to say it aloud.

Sian ran the program. Within seconds, it spat out two possible combinations for the priming sequence.

"Two?" Alice said, frowning.

The programmer gave a slight shake of his head. "I'm not sure how Klaus managed to get the sequence correct the first time." He turned in his seat. "The only thing I can think of is that he must have used Yaxche's grandson's recitation, whereas we used Yaxche's—and yes, we have two recordings of it." Taking a breath, he said, "It's possible the old man's voice has become weaker over the years. He was off on one note."

"At least we don't have to worry about variables," Alex said. "Klaus didn't have access to me, or to Quantum Resources' trials, so he had to test for environment conditions, gravity, atmosphere, Kinemet volume and so forth. From the records of our trials, and from what Major Turner told me, I can recreate the necessary conditions."

Alice took a deep breath. "But it still means we only have a fifty-fifty chance of getting it right. Which means—"

Another voice cut through their discussion. "Which means there will have to be a necessary sacrifice."

Alex hadn't noticed the main door to the lab had opened. In the frame, standing up with the aid of his biomechatronic legs, Chow Yin put his hands on his hips and surveyed the occupants of the lab.

He gave them a disapproving glance. "Did you think I would leave you to your own devices without monitoring you every step of the way?"

"Sire!" Sian said in a gasp.

"I expected betrayal from Mr. Manez, but you, Sian? I rescued you from life imprisonment. I'm very disappointed."

Then he wagged an accusatory finger at Alice, his face pulled into an expression of disapproval. "And you, my daughter." Then his lips spread into a wide smile. "You were correct. All you needed to do was to play the damsel in distress who needed rescuing, and look, your knight in shining armor gave up all his secrets for you."

Alex's stomach did a lazy flip-flop. He'd been duped, and easily at that.

A crooked, satisfied smile on her face, Alice separated herself from the other two and made her way over to stand beside her father.

Shaking his head, Chow Yin motioned for the guards who had accompanied him to enter the lab and seize the prisoners.

Sian took a step back, and tried to resist when one of the guards grabbed his arm. "What are you going to do?"

Chow Yin, Emperor of Sol System, said, "It's quite simple. We have two possible formulas to create a Kinemat, and now we have a volunteer."

27

Cerro Azul :
Guatemala :

When Patli finished his story, Michael noticed Humberto's eyes boring not into the storyteller, but into him, as if trying to measure his reaction. It was an incredible story, and if Michael had not encountered Ah Tabai, Aliah, and the Kulsat, he would have immediately discounted the tale as nothing more than a fable. Now, however, he was inclined to believe the story had merit. From the description of the Grace's ship and its destruction to the radiation sickness caused by the piece of active Kinemet brought back to the camp, and ending with the villagers' rescue from the tall, bird-like aliens—it all made sense with what Michael had already learned.

It was obvious that he had not hidden his belief as he listened to the story; Humberto's expression as he considered Michael was proof of that.

For one fleeting moment, the thought of denying the story went through Michael's mind. After all, the fewer people who knew the truth of the galaxy's history at this point, the less chance of the information getting back to Chow Yin, who would use it to his advantage.

Humberto's track record of assistance and reliability prompted Michael to trust in the Cruzado.

As if sensing Michael had come to his decision, Humberto asked, "Do you think this is all true?"

"For the most part, yes." Michael rubbed at the stubble growing on his chin. "I'm not supposed to go into the details. It's a matter of international security, and I've been sworn to secrecy by my government. I trust you won't reveal what you learn here to anyone?"

Nodding, Humberto said, "So long as I have your word that our people won't be exploited anymore. It sounds like there is a connection between our ancestors and whatever it is out there." He pointed skyward.

"Let me put it to you this way," Michael said. "There's a very real and imminent threat in the galaxy, known only to a handful of people. The 'god' described in Patli's story is most likely a member of a powerful race of aliens who, at one time, could restrain the other systems in the galaxy. In the past millennium, they've disappeared, and the threat grew."

"I take it you are talking about something more dangerous than Emperor Chow Yin?"

Michael said, "We encountered this menace. They ripped our ship apart with a single strike, and from what we learned, the only reason they didn't destroy us is that they didn't consider us to be worth the effort."

Nodding toward Patli, Humberto said, "And you believe the only defense might be found within a thousand-year-old tale?"

Michael shrugged. "The formula for Kinemetic conversion was in this storyteller's tale, the Song of the Stars. Apparently, it was passed along to this Subo Ak by the dying alien. Perhaps Subo Ak left more clues that might help us."

Humberto spoke rapidly in Spanish to Patli, who then nodded and replied. The Cruzado said, "He says the shrine is in a mostly forgotten area of the Cerro Azul—the Blue Hills.

It is where the warriors of the lost village first learned of the fate of their loved ones. It is in the shrine where Subo Ak etched the story on stone columns. Patli has not made the journey there in more than twenty years, but he remembers the way."

The two spoke in Spanish some more, and Humberto said, "The shrine is just over the Guatemalan border. He says there is a horse trail that might be wide enough for our truck. There are no border guards out here."

"And he's willing to show us the way?"

Humberto nodded. "He seems more than happy to do so. Few people have shown this much interest in his story." He said something to Patli who, despite his age, sprang from his chair and hurried into his house. When he returned, he was wearing hiking boots and had a large sack full of food. He was ready to go.

Together, they went to the truck, and Yaxche and Patli squished themselves into the front beside Migel, while the other three piled into the back.

"We've probably got enough fuel to get there," Migel said as he pulled out onto the dirt road and headed north under Patli's directions, "but I doubt we'll have enough to get back to Copán Ruinas."

"No problem," Humberto said. "Los Amates is only twenty or thirty kilometers north of the border. We should be able to make it there to refuel. If not, I have some friends there who can bring us some hydro."

To Diego, Humberto said, "If this horse trail is passable, it will let us go back and forth to Guatemala discreetly."

As it turned out, the trail was passable, but only on foot or hoof. The truck was too wide, and the ground too soft for the tires to get traction. They all had to get out and walk. While the three Cruzados wore military boots, and Patli had hiking gear, both Yaxche and Michael had street shoes on. According to the old man, they were only a few kilometers away from the shrine. By the time they got there, Michael's feet were completely caked with mud, and his ankles burned with the strain of the hike. He was so miserable, he barely registered it when they finally reached their destination.

The area, as Humberto had told them while they hiked, was part of a national park. While there was a healthy tourist industry there, he didn't think many people would venture that deep into the hills. Even if they did, very few people could interpret the Mayan writing on the shrine.

"It doesn't look like anyone has been here in a very long while," Humberto said, pointing to the tall grass in the clearing, and the overgrown vegetation.

Near the tree line, there was a series of four stone columns, no more than two meters high. Mayan glyphs covered their entire surface.

Patli, barely winded from the hike, went to the columns and ran the palms of his hands over them. He gave Michael and the others a wide grin and started speaking in Mayan.

Yaxche, who didn't look like he'd managed much better on the journey than Michael, said, "He's telling us what each glyph means."

"The story he told us back at his place seemed much longer," Michael said, surveying the four columns.

Humberto nodded. "The glyph-style of storytelling is more like point-form. The priest telling the story would fill in the narrative when he recited it. There's a lot of room for interpretation."

"Tell me about it," Michael said. "When our linguists tried to decipher the Song of the Stars, we had a dozen different versions, and every translator insisted theirs was the correct one."

Humberto held up a finger, and a crease appeared in his forehead as he questioned Patli. When the older man replied, the cruzado spoke to Michael. "He says the only thing written on the columns that talks about where the alien might have been buried is that it took Subo Ak from sunrise to sunset to walk the distance across the valley from the Sierra de las Minas."

"Twelve hours." Michael looked behind him. "How far did we come from where we left the truck?"

"About ten kilometers. It took us a little under four hours."

"And we're not all exactly young and fit." In his head, Michael calculated. "If he could make better time than us, we're looking at a maximum range of, say, thirty kilometers from this spot." A moment later, Michael added, "Of course, that's based on our interpretation of the glyphs."

Humberto took out his holoslate and called up a terrain map. "In a generally northern direction, I would say we should be looking in this section, along the southern edge of the mountain range."

Michael blanched. "That's over ten-thousand hectares, easily. It could take us weeks to cover that much ground."

Humberto brought up another screen. "There's a mining operation supplier in Guatemala City. The Guatemalan Minister of Culture is one of our supporters." He glanced up at Michael. "I can trust him. I'll ask that he send satellite survey maps to us—we should be able to narrow down any caves in the area. We should get some equipment as well: laser scanners, that kind of thing."

"Get a radiation detector," Michael said. "The half-life of Kinemet is in the hundreds of thousands of years. That might help."

"Good." Humberto typed a message. "According to the topographical map, there's a tributary to the Motagua River a few kilometers from here, and a small village a few more kilometers downstream. I'll tell my friends in Los Amates to come get us there."

Michael's excitement was quickly dampened. "The fewer people who know who we are and what we're doing, the better."

"Not to worry," Humberto said, "I trust these men with my—"

He was cut off when the crack of a rifle shot split the air. Diego, who had been standing at the southern edge of the clearing, flew backwards as a bullet ripped through his shoulder, and he disappeared into the long grass.

Migel swung around and shot into the forest, but the bullet that struck was the one that hit him in the leg, spinning him around before he fell with a loud cry.

Before anyone had a chance to react, a loud voice yelled out in Spanish. *"¡No se mueva!"*

28

Gliesan Ship :
Centauri System :

Justine watched as the Gliesans maneuvered their patrol ship close to the shuttle. At the last moment, the shuttle veered to port and accelerated away.

"They think we're attacking them," Justine said. "Is there any way we can communicate with Red Spot? I could explain what we're doing."

Naila reached out a feathery finger to an open space on the wall beside him, and touched the flowing surface. A shimmering console molded itself out of the wall. The alien pressed a series of small squares on the device.

"It is rare that a Kulsat ship will respond to a hail, but you may make the attempt. Direct your message into this receptacle. Our communications program will translate to the Kulsat computers."

He ran his finger along a section of the console, and a thin protuberance formed out of the wall that Justine assumed was a microphone.

Justine stepped up to it and said, "Red Spot, this is Justine. If you can hear me, please respond. We are not trying to destroy you or your ship. The Gliesans have agreed to help us."

Just when Justine thought there would be no reply, a

monotone voice spoke. "There will be no help. They will torture us. Death is preferable."

"I promise that is not true," Justine said. "They have given me their word."

Several moments passed before Red Spot replied. "You cannot guarantee our continuance. Our enemies practice deception on you, Justine."

Trying to bridge these two very different worlds was frustrating. Justine gave Naila an exasperated look. "Is there anything you can do to prove to them they won't be tortured?"

Naila and Fairamai shared a look. The pilot looked back at Justine. "You show uncommon compassion for a violent species that shows no compassion for others."

Shaking her head, Justine said, "You can't judge an entire culture based on the policies of those in power. Red Spot proved that not all Kulsat are like the Risen. She protected her people from Three Crescents' murderous rampage, and she helped me—an alien—escape him."

Cocking his head in a manner that Justine interpreted as bewilderment, Naila bent toward the microphone.

"This is Naila of the *Fainne*. Do you have the ability to broadcast my words to your entire ship?"

"All Kulsat on board can hear you," came the monotone reply.

Formally, Naila said, "On behalf of the Collection of Worlds and the Parliament of Gliese, I am willing to offer you and the other members of your crew the right of asylum in return for your parole that you will renounce all hostilities against the Collection now and in the future. You will live, but you never be permitted to leave Gliesan space for the rest of your lives. Do you agree to these terms?"

A few long moments later, Red Spot replied, "All are in agreement. We accept your conditions."

"Cut your engines. We will latch your shuttle to our ship and enter Aetherflight."

"Thank you, Naila," Justine said.

Naila made a low throaty noise. "Do not thank me yet. Their shuttle is much larger than our patrol ship, and our scans indicated there are over one hundred of them. If the shuttle is secured to our ship, and we push our quantum drive to its capacity, we should be able to convert them to Aethersleep, but I cannot guarantee they will all survive the Aetherflight."

Justine opened her mouth to ask him to elaborate, but Fairamai got up from her seat and gestured to the corridor leading toward the back of the *Fainne*.

"If you will follow me down the passageway, Justine, I will take you to the passenger compartment. It is for your safety."

As Naila began the docking procedure, Justine followed Fairamai and asked her a question. "What kind of danger was Naila talking about?"

"I'm sure you are aware there can be disorientation when coming out of Aetherflight."

"Actually," Justine said as she trailed the Gliesan, "I've only been on a quantum ship once, and I was the pilot at the time. I had no idea what I was doing—though I learned quickly— but I seemed to be able to manage the transition all right."

"For our flight," Fairamai said, "only the pilot will be in Aetherform and remain aware. It is the way of it. All passengers and crew of our ships, regardless whether they are Aethers or not, are placed in Aethersleep before Aetherflight. It is for their safety. You will not be conscious during the flight, and neither will I. Unfortunately, Naila will not be able to put all the Kulsat into Aethersleep. He will only be able to maintain a link with a dozen or so." A moment later, she spoke in a low voice. "The Kulsat Risen apparently do not bother to induce Aethersleep in their crew, and let their quantum engines perform the conversion. The Kulsat may have more advanced technology, but that doesn't mean they are more enlightened."

Justine guessed that Aethersleep must be the term for quantizing another being, whether by a Kinemat, or by a quantum drive. Sensing the deep emotion behind Fairamai's last statement, Justine was curious about the difference. "Why don't you use the quantum drive to start the photonic change in passengers?"

The alien shook her head. "There is a significant risk of passengers not returning to the physical state if the Aetherdrive initiates Aethersleep."

"Uh…"

"Were you not aware of this problem?" Fairamai asked. "Did you experience a noticeable delay when your ship came out of Aetherspace?"

Gulping at the thought that there had been a chance that all of them aboard the *Ultio* could have been stuck in the quantum state, Justine said, "Yes. That was one of our greatest hurdles when we began experimenting with quantum drives." The more she learned, the more she realized how much more there was to learn. "Many of our test pilots died…"

Fairamai had reached the passenger compartment, and gestured for Justine to enter first.

"I am sorry to hear that," the alien said. "We undergo years of training to master Aetherform and inducing Aethersleep before we are allowed to take a ship into Aetherspace."

"Since we both have the ability to become photonic," Justine asked, "why are we going into Aethersleep?"

"Only one consciousness can pilot a ship in Aetherstate. If there are two consciousnesses, there will be conflict and instability. The chance of returning to normal space is severely diminished."

Justine felt her stomach sink at the thought. It would have

been another fatal lesson for NASA and Quantum Resources to learn. At the back of her mind, she was aware that, in the four years since she'd been in Sol System, any number of disasters could have taken place if Earth continued quantum experiments.

Fairamai said, "The report we received from the other patrol ship indicated that your journey to Centauri was entirely in Aetherspace. The risks of mishap would have been greatly increased if you had gone outside light. You are lucky to be alive."

Fairamai touched a spot on the wall, and a hammock-like seat formed out of the fluidic metal.

"You will be secure here."

Justine didn't move to the seat, however. Her mouth hung open in shock.

"Is there a problem?" Fairamai asked.

"What do you mean by 'outside light'?"

With a slight jerking motion of her head, Fairamai made a chirping sound. She sounded surprised when she said, "You were not aware of this, either?"

Justine shook her head. "I thought there was a problem with the translation computer when you said the other patrol ship had sent a report to you before traveling to my solar system. I thought maybe you meant they'd left a report here for you, in Centauri; but they actually *went* to Gliese, and then to Sol System, didn't they?"

"Yes." Fairamai nodded. "It is by the Grace that we travel outside light. Inside a system, we travel in Aetherspace—inside the speed of light—but once we reach the star beacons, we are able to arrive in another system instantaneously."

Justine couldn't wrap her head around it. "How?"

"Outside light, the star beacons all occupy the same space."

"Are you talking about quantum entanglement?"

"It is one theory. However, our experiments in that area have proven inconclusive."

Chewing her lip, Justine asked, "Could 'outside light' be another dimension?"

"That is not known. When we are outside light, none of us has consciousness. It is only by the Grace that we are able to return to Aetherspace in another system."

Stunned, Justine made her way to the seat and laid back into it. "I spent four years in a quantized state," she said in a hoarse voice. "And I could have made the same journey in the blink of an eye."

"It is unlikely," Fairamai said. "You do not have the training, and your ships do not have the proper technology. All of that will come in time."

Springing up to a sitting position, Justine said, "Then you must train me and show us how to use the star beacons correctly."

"We cannot." The alien shrugged her delicate shoulders. "We are forbidden to interfere in your technological evolution. It is a knowledge you need to discover for yourselves. Already, I am in ambiguous territory by warning you of the dangers."

"I really don't understand that policy," Justine said.

"It is because of the Kulsat that the Grace made non-interference a law."

"The Kulsat?"

Fairamai made a tapping gesture to the wall beside her, a console appeared showing writing that Justine couldn't read.

The alien said, "We still have some time before Naila is finished attaching the shuttle. I will tell you the history while we wait—it is not restricted material." She flicked her fingers across the panel, and it disappeared back into the wall.

Another reclining seat, similar to Justine's, formed underneath Fairamai, and she sank into it.

"The Grace, who called themselves Xtôti, discovered Aetherspace nearly a million years ago. They explored our galaxy, and erected a star beacon in every system with a life-supporting planet, or cache of the Aetherock, so that they would not have to spend years or centuries to return to those systems.

"The Kulsat were the second species in the galaxy to achieve space flight—we believe this occurred approximately eight-thousand-years ago. From your own history, you understand that societal evolution can take a very long time. The Grace were perhaps too impatient. They brought knowledge of Aetherspace to the Kulsat as a gift. The Kulsat had not matured as a society, and quickly splintered into a caste system of those who could achieve Aetherform, and those who were unable to make the change."

Justine interrupted. "The Deficients." She thought about Alex. "They weren't able to transform fully."

"Yes. It is rare for it to happen in the other races, but there is some kind of physiological issue with the Kulsat species. Less than one in ten thousand is able to transform into a 'Risen'."

"That is why the Risen have cultivated their elite status."

"That," Fairamai said, "and because of the lifespan differential."

"Lifespan?"

"A normal Kulsat has a life expectancy of approximately two to three years." The translator calculated the time equivalent for Justine's reference. "Those who fail the conversion process have their normal life expectancy reduced to an average of one quarter—it is the same rate with any other species when this happens."

Justine swallowed hard. "One of my friends from the *Ultio*, Alex, wasn't able to complete the transformation. Do you mean to say his life expectancy will be cut short as well?"

"Yes. I am afraid that is the case."

The average human lived to a hundred-and-twenty. Alex had been exposed to Kinemet when he was ten. That meant that he most likely only had twenty or thirty years from the time on Macklin's Rock left to live.

Fairamai said, "We make every effort to ensure those unconverted are comfortable. Though they can never exist within the gravity well of a planet or moon, we have many stations in our system where they work and live out their lives."

"There's no cure?" Justine asked, to which Fairamai shook her head.

She said, "The Kulsat call them Deficients, and do not treat them very well. Often, since they rarely have more than a year of life left in them, they are sent out to mine Aetherock, or they are used as front-line troops in combat missions against the Collection."

Justine was aghast. "And the Xtôti didn't do anything to stop the Kulsat?"

"The Kulsat did not begin their war with the Collection until after the Grace disappeared from the galaxy. Before that point, the Grace were able to keep the Kulsat reined in. No one knows how this was accomplished; otherwise, we would have used the knowledge long ago to stop them."

After a moment, Fairamai continued, "The Grace realized that interference could have unforeseen consequences. They decreed that all species would retain autonomy over their own affairs in all matters, especially when it came to technological advances. Only once a system Emerged could they petition to become a member of the Collection of Worlds and share technology."

Justine said, "That answers some of my questions about the Kulsat's internal culture, but why are they so aggressively paranoid about other species? Surely, there has to be a way to stop the war between them and the rest of the galaxy. You said it's been going on for a very long time." Justine shook her head in astonishment at the thought of a thousand years of war. "Does it have something to do with this 'final component' they kept asking me about?"

Fairamai gave a shrug of uncertainty. "At this point, there can only be speculation. Over the centuries, many of our records have been lost, and those that remain are in dispute. We believe the Xtôti—the Grace—possessed a higher level of technology concerning the Aetherock than any we have been able to develop. There are two aspects to this advancement that we have debated endlessly.

"While those who fail the Aether conversion have their life expectancies shortened, those who convert successfully often more than double their life span. There is a theory that, individually, each of the Grace had lived for a million years."

Justine blanched, unable to imagine living so long. Doubling life expectancy was a more familiar concept; humankind had been exploring that for all history. Primitive peoples often only lived twenty or thirty years. Currently, it was becoming more common for people to celebrate their hundredth birthday, and still be quite active and lucid.

For the Kulsat, the difference between five or six years as a Risen and the immortality of the Grace was a goal that would be hard to ignore.

"You said there were two aspects."

"The second thought is more speculative in nature," Fairamai said. "We hypothesize that the advanced technology gives the Grace the ability to remain conscious outside light. That is the only explanation we can think of for how they were able to create the star beacons. Of course, the last Xtôti disappeared from the galaxy nearly a thousand years ago, and when they were among us, they did not share their secrets. Many in the Collection of Worlds have tried to discover this technology, but so far, we have not advanced our knowledge very much since the time of the Grace. The war with the Kulsat has taken its toll on our societies and resources. If the Kulsat gain the technology, they will control the star beacons, and thus, control us."

Justine said, "In the message Ah Tabai left for my friend Alex, he indicated the Kulsat believe this technology was hidden on an un-Emerged world. Is there any validity to that?"

"Since the Collection of Worlds adheres to the Grace's galactic laws, we have not explored this surmise. So far, the few worlds that have Emerged before the Kulsat destroyed them have not yielded the lost secret."

Bringing the conversation back around, Justine asked, "If the Collection of Worlds grants Emerged status to Sol System, that means you will offer us protection from the Kulsat?"

"We cannot guarantee the safety of any system," Fairamai said. "Indeed, in the last century alone, we have seen the cultures of more than a hundred Emerged systems destroyed by the Kulsat armada. However, we will all offer what assistance we are able to, in order to shore up your defenses. There are ways to limit travel through your star beacon. It is a difficult process, and requires the combined effort of many Aetherbeings to accomplish this."

A chime sounded from somewhere in the wall, and Fairamai said, "Naila has secured the Kulsat shuttle. He will put us into Aethersleep soon. When we awaken, we will be in Gliesan space."

"One more question," Justine said. "Just because we've achieved what you call Aetherflight, that doesn't mean the Collection will consider us Emerged, does it?"

"For Gliese, it was years from the first discovery of

Aetherock before we were able to travel outside light."

Justine cursed to herself. The Kulsat were probably already looking for Sol System. Earth didn't have years to play catch-up.

Before she could form any other thoughts, she felt herself transforming into the photonic state as Naila induced Aethersleep in her.

29

Cerro Azul :
Guatemala :

Michael immediately rushed over to Yaxche and Patli, intending to push them out of the line of fire. Humberto pulled out his pistol, dropping to a crouch as he did so, and scanned the wooded area for their assailants.

"I said, don't move!" the gunman yelled out in English.

Michael froze and looked in the direction the voice had come from. He couldn't see anything. Glancing at Humberto, Michael said, "They have us surrounded."

"Put your weapons on the ground, step back, and put your hands on your heads." A moment later, the assailant added, "I don't want to have to kill any of you, but I will."

With a low growl, Humberto complied. Only once the four of them put their hands on their heads did two people, a man and a woman, step out from behind the bushes. With a measure of alarm, Michael recognized the tourist couple from the day before. They'd followed them all this way. Who were they?

He hadn't paid them much attention at the village, but now he got a good look at them. They were both of Spanish heritage, and both were tall and thin. The man's black hair was cut short, while the woman had her long hair tied back in a ponytail. Neither of them wore smiles, and their eyes radiated anger. There was something familiar about the man.

Both held high-powered rifles. The man aimed at Humberto, while the woman slowly slung her weapon at the rest of them one at a time.

"Who are you?" Humberto asked. When the two didn't reply, he continued, "Can I check on my friends?"

The man gave a slight shake of his head and spoke English with a heavy Spanish accent. "I am an excellent marksman. I did not shoot them in any vital areas. Shoulder and leg. Both will live. If you do not do precisely as I say, however, then I will ensure they do *not* survive."

Careful not to let his aim waver in the slightest from his target, the man walked toward Humberto. Only when he was right in front of the Cruzado did he stop. Without glancing behind him to make sure his partner had him covered, the man slung his rifle over his shoulder. Standing tall, keeping his eyes fixed on Humberto, he reached out and grabbed the holoslate, which the Cruzado had slipped into a belt pouch.

He flicked it on with a swipe of his finger and looked at the readout. "It is fortunate for you that you did not have time to send your message; otherwise, we might have had to take more extreme measures."

"Who are you?" Humberto asked again.

Continuing to examine the holoslate, flipping through the screens to read the history, the man said, "What is this map of? Why is that area so important to you? Why do you wish to excavate there?"

A wave of relief went through Michael. If these were Ruiz's people, then his organization had no idea what he was doing in Honduras and Guatemala. The attempt to kidnap him and Yaxche was nothing more than a fishing expedition. Under no circumstances could he let them know his true mission.

"It's a jade deposit," Michael said.

The woman narrowed her eyes. "Jade?" She let out a laugh of disbelief.

"I used to work for a Canadian resources company," Michael said. "A mineral satellite that ran over the area several years ago indicated there might be a deposit there. It was too small for my company—it wouldn't have been worth it for a big company like that to lease the rights. It might be valuable for a smaller operation, though. If I can find it, I can sell the information for a ten-percent finder's fee. At my age, I have to think about my retirement."

The man and woman didn't look convinced, and Michael added, "I asked my friends to help me find the deposit."

"If we've mistaken you for someone else, I'm afraid we're going to have to kill you all." The man smiled conspiratorially. "After all, we do not need witnesses." He raised his rifle to Humberto again.

"No, wait!" Michael said, holding out his hand.

"Why?" the man asked, lifting one eyebrow. "Do you have a different story to tell me, Mr. Sanderson?"

Michael gaped. How did he know his name?

The man nodded, and his smile widened. "Yes, we know all about you. Your government's attempt at misinformation might fool the newsvids, but not us."

"What do you want?"

"Do you remember Señor Oscar Ruiz? He offered you his hospitality and protection, and in return, you led the police to his plantation, ruined his name, and stole the knowledge possessed by Señor Yaxche for your own purposes."

Michael glanced at Humberto, and then back. "You work for him?"

"Work for him?" the man said, looking offended by the suggestion.

Humberto narrowed his eyes. "He is your father. You must be Alondo and Nadia. I see the resemblance now."

"And so," Alondo said, finally, "now that we all know who everyone is, let us try this again."

"What do you want with us?" Michael asked.

Nadia spoke. "Once, you came to Honduras and stole from our nation. You took knowledge from us, and you and your country prospered. Now, you are back, and I think you are here to steal more. This time, you will steal it for us. We will carve out our own legacy."

"I'm not here to steal anything."

With a sneer, Nadia said, "You are looking for information, as you did before. Do you deny this?"

Michael couldn't, not without giving away the lie—he was too physically exhausted from the march and too emotionally wrought from the violence to be a convincing actor.

Alondo said, "You will explain what you are doing, illegally crossing the border to Honduras, and what is really buried in this mountain range. I promise you, I have more bullets than you have friends."

Expecting that Alondo and Nadia would think he was still lying and kill him anyway, Michael said in a flat voice, "Based on a folk tale, we believe an alien creature was buried somewhere in those mountains over a thousand years ago."

"An alien, you say?" Alondo grinned. "That is quite the story. Let's investigate this fairy tale, shall we? I will make the arrangements."

∞

Alondo permitted Humberto and Michael to tend to Diego and Migel, and they did their best to bind the men's wounds. The two carried the injured men closer to the stones one at a time, where there was more shade. After asking if it was all right with Alondo and Nadia, they left the two men with a few canteens of water.

"I will send someone back to fetch them," Alondo said, and instructed his remaining prisoners to march north overland to the small village Humberto had spotted on his map earlier.

As it turned out, Alondo Ruiz and his sister were not without resources. Along the way, once he received a decent satellite signal, Alondo made several calls on his commlink. He didn't attempt to hide his conversations from his prisoners.

He contacted a mining operation they partly owned, and ordered them to start the paperwork to excavate the area.

Sensing Michael's confusion, Alondo laughed. "What, did you think you were just going to walk into a national park with a few shovels and start digging? The police would be on you before you broke a sweat. No, for appearances' sake, it will all be legal. The CEO knows how to grease certain Guatemalan officials to get the permits quickly. Fear not, we will begin surveying by this time tomorrow. Once you've found the location for us, we will excavate."

After three more grueling hours of marching, they arrived at the village and were greeted by two armed men driving a two-ton cargo truck. The captives were herded into the canopied bed. Michael sat on the floor, welcoming the relief from his blistered and burning feet. Both Patli and Yaxche looked worse for wear. Humberto was more angry than exhausted, but he kept his head down.

The siblings rode up front with the driver, and the other armed man sat in the back with the prisoners, his rifle at the ready.

They drove north for half an hour, and stopped when they reached an isolated farmhouse.

Michael and the others got out of the truck. Alondo led

them to a barn and motioned for them to go inside. There were several stalls with straw on the ground. The doors were chained and bolted, and the one window in the loft was sealed shut. There weren't any animals in the barn, but there were a few barrels filled with what Michael hoped was drinkable water.

Alondo looked outside and waved his hand. Another man entered, holding a large cooking pot. Placing it on the floor, he removed the cover to reveal a corn, bean, and rice mix. It didn't look particularly appetizing, but it had been a long time since they had eaten last, and Michael was ravenous. There didn't seem to be any cutlery, as if Alondo expected them to eat with their hands.

He said, "My father believed in treating his guests with courtesy." He glared at Michael. "You, however, are not guests. I trust you will *not* have a comfortable stay."

30

Gliese Outpost :
Gliesan System :

Justine came out of the photonic state—Aethersleep—immediately. There was no delay between the intangible and physical states of being that she'd experienced on her last journey. While some people experienced momentary disorientation when waking up from normal sleep, Justine had always been one of those people who were instantly alert. This process was no different.

She opened her eyes and looked around the passenger compartment. Fairamai took a few moments to open her eyes. The Gliesan made a quick ruffling movement with her head, as if to shake off the effects of the Aethersleep, and then she looked at Justine.

"We are here," she said. "Home."

Pushing her *sight* out, Justine quickly sensed that she was in a new solar system, one with a red dwarf star at its center. There were several small planets orbiting close to the star, and four larger bodies outside those. A number of tiny planets that would most likely be considered dwarf planets orbited the outer edge of the system. From what she could sense, there weren't any gas giants in Gliese.

"I would love to be able to visit your home world," Justine

said to her, wondering which one of the four planets in the habitable zone was their prime.

"Even if it were permitted, you would not be able to survive for more than a few days."

"Oh?" Justine asked. "How come?"

Fairamai got up from her hammock, and it melted back into the wall. "Our physiology has been altered by the Aether process. The gravity of a planet, or even a moon, puts an incredible pressure on our cells. It interferes with the Aether, and dampens its ability to sustain us. Our internal systems begin to shut down."

"Alex, the first of us to be changed by the Kinemet, lived several years on our moon before his health deteriorated," Justine said.

"As you said before, he is not fully transformed. He might even be able to survive several months on the surface of a planet. We are beings of light, Justine. We are no longer true members of our own species."

There was one question that Justine hadn't asked yet, and she realized it was because it was something she wasn't certain she wanted to know. Kinemet was a miracle element, and would give any world the ability to venture beyond the borders of its solar system. For those who successfully underwent the Kinemetic change, and were forever altered, there were numerous benefits: the ability to pilot ships between the stars, electropathic control, and enhanced memory. It was a dream-come-true on many levels.

The change came with some serious disadvantages. There were many dangers involved with utilizing the Kinemetic power itself, but it was the secondary effects that would give potential candidates pause. Never being able to set foot on her home planet again without risking death was a significant downside. If Justine had had a choice in her conversion, and had known about this drawback, she would've had a very tough decision to make. It was a big enough issue that it would deter many from going down the path to becoming an interstellar pilot.

The Kinemetic change altered a person at the cellular level. What other side effects would this change produce?

Hesitant to ask the question, Justine nevertheless spoke it. "Whatever you want to call us—Risen, Kinemats, Aetherbeings—we can't have children, can we?"

"Not once we are altered," Fairamai said, as if that were a well-known fact.

The confirmation was like a punch in the stomach to Justine. Though she'd made the decision not to have a child of her own long ago, the option had always been there if she ever changed her mind. Now, there was no hope. Klaus had taken away a great deal more than anyone thought when he'd forced Justine into the change.

The anger surged in her, but she had no place to direct it. Klaus hadn't survived Lucis Observatory, but if he had, she would track him down and make him wish he hadn't.

Fairamai led her back to the bridge, and by the time they arrived, Justine had managed to regain control of her emotions.

The display on the main console panel showed dozens of Gliesan patrol ships in the vicinity around the star beacon. A distance away, there were a number of larger ships that looked like they were military cruisers of some kind—she could sense a variation of weaponized Kinemet on board them. Considering the ongoing war with the Kulsat, Justine assumed that if an enemy ship were to travel to their system, they would quickly be engaged in battle.

Naila said, "I have transmitted our report to Commander Analock. We will be escorted to Skanse Aerie—our outmost station." Glancing over his shoulder at Justine, he added, "The

Commander is not pleased that we brought the Kulsat shuttle with us ... or that I offered them asylum."

Setting her jaw, Justine asked, "What did he have to say about me?"

"With Ah Tabai and Aliah breaking protocol—and galactic law—and with my decision to spare the enemy, his response to your presence was ... not repeatable. He has, however, dispatched a courier ship to Gliese Prime for further instruction."

Justine felt acutely guilty at the mention of the 'enemy', remembering Fairamai's warning about how unstable the conversion to and from Aetherspace was for normal beings. "The Kulsat," she said. "Did they all make it?"

"There is one less life form registering on our monitors," Naila said.

Gritting her teeth at the news, Justine was silently thankful that her ignorance had not cost any of her passengers on the *Ultio* their lives.

As Naila plugged in the course to the station, Fairamai stroked her long, taloned finger on the control panel on her side of the bridge. A workstation of sorts emerged from the wall on one side of the bridge and a contoured chair rose up and floated above the floor. The Gliesan motioned for Justine to take a seat.

"Skanse Aerie is approximately two-hundred-thousand kilometers away—too short a distance for quantum travel. We'll have to use normal space engines. It will be at least forty minutes before we arrive. Perhaps you would like to access some background material on our history before you meet a representative from the Collection of Worlds and present your case. It would be best if you were as informed as possible."

"Thank you, Fairamai," Justine said, and settled herself into the floating chair. When she'd been standing up, the display screen had looked like a two-dimensional representation; once she sat down, the image before her expanded into a volumetric holograph. Haptic technology had just started to become popular on Earth, and Justine extended her hand to manipulate the image in front of her.

"No," Fairamai said, "the educational database has a synaptic interface."

"How do you operate it?"

"Simply focus your concentration on any rendered object or word." She pointed to a small antenna above the display. "It will receive your neuropulses. To manipulate the display, form one of the basic commands in your mind. I've entered translations of 'Go', 'Back', 'Follow', and 'Return'. You can customize other commands with the interface at the bottom. Subvocalize searches to begin. I would suggest that you start with the Xtôti entries before moving on to Kulsat history."

Silently amazed at the remarkable technology, Justine looked at the display. There was a single phrase hanging in three-dimensional suspension: *Please supply search parameters.*

"Xtôti history," Justine said under her breath, and the display launched the first page in the database, comprising text as well as a dimensional image of what looked like a humanoid turtle without a shell. For a moment, Justine gaped. In her mind, she hadn't really formed an image of the Grace, but this was not what she had expected.

Before reading the text, however, she wanted to be sure she had a handle on the interface. She focused on an arrow on the bottom of the display and thought, *next.* Immediately, the page transitioned to a topic list. *Back,* she thought, glancing at the right side of the page. The first page returned. The top line of the text read, 'Introduction', and Justine focused on that and thought, *go.* A generic definition of 'introduction' appeared on the display.

She played with the controls for a few more seconds until she was confident she could navigate the database.

The synaptic interface was as close to a telepathic link as technology could get. On Earth, thought-link implant surgery allowed for a very rudimentary Meshstream to be uploaded through the optic nerves, with commands still based on vocalization. A true synaptic interface had never been developed.

Turning to Fairamai, Justine asked, "Can you use this for communication?"

Shaking her head, Fairamai said, "Far too many conservatives in the Parliament. They've banned synaptic technology for anything other than databases and medical emergencies." She made a short screeching sound that Justine took for amusement. "One of the first demonstrations proved embarrassing to a certain member of Parliament..."

Justine turned back to the display and immersed herself thoroughly in the history of the galaxy.

∞

The amount of information she absorbed was incredible, but she knew she had only uncovered the tip of the iceberg. Even with her accelerated learning ability, it could take her years to learn everything available in the database.

A few key points stood out from the research.

Although there wasn't a direct match in the species catalogs between the evolved worlds throughout the galaxy, there were significant similarities among them. With a few rare exceptions, the animal kingdoms of the diverse worlds could be categorized along the same basic families. As humans evolved from the primate family and became the dominant species in Sol System, the Gliesans—whose home world's geography was dominated by mountainous regions and forests—evolved from a species of flightless birds that was something of a cross between an ostrich and an owl.

The anthropology of the *Aves,* as they called their species, was fascinating, and Justine had to stop herself from spending the entire session learning about them. There was time for that later. She needed to learn about the Kulsat.

Ninety-two percent of the Kulsat home world's surface was water. The cephalopods on that planet were the first to use tools for survival. They had created underwater cities and developed agriculture around the same time as humans were still living in caves. The Kulsat had discovered electricity thousands of years before the first human hut had been erected in Mesopotamia.

One statistic that surprised her was, among the thirty-thousand species that had developed space flight—or were on the cusp—less than twelve percent had evolved from land-based mammals. By far, the majority of dominant species evolved from oceanic environments. It only followed, Justine thought; after all, mammals were latecomers on the evolutionary scale of Earth.

As Fairamai had mentioned earlier, the Kulsat had been the second species to expand beyond their planet's surface and into the space of their solar system. A million years ago, the reptilian Xtôti had already mastered light-speed travel, and had discovered a way to circumvent normal space. Justine had difficulty imagining spending that amount of time alone in the galaxy, knowing that there were tens of thousands of other sentient species with the potential of becoming galactic neighbors.

If the Xtôti had not provided technological advancement, the Kulsat might not have developed light-speed travel for many more millennia—their system was barren of Kinemet.

The nearest solar system was eighty-seven light-years away. With the short lifespan of the Kulsat species, they would've had to develop generation ships to explore the systems in their sector.

Without Xtôti interference, the Kulsat would most likely have Emerged around the same timeframe as the majority of the other members of the Collection of Worlds. According to the database, there was a mass confluence of advancement throughout the galaxy. The majority of worlds had emerged between two and four-thousand years ago—it was practically simultaneous, in the context of galactic time.

Sol System was a straggler. A question arose in Justine's mind, and she did a quick search. While interference in un-Emerged systems was against the law, observation was not. The Xtôti had been notoriously close-lipped about the existence of other systems, having learned their lesson with the Kulsat.

A question occurred to Justine, and a few thought-strokes later, she found her answer. Galactic scientists estimated there were over two thousand more un-Emerged systems in the galaxy. When Justine read this, she wondered how they'd arrived at that number. With her mind, she focused on that fact and thought, *follow*.

The monuments housing the star beacons, she read, all contained the same catalog of language samples. Apparently, the Xtôti kept a close watch on developing systems. At some point in the evolution of that culture, the Xtôti would sample local languages and leave a message on the monument housing the star beacon as a way to welcome them to the galactic fold. There were 2,341 unidentified writing samples.

Justine wondered at the translation they'd found on the *Dis Pater*. She knew the Mayan language had dozens of dialects, and even modern-day linguists argued over the meaning of many of the symbols and icons.

'Behold the Mighty Door of Kinich Ahua; Eternity is Now Before You; Beware the Power of Kukulcan.'

It sounded ominous, and she wondered what the message really meant.

She turned to Fairamai. "I have a question about the writing on the star beacon monuments. Actually, I have two, but the first one is, 'What do those messages really mean?' "

"I am not certain the translation program will give you the correct context of our message," Fairamai said. "The line was written in one of the earliest languages from our southern continent. No one has spoken it in thousands of years, but according to our linguists, it reads, *'Observe the gate of creation and the endless sky of your future. Great and terrible is the power of Aether.'* "

Justine deduced that, in a rudimentary form, the messages were similar, and could be written in any number of ways. *Here's the star beacon. With it, you can travel to other solar systems. Use the technology with care.*

"The database says all the monuments have the same writing samples," Justine said. "So yours, out here, has our Mayan message on it. Did the Xtôti write on all the beacons?"

Shaking her head, Fairamai said, "You still do not comprehend. The star beacons all share the same space outside light. Some of our scientists believe there may only be one star beacon, and what we see in normal space is a metaphysical representation. Our technology cannot accurately measure the star beacon. We can only hypothesize. The monuments are connected to the star beacons on a level we do not understand."

"So, if the Xtôti wrote on one, the writing would appear on all of them?"

"That is our theory," Fairamai replied.

"So," Justine asked, drawing her words out, "if one of them

were destroyed…?"

Giving that amused screech of laughter, Fairamai said, "They cannot be destroyed. Believe me, it's been attempted many times by many different systems."

31

Sierra de las Minas :
Guatemala :

In the morning, Nadia came for Michael.

"Your friends will remain here to ensure your cooperation," she said, casting a suspicious glance at the others. Her rifle was crooked in her arm, and it was as if she wanted someone to try to escape.

"You said you would send someone back for Diego and Migel," Michael said.

"Yes. We brought them here last night. They're in the main house." She glanced at Humberto. "They will both live as long as you all continue to cooperate."

Michael didn't want to give her any excuse to follow through with the threat. Sharing a concerned look with Humberto, he got up and followed the young woman out of the barn. Before he left, he looked back. "It will all work out," he said. Yaxche gave him a nod.

Outside, there were several more people than the day before. A second cargo truck was there, and it was filled with both electronic and digging equipment. Tucked deep inside the cargo area was a compact excavator.

Alondo was standing near the rear of the truck, going over an inventory list. He looked up as his sister and Michael approached.

"I think we have everything we will need," he said to his sister, "provided it is not too deep a cave."

"So long as we are not chasing a fairy tale," Nadia said, raising an eyebrow at her brother.

"I can't guarantee what's there," Michael said, and felt a shudder go down his spine at the malevolent scowl he got from the siblings.

Nadia practically spat out her words. "For you and your friends' sake, let us hope we find something worth our while."

In a businesslike manner, Alondo said, "We have four laser radiation detectors. Once we reach the mountains, you will program the frequency into them, and instruct the teams what to look for. Your map showed an area of ten-thousand hectares. We have used a recent satellite scan to eliminate more than eighty-percent of the area that does not show any subterranean gaps. I've marked the remaining possible locations on these maps. With four teams, we should be able to survey all possibilities in one or two days. We've paid the local authorities to look the other way for that amount of time. If we haven't found what we are looking for by then..." He gave Michael a hard look.

They all turned around at the sound of a third truck rumbling up the dirt road. It pulled a long trailer, on the back of which were four military-style all-terrain vehicles.

"A loan from a colonel in the Guatemalan army," Alondo said.

A knot formed in the pit of Michael's stomach. Once again, he was being swept along with the tide of events. At one time, he was the CEO of one of the most important corporations in the world, and was at the forefront of future exploration. Now, in less than two decades, he was nothing more than a pawn in an international and interplanetary power struggle.

How was he possibly going to be able to save Sol System from the Kulsat when he hadn't been able to save Kenny or Alex from Chow Yin? Even Humberto's intervention had only delayed his being abducted and used by Oscar Ruiz's children.

Now, if he didn't cooperate, more innocents would die. There was every possibility they would all die anyway.

Michael couldn't remember ever feeling so low.

∞

The troop set up a base camp fifty meters outside the tree line at the base of the mountain range and waited while Michael calibrated the radiation detectors.

While raw Kinemet gave off ultra-high electromagnetic radiation—more so than gamma rays—and could disrupt any electronics in the nearby area, the radiation of a Kinemat, such as Alex, was non-ionizing electromagnetic in the extremely low-frequency range. If a Kinemat was not utilizing the radiation, the only means to detect it was with highly sensitive detectors.

When Michael was finished, Alondo split up the men into four teams and handed out coordinates of the most likely locations. Nadia stayed at the camp with the trucks and the excavator. Her task was to coordinate the search with the teams, and provide a communications hub for them.

Alondo took Michael with him. After taking his place in the back seat of one of the terrain vehicles, Michael sat back and kept quiet. Until they found the cave that entombed the alien— if it did, indeed, exist—he didn't have much to do other than go along for the ride.

The forest of the range was sparse, and the trees were spaced far enough apart for them to ride between the trunks. There was also an intricate pathway system the park officials had maintained for years. From the story Patli had told, it was doubtful the cave would be too far up any of the mountains. Michael doubted they would have to walk any great distance from the vehicles.

While he concentrated on keeping his teeth from clattering together, and his bones from rattling from the jarring ride, Michael considered the younger man beside him. It was alarming how much groundwork Alondo had done in such a short span of time. His attention to detail was meticulous, and he commanded the men with an ease that seemed to be an inherent trait. If he'd put his skills to legitimate trade, Alondo could easily have led a company to prosperity. It was too bad he had baser motivations. Internally, Michael sighed. It seemed the universe ran on greed, jealousy, and revenge.

When they arrived at the first prospect—a small area of rock surrounding an outcrop—Alondo got off the vehicle and motioned Michael to grab the radiation detector from the storage compartment on the back.

As they approached the outcrop on foot, Alondo called his sister to let her know where they were. Once he'd finished checking in, he turned to Michael.

"All right, let's see if there's anything there."

Michael set the laser radiation detector on a tripod in front of the rocks, turned it on, and aimed at the center of the pile of rubble. It was a similar device to the ones surveyors used on asteroids. Idly, Michael wondered if the Kinemet would react to the laser and produce an effect similar to the one that had quantized Macklin's Rock.

After the initial discovery of Kinemet, every mining company on Earth went on the hunt for the element in the hopes of improving their fortunes. After years of surveys, however, no sign of Kinemet was found.

Now, here they were searching again, but this time it wasn't for the element itself, but the residue of the element. They were working off a lot of assumptions, but the one thing Michael clung to was that if there had, indeed, been a Kinemetic being buried here, he would give off the same electromagnetic signature as Alex. It was a well-documented frequency.

It took several seconds before the readout spat out the results of the scan. Every spec of matter on the Earth gave out its own form of radiation, and the computer listed every frequency it found: oxygen, silicon, iron, calcium, magnesium, and many other innocuous elements.

Michael adjusted the laser a few degrees and waited for a second readout, which ended up being similar to the first except for a trace of jade—a quantity much too small to warrant the effort of excavation. He continued to play the laser around the area, and only stopped after half an hour of searching.

All the while, he could feel Alondo's hawk eyes watching him.

"Sorry," Michael said finally, "there's nothing in there. From a geological standpoint, it's probably nothing more than a crevice caused by a natural shift."

He expected an outburst, but was surprised when Alondo spoke into his radio to touch base with his sister and inform her that the first coordinate was not a hit.

Alondo crossed the spot off his map. To Michael, he said, "One down, fourteen more to go."

∞

By late afternoon, they'd surveyed five locations. Some of the areas were buried by rock slides, some from sunken earth, and one had been a wide-open tunnel whose opening was half a meter in diameter. Both Alondo and Michael had started when a lowland paca darted out. The rodent had obviously adopted the cave as a home, and was more frightened by the encroaching humans than they were of it.

After their pulses returned to normal, Alondo said, "We'll do two more today, then complete the rest of them tomorrow. You look dehydrated. Have some water, and I'll check in and see how the other teams are doing."

Michael had just enough time to find the canteen on the seat of the vehicle and take a sip before Alondo hollered at him.

"Team Three thinks they may have found something." He hurried toward Michael, trying to read his map while he moved. When he got to the vehicle, he put the map on the seat and found the location of the other team. "There. We can get there in ten minutes."

Despite himself, Michael found his heart thrumming with excitement. Was their long shot really going to pay off?

He climbed onto the back seat, and held on while Alondo drove to the site.

∞

By the time they got there, the other two teams had arrived, and within minutes, Michael could hear the engine of the compact excavator as it slowly picked its way through the forest to them. Nadia stood on a riser outside the cab, one hand holding her close to the vehicle. She had her rifle in the other hand.

A dozen meters out, she jumped from the excavator and trotted up to meet her brother.

Alondo smiled at her, and then turned to Michael. "All right, let's verify the findings."

They scaled a short rise to an area where there had been a

massive landslide. From the looks of the overgrowth, it could have been decades or centuries since anyone had been there. There was only one way to tell whether this was the spot.

Michael approached the laser operator, but his eyes were on the readout. "What did it find?" he asked.

"Kinemet," the man said, and Michael gave him a sharp, questioning look.

"Surely, you mean you detected the ELF radiation?"

Shaking his head, the man pointed to the readout. "See for yourself."

Michael refreshed the screen and read the results. It was positive for the high-frequency radiation of Kinemet. The laser indicated there was a very tiny amount of the element, but left no doubt that it was there.

Perhaps the story had been wrong, and there wasn't an alien buried beneath the mountain. There were dozens of other possibilities to explain the presence of Kinemet, the least of which was an alien visitor.

Seeing Michael's expression, Alondo asked, "What does this mean?"

"It's possible there's a natural deposit of Kinemet here. Perhaps a meteorite heavy with the element fell to the Earth a long time ago." He shook his head. "For all we know, someone could've stolen some and buried it here sometime in the past twenty years."

Alondo and his sister shared a greedy look. "A gram of Kinemet is worth a million on the black market, what with the Emperor's embargo. Perhaps, if we continue to search, we will find more than that."

Nadia turned and signaled for the excavator operator to move closer.

Slapping Michael on the shoulder in congratulations, Alondo said, "It seems we may have found the pot of gold at the end of your rainbow." He laughed. "An alien grave site. What a story! I knew you were trying to—how do you say it?—pull a fast one."

∞

It took the excavator operator nearly half an hour to remove enough of the rubble to reveal a narrow crevice in the face of the mountain. A blast of fetid air rolled out, and Michael had to hold his nose together with his fingers.

From a case on his belt, Alondo produced a handheld spectrometer and leaned over to make himself small enough to fit in the crevice. In his free hand, he aimed a high-powered flashlight into the darkness within.

Nadia, with her rifle, motioned for Michael to go next, and she followed right behind him.

The cave was dark, and the flashlight cast eerie dancing shadows on the walls. They didn't have far to go before the spectrometer lit up, indicating they were right on top of the source of the Kinemet.

To everyone's surprise, there wasn't a deposit, or a vein from a meteorite, or even a buried cache of the kinetic element.

What they found was a perfectly preserved body, covered in a thick layer of dust.

The figure was short, like a boy, but the head was reptilian in shape, with a curved eye ridge that traced around the sides of its bald head. It had large, wide-spaced eyes and a beak for a mouth. Its skin was leathery; pale white and mottled with blue patches.

Michael was the first to recover from the shock, and he knelt beside the creature, feeling at its neck and wrist for a pulse.

It had to be the alien from Patli's story. The Grace? If so, he'd died over a millennium ago.

32

Skanse Aerie :
Gliesan System :

"We've arrived," **Naila** said, breaking Justine's concentration.

When she looked up at the front display, Justine saw that the *Fainne* was approaching the deep space orbital the Gliesans called Skanse Aerie.

While Earth stations were largely built using basic architectural forms as their foundations—a collection of tubes, like Canada Station Three, or wheel-shaped with spokes, like Lucis Observatory—the Gliesan station looked like a starburst, with hundreds of spires extending from the central hub. It was an immense, brightly lit construction, set against the backdrop of the stars.

"How many people are there?" Justine asked in wonder.

"About one-hundred-thousand." On the display, Fairamai pointed to a spot halfway up one of the long spires, which must have been nearly a kilometer in length. "I live there with my mate, Havena. He's one of the gravimetric technicians."

"This is your permanent home?" Justine asked.

"Yes." Fairamai clicked her taloned finger on an icon at the bottom of the display. A series of images in a small sub-window showed several portions of the station: markets, offices, workshops, hallways, and hundreds of elaborate gardens. One of the last sets of images showed dozens of hangars with several spacecraft. "The aerie is primarily a military outpost, and also serves as the first stop for visiting emissaries from other worlds—the population is mainly transitory. Several spires are set aside for Aethers, since we cannot live on our home world."

As they approached the central area of the aerie, Justine spotted a landing bay. A tug emerged from it and latched on to the Kulsat shuttle. It towed the shuttle off to another section of the station.

"Where are they taking them?" Justine asked.

"We have … facilities to house them," Fairamai said. Before Justine could ask, she added, "They are not the first Kulsat we've had here, but they will be treated according to our highest diplomatic conventions. Rest assured, they will not be harmed."

Relaxing at the Gliesar's assurance, Justine watched as the *Fainne* completed its docking procedures. As they pulled into their assigned bay, Naila spoke through his communicator. The translation machine didn't interpret for Justine, and she wondered if they were talking about her.

When he'd finished his conversation, Naila said, "We will disembark now. An ambassador from Gliese has been assigned to escort you from this point on—he will meet you at the main gate. They've set aside quarters for you on the station while the Collection's assessment council deliberates on your situation. I'm sure they will contact you for debriefing at some point, though I can't say for certain; I am simply a pilot, not a politician."

Justine smiled. "How long do you think they'll take to decide?"

"I have no idea," Naila said. He motioned to the

communication console. "I've been given some instructions. Before we can let you off this vessel, I must formally inform you of the following:

"On behalf of the Collection of Worlds, the Gliesan Parliament extends you, Major Justine Turner, political asylum and shelter from enemy attack. In return, you will not undertake to acquire our Aether technology, and you will give your oath that you will uphold all Gliesan and Galactic Laws. You will be restricted from traveling to or contacting any being in Sol System until said system is granted Emerged status and membership to the Collection of Worlds. Do you agree to these terms?"

At first, Justine balked at the official words. What if the Collection decided Sol System wasn't Emerged? She would be stuck out here, alone and away from home, for the rest of her life. What other choice did she have, though? She would just have to do everything in her power to convince the politicians to come to a favorable decision.

"I accept," she said.

Fairamai put a feathered hand on Justine's shoulder and made a soft whistling sound. "Welcome to Gliesan System."

∞

From the moment Justine had re-materialized in physical form aboard the *Fainne,* there had been a nagging thought in the back of her mind. She'd been so caught up in the excitement and wonder of making contact with an alien culture that it took her until now to realize something. Naila and Fairamai had been completely composed when she—an alien life form to them—had appeared on their ship.

Was it so commonplace to meet a new species that there wasn't any exhilaration left in the occurrence of first contact?

Ah Tabai and Aliah had briefly jumped into Gliese System to give their report before heading to Sol System, but from what Justine gathered, they would not have remained in the system, since what they planned on doing was breaking galactic law. Certainly, they would have transmitted images of the 'Solan beings'; but even at that, why would Naila and Fairamai have been so casual at Justine's arrival on their ship?

When Justine disembarked from the scout ship, and followed the walkway to the main gate, she quickly learned why her appearance had not elicited any surprise in the Gliesan pilots: They had seen humankind before.

Justine stepped through the doorway into the gate room, and a human male stepped forward, a huge grin on his face as he extended his arm toward her to shake her hand.

Though there was the distinct possibility that humaniform beings had evolved from primates on another world, Justine knew this was not the case in this instance. The man could have been a brother or cousin to Alex Manez or Yaxche. He was most definitely Mayan in origin.

"Good Morning, Major Justine Turner. I am Yoatl Cen, the Gliesan ambassador to Sol. I must apologize if my etiquette is not correct. I've never had the pleasure of visiting Sol System, and I have only been able to reference the data we received from Alex Manez's ship."

Justine's mind spun. There was so much conflicting information, she couldn't process it. The Gliesans had spent a great deal of time telling her that Sol System was off-limits, and that interference was strictly prohibited. Yet, here before her, was evidence to the contrary.

Numbly, she reached out to shake his hand.

Yoatl, shorter than Justine by a few centimeters, nodded to her, a wide smile on his lips. "You must have many questions. I have even prepared a speech to explain it all to you. We have set aside quarters for your stay; you may wish to tend to personal needs or perhaps meditate for a few hours. When you are ready, I will give you a tour of the aerie, and bring you up to velocity before your briefing with the Collection representative."

"Thank you," Justine said absently, and gathered her makeshift toga around her as she followed the—*her*—ambassador through the processing area and into the corridors of the station.

One of the first things she noticed was the aesthetics of the station. The organic décor of the interior was a sharp contrast to the futuristic architecture of the outside of the station. Many of Earth's space stations were designed for efficiency, and while there were attempts to make it seem a little more homey for the long-term residents, no one who visited any of the stations made of the mistake of forgetting they were in space.

The corridors of Skanse Aerie station were anything but straight. The path wound left and right, sometimes gradually, sometimes sharply. Sculpted to resemble the walls of a canyon, the surface had rocky areas with outcroppings housing plants and flowers. Justine was surprised when a small bird she thought was a decoration flapped its wings and flew off ahead of them. The floor rose and fell unevenly, and the base narrowed and widened randomly. Above them, a wide-open green-blue sky housed several cloud formations and the image of a small, red sun. The ceiling obviously used some kind of projection technology. Although the expense must have been enormous, the Gliesans must have believed it was worth it to create a natural-looking environment for those who were stationed on the outer rim of the system either temporarily or permanently. To Justine, it felt as if she were taking a stroll through a national park on Earth.

"On the other side of the wall to our right is a transport

conveyor for those carrying supplies, or for those who do not wish to walk the distance from the central hub to their destination. You can access them here."

He pointed to what looked like a sawed-off branch coming out of the wall. With a quick motion, he waved his hand over it, and a section of the wall vanished, revealing a short passageway to the transport tunnel. There were two pathways there; one leading up to the far side of the tunnel, the other descending a shorter distance to the lower level, where the floor itself moved slowly up the length of the spire. Though she couldn't see the floor on the upper side, she assumed it held a similar moving floor heading the opposite direction.

"The upper pathway," she said. "How is it suspended?" There wasn't any scaffolding propping it up, and she couldn't see any wires leading from it to the ceiling of the tunnel.

"There's an electromagnetic field, though I can't pretend to understand the specific technology; it's not my area of expertise."

Stepping back into the main corridor, Yoatl gestured to another cutoff branch sticking out of the other side of the wall, though he didn't wave his hand over it.

"On the left side of the wall are the compartments for living quarters, working environments, industrial complexes, life support gardens, or storage facilities."

Justine said, "I'd love to see those gardens."

"Once we've completed the briefing, you'll be assigned a security level coded to your biosignature. I assume you'll be granted access to all the common areas—which includes the gardens—in addition to your quarters. You may visit any unrestricted areas at your leisure. Until then, you'll need me to escort you around the station."

"Understandable."

He nodded and then gestured to the branch marker on the

wall. "Temporary visitor quarters are inside here. They are fully equipped with every amenity you should require, though I'm sure once we've established your diplomatic status, you'll be assigned a more appropriate dwelling." Waving his hand over the branch, he took a step back when a portion of the wall vanished, and motioned for her to enter first.

Inside, there was another corridor, though this one did not look quite as natural as the main pathway through the spire. The walls and floor were smooth and straight, but the ceiling still benefited from the projection of the sky. It was a very comforting illusion.

There were several apartments along the corridor, and when they reached the last one, Yoatl opened the door for Justine and politely waited at the entrance for her to enter.

"My wife, Ekthin, did not have much time to synthesize clothing for you; I hope the garment style she selected is to your liking. There is nutritional refreshment in the cold storage unit, a sonic shower, and a reclining platform if you wish to rest or meditate. I have reserved a private space in one of our most popular eateries where you can sample some Gliesan cuisine, and we can talk. I will return for you in two hours."

Justine shook her head. "But I have so many questions."

"I am sure everything you've experienced must be overwhelming, even for an Aetherbeing. You will benefit from some time to gather your thoughts and—how do you say it?—'catch your breath'. Besides," he said, giving her a conspiratorial wink, "I must report my first impressions of you to the Solan Society. Your arrival has created quite a stir among us, and I fear there might be an uprising if their curiosity is not satisfied."

She wanted to protest again, but Justine realized that he was right; too much had happened in too short a time. She needed a few hours to clean herself up and get her head straight.

Whatever the Kinemet had done to alter her on a cellular level, one of the side effects was that her suprachiasmatic nuclei stopped inducing the sleep aspect of her circadian rhythm. While she'd only spent a small portion of her time since the Kinemetic change in physical form, she realized that quieting her mind was still a necessity. Even Alex had spent several hours a day in a meditative state. Since arriving in the Centauri System, the only time Justine had not been conscious was when the Kulsat had quantized her, and that had been more like a state of suspension than affording her any real rest.

When she entered the small apartment, and Yoatl closed the door behind her, Justine's first impulse was to review everything that had happened over the past few days; but when she saw the reclining platform set into a small alcove at the back of the room, she changed her mind. Instead of a flat mattress, there was a hammock-like bed that looked irresistible.

One thing she had to do first, however, was clean up. She'd spent several days in the Kulsat terrarium. Yoatl had been polite not to mention how badly she smelled. There was another recess on the other side of the room, and Justine stepped out of her makeshift toga and entered the sonic shower. It was simple to figure out. A single lever turned the device on and off. She didn't know if there was a time allotment, but she figured she must have spent a good half an hour letting the sound waves wash over her. Never in her life had she been so thoroughly scrubbed and cleaned.

While she showered, she thought about sonic technology. Scientists on Earth had long thought that sound was one of the most powerful forces in nature. At the right frequency, sound waves could melt metal, shatter glass and rock, and—as she had witnessed—explode organic cells. For over a century, engineers had used sonic welding in electronics to bond metals.

The nature of the star beacons suggested that the Grace had somehow tapped into the sound frequencies of all stellar objects, using that technology to help those attuned to it to navigate between the beacons. It was no wonder the Kulsat had developed sonic weapons and tools.

If Justine listened hard with her newfound ability, she could hear more than the Song of the Stars, or the Music of the Spheres—she could hear something beyond. When she had time, she would have to discuss it with other Aetherbeings.

Her skin tingled from spending so much time in the sonic shower. She turned off the device and stepped out.

Naked, she went back to the reclining platform, crawled in and was surprised when the foam wrapped itself around her in a form-fitting cocoon. It felt as if she were floating, and she was able to put herself in a relaxed state very quickly.

It was the very thing she needed, and she remained there right up until a soft chime sounded. She assumed Yoatl had come to retrieve her.

"Just a moment," she said, wondering if he could hear her. She took a one quick glance at the makeshift toga lying in the heap on the floor. No matter what the fashion in the Gliesan System was, she was sure it didn't include long swaths of fabric tied haphazardly around her torso.

A few moments searching was all it took before she found a small closet with half a dozen clothing selections. She picked the one that looked most appealing to her—she was always drawn to darker colors; perhaps a carryover from wearing her military uniform for so many years.

After slipping on a long one-piece outfit with baggy leggings that seemed to produce the dual effect of looking like a jumpsuit and an ankle-length dress at the same time, she went to the door and opened it.

Yoatl bent his head in admiration and smiled. "Perfect

selection."

"Thank you," Justine said, and followed him back out to the main corridor.

∞

The hub of the aerie was bustling with activity. If the station had over a hundred-thousand people, the majority of them had congregated in the central area.

When they exited the spire, they were several dozen meters above ground level, and at a perpendicular angle. They had to use a floating platform to descend, and Justine was completely unaware of any gravitational shift as the platform altered pitch to match the common area's perspective; the Gliesan technology was seamless.

The architecture of the hub followed the nature theme of the corridor. Like a multi-layer landscape, replete with canyons, grottos, forests, cliffs and waterfalls, it was enough to put any of Earth's theme resorts to shame.

"This is primarily a military outpost?" Justine asked.

"The well-being of our citizens is of utmost importance. We have a number of permanent residents. They can be proud to call this home. Besides, we need to set a good impression for ambassadors from other worlds."

Although she'd read about the proliferation of alien species, Justine was still taken aback seeing the variety for herself. While the majority of the population was Gliesan, she spotted a number of people who had evolved from other species. A being with four short legs, a squat body, and a round head on a long neck sauntered past them. He had no arms, but he had a long prehensile tail with a half-dozen 'fingers' on the end of it. He turned his head and bowed to them, while waving his tail-hand.

Yoatl nodded back. "Ambassador Etrevius," he said to Justine. "From Beta Monocerotis. And yes, he's a dinosaur—mammals never evolved on his planet at all."

"So many people…" Justine could spend a lifetime learning about all the denizens of the galaxy, but she would have to wait for another time. They had arrived at the restaurant.

Quickly, Yoatl ushered her in and they found their cubby. It wasn't a typical chair and table setup, however, and it took Justine a moment to figure out that the space was a representation of a bird's nest. Following Yoatl's example, she climbed in and sat on the floor of the nest, resting her back against the curved wall, which was lined with a foam-like material and was quite comfortable.

Yoatl settled himself in, crossing his legs. "I've taken the liberty of ordering for us. The main entrée should arrive soon. In the meantime, if you want water or another beverage, simply use the control panel there to indicate your preference." He demonstrated by tapping one of the icons on the panel, and a section of the wall folded out. The platform held a bowl-shaped container of liquid. "A form of wine, quite sweet, like nectar. Did you want one?" he asked, and Justine nodded. He closed the panel and tapped the icon again to produce another drink for Justine.

She sipped it, and found it extremely pleasant-tasting.

"Thank you," she said, and then waved one hand to encompass the station. "All of this is fantastic, and the explorer in me wants nothing more than to spend the rest of my life experiencing all these wonderful new worlds. But…"

Smiling, Yoatl said, "But we have more pressing matters, and I promised you a story."

"Yes. And start with how there are humans here, in the stars."

"Very well." He took one more sip of his nectar wine. "I

264

hope this answers most of your questions."

Taking a moment to gather his thoughts first, he began:

"According to the report Naila filed, you have accessed some basic history of the galaxy, correct?"

Justine nodded.

"Let me give you a bit of background on the Grace, the Xtôti. A million years before the Mass Emergence—which is what we call the era when the majority of systems began to discover light-speed travel—the Xtôti home system was destroyed when their star went supernova. They were unable to evacuate their system, and the tragedy decimated their population. The survivors were those who were at the edge of their system, or in other solar systems: namely, Aetherbeings. Some speculate that the supernova may have been caused by experiments. We only have scattered accounts of what happened at that time. You must remember, this was a million years before most of our species began to evolve into sentience.

"There is a theory that those Xtôti who were in the system at the time of the supernova became the Grace. Slowly, over time, as each Xtôti who was outside the system—and who had not ascended to the Grace—reached the end of their life cycle, their numbers dwindled, leaving only the Grace to remain."

Yoatl paused as a chime in the back wall sounded, and he touched another icon on the control panel. A length of the wall folded down out formed a long, narrow table. Several dishes of food slid out from inside the wall, and the smells wafted up to Justine's nose. Her stomach growled with hunger.

She couldn't identify the type of food Yoatl had ordered for them, and gave him a questioning look.

"It's called *biantha*. A vegetarian mash baked in a crusted bread container, which is also edible. Try it."

Justine did so, and the flavor exploded in her mouth.

"Delicious," she said. "Tastes like a pot pie."

Yoatl took a bite before continuing his story around mouthfuls of food. "The Gliesans discovered Sol System by accident twelve-hundred-and-seventy-nine years ago."

Justine gaped. "You know that exactly?"

"Yes." Yoatl nodded. "The Galactic Law of non-interference had been in place since before the Gliesans Emerged. One of the ways that was enforced is through the star beacons themselves. Somehow, the Xtôti were able to 'lock' those beacons orbiting developing worlds. They are completely masked; our computers can't even detect them in the galactic grid. Any radio signals you send out are dampened at the outer limits of your system. You are, for all purposes, invisible to us until you Emerge.

"One Gliesan scouting ship, however, had been monitoring a lone Xtôti—even back then, they were rare. I do not blame the pilots for being curious. The Grace were so much more than celebrities; they were—are—like gods to us. So, when the Xtôti traveled to your system, temporarily activating your star beacon, the Gliesans recorded the location of your beacon. I'm certain they had no intention of breaking Galactic Law, but were rather 'star struck', as it were, and did the unthinkable: they followed the Xtôti to Sol System."

"They remained near your beacon while the Xtôti went to your planet. No one knows what his purpose was. However, there was a noticeable Aether event on your world several days into the visit, and the Gliesans raced to investigate. If the Xtôti were in trouble, they would try to help.

"Even though Aetherbeings cannot survive on a planetary body for long, the Gliesans took the risk and landed at the location where they'd detected the explosion. There was no sign of the Xtôti, but a small village had been irradiated by Aether. If left unaided, they would all die. The Gliesans are a very compassionate people, and though they knew their actions could be subject to penalties, they offered to take the afflicted villagers away to save their lives.

"Those humans," Yoatl said in conclusion, "were members of a Mayan tribe near Copán, Honduras."

"The 'Song'," Justine interrupted. "One of my friends who came with us to Centauri, Yaxche, was the keeper of an ancient story called The Song of the Stars. It contained the key to unlocking the power of Kinemet, but the story in it told of a time when the 'gods' abducted their people."

Smiling, Yoatl said, "I'm certain it would have seemed so to them."

Finishing the vegetable mash, Yoatl picked up the bread plate and took a bite out of it. "Many of the villagers had been exposed to lethal levels of Aether radiation. In such cases, transforming a person into an Aetherbeing is the cure. Once they cured the villagers, the Gliesans brought them here, to Skanse Aerie, where they lived out the remainder of their lives in comfort.

"There were several pairs of humans who had only been partially affected, and they were otherwise physically normal. They chose not to become Aetherbeings, and made their homes on Gliesan Prime. They were welcomed into their society, married and had children. Over time, our numbers grew to over six-thousand. Though our citizenship is officially Gliesan, many of us remember our Solan roots, though we may never visit the planet of our origin."

Justine had finished her bread plate as well, and a moment later, a second dish slid out from the recess in the wall. It was in a cup that looked like the same kind of bread as the entrée.

Yoatl made a happy sound. "Ah, desert. It's a kind of whipped desert made from the sap of one of their tropical plants. You can eat the utensil as well as the cup."

Justine tasted it and smiled. It had the consistency of rice pudding with a slight hint of syrup.

"About a century ago, several of us sought to reconnect with our roots. We formed the Solan Society. We petitioned the Parliament for permission to set up a spaceport in the nearest system to you, Centauri, for when you Emerged. Historically, most systems who discover Aetherflight naturally attempt to visit their closest neighbors.

"It was a little over ten years ago that our sensors detected the first traveler from Sol System, Alex Manez. Ah Tabai, one of the Solan Aetherbeings who had volunteered to become a Sentinel, had the privilege of making first contact. It was from his ship's computer that we were able to find out about your history. We have all been waiting for a second meeting with excitement."

"Ah Tabai is human?" Justine remarked. She'd originally been under the impression that he was a Gliesan.

Yoatl lowered his voice. "Yes. He is young and impetuous. I do not know how he convinced Aliah to accompany him; but should they return to Gliese, I fear they will be arrested."

"They were only trying to help us," Justine said.

"The Law is the Law." Yoatl raised both of his open hands in front of him. Then he offered Justine a conciliatory smile. "I will do what I can for them."

"Thank you."

Having finished dessert, Yoatl tapped on the console one more time, and the recess produced two small glasses of liquid, which seemed to change color from red to yellow.

"It's called *ljúka,*" he said as he passed one of the glasses to Justine. "The final course." With that, he picked up his own glass and drank it down in one motion.

Following suit, Justine was surprised at the taste. She'd been expecting something fruity and sweet, but the drink was slightly spicy. As it hit her stomach, she felt a tingle go through her. Whatever the drink was, it had the effect of reinvigorating her. Yoatl placed his empty glass back in the recess, and Justine did the same.

"That was very nice," she said, and Yoatl smiled. "Thank you for the meal."

"No thanks are necessary. It was my pleasure."

"So," Justine said, "what happens now?"

Considering his words, Yoatl rubbed a knuckle on his chin. "Now comes the hard part."

"Oh?"

"While you were resting, I received a message from the Collection's ambassador. One of the requirements before a system can be granted Emerged status is that you are able to travel outside light, utilizing the Grace. Since you did not, they have decided that Sol System has not yet Emerged."

Justine stared at him, wide-eyed, as she heard the news. The Collection had not even debriefed her. "Then they won't help us?"

"I'm afraid they will not. Not yet, anyway." He had a pained look on his face.

"And they won't let me go home, either," Justine said.

Yoatl nodded, his eyes cast down. "I'm sorry. You have been exposed to too much of our technology."

Feeling the frustration and anger grow in her, Justine willed herself to remain calm. From the moment she'd escaped from Lucis Observatory, everything that had happened had been out of her control. She'd done the best that she could to survive, but her personal survival wasn't enough, especially if the Kulsat invaded and destroyed Sol System.

Yoatl said, "Every effort will be made to ensure your comfort. They've assigned you permanent quarters on the station. Should you choose to, you may request work duties, though it is not mandatory. I would be honored if you would consider taking a position in the Solan Society."

"I don't want a job here," Justine said, then she gave him a hard look. "You're human; how can you just sit there when you know the Kulsat are going to wipe us all out?"

"I don't want that to happen any more than you, but I believe in the Law. Ah Tabai's scout ship accessed your database. The Collection is aware of your history. There are many conflicts in your world; it was one such that caused you to flee. If we were to extend the knowledge of Aether technology now, who can say if humans won't become the next Kulsat?"

She didn't want to hear those words, and though her first impulse was to deny the possibility, in her heart she knew humanity still had some maturing to do.

However, she believed they needed the time and opportunity to find their way in the galaxy. The Kulsat would destroy their future.

There had to be a way for Justine to stop them...

33

Sierra de las Minas :
Guatemala :

Alondo swept the spectrometer over the alien, and nodded to Michael. "It is made of Kinemet."

"How can that be?" Michael gasped. Kinemats, such as Alex, were altered at the molecular level by Kinemetic radiation. It seemed as if this creature—the Grace?—had a quantity of the element as part of its physiology.

What did that mean?

Michael's mind raced. Did the Grace have Kinemet as part of their natural biological makeup? Or had they figured out a way to infuse themselves with the element, and alter themselves on a genetic level? Was it because of this that they were able to create the network of star beacons? Or had the star beacons been there all along, despite the legends, and the Grace had somehow changed from a million years of exposure? If the Grace were made of Kinemet, then perhaps they would not decompose like a normal biological being; it was possible the Kinemet in them would sustain the body's cells until the element decayed slowly over hundreds of thousands of years, though the creature's brain would cease to function.

Another question entered his mind: if the Grace decayed

rather than decomposed, then there should be millions of alien bodies strewn throughout the galaxy. There were not; what had happened to them? He recalled the story, how the alien had asked Subo Ak to cremate him. Is that how the Grace slowly disappeared? They came to a planet and arranged for their own death? Go out in a blaze of fire? Michael initially balked at the thought, but then he realized that he didn't truly understand their motivations.

He needed more information on the Grace, the Kulsat, and the origins of Kinemet. Everything he knew, he'd surmised from what little Ah Tabai had divulged before his death.

He wished fervently that George and Kenny were still alive. Both loved to speculate on such things. Often, throwing around ideas led them down paths none of them would think of on their own. Both were friends as well as colleagues.

As if assuming Michael had all the answers ready for the asking, Alondo waved his hand over the alien's body. "What does this mean?"

"It means there is no deposit of Kinemet for you to mine."

The other man frowned, and Michael could almost read the thoughts going through his mind. How would they be able to monetize this discovery? Selling Kinemet would be a straight black market trade, with a definitive value per quantity. Who wanted the alien body, and how much would they pay for it? It was a more complex proposition for Alondo, and he looked at Michael as if to ask for a hint on what the next step should be.

"There are only two governments that have the experience and resources to explore this discovery," Michael said. "USA, Inc. and Canada Corp. Do you want me to contact my superiors and set up a meet?"

Alondo scoffed at him. "Nice try, Mr. Sanderson. But I think we will make our own plans." He pointed at the alien. "How do you suggest we handle the body?"

"I would recommend we leave it as is for now. We have no idea what will happen if we alter the environmental conditions. Kinemet can be a volatile element. Exposure to sunlight can have a detrimental effect. We need to be extremely careful."

Together, the three of them filed out of the cave through the narrow crevice, Nadia taking the lead, followed by her brother, with Michael last.

When he reached the opening, Michael was blocked by Alondo's legs, and he suffered a moment of claustrophobia, wondering if the young criminal had decided to cut him out of the equation and leave him there.

Someone from outside the cave barked out an order in Spanish, *"¡Alejese!"* A moment later, Alondo stepped out of Michael's way.

Holding his breath, Michael pushed himself outside. His stomach knotted when he stood up and looked around. The entire area was surrounded by Guatemalan soldiers, all pointing their rifles at them.

The captain of the soldiers and Alondo exchanged several heated words in their native language, speaking too fast for Michael to understand. Even still, he got the impression that both men were familiar with each other.

After they finished their exchange, the soldiers put down their weapons. Alondo turned to Michael, his face red and his eyes narrow. "It seems our plans have been made for us."

Alondo shared a sour look with his sister. "All right. Let's get packed up."

∞

The captain left one squad of armed soldiers to secure the area while he directed the rest of his men to escort the Ruiz's and the others back to the base camp. Several more military trucks were in the area. A squadron of Guatemalan soldiers had taken over the operation.

Michael and the Ruiz siblings rode in one truck with the captain and four of his guards. Together, they headed away from the camp. Once they reached Los Amates, they turned east. A little over an hour later, they arrived at their destination, a beachfront estate on the Caribbean Sea.

During the trip, none of the soldiers spoke to them, and though both Alondo and Nadia whispered to one another, they ignored Michael.

Once they got out of the truck, the three of them were greeted by a small squad of Guatemalan soldiers, who escorted them to the main building.

Inside, dressed in the uniform of a general, a dark-haired, middle-aged man with a thin, black mustache, which drooped at the corners of his smiling mouth, stepped out from a side room and gave Michael a conciliatory nod of his head.

"Once again, I must apologize for your treatment. Welcome to my home."

Michael couldn't believe his eyes, and though he opened his mouth, no words came out.

Nadia, her voice cracking with shock, said, *"¿Papá?"*

"What are you doing here?" Alondo asked, more outraged than surprised. "I thought you were still in prison?"

Obviously enjoying himself, Oscar Ruiz made a dramatic bow and said, "I haven't been there for years, my son. It suited me to let the world believe I was still incarcerated. It gave me freedom to accomplish a great many things."

"Why didn't you tell us?" Nadia asked, then she frowned. "Is this why you would not permit us to visit you in La Granja?"

"I assure you, it was necessary. My apologies, my children. Of course, you will forgive me."

Both the siblings looked hesitant.

Then Oscar waved his hand at them. "Come, we have much to discuss, and my other guests are waiting."

Numbly, Michael let himself be led into the adjacent room. He guessed who was in the room before he got all the way inside.

Yaxche, Patli, and Humberto were sitting beside one another on a long couch, looking refreshed.

"Are you all right?" Michael asked Yaxche, his eyes encompassing all three of them.

"Ahyah," the old Mayan said with a grin. "We've been here since noon."

Humberto glared at Señor Ruiz. "Where are the others?"

"Do not worry yourself. I 'liberated' everyone from my children's custody and brought them here. Your injured friends are in another part of the complex being treated as we speak. You see, I am not an uncivilized man."

Oscar Ruiz gestured to a table with trays of meats, fruits and pastries. "Please, eat something. I must apologize if the coffee is not quite as good as what we grew on my plantation."

Alondo and Nadia made no move toward the refreshments, but Michael's stomach growled. He wasn't certain what Oscar's intentions were, but from his last encounter, he decided the man's sense of hospitality would prevent him from having his guests harmed out of hand.

Michael picked up a small dish and filled it with a few choice selections from the table. He found a chair and sat down.

Around the food in his mouth, Michael said, "You arranged to have me abducted at the airport."

"I prefer to say that I tried to extend an invitation to you, Mr. Sanderson, without the knowledge of the Honduran or Canadian authorities. I've been paying a great deal of money to ensure everyone thinks I am still incarcerated in La Granja

Prison. If my 'old friend' Humberto had not interceded, we all could have saved a great deal of time."

He glanced at his children. "I am sorry if you have suffered in the past few years, but it was necessary to maintain the fiction. I know you are angry with me, but now that you are here, we will combine our efforts, and once again become prosperous."

"In Guatemala?" Alondo asked.

"Honduras is aligned too closely with the northern countries. The Cruzados are now nothing more than a group of nostalgic farmers and peasants—I'm sorry if that insults you, but it is the truth," he said to Humberto. "However, the CEO of Guatemala Departmental understands where the future is, and together, we are working to ensure our place in the Empire."

Michael had a sinking sensation in his gut. "The Solan Empire?"

He couldn't believe it. Somehow, Chow Yin had aligned himself with the government of Guatemala. Had this been his plan all along? Was this why he had really let Michael go, rather than simply to appease Alex? If so, how had Yin known what Michael's purpose was? Even Michael hadn't known what he was looking for until he got here. Or had Chow Yin merely been playing the long odds?

Oscar smiled. "I will answer all of your questions, Mr. Sanderson," he said, "and I will ensure your friends are returned to their homes in Honduras unharmed."

"I sense a condition," he said.

Nodding, Oscar said, "And I'm certain you can guess that condition."

During the long ride in the truck, Michael had plenty of time to think through the various possibilities. It all came down to one, however: possession of the alien body. Michael had hoped that no one knew the true purpose of his journey. Now that Oscar revealed that he was working for the Solan Empire, he knew a message would have already been dispatched to Chow Yin, informing him of the discovery.

He suddenly lost his appetite. "You want me to work for you."

"His Highness has sent word to provide you with the most state-of-the-art laboratory facilities and equipment available, and to extend every convenience to you. Your stay with me here will be comfortable, I assure you. Once you have completed your work, we will make arrangements to send your friends home."

Michael felt like he'd been kicked in the gut.

Alondo, the look of anger having changed to one of anticipation during the course of the conversation, said, "What of us, Father?"

"Ah," Oscar said. "I would like you to return to the dig site and take over once again. I am certain Mr. Sanderson will instruct you on the precautions you need to follow in order to transport the alien body here safely." He winked at his son. "It is time for me to take you under my wing, and mold you to become my heir in the new empire."

To Nadia, he said, "My daughter, I have a very important mission for you. With all our new guests, I require someone to run the household—" At her sour look, Oscar held up a hand to forestall any protest. "—and to liaise with the Guatemalan CEO's office as an official ambassador of the Solan Empire. Do you think you are up to the task?"

For the first time, Michael saw the young woman's eyes light up. It would be a prestigious position.

"Now," Oscar said to Michael, "you have to excuse me while I report the good news to His Highness."

Michael dropped the plate of food on the table, its contents uneaten, and shared a miserable look with Humberto. He'd been a pawn in Chow Yin's game all along.

34

Skanse Aerie :

Gliesan System :

Justine accompanied Yoatl to his apartment on another spire, where she met his wife, Ekthin. She was a dainty woman, who spoke with a very soft voice.

"Welcome to our home," she said by way of greeting. "I hope the outfits I chose are to your satisfaction."

"They're perfect." Justine grabbed the fabric of her top and stretched it out. "What's it made of?"

"There's a small species of animal on Gliese, similar to the opossums of Earth, that produces this for their nests. We've managed to synthesize the material. It's very durable and warm. We call it *swa.*"

Yoatl gestured to a living room area. "Come, make yourself comfortable. I hope you don't mind, but before I take you to your quarters, there are several of the Solan Society's members I would like you to meet. I hope that will be all right."

"After I retired from NASA, I got a job as a public relations hostess for diplomats and ambassadors." Justine laughed. "I am more than comfortable with crowds."

Smiling widely, Yoatl said, "Excellent. I will let them know you are ready to meet them."

∞

Justine spent the better part of the evening chatting with the dozen guests Yoatl invited. For the most part, they were more interested in her personal history than world events. They wanted to hear stories of her time in NASA as a pilot. Her history with Alex and Michael was a hot topic, but when she spoke about Yaxche, everyone grew excited.

"From what we've learned, we share common ancestry with him; his forefathers and ours were from the same region on Earth," one of the older men said. "I would have enjoyed meeting him."

"I didn't spend a lot of time with him," Justine said. "But he is very wise. I'm sure he'd love to meet you someday."

The evening went on for longer than Justine had expected, and when Yoatl finally announced that it was time for their guest of honor to retire, she was more than grateful.

Saying goodbye to the visitors took another hour, and by the time the last one was gone, Justine was exhausted.

He escorted her to another apartment at the end of the spire. "There was some debate on where to house you," he said. "The commander of the station thought you might be more comfortable with the other Aethers, but we convinced him you would adjust to life here faster if you were surrounded by Solans."

Justine didn't want to tell him that it didn't matter to her where they put her; she had no intention of adjusting to life on Skanse Aerie, as wondrous as it was. Instead, she smiled at him and shook his hand as they stopped outside the apartment door of her new quarters.

"Thank you," she said to him.

"I will come by tomorrow morning, and we can begin your orientation."

"That would be perfectly fine." Justine waved her hand over the protrusion on the wall—as she'd seen Yoatl do at his apartment—and her door slid open. They both said their good-nights, and Justine went inside.

She was too tired to take a full tour of the apartment, and only looked around long enough to spot the reclining platform. A few hours' meditation there was just what she needed.

∞

After resting, she explored her new quarters. There were four rooms. Besides the lavatory and reclining platform, there was a kitchen with a nest-shaped area for eating. Justine climbed on and played around with the console until the panel in the wall folded out. Pressing a few other buttons on the console produced a breakfast dish—at least, she hoped it was breakfast. A shallow container appeared in the recess, filled with something that looked to be of the same consistency as the vegetable mash from last night. She tasted it, and decided it was palatable. She remembered how to order water, though she would have preferred coffee—she had no idea if Gliese had anything like caffeine.

Once she'd eaten, she went to the large, central room that she decided was the main living area. There was some odd-looking furniture placed around the room. Instead of chairs, there were soft pedestals. She assumed the Gliesans were more comfortable perching on these than sitting. Yoatl's apartment had more earth-style furnishings, all designed for humans. She'd have to ask him about getting some for herself.

Along one wall, she recognized a computer area, set up similar to the one aboard the *Fainne*. Immediately, she sat down on the curved chair, and the holographic monitor flickered on.

It didn't look as if the computer had a synaptic interface, but she was just as comfortable tapping the controls with her fingers.

Previously, she'd researched the ancient history of the Kulsat. She needed more current information, and she spent the next hour scouring the Gliesan database for anything that would help her understand them, and provide her with a means of stopping them from destroying Sol System.

The Kulsat home world was largely a mystery to the rest of the galaxy. They were a highly paranoid society, and they had a contingent of several hundred warships guarding their star beacon at all times. The Collection sent Sentinel scout ships on reconnaissance to the Kulsat System on an unsystematic cycle. The ships would materialize in Kulsat space, take as many readings as they could, and fly back seconds before the Kulsat Risen could close access to the star beacon, and before the warships could fire on them.

Over the past several hundred years, major offensives had been launched. At one time, before the Aetherbeings worked out how to limit access to the star beacon, more than a dozen systems had sent thousands of Collection ships to attack Kulsat in a concerted effort.

They'd managed to get past the first line of defenses, but before they could meet the bulk of the Kulsat armada, every Kulsat ship that had been in other systems returned home. The Collection ships were trapped between the two forces, and had been decimated. It was the last time anyone had attempted to bring the fight to the enemy.

The Kulsat, with their numbers and technology, had attacked and destroyed over ten-thousand cultures since the war had started a millennium ago.

So far, the only effective defense against them was to remain as unnoticeable as possible, and not to pose an immediate threat. As in Gliese, all star systems maintained a permanent patrol around their star beacon. Should it activate from any Kulsat-occupied system, the Aetherbeings would all work together to suppress access through the star beacon. Although the technique was effective against an armada, it would not stop a small number of ships from passing through. There was always a military presence on hand to deal with such situations.

In order for Sol System to defend itself, it would require enough Kinemats to do the same thing to their star beacon, and they would need a fleet of warships to interdict any Kulsat who managed to get through the restricted opening. Also, they would need to understand the technology the other systems had developed to read and control the star beacons. For all Justine knew, that could take years...

Growing despondent in the knowledge of what seemed like insurmountable odds, Justine called up some non-military information, wondering if there was some other way to defeat the undefeatable force.

As a society, the Kulsat evolution was driven by necessity. Their home world, mostly oceanic, was a harsh environment, filled with dozens of underwater predators. In their history, the Kulsat were easy prey, and had needed to develop the ability to use tools and weapons to ensure their survival.

Their progress had been geared toward industrial endeavors, and their social structure was based on technological merit; the more advanced they were, the higher their chance to protect their species against their enemies— and they considered any non-Kulsat an enemy. It was almost as if they had a genetic predisposition toward paranoia.

One social theorist in the Collection posited that meeting the Grace would have been one of the most frightening experiences in Kulsat history: a force so far advanced that they were completely at their mercy. As with many militaristic cultures, the Kulsat, realizing they were powerless, had become subservient to the Xtôti, biding their time until their own

233

technology advanced to the point where they no longer felt threatened.

Once the Xtôti died off, the Kulsat had begun a thousand-year campaign of expansion and domination that terrorized the galaxy.

Justine lifted her head when she heard the chime at her door, and quickly stepped over to answer it. Yoatl was waiting for her.

"I trust you had a restful night?" he asked.

Nodding, Justine said, "Yes. I have to say, that hammock is one of the most comfortable beds I've ever been in. I just wish I could experience sleep; then I could take full advantage of it."

"It's an extension of the nests the prehistoric Aves made. Warm, supportive, and protective." Yoatl crooked his head. "Have you thought about my offer to join the Solan Society? We're much more than just a casual affiliation of humans; many Aves are also members. We are strong advocates for future ties between Gliese and Sol, when they eventually become members of the Collection."

"That does sound promising," Justine said. Although Yoatl had already shown that he was a man who believed in the Galactic Law, and would not go against it, there might be others who were more sympathetic, and could provide Justine with other means to accomplish her goal: stopping the Kulsat.

"Before we do anything else, is there any way I can see Red Spot, and see if she's all right?"

"Of course," Yoatl said with a kind smile. "Though they have not been afforded nearly as much privilege as you, the Kulsat have been granted official refugee status from the Parliament. We can head there right away, if you like."

"Yes, please."

Stepping back to give Justine enough room to exit her apartment and join him in the long hall, he said, "On an interesting side note, Gliese has been, historically, very welcoming to species from other worlds. I believe nearly eight percent of the Gliesan citizenship are xenomorphic in origin. Should Red Spot and the others desire to work toward citizenship, they would be the first Kulsat in the history of Gliese to do so." A moment later, he added, "I'm sure, if you should decide to apply for citizenship, we could push for a quick approval. There are only five Solan Aetherbeings— including Ah Tabai—I'm certain you could become a role model, and perhaps convince others to attempt the conversion."

"Only five?" Justine asked.

"The Solans on Gliese are highly family-oriented, and we have kept many of our ancestral traditions, including a great reverence for nature. The sacrifice of being away from home and hearth for the rest of one's life is a difficult decision to make. I believe the Solan Society would gain political status with the Parliament if we could contribute more to space industries."

They'd reached the central hub of the station, and Yoatl directed Justine to another platform that floated above the large area and ended near the entrance of a guarded spire.

Two Gliesans looked up as they approached, and one of them faced Yoatl. "Ambassador," he said, shooting a glance at Justine. "We weren't expecting you."

Yoatl gave the guard a polite nod. "Last-minute decision to see to our other new guests."

"One moment, please."

The other guard tapped something on a podium in front of him. Justine assumed it was a computer or a communications console, because a few moments later, the guard nodded to his colleague. "The commander has cleared them for visitation."

The first guard stepped aside for them. "I trust you know

the way, Ambassador?"

Yoatl said, "Thank you, yes. I promise, next time, I'll get my office to clear it first."

"Pleasant day to you," the guard said, and then took up his position in front of the entrance once again.

The spire itself was far more utilitarian than the others, designed more for efficiency than for esthetics. It was unmistakably a military area. The long canyon-like hallway with the ceiling projection of the other spires was not in evidence. Yoatl led Justine to the automatic transport platform and both stepped on, patiently waiting as the conveyor took them all the way to the top of the spire. Instead of narrow corridors connecting the transport platform to the main body of the spire, there were wide hangar-like bay doors. Many of them were open to allow quick access for the hundreds of Gliesan soldiers, mechanics, engineers, clerks and supervisors as they went about their duties.

"Kulsat gravity is slightly higher than Gliese," Yoatl explained. "We have the last segment of the spire sectioned off and converted to a self-contained water environment as closely matched to their home world as we could. There's plenty of space for all of them, though quite of few of the Kulsat have had to double-up until we can install more individual domiciles."

When they reached the last section, they were stopped again by two more guards who took biosignature readings before allowing Yoatl and Justine in.

A small hallway led to a glass viewing area.

"There's a visual monitor on the inside and a computer interface for the Kulsat to use. Their interpersonal communication is based entirely on a complex sign language. Their written language is technical in nature, and was developed mostly to forward their industrial advances. Even with our communication computers, things sometimes get lost in translation."

Though the glass covered the wall in the room, it didn't show the entire water environment on the other side. There was a rocky wall that obscured the view. Even the Kulsat deserved a little privacy.

As a small Kulsat swam by, oblivious to the two humans standing on the dry side of the glass, Yoatl, raising his voice a notch, spoke in the direction of a receiver jutting out of the floor in front of the glass.

"Hello, my name is Yoatl. I am the Gliesan Ambassador to Sol. I would like to speak to Red Spot, if she is available."

The small Kulsat turned to them, approached the computer on his side, and tapped on the console.

"I will inform her of your presence. You will wait here."

He swam off, and Justine shared a look with Yoatl. He said, "They are a very old society. Even though they are in our space, and confined in our facility, Kulsat sensibility still considers all non-Kulsat beings as inferior. Diplomacy is not one of their priorities."

Soon, a familiar Kulsat approached. Justine recognized her from her unique marking right away, but she saw that one of Red Spot's tentacles was hanging limp under her as she swam closer.

"Are you injured?" Justine asked, casting a glance at Yoatl to see if he was aware of this development. He looked as concerned and surprised as she was.

Red Spot typed. "We have had a minor conflict between us. Several of the other Potentials were outraged that we surrendered. They launched an attack. There were casualties. Two Deficients and one Potential were killed in the fighting."

"In the fighting?" Justine said. "When did this happen?"

"We resolved the situation," Red Spot responded.

At that, Yoatl said in a tight voice, "I'll alert the guards. There should be safeguards in place to prevent this. I'll be right back." With that, he strode out of the room.

Turning back to Red Spot, Justine said, "I'm sorry this happened to your people."

"It is fortuitous it occurred," Red Spot typed. "I have established command as senior Potential. The other Kulsat will not rebel again. The Deficients have sworn fealty to me as well. We will continue."

"I don't know what to say." Justine took a step toward the glass and put her hand on the surface. She had no idea if Red Spot could sense her sincerity. "You saved my life; I don't want to see you—or any of the others—hurt."

"Gratitude, Justine. The Gliesans have provided the necessities. There is no cause for further concern."

Just then, Yoatl came back into the viewing room. "It looks like the fight took place out of sight of the security monitors. The guards are sending in medical staff to see what they can do to help, and to retrieve the bodies. Unfortunately, there was nothing they could do to prevent the fight."

Red Spot typed. "It is an internal matter, Ambassador. Interference is not required."

"Of course," Yoatl said.

To Justine, it seemed as if Red Spot had not extended her trust to anyone besides her. She asked, "Is it possible for Red Spot and me to speak in private? Do the translators record our conversation?"

Yoatl gave her a considering look. "As refugees, and not prisoners, the Kulsat do have more rights under Gliesan law. Privacy is one of those rights." He seemed on the verge of asking a question, but then smiled and gave Justine a bow of his head instead. "I'll wait outside for you."

"Thank you, Yoatl."

When he'd gone, Justine spoke to Red Spot. "I don't want to ask you to do anything to betray your people, but I need to protect my world. I need to warn them that your military will attack them."

"It is understandable. While I do not agree with our policy to attack un-Emerged systems, I do not know how I may assist you, Justine."

Taking a deep breath, she said, "I have given the Gliesans my word that I would not seek to learn about their Aether technology, and I don't believe in breaking my word. Their Galactic Law forbids sharing, but since the Kulsat do not subscribe to that Law..."

"Of course, Justine," Red Spot typed, catching on to the loophole. "I will be glad to teach you everything I know about the Gift and the path to becoming a Risen being."

"Thank you," Justine said, but she was interrupted. Red Spot continued typing.

"However, warning your system of our attack will be futile. Our warships are far too powerful. They outnumber you. They will crush anything your technology can send against them. If you wish to save your home system, there is only one way."

"What do I have to do?"

"You must stop the Kulsat Risen."

Justine laughed. "That's the number-one question on everyone's mind: how to accomplish that."

"The answer is obvious, Justine," Red Spot typed. "Obtain the final component."

35

Caribbean Coast :
Guatemala :

Over the next few weeks, Michael worked in an underground laboratory on the coastal property.

True to his word, Señor Ruiz provided him with the most up-to-date diagnostic equipment with which to study the alien. Michael's expertise was more in the fields of planetary geology and astrophysics.

Two lab assistants arrived to assist. When they saw the alien body for the first time, they both stood and stared for several minutes, their mouths open in shock. After recovering, they started to babble uncontrollably, as excited as children in a theme park.

One of the assistants was a biochemist from the Universidad de San Carlos de Guatemala. His name was Felipé, an older man who spent a great deal of his time talking about his fishing boat, and where he was going to sail once he retired with the money he was making from this job.

The other was Tristán, a young biologist from La Aurora Zoo who had spent a few years in oceanographic exploration. He was the one who quickly categorized the alien, surmising it had evolved from a creature much like the *protostegidae* family."

"A sea turtle?" Felipé asked. "But it has no shell."

Tristan smiled. "Look at this x-ray." He pointed. "Obviously, over time, it no longer needed the shell for protection, and it gradually shrank. There's still the remnant of a carapace running along the spine of the creature. It's subdermal, but it's most definitely a shell under its skin. Very similar to the *dermochelys coriacea*—the leatherback turtle."

The two debated and speculated on the origins of the species. What kind of environment did it come from? What level of intelligence had it achieved? What cultural dynamic had it developed? How had it managed to be buried on Earth? The one thing they agreed on was that it had evolved on a different planet, in another solar system.

While Michael listened to their conversations, and sometimes joined in the discussion, he was far more interested in a completely different aspect of the alien's physiology. Namely, that every cell in its body contained a single molecule of altered Kinemet.

Very quickly, they determined that the element would have to have been introduced some time after physical birth; the Kinemet, while providing a constant source of energy to the cells, also had the effect of halting the aging process.

It took Michael well over a week of inputting and collating data from the thousands of diagnostics they performed to conclude that the infusing of raw Kinemet into these creatures would increase their normal lifespan by a factor of thousands.

Was that the legacy the Kulsat sought? Virtual immortality? If that conclusion was accurate, then where had the Grace gone? Certainly, not all of them had strayed too close to the gravitational well of a planet, where the forces that played on the cells would be too strong for any physical being to endure. That, they decided, had been the cause of death in this case. Kinemet was such a heavy element that the proximity to Earth, and the strain of its geomagnetic force, had caused the cells to overload.

No, there had to be another explanation for the fate of this race, the ancient beings that had explored space and created tens of thousands of star beacons to connect the galaxy.

Michael wrestled with these questions during the day, and they even pervaded his thoughts in the evenings, when he ate dinner with Yaxche and Patli. Michael wasn't permitted to speak to anyone else. All information about the outside world was restricted from them.

Humberto was secured in another building with his two Cruzado friends—they were all still considered a threat. Humberto had effected Michael's escape once before. Señor Ruiz would not make that same mistake again.

Every morning, Michael had to give a progress report to Oscar Ruiz, who would then presumably pass it along to Chow Yin.

Michael dreaded the day he made the final connection. His initial exultation at the realization of the relationship between the Xtôti and Kinemet was quickly marred by the fact that he knew he could not keep the information from his captors for long.

He suspected the Kulsat did not want the secret of the Grace merely to extend their lives. They wanted it for something far more powerful. Something that could, and would, change the entire order of the galaxy.

The discovery happened quite unintentionally.

Since Michael did not have access to any Kinemet for experimentation, he extracted a few of the alien's skin cells— using a high-density laser set a frequency he knew would not cause a reaction with Kinemet.

The problem arose when he tried to separate the Kinemet from the biological cells. The element was bound to the cell at a subatomic level.

For two days, Michael struggled with the problem, but nothing he did could extract the Kinemet. It was as if it had become an integral part of the alien's physiology.

One of the known reactors to Kinemet was hydrogen photons. Michael decided to see what would happen to the Kinemet-infused cell when bombarded with hydrogen photons.

He set up his experiment on the other side of the lab, away from the alien's corpse, in a vacuum-sealed container.

Before he initiated the emitter to produce the photons, there was an explosion from outside the lab. For a split-second, Michael thought his experiment might have caused it, but there was no possible way for that to happen.

His alarm turned to fear when he heard the distinct sound of machine-gun fire. The complex was under attack.

He ran to the window and lifted one of the blinds to look outside. It looked like a battlefield in the compound. Dozens of guerrilla soldiers were storming the property. Cruzados? How had they tracked the captives here?

A stray bullet splintered the wall beside Michael, and he jumped back with a start.

Something bright caught his eye, and he realized the bullet had hit the hydrogen emitter. Sparks flew from the unit, and it caught on fire, which spread quickly.

When the fire burned through the container, the Kinemet in the skin cells he'd extracted grew bright.

Instinctively, Michael backed away, remembering Patli's story. Even though there were only a few molecules of Kinemet on the table, the reaction could be highly energetic.

Then Michael felt a sudden heat from behind him, from the alien body. It was glowing.

He checked the computer display monitoring the cells. Somehow, the Kinemet in the skin cells Michael had removed were entangled with the Kinemet still in the alien's body. What happened to one cell, happened to all the cells.

That was his last thought before a wave of Kinemetic radiation rapidly filled the room, completely encompassing Michael. He did not even have time to scream before he was entirely consumed.

∞

When Michael woke up, he felt like the weight of the world was pressing down on him. He was being crushed, but when he opened his eyes, he saw that there was nothing on top of him.

A sensation went through him then, and for the first time, he felt a tiny fraction of what Alex felt, of what those soldiers Klaus had experimented on felt, and what the ancient Mayan villagers had felt.

Michael was irradiated. He didn't have any of the powers of a Kinemat, because he wasn't converted.

There was a tickle at the edge of his consciousness. But, like a half-formed thought, whatever was there eluded him. He could not fully identify what the connection was.

There came a sober realization, though, when Michael struggled to breathe.

He was going to die.

A stream of light cut through the room, and a shadowy figure entered. Hastily, it approached him.

"Michael?" Humberto asked. "You are alive. The Cruzados have found us. They are liberating us. We will be home soon."

"How?"

Smiling, Humberto said, "At Alondo's ranch, Diego and Migel managed to get word to my men in Honduras, who contacted some of our friends in the government here. There's a revolution going on in the Guatemalan capital—it seems not everyone was on board with the CEO's policies, nor his involvement in the kidnapping of Honduran and Canadian citizens. Both our governments are sending troops to police the transition. The Guatemalan army got new orders this morning to liberate this complex. They've already arrested Oscar. Both Alondo and Nadia have been killed."

Then he gave Michael a concerned look. "Are you all right?"

Michael was barely able to whisper. "Something's wrong. I can't move."

"Are you paralyzed?"

"No," Michael said. "I can feel everything, but it feels like I weigh a hundred kilotons."

Humberto looked down at him with a helpless expression.

"The alien," Michael said. "Is it still there?"

Standing up, Humberto glanced at the metal table that once held the alien body. "No. Where did it go?"

"It reacted when the emitter caught on fire. Now, I'm irradiated with Kinemet. I won't survive this."

"I will get one of the other scientists—"

"No. Listen to me," Michael said. "Come closer."

He was finding it more difficult to breathe with every passing moment.

"What is it?" Humberto asked.

"You need to get a message to Alex Manez. I don't know how. He's being held on a mining station in the asteroid belt by Emperor Yin."

"What do you want me to tell him?"

"Tell him what happened here, that the alien's DNA was infused with Kinemet." His lungs felt thick, as if he were drowning. "It's some kind of entanglement. That's the secret."

Humberto grasped Michael's arm. "What's happening to you?"

"Promise me," he said to Humberto. "Only for Alex's ears. No one else must know."

"I promise," Humberto said, but Michael could not hear him.

36

Qin Station :
Sol System :

Over the next two weeks, the guards shadowed Alex's every move. He was confined to the lab, and Sian was locked in the experiment room with guards of his own. Apparently, Emperor Yin didn't want the young programmer to do anything foolish, such as harm himself. Sian was no longer trusted to work on the project independently, so the final setup was left to Alex.

Checking Alex's progress every step of the way, Alice never failed to flash him a condescending smile. The entire time he was setting up the first trial, Alex couldn't stop remonstrating with himself. If the situation hadn't been so dire, he could have blamed it on his screwed-up physiology causing him to think with his emotions rather than his logic. A part of him recognized that he might have wanted to believe in Alice's change of heart despite her history.

The game hadn't changed, just the players. The Kulsat were still on their way at any moment in the future, and Alex could not hold out hope that anyone on Earth would be able to crack the code and develop an army of Kinemats to stop both Chow Yin and the impending alien invasion. For all he knew, Justine was dead, and no one on the Gliesan home world had any idea what had happened.

At the back of his mind, he still nurtured the possibility that he would be able to find a way out of his predicament. He couldn't give over to despair.

While he prepared for the first experiment, he kept coming back to the conversation he'd had with Alice. Her theory that the star beacons were inter-dimensional devices had some merit, but there was a nagging thought that it wasn't exactly the correct answer.

Back on Canada Station Three, when he and Kenny performed their unauthorized experiments, Alex had been lost in some otherness that he couldn't explain. Yaxche had called it a spirit walk, a dream state—though Alex had not been able to sleep or dream since the moment he'd been exposed to Kinemet on Macklin's Rock.

There were so many ancient myths and legends about the nature of the universe that it was difficult to sift through all of them. One aspect penetrated them all, however: that there was a level beyond the physical plane, something to which all humanity could and should endeavor to attain.

The problem Alex had with that idea was how the star beacons played into it. Were they some kind of bridge to an alternate level of existence? He found it hard to believe that something so tangible and prevalent was the answer.

Though he only had Ah Tabai's very brief account of the history of the galaxy, it seemed the Grace were a terrestrial species. They were not gods; they'd merely attained a significant level of scientific advancement.

If they had created the star beacons, then there had to be another explanation for how they worked. The words 'outside light' kept playing over and over in his head.

He knew there was some kind of physical explanation for the star beacon's mechanism; there was no need to get into the metaphysical or mystical to find the answer.

Once Alex had completed all the calculations for the first Kinemetic conversion trial, he informed one of the guards, who immediately spoke into a communications chip on his wrist.

Within a few minutes, Alice arrived.

Behind her, several workers carted in a large container made of a transparent thermoplastic. Big enough to fit a person, it was hooked up with several electronic wires and circuits. A small tube inserted in the back of the container led to an oxygen tank. The only opening was the door, which was electromagnetically sealed.

Alex instinctively knew what the container was. "A Kinemetic damper?"

Nodding, Alice said, "Well, we want you on hand to observe the experiment, but the moment we lift the damping field in the lab, you would have the ability to thwart the experiment."

Sourly, Alex spoke in a low voice. "We can't have that, can we?"

Pretending not to hear him, Alice said, "Unfortunately, my father is attending other business, so we'll postpone the trial until later this evening."

From the small room, Sian watched on through the window. Alex could feel his despair.

Another person entered the lab. Doctor Naysmith, his perpetually good-humored smile on his face, gave Alex a nod as he passed by and headed for Sian.

"What's going on?" Alex asked.

Alice said, "We need to be sure there's nothing physically wrong with him. There can be nothing that will skew the results of the test."

While the doctor performed a thorough examination of

Sian, Alice ordered the guards to set up the lab for the experiment, placing chairs facing the experiment room window, and setting up monitors so everyone watching could follow the progress of the trial. Alex wondered how many people were going to be there.

Since no one seemed to be paying attention to him, Alex took a step toward the lab door, but a sharp-eyed guard spotted him and snapped his weapon up, the barrel of his rifle pointed at his head.

Alice snickered. "Perhaps you would be more comfortable waiting on the other side of the lab. Lie down on your cot and get some rest. You don't want to miss the show."

Feeling as helpless as he'd ever been, Alex retreated to the cot and sat down, but there was no way he was going to get any rest. Inside, he was far too frustrated and angry.

He willed himself to think about something else, and came back to that nagging sensation that had been haunting him since CS3.

How could something be 'outside light'?

Light was simply electromagnetic radiation. Human senses could only detect a relatively small band of its wavelength.

Was Ah Tabai talking about the absence of light? If so, then how did that relate to being in a photonic state? Did the star beacons negate the effects of the quantum drive?

Alex shook his head. That didn't explain anything. The travel between the star beacons was, as far as he knew, instantaneous.

What about the opposite end of light? Gamma rays were at the top of the spectrum. The galaxy was flooded with their bursts, whether from black holes or hypernovae. Many of the corresponding frequencies in the Song of the Stars were charted among the gamma wavelengths. It was these frequencies they were going to use on the sample of Kinemet and change its physical properties to the point where, once bombarded with hydrogen photons, it could properly irradiate a person, in turn altering their physiology where they became sensitive to light and all things in the electromagnetic spectrum.

Was there something beyond gamma rays? Some high-energy wave that had previously been undetected, which was somehow used to create the star beacons, much as a Kinemat was created? When Macklin's Rock had traveled through Sol System at near light speeds, the readings Justine's crew had taken of the star beacon they'd dubbed *Dis Pater* was off the charts.

What could possibly produce that much energy?

The thought vanished from his mind when he realized someone was standing over him, a personable smile on his face.

"Doctor Naysmith?" Alex said.

"And how are you today, young man?"

Frowning, Alex glanced over at Sian. "How can you pretend to care, when you know he could die from this experiment?"

The perpetual smile on the doctor's face wavered for a fraction of a second. He cocked his head. "From my understanding, he could live."

Looking up sharply, Alex stared into the doctor's eyes.

Doctor Naysmith said, "Everyone has the right to medical treatment. Now, your checkup has been overdue. If you will permit me, I would like to scan you."

His first impulse was to continue haranguing the doctor, but then Alex realized he would only be wasting his breath.

The doctor pressed a sensor against the side of Alex's neck and looked at the readout on his holoslate.

"Hmm," Doctor Naysmith said, for the first time looking concerned.

"What is it?" Alex asked, wondering if the time away from

the influence of Kinemet was starting to drain him.

"Your blood pressure is a bit high."

Laughing involuntarily, Alex shook his head. "Is that it?"

"Well," the doctor said, reaching into a pocket of his lab coat and withdrawing a hypodermic gun. "According to my records, your diet is well within guidelines. It could just be the stress of the day, but there's always the possibility of hypertension. I'd like to inject you with a micro-monitor. It will record your blood pressure over the next twenty-four hours and send the results to my lab."

Without waiting for consent, the doctor pressed the tip of the gun against the inside of Alex's wrist and pressed the trigger. Alex let out a short cry and rubbed the spot until the pain dissipated.

Putting the hypodermic gun back in his pocket, the doctor said, "If the area becomes irritated, let me know."

Alex looked up as Alice approached. She glanced back and forth between him and the doctor. "Everything all right?" she asked.

The doctor gave her a warm smile. "Right as rain."

"Good," she said, and looked at Alex as she pointed to the glass cage. "My father will be here soon. It's time to start."

∞

When Alex realized he was pacing like a caged animal in the glass encasement, he willed himself to stand still. He watched as Alice and several technicians set up for the first trial on Sian.

Though the young programmer was in the experiment room on the other side of the laboratory, Alex could see the worry on his face. He didn't blame him. There was an even chance that Sian would suffer an agonizing death by being subjected to the Kinemetic radiation. Going through all of his calculations in his head once more, Alex could not think of any way to eliminate one or the other of the two sequences. The trial was the only way.

When Alex had been exposed to the Kinemetic radiation on Macklin's Rock, he'd been partially shielded by the electromagnetic barriers in the TAHU, which was specifically designed to protect against the numerous radioactive waves floating through Sol System. If not for that shielding, Alex knew he would have died as his parents had, since the Kinemet had not been primed before activation. It was a cruel truth.

Absently, he scratched at the spot on his wrist where Doctor Naysmith had injected the micro-monitor. When he looked down, he saw the skin had turned a faint shade of red. It was probably caused by the rubbing and scratching.

Alice stood in front of the communication panel on one wall, her hands balled into fists and resting on her hips. She exchanged a few heated words with whomever was on the other end, but Alex couldn't make out what she was saying through the glass.

Finally, she turned to look at Alex, and then a moment later strode over to him. There was an intercom system set up on the encasement, and she pressed the button to turn on the microphone. Her voice came through the speaker set high up on the glass wall.

"Well, it looks as if we're going to have to start without His Highness." She did not attempt to hide her bitterness. "We're to record the trial for playback later. I can't imagine what is more important right now."

"Why not postpone?" Alex said.

She gave him an irritated glare. "No. We'll do this now. It will only take a few more minutes to set up the recorders. I'll have a monitor brought up here so you can follow the progress of the trial. If there is any anomaly, you will let us know right away."

"Of course," Alex said with a terse nod.

Alice narrowed her eyes. "Do I need to remind you that any trickery will earn you swift punishment?"

Though Alex did not want any harm to come to Sian, the logical side of him knew this trial was necessary. Once the procedure for creating a Kinemat was ascertained, they could begin creating a defensive force against the Kulsat.

"I know what's at stake," Alex said. "You don't have to threaten me."

A look of annoyance crossed Alice's face, showing Alex that she didn't completely believe him. Someone who had gone through what Alice had would most likely never lose that level of paranoia.

As the Emperor's daughter walked off to oversee the last-minute details, Alex found himself scratching at his wrist again. The skin was turning bright red. He wondered if he should get the doctor back into the lab to have a look. Instead, he made a conscious effort to thrust his hands in his pockets and not scratch.

After fifteen more minutes of prep, Alice and a technician wheeled a monitoring station over to the glass cage and positioned the screen so that Alex could see the readout. The display showed a score of diagnostics, including Sian's vital signs, the ambient temperature in the experiment room, the luminosity, gravity, air pressure and content levels. From his first summary glance, Alex couldn't see anything out of the ordinary.

"All right," Alice said through the intercom after one of the technicians gave her thumbs-up sign. "Alex, we're going to bring in the Kinemet sample now, so we'll be turning on the damper in your encasement. The shielding will cut off all electromagnetic waves, including the speaker system. If you feel the experiment needs to be aborted before the priming, knock on the glass three times. Once I engage the priming sequence, there's no turning back."

Alex nodded that he understood her. She took a few steps away and sat down at a nearby workstation.

A minute later, he heard a slight hum of the electromagnetic shielding indicating the Kinemetic damper was engaged. He saw Alice press another command on her console, presumably to disengage the lab's damper.

A technician wheeled a trolley, with a sealed container resting on top, through the main door. It must be the Kinemet. Though it was very close, Alex could not sense the radiation from the metal. Just knowing it was there sent a sensation of longing through him. It'd been days since he'd been in the presence of the Kinemetic radiation. Like a junkie, his entire body ached for it.

Pushing the trolley into the experiment room, the technician donned a radiation suit before transferring the container to the priming station. Sian, strapped onto the operating table in the middle of the room, tried to turn his head to see what was happening, but he couldn't find the right angle. Alex could imagine the man's fear, and he swallowed the sudden surge of guilt that coursed through him.

Exiting the room, the technician closed the door behind him. Alice hit another command key, and the window blackened. The only images those in the lab could see were on their monitors, which would blank the moment the reaction took place.

Alice programmed in the first formula sequence, and Alex watched on his monitor as the milligram of Kinemet—magnified several hundred times by the camera—was bombarded with a series of electromagnetic waves. The display indicated the Kinemet was transforming its elemental signature on a microscopic scale.

Everything was going as Alex expected, except that his wrist felt like it was on fire.

He pulled his hands out of his pockets and grew alarmed when he saw the red blotch on his skin had tripled in size. There was a large lump forming, as if he'd developed some kind of sebaceous cyst.

Was the minute amount of Kinemetic radiation in his system reacting with the micro-monitor?

Unable to help the impulse, Alex scratched at the spot, which was turning white at the top. Pressing down, he detected something hard under his skin. It felt like a metal sphere. There was a sudden flare of heat, and the capsule popped open.

The sensation that went through Alex was completely unexpected.

It was raw Kinemet inside the capsule, at least a half a gram. The doctor had not injected him with a monitor. He'd given him a strong dose of the kinetic metal—enough to power him for several months. The doctor? Alex wondered. Was he a saboteur? An agent? Whatever his motivation, had he not known that the greatest weapon against the Emperor was a fully irradiated Kinemat?

Starved from the lack of radiation, Alex could almost feel every fiber of his being soak in the effects.

The electromagnetic shielding around the cage was set to the lowest level in an effort to minimize any effect it might have on the trial. That level was more than enough to contain the trace radiation Alex previously had in his system. Now, however, with raw Kinemet surging through his system, the damper field was like a thin sheet of paper against a hammer.

Instinctively, Alex pushed against the shielding, and the damping coils burst above the glass encasement.

Alice and the other technicians jumped at the sound and

spun around to see what was happening.

The door of the cage was no longer electromagnetically sealed, and Alex slammed his shoulder into it. Bursting open, the door hit a technician who had rushed over to stop Alex.

The impact sent the technician reeling backward toward Alice and her command console.

She shrieked as the man flailed about to get his balance, and threw up her arms protectively.

In the chaos, the tech must have hit the door lock command to the experiment room, and it unsealed and rolled back with an electric hum.

Out of the corner of his eye, Alex saw on his monitor that the priming sequence was complete.

"No!" Alice screamed, trying to reach for the failsafe button on her console to stop the Kinemetic trigger.

Without the Kinemetic damper in the experiment room to shield them from the reaction, they would all be exposed to the Kinemetic process.

The entire lab was bathed in a blinding light as that section of Qin Station, and everyone in the area, quantized.

37

Skanse Aerie :
Gliese System :

Over the next few weeks, Justine acclimated to life on the station. During the days, she worked with the Solan Society in a diplomatic capacity, meeting with ambassadors of hundreds of other worlds to strengthen future ties between Sol and the other systems when the day finally came that Sol System gained membership in the Collection of Worlds.

At first, encountering so many new life forms had been overwhelming, and she was certain she'd committed dozens of social *faux pas,* but with her increased capacity for learning, she quickly overcame her anxiety and awkwardness.

Within a short time, Yoatl was able to get the Collection to recognize Justine as the Envoy of Sol System. While this did not give her any significant power in the Collection, it did give her a voice, and increased her status in the Solan Society.

When she wasn't establishing relationships with other worlds, Justine spent time with the Gliesan-humans, talking to them about Solan culture, history, science and politics. As Yoatl had hoped, her stories of their home system inspired several of their younger members to enlist in the Gliesan Space Force and undertake Aether training. It would be years before they were ready to become pilots, but it was a step in the right direction.

Justine also spent some time with the other human Aetherbeings in the system, and though they were restricted from discussing Gliesan Aether technology, they were allowed to help Justine learn more about her altered physiology— aspects common to all beings who had undergone the quantization process.

While in physical form, Aetherbeings were unable to sleep in the classic sense of the term, but they still required rest and time for their minds to process all the information of the day. They showed her meditation techniques that proved quite effective in giving her both requirements. During her four-year flight from Sol to Centauri, Justine had been fully conscious; there had been times she thought she was going to go mad from boredom and loneliness. When they'd learned of her extended time in Aetherspace, the others had been alarmed, and wondered that she hadn't gone insane. Aethers rarely spent more than twelve hours at a time in the Aetherstate.

"Books," Justine told them. "I was able to recall every book I ever read. They kept me company."

One of the human Aetherbeings, Na Huama, told her that word had come through the ranks that the Kulsat had posted a single warship to patrol the Centauri System. It was likely the ship would remain there for months, perhaps even years. The Sentinels, Fairamai and Naila, decided to go on reconnaissance trips to Centauri once every few days to check on their enemy's status.

In her off-hours, Justine visited Red Spot and went over the plan to get back to Sol System. She also undertook the training she needed to accomplish that goal.

One of her first questions was what the final component was.

"We do not know, specifically," Red Spot told her. "It was

a tool of subjugation. With it, the Xtôti were able to nullify the Gift."

"Like a damper?"

"A damper will only suppress the power. We have devices that will quell the Gift from an enemy or their vessel, but it is a temporary effect. Whatever technology the Xtôti had, if they used it on a ship, it would render the Gift permanently inert—whether it was in a quantum engine, or in a Risen. If a ship were too far from a station or planet, it would never return. Any Risen exposed to this technology would perish."

If the Kulsat had that technology, they would be able to eliminate any other system's ability to travel between stars. With that kind of threat, no world would dare to resist the Kulsat.

The alien didn't have any more information other than that, and Justine was left with only speculation on how she could identify the final component.

"What if it's not on my home world?" Justine asked.

"Then you will have to continue searching other worlds until you find it. Our people have the advantage in that we are the only race looking for the final component."

She listened as the alien went into minute detail over the Kulsat training exercises for Potentials. Though Red Spot only knew the theories, she was able to convey to Justine many techniques of control while in Risen form.

Justine practiced quantizing herself. Red Spot, along with several other Kulsat, volunteered to let her practice on them as well. Soon, Justine could quantize twelve of the aliens at a time, maintaining a photonic link with them for over an hour without becoming depleted.

She learned several other techniques besides quantizing objects and beings. The first was how to hide her quantum signature while in a photonic state.

When she'd escaped from the Kulsat mining ship, luck was on her side in more than one way.

If the ship leader had extended his *sight*, he would have detected her moving about the ship. He would have initiated a section-by-section damping field to trap her and return her to her physical self. In that event, she would have drowned.

Red Spot remarked that the hull of their ships had an external damper—a basic defense against alien Aethers boarding their vessels. To conserve energy, the shields were not normally charged unless there was cause. She was lucky to have passed through the hull without being converted to her physical self out in the cold of space.

Another ability, which many Risen were unable to master, was to learn how to resist being quantized by another being. Three Crescents had not yet perfected the technique, since Justine had been able to quantize him.

Justine could not practice hiding her signature or resisting being quantized by another. There was no one to practice on, or against.

She'd promised the Gliesan Parliament that she would not try to learn their—or the Collection's—technology, but there was no rule that said she couldn't learn how the Kulsat did it. If the Collection of Worlds or the Parliament of Gliese found out she was learning the techniques, however, they might decide she was going against her oath by using that loophole, and restrict her from visiting Red Spot.

The most important ability she needed to learn was how to travel outside light. Red Spot informed her that the technique was universal, no matter how the quantum engines had been constructed.

Once again, however, Justine could only learn the theory; there were no Kulsat quantum engines for her to practice on. She hoped the theory would be enough when the time came.

The skill was a compound of all the attributes of becoming a Kinemat.

The navigational principle was similar to when Justine had flown the *Ultio* from Sol's star beacon to Centauri's. Her *sight* was able to mark the spacial locations of the two beacons, and her enhanced memory kept the two points in her thoughts when she engaged the star beacon.

In order to travel outside light, the pilot would have to use the electropathic ability to link herself to the star beacon much the same way she linked herself to the quantized passengers on her ship. In this regard, it was akin to quantum entanglement. For a brief time, she, her ship, her passengers, and the star beacon would be a single entity. The star beacon would 'know' her navigational intentions.

Once she reached the star beacon, instead of sling-shotting past as she'd done before, the star beacon would take over, and absorb the photonic energy of the ship and its passengers.

That's when the mystery began.

Everyone she spoke to gave her an identical explanation: outside light, the star beacons shared the same space. That made no sense to Justine.

If it were a form of dimensional travel, then the star beacon would simply transfer the photonic signature from one beacon in this plane of existence to its counterpart in another dimension, then back to another beacon in a different region of space. There was no way Justine could conceive of this without there being a delay. Travel between two star beacons was instantaneous; therefore, it wasn't dimensional transference.

It couldn't be true entanglement, which would mean the star beacons were, in effect, the same beacon existing in different places at the same time. If that were the case, anytime someone activated a star beacon, they would all activate.

No one knew the secret, or how the Xtôti had built the star beacons. The only thing they agreed on was that they had developed the technology nearly a million years ago.

Justine wished she had Alex and Michael to talk to about it; perhaps they would have some theory to explain it.

Each day, she went over the lessons with Red Spot, but without a practical application, she wouldn't know if she had mastered the abilities. Under no circumstances would she share the fact of her knowledge with anyone outside of Red Spot and the other Kulsat.

Learning the techniques without being able to practice them was a significant obstacle, but a bigger hurdle was managing to get on board a vessel heading for Sol System.

No ship from the Collection of Worlds would break protocol and travel there. Speaking with Na Huama, Justine had learned that Ah Tabai had always been something of a rebel. As much as the human Aetherbeings wanted to help, they would not follow down their colleague's path.

Justine had given her word that she would not break Gliesan Law, and she was not one to go back on her word. She'd worked hard over the past few weeks to establish relations with nearly one-hundred systems; if she broke the Law, she would also break the trust she'd engendered with those races. Of course, if Sol System were ravaged by the Kulsat, those diplomatic relations would be meaningless. Justine was torn.

When she related her concerns to Red Spot, the alien's reply hit her like a bombshell. She couldn't believe what she heard. For a brief moment, she thought that, despite all the time they had spent together building trust, Red Spot had been secretly plotting against her all along.

It was only after the initial shock began to wear off that Justine realized it was the only way for her to uphold the Laws of Gliese and the Collection, and to get home and try to find the final component.

Red Spot told her, "If no Collection ships will travel to Sol System, and you will not commandeer a ship, then you must be on board a ship that is already heading there ... you must find a way to board a Kulsat ship."

38

Qin Station :
Sol System :

For the first time in months, Chow Yin took no pleasure in walking around the station with the aid of his biomechatronic legs. The sense of freedom that came with the technological prosthetic paled in comparison to another, more unfamiliar feeling.

Loss.

From the time he was a child, he'd never formed a close attachment to another person like the one that had developed between him and his daughter. They'd only been reunited for the last few years; their time together had been painfully short.

He'd imagined grooming her as an heir to the Solan Empire once he moved on to conquer the galaxy. Now, there was no one left to pass his legacy on to.

It was all because of Alex Manez and Doctor Naysmith.

Chow Yin had reviewed the recording of the last hours of his daughter's life a hundred times while his technicians and engineers repaired the damage that had nearly destroyed Qin Station.

Though Chow Yin had done his share of betrayal over the years, and uncovered more than a few traitors in his ranks, the doctor had been singularly successful when he'd slipped Alex a small quantity of Kinemet.

It had restored the boy to his full powers, which he'd exercised at the most unfortunate time: simultaneous with the activation of the Kinemetic process on Sian.

The photonic explosion quantized the lab and the top few levels of the space station. Unlike the accident on Macklin's Rock years earlier, there was not nearly enough Kinemet to launch the affected section toward the star beacon at near-light speeds. Less than a day after the event, Chow Yin's sensors picked up fragments of the station hull several thousand kilometers away.

The salvage mission recovered the bodies of all those affected by the photonic conversion, including the technicians in the lab, several other workers in the nearby levels, as well as Sian and Alice. Medical staff quickly determined that all of them had been partially converted to Kinemats, as had those who were subjected to Klaus's first trials. Of the two priming sequences, their first attempt was the wrong one. Even if the cold vacuum of space had not killed his daughter and the others within moments of returning to normal space, the unsuccessful conversion would have killed them soon enough.

The only body they had not recovered was that of Alex Manez. Chow Yin could only surmise that his previous conversion somehow kept him alive. Perhaps, as his records indicated, Alex managed to remain quantized. There was no way to tell how long he could maintain himself in a photonic state. According to those reports, Alex had no awareness in that form. Depending on how much Kinemet the doctor had injected him with, Alex could remain out of Chow Yin's reach for months or even years.

At least Chow Yin had been able to arrest the doctor before he escaped the station. Though Chow Yin did not believe in torture, he believed in poetic justice, and he'd had the doctor launched out into space to suffer the same fate as his daughter.

There was a silver lining to the entire tragedy, and Chow Yin clung to it. Now, they knew the priming sequence for converting a person into a Kinemat. Once they finished rebuilding the Kinemetic conversion chamber, Chow Yin could create as many squadrons of quantum pilots as he needed to subjugate Sol System, and later, the galaxy.

Chow Yin had never been a superstitious man, and did not hold with the power of chance, but he thanked his lucky stars that he'd received word about the liberation of Michael Sanderson in Guatemala. That had prompted him to speed up work on the quantum ship his engineers were building in the dry dock station several kilometers away from Qin Station. Chow Yin had decided to oversee the final stages of the operation.

It was a grand warship. With a crew of only twelve, it had enough firepower to take on any of the USA, Inc.'s space destroyers and win. Chow Yin's engineers had long ago learned to weaponize Kinemet into torpedoes, and the warship carried thirty-six of those, as well as an additional twenty-four conventional and nuclear missiles. A believer in stacking the odds in his favor, Chow Yin also had a dozen twenty-pound gun turrets installed, each with a five-kilometer range, just in case of those rare times the ships came within proximity to one another.

Chow Yin visualized its maiden flight, once he'd successfully undergone the Kinemetic conversion to become a quantum pilot. His first target would be Canada Station Three, in revenge against Alex and his country. Even though his Solan forces had already taken over that station, he would destroy it as a symbol of his power and will. The United Earth Corporate would know the temerity of his purpose. If they did not immediately surrender the corporate nations of the world to him, he would launch Kinemetic warheads at their capital cities until they capitulated. Once he had bent Sol System to his will, then he would focus on these Kulsat Alex had told Alice about.

Though the information he had on them was thin, he'd already developed a plan of attack: if they were so interested in some artifact on Earth, he would offer them free access to the planet to search for it. Why not feign cooperation, make them drop their guard? Once they'd found whatever it was they were looking for—presumably some kind of weapon they feared—then Chow Yin would swoop in and take it from them, and use it against whatever armada they sent against him. With that weapon in his arsenal, the galaxy was his for the taking.

"Your Highness," someone behind him said. "There you are."

Chow Yin stopped walking and turned to see General Leong hurrying to catch up.

"General." He gave a slight bow of his head. "I was on my way to inspecting the progress on the lab repairs."

The general said, "They should be complete by the end of today."

Resuming his pace, with full expectation that the general would follow, Chow Yin said, "And the warship?"

"We're going through final diagnostics. The quantum drive has passed all tests. The ship will be ready for its maiden voyage by this time tomorrow."

"Ensure there is ample Kinemet on board. I fully expect to test the quantum drive at that time."

"Are you certain it is wise to undergo the conversion yourself?" the general asked, raising a concerned eyebrow. "Perhaps it would be more prudent to test the formula on someone else first."

Chow Yin turned his head and growled, "And sully the memory of my daughter? She gave her life to prove which sequence is valid. No, I shall make the conversion tonight."

"Of course, Your Highness."

∞

It was the first time since he was a child that Chow Yin felt apprehension. He knew, in his mind, that the priming sequence was the correct one, but there was a small nagging thought that there could be another factor which might cause the trial to fail.

For a fraction of a second, he wanted to heed the general's advice and have someone else undertake the first trial, but then his pride drowned the notion. How could he face his men if he showed even the smallest hint of fear?

Purposefully, he strode into the lab, taking pleasure in the heavy thumping sound of his biomechatronic legs as they stomped against the ceramic floor. It was a grand way to make an entrance; no one could mistake who had arrived.

The general was there, as well as several of his top officers, watching on as the technicians made the final preparations.

Without any sign of hesitation, Emperor Yin continued through to the Kinemetic conversion chamber. Inside, instead of an operating table with straps, there was a chair. Chow Yin would not be able to wear his biomechatronic legs during the event. The electromagnetic signature could interfere with the Kinemetic priming sequence.

With the assistance of two technicians, Chow Yin unlocked the legs and, leaning heavily on the men, allowed himself to be maneuvered into the chair.

Beside the chair, the Kinemet was already placed inside the priming device. Chow Yin imagined he could feel the radiation penetrate through him.

He looked out through the viewing window at the general

and the other officers, taking on a look of supreme confidence, as the technicians hooked up sensors to him.

When all was ready, one of the technicians nodded. "We can begin whenever you are ready, Your Highness."

Chow Yin waited until everyone had exited the chamber and sealed the door behind them.

Once everyone in the lab focused their attention on him, Chow Yin said, "Gentlemen, today marks the beginning of the greatest era in our history. From this day forward, the course of human existence will be shaped by us. Burn the memories into your minds; you will be able to tell your grandchildren that you were among the honored witnesses to the birth of the first galactic empire."

Having finished his speech, Chow Yin slowly raised one hand, lifting one finger and, after a dramatic pause, pointed to the technician to begin the priming sequence.

The chamber became eerily silent as the Kinemetic damper engaged, and the room sealed electromagnetically. Beside him, the milligram of Kinemet in the conversion device, which was so small when dormant that Chow Yin had to squint to see it, began to glow as it was primed with the sequence of light waves. Once the procedure was complete, and the Kinemet was too bright to look at directly, the bombardment device opened a thin tunnel from which a beam of hydrogen photons penetrated the kinetic metal.

The reaction was all-consuming.

∞

Chow Yin had never been much of a patron of the arts, and held little interest in music. The sound that filled his mind and body when he became a photonic being transcended everything he'd experienced before in his life, and the music penetrating his soul was beyond description. It was the end-all of all things. Forevermore, the elegant symphony of the heavenly bodies throughout the universe would be an integral part of him. He was the song, and the song was him.

He could sense the subtle signature of the Kinemetic damper around the chamber, and with a mere thought-impulse, he penetrated through it and turned off the electromagnetic seal.

A collection of photons, Emperor Yin pushed himself out of the chamber and into the lab, reveling in the looks of awe on his men as they watched a being of light appear before them.

Chow Yin knew he truly was a god.

Just as the thought came to him, he became aware of something else in the vicinity, another presence, and he instinctively knew it was of a magnitude more powerful than he was.

For the first time in his life, Chow Yin felt fear.

39

Unknown :
Unknown :

Nothing.
Then something.
The smallest whisper.
A crescendo of sound.
Everything inside him was outside.
The infinite universe filled his essence.
Answers just out of reach.
Music of the Spheres?
Song of Stars?
Cosmic Opus?
Key.
A rift.
Absence of light.
The inexistence of time.
A dichotomy of spacial matter.
Convergence of light, space and time.
Everything outside him was inside.
Simultaneous divergence of matter.
Invariance and covariance.
Quantum absence.
Everything.

40

Low Earth Orbit :
Sol System :

His first thought was that he had died and gone over to the other side.

A feeling of completeness came over Michael as he regained consciousness. The soft, crackling warmth that flowed through his body was unlike anything he'd experienced before.

The ever-present ache he felt in his knees and hips as he grew older came back, and that was when he realized he wasn't dead. Every cell in his body was on fire, and he knew this was because he'd been irradiated by the reaction to the Kinemet in the alien. It had not been enough radiation to kill him immediately, however. Then why had he felt like he was going to die?

He opened his eyes and looked around. To his confusion, he realized he was in officer's quarters on a ship. There was a desk with an old-fashioned DMR casement. The screen held orders for the captain of the ship, and the name was all too familiar.

Michael struggled to understand how he'd ended up back on Lieutenant Gao's ship.

In space?

His disorientation and confusion sent his heart racing. What was going on? How did he get here?

Fighting against the feeling of weakness running through him, he got up, and a wave of pain coursed through his torso.

He had a broken rib. Something must have fallen on him during the explosion. That was why he'd felt heavy. Shock had tricked him into thinking he was going to die.

With one hand, he felt the bandage around his ribs. It still hurt to breathe, and it took him a bit of time to approach the computer console. There, he read the status report on the screen.

The ship was in orbit at the L3 point on the opposite side of the Moon from the Earth. That region was long-held as a launching point for missions to the outer planets. It had been one of Chow Yin's first targets.

The status report indicated that there were dozens of ships sharing the same orbit, and the majority of them were models used by USA, Inc., Canada Corp., UK PLC, and Deutschland, AG. More than half the ships, however, were of Chinese manufacture. Was Chow Yin massing an armada to invade Earth? Had he captured all these ships? Had he captured Michael?

His confusion heightened when Lieutenant Gao entered the quarters and smiled at him.

"I see you are awake and well, Mr. Sanderson."

Dropping all pretext of civility, Michael demanded, "What the hell is going on? How did I get here?"

Putting up a hand to calm his guest down, Lieutenant Gao said, "You are safe, I assure you. If you feel up to it, I can explain."

Though he knew the radiation in his body, combined with the broken ribs, was sapping his strength, he felt more than up to an explanation.

"Please do," he said, bringing himself to a sitting position on the edge of the bunk.

Lieutenant Gao pulled a chair out from a small desk set into an alcove on the wall, and eased himself down. "We only have a few minutes, so pardon me if I give you the highlights."

"Go on."

"I am, and always have been, an agent for the PRC, planted among the Solan Empire to undermine Chow Yin's rule. When you arrived in Sol System, we sent an alert to avoid the mines, but the alien vessel did not receive the warning in time. When I saw it fly toward another mine, I sent a warning missile to get it to change course. I had no idea the vessel would explode. I am so sorry about your friends."

A mix of emotions went through Michael at the admission, but soon enough, he nodded to Lieutenant Gao to continue.

The lieutenant said, "Over the past few months, we have been secretly amassing a fleet out here, launching during solar flares to mask our movements. In one hour, we will begin to take back Sol System, and we require your help."

"Me? What do you think I can do?"

"You were captured by rebels in Honduras, who were working for Chow Yin, is that correct?"

"Yes," Michael said. "The last thing I remember, the complex was under attack. Humberto, a friend of mine, said the Guatemalan army was liberating us." He gave the lieutenant a hard look. "How did I get from there to here?"

"When the authorities found you, the Cruzado informed them that you had sustained injuries and would only speak to Alex Manez. Of course, that was impossible at the time, but he finally agreed to speak to Minister Calbert Loche, one of your top officials."

"What did he tell him?"

"You had sustained a few broken ribs, and that you had been exposed to Kinemetic radiation. Word was sent through diplomatic channels from your government to the Americans, then to my government who has been working in cooperation with them. My ship was in low-Earth orbit on a routine patrol when I received instructions to break my cover and take you aboard. The Guatemalans launched a small vessel to rendezvous with our ship. You've been here for several days, drifting in and out of consciousness. Now, our ship's doctor has verified that you are well on the road to recovery from your physical injuries."

Michael, his mind racing with all the information he'd just received, reached the most vital conclusion. "You broke cover. That means—"

"Chow Yin is aware of my duplicity. We already have information that he is gathering his forces at Qin Station—he is obviously protecting something very important. Our fleet will launch within the hour, but General Gates, the commander of the flotilla, needs to debrief you before we finalize our mission specs."

"Debrief me?"

"You may be the only person who can contact Alex."

"Alex?"

The lieutenant nodded. "I was able to send off Humberto's encoded message to an agent at Qin Station; Doctor Naysmith. We have no way to verify whether Mr. Manez received it, and we've lost contact with the doctor."

It took a moment for Michael to wrap his head around all the new developments. He asked, "What about the others, Humberto and his men, and Yaxche and Patli?"

"As far as I know, they have been escorted back to Honduras, and are under the protection of their military. They are fine."

A chime sounded, and the lieutenant stood. "Ah, it's ready."

"What is?"

"We have prepared a shuttle to take you to the general's flagship."

∞

The *Liberty* was the largest battle cruiser in the US Space Force. It had eight torpedo tubes with both nuclear and conventional warheads, twelve short-range missile launchers, and two dozen heavy gun batteries. There were six portals on either side of the ship for small fighter shuttles to dock. The ship utilized the latest high-tech countermeasures, and was equipped with state-of-the-art computer technology.

What got Michael's attention was not the weaponry or the firepower. As his shuttle neared the warship, he saw on the monitors that someone had installed a quantum drive. From what he could tell, it was the same configuration as the prototype he had installed on the *Ultio*.

This was the first he'd heard of a light-speed capable military ship—of course, all they were missing was a Kinemat who could pilot it.

By the time he docked, disembarked from his shuttle, and was led to the bridge to meet General Gates, Michael was bursting with questions.

Before he could say anything, however, the general pulled him into a small conference room away from the other officers.

"Mr. Sanderson, welcome to the *Liberty*. Thank you for assisting us."

"How can I help?"

"We plan to attack Qin Station, which is Emperor Yin's base of operations. We have reports coming in that Emperor Yin has four times the number of our ships, but most of them are scattered around this area of space. If we stand any chance, we must arrive in force before he has a chance to gather his fleet. Our attack must be unexpected. No doubt, you are aware that our ion engines have improved over the past few years. It should only take us two or three days to arrive there once we launch."

"What is it you want from me, then?" Michael asked.

"It is our belief that Emperor Yin is building a quantum ship of his own. Should he successfully create a Kinemat, he will have an advantage over us. We know he has coerced Alex Manez into assisting him; we must retrieve him alive if we are to have any chance of creating our own force of Kinemats."

"Alex had no choice…" Michael said.

"We know. That's not important. What's important is that he may not know whom to trust. That's where you come in."

"Of course. I will do anything to help."

"Good." The general nodded, and then took a moment to form his words. "We don't believe we've been able to contain news of the Guatemalan revolt, which is why we believe Emperor Yin has moved up his timetable. Once he has what he wants from Alex—"

"He'll kill him," Michael finished.

41

Qin Station :
Sol System :

There was no sense of time or space. It was a complete metaphysical metamorphosis. Alex was unaware that he'd ever been a corporeal being. His consciousness was filled with the entire scope of the universe's existence. At the same time, he was suspended in a moment of a pure energy.

He could have existed in that state for all time, and not known the difference—or cared, for that matter. It was the end and the beginning of all things for him.

In an instant, he became aware of his unawareness, and he willed himself to become conscious.

There was another sentience near him, and the edges of his perception told him it was a presence similar to him.

The overwhelming bliss called him back, and he was very near to dismissing the anomalous sense that there was someone or something near him. All he wanted was to exist in that glorious fragment of time and space for all eternity, the suspension of all reality.

Still, there was something in his psyche that would not let him remain in his current form. What was it? If he had the perception of consciousness, did he not have an obligation to embrace it? Otherwise, the infinite inexistence was a lie.

He concentrated, and became cognizant that there was a material universe surrounding him.

Galaxies, solar systems and planets. Elements, particles, molecules, and quanta.

Time slowed down and returned to him, and his memories were restored.

From one moment to the next, he realized a great many things.

He was different from before. For nearly twenty years, he'd been affected by the radiation of Kinemet. Now, the Kinemet was a part of him. Every cell in his body, his very DNA, was altered. Kinemet was part of his fundamental physiology now. He was no longer a failed conversion, no longer a half-human, half-Kinemat—he was different enough that he'd become another species, even though he knew his physical appearance would not show the changes.

The Grace! Was this what the Grace were? Alex sent his consciousness out. Though he could always sense every planetary body in Sol System, he could not send his awareness more than a hundred-and-fifty kilometers away from his photonic self. Beyond that limitation, the details were completely obscured. Now, if he concentrated, he could push his awareness out to every point in Sol System.

Like a lighthouse beaming directly into his soul, the star beacon on Pluto shone brightly. No longer was it a distant pin of luminescence in the farthest reaches of his *sight*.

And … Alex could see beyond it. Not in the physical sense. It wasn't as if he could see past it on a spacial basis. Though he could still detect other star beacons throughout the galaxy, his new perception of Sol System's beacon was beyond anything he'd imagined before.

An ethereal symphony emanated from it, something much more majestic than the Music of the Spheres, or the Song of the Stars. It was all-encompassing perfection, and it called to him. The message had been there since Macklin's Rock, but now it was much more powerful than ever before.

Alex, come home.

How had he changed? The doctor! How had Doctor Naysmith known that injecting Alex with Kinemet before the conversion process would have this effect? Or had it been an accident?

That was the final key, Alex knew. Priming the Kinemet to match the Song of the Stars was only half the equation. Exposure to its radiation would convert a physical being to a Kinemat, but a Kinemat was merely the halfway point. Infusing the converted Kinemet during the conversion process changed Alex into a full quantum being.

Was this the secret the Kulsat had been searching for over the past thousand years? In theory, it sounded right, but there was a seed of doubt in Alex's mind. He would need to think about it more.

Another realization came to him, this one more immediate. There was something important about the secondary presence he'd sensed.

There was a physical distance between him and the other photonic being. Several thousand kilometers. Before he could think about the question, he had the answer. Alex, in his quantum state, had drifted outward from the Sun. A quick calculation of his position among the planets told him he'd been in the alternate awareness for several days.

Using his *sight*, he focused on the presence, and realized it was very near Qin Station.

It was another Kinemat, and Alex focused his perception to identify it.

When he realized it was Chow Yin, Alex pushed his photonic self forward.

At one point, he'd thought the only option for saving Sol System was to help the self-styled Emperor of Sol System. Now that he'd discovered how to create Kinemats, Chow Yin would not stop in his mad quest. The last thing they needed was a maniac running around with that power.

Chow Yin had to be stopped.

Though his perception traveled at near-light speeds, Alex still had limitations, and could only push his photonic self at a fraction of that speed.

As he neared Qin Station, Alex felt the presence of a significant quantity of raw Kinemet, the entirety of which was loaded on a large warship. He could sense Emperor Yin's Kinemetic presence on that warship, and he detected there was a quantum drive installed in the vessel.

By the time Alex's essence had reached Qin Station, the warship had moved a few kilometers away and was coming about.

Chow Yin's ship launched a Kinemetic torpedo at the station.

As Justine had caused the torpedoes to explode years before when they were being chased from Canada Station Three, Alex pushed his senses out at the weapon and detonated the Kinemetic torpedo before it hit the station.

Immediately, the Emperor's ship launched a conventional missile, and Alex could do nothing but watch in horror as Qin Station was obliterated.

How many innocent people had been on that station?

No! Alex raged. He had a crazy thought: as he'd detonated the weaponized Kinemet on the torpedoes, perhaps there was a way he could detonate the Kinemet on the Emperor's warship.

Before he could push his senses out, Chow Yin activated his quantum drive, and the warship disappeared in a streak of light.

It was then that Alex sensed another quantity of Kinemet. A fleet of ships were coming his way. His first thought was they were the Emperor's reinforcements, since many of the ships carried markings of the People's Republic of China.

When he looked closer, he realized the ships did not carry weaponized Kinemet warheads. One of the ships bore a USA, Inc. signature and had a quantum drive installed, and several hundred kilograms of Kinemet on board—more than enough to power the ship for years.

At the same time, another group of ships converged on the newcomers from another direction; they must have been the remainder of Chow Yin's forces.

As the two fleets met, they began to fire on one another. Alex was helpless in the fight.

If this had been a vid, or a rendition of Nova Pirates—the game Alex had loved to play as a youth—he would have enjoyed the epic space battle that ensued. He would have reveled in the conflict, cheering his side on.

Now, Alex could only watch in horror as dozens of ships, and hundreds of soldiers on either side, were destroyed in the fight.

After what seemed like hours, but was in truth less than five minutes, the battle was over.

Chow Yin's forces, without the Emperor at their head, quickly broke ranks, the ships turning away from the fight and fleeing from certain death.

The Earth forces had won the battle.

But what of the war?

Certainly, Alex knew, there were pockets of imperialists throughout Sol System, but without their Emperor, the odds favored Earth.

Alex had been distracted by the fighting, but now that the

conflict was over, he scoured the main Earth ship. Were they truly from his side?

When he focused his perception on the bridge, he felt a surge of relief.

Michael!

Pushing himself forward, Alex passed through the hull of the ship and onto the bridge.

Michael, as if expecting him to arrive all along, said, "It's so good to see you, Alex."

His warm smile was in complete contrast to the look of shock on the officers' faces when Alex materialized into physical form.

∞

In the captain's cabin, Alex sipped a cup of hot chicken broth while Michael and the commander of the fleet, General Alan Gates, brought him up to date.

"And so," Michael said, "Chow Yin must have initially prepared to repel us—"

"But then he sensed me," Alex said, and shook his head.

Michael said, "With you on one side, and us on the other, he would have realized he was outgunned without the bulk of his fleet. Like any coward, he fled."

General Gates growled. "Not until he was sure to destroy Qin Station behind him, whether to distract us, or to hide his research."

Giving Alex a level look, Michael asked, "Where do you think he went?"

"He went to look for more allies."

"Where?" the general asked. "The Jupiter moons?"

"No," Alex said, and took a deep breath. "Centauri. He knows about the Kulsat. He thinks they will join forces with him, if he gives them what they're looking for."

General Gates frowned, and looked at Michael. "None of this was in your report. The Kulsat?"

"It's time you heard the truth," Michael said. "I briefed my government, but my report was discounted as a fabrication."

Together, Michael and Alex told the general everything they knew about the Kulsat threat.

When they were finished, the general didn't question the truth of their story. He asked, "What about these Gliesans you mentioned, the ones that saved Alex on his first trip, and the rest of you this last time?"

Michael said, "I'm not sure if they have the resources to stand against the Kulsat. I got the impression they're severely outgunned. Their Kinemats have helped us, but I believe they have done so of their own accord. Their actions might be unofficial, and they might have been breaking their own laws to assist us." He shook his head. "There's no way to guess what stance their government has adopted concerning us."

Alex said, "Up until now, the Kulsat haven't had any idea where in the galaxy Sol System is. The star beacons have a kind of interstellar cloaking mechanism, hiding our location from anyone who doesn't know our coordinates."

"And hiding them from us," Michael added. "This is why none of our long-range sensors have recorded anything outside our system."

General Gates stood up and paced in the small room. "And you say this was set up by these ancient aliens, the Grace?"

"As far as we know," Michael said. "We weren't able to debrief the Gliesans in full before Chow Yin's mines struck. And the only other information we have is the stories from Yaxche and his friend, Patli. It's possible some parts of the story could have been altered or lost over the past thousand years."

Drawing himself up to his full height, the general nodded to himself. "I will send a report to HQ."

"We don't have time to wait for them to debate this," Alex said. "If we don't follow Chow Yin and stop him, he'll lead the Kulsat right to us."

"I don't have the authority to do that," the general said, and then glanced at Michael. "Besides, if your government has discounted your story, my government might do the same. I can't just run off to another solar system based on conjecture."

"What if I could prove it?" Alex stood up.

Raising one eyebrow, the general asked, "Prove the Kulsat threat?"

"Yes."

"How?"

"You have a quantum drive on board."

Slowly, the general nodded. "Yes, but I understand neither of you are fully capable of piloting the drive."

"Things have changed," Alex assured him. "Don't worry; it will be a short trip."

"A short trip?" The general frowned. "To where?"

Alex smiled. "Back to Pluto."

∞

When the general went to send in his report, insisting he needed someone higher up the food chain to sign off on the proposal, he left Alex and Michael alone in the cabin.

"You've been irradiated by Kinemet," Alex said.

"I have, but I don't seem to have any of the powers of a Kinemat. I just feel the bad side effects. If they hadn't got me off Earth, I'm sure I would've died. Now, I can handle it—at least for the time being. Judging from past cases, I might not have more than a few days or weeks before the radiation starts to kill me."

"Tell me what happened?"

Michael quickly outlined everything that had happened since they'd parted ways after Kenny's death. "I realized that the alien had Kinemet infused in his DNA. Of course, that revelation came seconds before the lab blew up."

"It wasn't natural Kinemet," Alex said. "It was already altered, as if it had undergone the priming sequence."

"Yes." Michael frowned. "I got Humberto to send the message to you letting you know that was the final key. I assumed…"

Shaking his head, Alex said, "Doctor Naysmith must have snuck Kinemet into my bloodstream just before the first trial. The sample they used on Sian was incomplete—everyone else in the lab died. I was insulated against that; I assume because I've been previously irradiated. I quantized myself moments before the explosion. Somehow, while being quantized, I managed to process the Kinemet in my system. The conversion must have altered it. If you were to take a genetic sample of me now, you'd most likely find that I share the same Kinemetic DNA markers as the Xtôti you examined."

"So you…"

Alex nodded. "Technically, I'm no longer a human. I'm one of the Grace." He laughed. "Unfortunately, I have no idea what that entails. Other than being aware in the photonic state, the only other ability I seem to have is to be able to extend my awareness throughout the solar system."

"So that was the legacy the Kulsat were looking for? The infusion of Kinemet? It was the alien's body that gave us the clue."

Alex frowned. "I think the infusion may only be a part of the legacy, an important step. There's a piece missing in this equation, and for the life of me, I don't know what it is."

"We need a lab, and a lot of time," Michael said. "We have neither." A moment later, he added, "I don't know how much time I have, either."

"I'm sure you'll have all the time in the world," Alex said.

Michael squinted at him. "What do you mean?"

"You told me Patli's story, about how other aliens abducted the irradiated villagers a millennium ago."

"Yes."

"I believe the rescuers were Gliesans, and the villagers were Ah Tabai's ancestors."

Nodding, Michael looked at the floor, thinking it through. "That makes sense."

"So, all we need to do is get Ah Tabai and Aliah to fix you, as the Gliesans fixed the villagers."

Michael jerked his head up. "What?"

"What better way to prove our story than to get it straight from the horse's mouth?"

"Ah Tabai? Aliah? They survived?"

Alex nodded. "Yes. The same way I did when I first went to the Centauri System. They're waiting out there, in the photonic state. Why else would I want to go to Pluto?"

∞

At first, the general wanted to get authorization, but Alex pointed out that a message sent to Earth from their position would have taken nearly fifteen minutes each way, and adding in the time it would take for someone in command to make a decision, Chow Yin would most likely be an hour or two ahead of them, traveling at very near the speed of light.

"Also, if he is fully converted to a Kinemat, he can utilize the star beacons. The moment he travels to the Centauri System, he could signal the Kulsat."

"My original mandate was the capture of Chow Yin," General Gates said after considering Alex's words. "Technically, nothing has changed." With that, he gave the order to get the quantum drive online.

It only took the engineers a few minutes to prepare everything, and when the general was notified that all systems were ready, he nodded to Alex. "You're sure you can do this?"

"Yes," Alex said, finding his way to the console area built specifically for a quantum pilot. "Now more than ever."

"Very well, I'm transferring navigation to your station. Let us know when you're going to engage the drive."

Taking a deep breath, and familiarizing himself with the controls, Alex was suddenly reminded of the first time he'd piloted a luminous vessel, when he'd hijacked the *Quanta*.

He closed his eyes, and could feel a connection to the Kinemet already loaded aboard the quantum engine. At the same time, he became acutely aware of Michael and the other three officers on the bridge, as well as the six engineers on board the ship. It was almost as if he could reach out with a thin tendril of his own essence and touch each of them.

Alex hesitated as something revolutionary occurred to him.

"What is it, Alex?" the general asked.

"Something's not right."

Michael got out of his seat and stepped over, looking over Alex's shoulder at the console. "It looks fine to me."

"No," Alex said, "not with the drive; with the procedure." He glanced up at Michael. "Do you remember one of the primary reasons I took the place of the first pilot of the *Quanta?*"

"You thought a pilot who had not undergone the Kinemetic conversion process would not be able to dampen the secondary Kinemetic reaction."

"And I was right." Alex looked back down at the quantum

drive controls. "Since that time, I've always thought there was something fundamentally wrong with our theory, that the secondary reaction should never have been an issue."

General Gates approached, a harried look on his face. "What's the delay? Weren't you the one who convinced me time was of the essence?"

"All this time we've been using the theory a quantum pilot is for navigation and to control the ship's return to physical space." He smiled. "But there's much more to it."

"What do you mean?" Michael asked.

Alex waved the two men back to their seats. "Not to worry. I think I know what I have to do."

"You think?" the general asked, his eyes wide and disbelieving.

"Instinctually," Alex said and gave him a firm nod. "Trust me."

Slowly, the two men returned to their seats, and Alex faced forward.

Closing his eyes, Alex reached out with his photonic essence and connected with the crew. Then he formed a bridge between them and the quantum drive.

Michael said, "We're ready—"

As Alex had been able to quantize himself in the past, he knew, deep down, he could convert the crew to photons by willing it to happen. He did so, and a moment later, he quantized himself. He was fully aware in that state, and with his electropathic senses, he engaged the quantum drive…

…A little over four hours later, he disengaged the drive, then returned himself to physical form moments before rematerializing the crew.

It had been the smoothest flight Alex could ever have hoped for.

"—when you are," Michael finished, then paused with his

mouth open when he saw the main casement on the bridge showing him that the ship was in orbit around Pluto.

"We're here?" General Gates said in a breathless rush. With a slight shake of his head, he added, "It felt instantaneous."

"It's just a matter of perception," Alex said. "To me, the flight took four hours, eight minutes, and twenty-seven seconds."

"Pluto." General Gates stared at the image on the casement screen. "I never truly thought I would see it."

"If you think that's remarkable," Alex said, "prepare to be amazed."

"What—?" the general began to ask.

Two photonic essences came out of the bulkhead and floated down in front of the officers on the bridge. Slowly, both of them coalesced into bipedal forms.

"I'd like you to meet Ah Tabai," Alex said, standing up and approaching the two. He shook hands with the shorter of the two beings, who looked Mayan in appearance. "And Aliah, of the Gliese System." He bowed to the tall, bird-like alien who gave him an excited chirp of greeting.

"Alex," Ah Tabai said. "I didn't know if you would realize we were here, waiting. Thank you for rescuing us."

Smiling, Alex clapped a hand on his shoulder. "It was my turn to save you."

Aliah spoke in her whistle-like language, and the words came out from the translator at her collar. "You are more than an Aetherbeing, Alex. I can sense it." She and Ah Tabai glanced at each other.

Ah Tabai nodded. "Yes, I can feel it, too. You are—" Then his eyes widened. "—you are in a state of Grace! How—?"

Aware that all eyes were on him, and not certain if he should be telling anyone the secret, Alex realized that it was only a matter of time before the truth came out.

341

"Michael discovered the body of one of the Grace on Earth, and saw that he'd infused Kinemet with his DNA. I was injected and exposed to a conversion." He shook his head. "I'm surprised no one else has ever stumbled on that."

"No," Ah Tabai said. "That has been attempted before. It never resulted in ascension to the Grace." With a concerned look at Aliah, he added, "The results of that experiment have always been fatal."

Michael asked, "Then how did Alex survive it, and become—how did you say it—ascended?"

"That is the question," Ah Tabai said.

Aliah spoke. "We sensed another activation of the star beacon a little while ago. It was on course for the Centauri System."

"Yes," Michael said. "That was Chow Yin." For Ah Tabai's and Aliah's benefit, he added, "He's a criminal who is trying to contact the Kulsat."

His expression turning alarmed, Ah Tabai said, "You must not allow that. The Kulsat will not make allies with him. They will destroy him, and then come here. We must stop him."

"My sentiments, exactly," the general said. Up until that point, he had not spoken. Instead, he'd been staring at the alien on his ship. "Perhaps we can all formally debrief later. Right now, can we get to Centauri and stop Chow Yin in time?"

Alex took a deep breath. "We had better." He turned to Ah Tabai. "I've never used a star beacon correctly before. I don't think we have time for a lesson. Would you do the honors?" he asked, glancing at the general for approval.

Once General Gates nodded, Ah Tabai said, "Of course."

…And then Alex became aware that he, the crew, and the entire ship, now existed in deep orbit around the Centauri star beacon.

To his perception, the trip had been instantaneous.

The next moment, they were under heavy fire.

42

Aerie Skanse :
Gliese System :

Deep down, Justine had hoped the day would never come, but when she received the message from Naila, she held her breath as she listened.

"We have picked up a signal from the Centauri star beacon. It is activating, indicating a new arrival. It could be a Kulsat ship coming to relieve the other one, but from what our sensors could detect, the warship in the system has raised Aethershields and primed its weapons systems. We presume the new arrival is not expected. If you are coming, you had better hurry. We're flying into Centauri in fifteen minutes to investigate."

Justine, who had been at dinner in Yoatl's apartment, looked to the Ambassador. "It's time. Are you still willing to help me? I know you've had your doubts."

Yoatl wiped the corner of his mouth with a napkin as his wife started to clear the table. "It is a terrible risk. If the Parliament finds out, you'll have sacrificed your position here for nothing. It's not too late to back out."

Standing, Justine forced a smile. "This might be my only opportunity. I'm willing to take the chance."

"Just remember," Yoatl said as he went to the computer

console on the other side of the room. "If it is one of your ships, and they have arrived using the Grace, you still may not share any Aether technology with them until the Collection verifies their method of travel. Warn them to return to Sol, and then come back here immediately." He began typing a series of commands into the computer, granting her permission to accompany the *Fainne* on their reconnaissance mission. "If the Parliament finds out I did this, they'll revoke my ambassadorship."

"Don't worry, Yoatl. I won't break Galactic Law. It's the same loophole Naila and Fairamai used to save me."

Yoatl faced her, taking a deep breath. "Be careful. The Kulsat will be quick to attack." He gave her a long look. "I would hate myself if anything happened."

"You've been a wonderful friend, Yoatl. I will do everything I can to return to Gliese safely."

∞

By the time Justine got to the area in the space port where the *Fainne* was docked, Naila and Fairamai had the ship prepped and were ready to fly. The spaceport controller noticed her striding purposefully toward the ship. He was a tall Gliesan with red plumes on the top of his head.

With his long legs, he quickly caught up to her. "Envoy Turner, you aren't supposed to be here," he said. "You don't have clearance."

"Actually," she said to him, "I do. There is a possibility the new arrival is from Sol System. As envoy, it's my responsibility to be there to warn them of the Kulsat danger."

The controller cocked his head in doubt.

Justine shrugged. "Call Ambassador Yoatl, if you like. He'll verify the orders. But you're delaying the *Fainne*. We only have a small window of opportunity."

As if imagining the effort of going through official channels to get verification of Justine's statement, the controller nodded. "All right. Go ahead."

"Thank you," Justine said, and hurried to the ship. The portal closed behind her, and the vessel launched a moment later.

Fairamai was in the bay, and motioned for Justine to follow her to the passenger compartment where she helped secure her in the molded seat.

"You remember what we talked about?" the bird-like alien asked, and continued to spell it out before waiting for a reply. "Once the *Fainne* arrives in Centauri, Naila will scan the area for ship signatures. If it is Kulsat, he will return us to Gliese immediately. Should the new arrival come from Sol System, you will have less than twenty seconds to send them a warning; that is the amount of time a Kulsat ship needs to lock on to our ship, charge weapons, and fire."

"Yes," Justine said. "I know. I'll be ready."

Frowning, Fairamai said, "We are more than capable of sending the transmission. You do not need to come on this mission. Remain here, be safe. We will return with news."

"No." Justine shook her head. She could feel the vibrations of the *Fainne* as it banked around the Skanse Station, lining up for the run at the Gliese star beacon. "It's my responsibility."

A communication speaker in the room hummed, and a moment later, Naila said, "Engaging Aethersleep in 5 ... 4 ... 3 ... 2 ... 1—

∞

Justine had conditioned herself to react the moment she came out of the photonic state. She did not wait to find out the origin of the arriving ship, because it didn't make a difference to her plan.

A split-second after returning to normal space in Centauri, Justine quantized herself and pushed her particles outside the hull of the *Fainne*. Utilizing the technique Red Spot had taught her, she shielded her photons—essentially making her invisible to detection—and used her *sight* to scan for the other ships in the area. She figured there would be an even chance between one of two possibilities.

If the new ship was Kulsat, Justine's intention was to stow away on board. So long as the Kulsat didn't suspect their unseen passenger, Justine would be able to feed off the Kinemetic radiation of the ship and exist in her photonic state indefinitely. At such time as the Kulsat discovered Sol System, Justine would hitch a ride and return to her home world, and there do the best she could to aid in the defense of her people—by finding the final component, if it existed on Earth.

If the ship were from Sol, Justine would go on board and do everything she could to evade the Kulsat warship, and return to Sol, even if she had to commandeer the ship and pilot it herself.

She felt guilty for deceiving Yoatl about her intentions, but her promise held: she would not share technical knowledge of Kinemet. It was possible she wouldn't have to. It had been a while since Alex, Kenny, Michael, and Yaxche had returned to Sol System. They would do their best to prepare for a Kulsat invasion, and to advance their own Kinemetic technology as far as they could.

No matter what they did, though, she knew the one thing that could save her system was to do what Red Spot had suggested: possess the only technology more advanced than the Kulsat's, and make them surrender.

The first ship she sensed was the Kulsat warship, a

behemoth compared with the mining ship that had abducted her when she first arrived in Centauri. She could feel the overwhelming quantity of Kinemet on board—they were stocked, enough to supply a fleet for years. To her surprise, they were already firing their weapons, not at the *Fainne,* but at the Solan ship that had just arrived.

She became aware of several things at the same time:

The Solan ship had traveled from Sol to Centauri outside light. For the first time since she'd left her home system, Justine could momentarily sense the star beacon from Sol, attached to the *Dis Pater* monument. It was faint, and the signal dissipated quickly, but it was there nonetheless. The technology that had hidden it and Sol System from the awareness of the rest of the galaxy had been tripped by the very act of using the star beacon. In the back of her mind, she knew it would only be a matter of time before the Gliesans became aware of this and, with Justine already having laid the diplomatic groundwork, ratified Sol System into the Collection of Worlds.

Those thoughts came and went in a blink. What captured Justine's attention was when she realized the Solan ship had the same markings as the ship that had chased her and the *Ultio* out of Sol System.

The flashback of narrowly avoiding destruction from a Kinemetic torpedo gave Justine pause. For a very brief moment, she didn't know which ship she would rather see blown apart.

Only a few thousand meters apart, the Kulsat and the Solan ship were firing on each other, the Kulsat with their sonic energy beams, the Solans with the Kinemet-modified nuclear warheads.

To Justine's surprise, the Solan ship was holding its own. Many of Earth's industrial ships, especially the long-haul vessels which traveled between planets, were still heavily reliant on electroceramics—a highly durable material which provided insulation against solar radiation and other forms of energy, including sound—to bolster the titanium hulls. The *Ultio,* being a private yacht designed for short excursions, did not have the electroceramics shell over its titanium hull. The mining ship, with its sound energy beams designed to rip through asteroidal metals, had torn the *Ultio* right apart.

Even still, the sonic blast was enough to cripple the Solan ship. Panels of the hull shattered and flew off. The vessel listed, as if its internal stabilizers had malfunctioned.

As she pushed her photonic particles forward toward the battle, she could sense the Kulsat ship changing the aim of one of its energy beams. She had not noticed, but the *Fainne* was coming about and attacking the Kulsat warship. Their weapons were no match by themselves, but in concert with the Solan ship, they helped to even the odds.

The distraction gave the Solan ship enough of an opportunity to shift itself a few degrees below and to the starboard of their enemy.

The Solans fired a conventional torpedo at the belly of the alien ship where, by Justine's estimation, their quantum engine was.

Unlike the Kinemetic ordnance, the conventional torpedo caused damage. It didn't disable the warship, but it shredded a section of the Kulsat's hull, and Justine could sense a level of protective radiation diminish. If the Solans followed up with another torpedo in the same spot, or if the *Fainne* fired its weapons, they might be able to inflict heavy damage.

Apparently, the Kulsat were aware that if they suffered another hit they would be dead in space; instead of returning fire, the ship changed course, pointing toward the star beacon, and engaged its quantum drive. It vanished from Centauri space.

Justine watched as the *Fainne* moved off from the Solan ship. There was no way for Naila or Fairamai to know where Justine was, or if she was still in Centauri space. They also had no way of knowing if this Solan ship were friend or foe. Their only two options were to go back to Gliese for further instructions, or stand by and see what happened. They chose to wait.

Not wanting to contact Naila, since he would most likely charge her to return to Gliese, Justine approached the Solan ship, and experienced a moment of trepidation.

This group was the same that had tried to destroy her four years before. She knew they had not followed her right away— the reappearance of the Sol System star beacon in her photonic consciousness proved that whoever piloted the ship had not only developed the ability to create Kinemats, but had also discovered how to travel outside light.

She could only come to one conclusion: one of Earth's more aggressive nations had mastered the ability to travel faster than light. The fate of her friends suddenly became uncertain to her.

Under her current circumstances, however, she did not have another option. Now that the Sol System star beacon had activated on the interstellar grid while the Kulsat monitored it, the armada would head there as soon as they marshaled their forces.

Mentally steeling herself, Justine pushed her photons through space toward the Solan ship. It took her quite a while to get there. At first, she had the impression the ship was flying away from the star beacon, but as she got nearer, she realized it was drifting. It had not come out of the fight unscathed. Perhaps the ion engines had been damaged in the fight, she wondered.

She could also sense that many of the electrical systems on board were blown out. Once she pushed herself through the hull and into the ship, she heard the cries of the crew who were badly hurt; some of them were dead.

As she floated near one section with several bodies on the ground, she examined them. The first thing she noticed was that they were multiracial. Pausing near one man, she looked closer. The style of uniform and the insignia on the sleeve were unfamiliar to her, but the words written on the epaulet sent a wave of dread through her: her Chinese was rusty, but she swore it translated as 'Solan Empire Space Force'.

The hallways were strewn with metallic rubble, overhead lights sparked, and smoke filled the air. Still in her photonic state, Justine was able to navigate through the ship to the bridge.

It was there that her suspicion was confirmed. The captain of the ship was, indeed, a Kinemat. Justine could sense the radiation emanate from him. When she saw who it was, she couldn't believe her senses.

Standing with the assistance of a bulky set of biomechatronic legs in front of a bank of computer consoles, Chow Yin shouted orders to the half a dozen men to get the ship's controls back on line. Justine was glad she'd learned how to mask her photonic form from other Kinemats and Kinemetic sensors. She was free to eavesdrop until she had enough information before she decided what course of action to adopt.

An older uniformed man, with general's stars on his collar, stood at a console beside Chow Yin. He looked up and said, "Emperor Yin, we have reports that the fires in the ion engine room have been put out, but it will take several hours to repair the damage."

"What about the quantum drive?"

"Intact, Sire."

"What about torpedoes."

The general called up a readout. "Two conventional, four Kinemetic, Sire."

Chow Yin pointed to him. "Ensure they are all armed. That other ship could decide to fire on us at any time. Meanwhile, put as many men as you can on repairs." He let out a throaty growl. "And keep your eyeballs on that star beacon readout."

"Yes, Sire. That other ship is maintaining its distance. It doesn't look like it's attacking."

"If it changes position, let me know. Otherwise, ignore it. We don't know if they are the Kulsat or another race."

Everything was happening far too fast for Justine to figure out what was going on. She needed more information. Coalition? Solan Empire Space Force? Emperor Yin? What had happened in the years since she left Sol System?

She watched for the next several minutes as the crew desperately tried to repair their vessel.

In a panicked voice, one of the helmsmen called out. "Sire, the sensor indicates the star beacon is activating. We have no way of knowing if it is the aggressor returning, or the Coalition."

Waving his hand dismissively, Chow Yin said, "It doesn't matter who it is. Prep the torpedoes. Fire both a conventional and a Kinemetic warhead the instant any ship rematerializes."

Justine felt a moment of panic. She didn't know who the Coalition was, but if they were opposing Yin, then they had to be the good guys. She highly doubted the Kulsat would return to Centauri; now that the Sol System beacon was revealed to them, they would be able to head there from any point in the galaxy.

The general said, "They should be arriving in five seconds. Three ... two—"

With a thought, Justine shifted to normal space.

"Stop!" she yelled.

She expected Chow Yin and the officers would be surprised at her unexpected appearance, at the very least. The moment she became a physical being, however, the general pivoted toward her. He had a phase pistol in his hand, and fired without hesitation.

The only thing that saved Justine was that she was close enough to Chow Yin that the general aim was off to avoid hitting his Emperor.

Outraged, Justine quantized him.

Chow Yin's reaction was a fraction slower than his officer's, but much more effective. He tapped a control on the console on the arm of his computer and activated a Kinemetic damper.

The entire bridge became a null zone for the Kinemetic energy.

When Klaus had used the damping technology on Justine on Venus, she'd been in physical form. The effect was that she'd been unable to shift into light, or use the energy.

The general, already in a photonic state, suffered a much different effect.

Without Justine's Kinemetic link to guide the reversal, the photons became physical, but they did not realign with the general's original form.

A mass of flesh appeared in midair, hung there for a moment, and then fell to the deck in a bloody pile. Justine gagged and looked away before she threw up.

Ignoring the dead general, Chow Yin barked an order to the nearest other crew member on the bridge. "You, put a gun on Major Turner. If she moves, kill her."

The man drew a gun and pointed it at Justine. She put her hands up.

Chow Yin pointed to another officer and yelled, "You! Get

over there and fire those damned torpedoes."

Justine looked up at the holo casement on the front wall. Another ship had entered Centauri space, and its architecture was familiar. It looked like one of the U.S. Space Corps' warships.

Just as the crewman raced to the general's station and launched the torpedoes, the U.S. warship opened fire, spraying Chow Yin's vessel with thousands of projectiles that ripped through the already damaged hull and breached the inner compartments. On the screens, the two torpedoes exploded halfway between the two ships.

The blowback rocked Chow Yin's warship. Alarm klaxons sounded. The ship was venting atmosphere.

The helmsman called out, "Sire, we must abandon ship."

"The hell you say! We can send repair crews to patch those holes. Launch more torpedoes. Their countermeasures can't possibly stop all of them. Blow them out of space. Damn it!" he yelled, and pressed a control on his console. "I'll do it myself."

The U.S. warship launched a torpedo of its own; it wasn't weaponized Kinemet, but it carried enough of a conventional blast that the force knocked everyone on the bridge back. Chow Yin started to tip over, and the self-styled Emperor fought to keep his balance.

Some of the electrical systems were going offline because of the widespread damage. To Justine's amazement, one of those systems had been powering the Kinemetic damper. Her power came back to her in an abrupt rush, and she didn't waste a moment.

She quantized everyone on the bridge.

∞

The U.S. ship was launching another volley of projectiles. In a panic, Justine raced for the communications console and looked for the radio controls. From her days at NASA, she remembered which emergency channels the military used during conflicts, and hoped they had not changed protocol.

"U.S. vessel, this is Major Justine Turner aboard the enemy ship. I have secured the bridge. Cease fire. Cease fire. I repeat: I have secured the enemy bridge." She tried two more channels before she received a reply.

"Major Turner, this is General Gates. Verify your identity."

"Recall code: seven-alpha-seven-five-five-alpha."

"Verified."

Justine breathed a sigh of relief. "Welcome to Centauri, General."

"It was quite the welcome," the general said wryly. "What is your status, Major?"

"Chow Yin and the bridge officers are quantized. The ship itself is badly damaged; it may not be salvageable. There are at least a dozen wounded, several dead."

The general said, "If you have access to the internal communications, inform the crew to surrender and prepare to be boarded."

"Understood, General." Before Justine complied with the orders, she asked, "Do you mind if I ask, who is the Kinemat on your ship?"

"I'll let you talk to them yourself," the general said.

"Them?"

A moment later, a very familiar voice came over the speaker. "Justine," Alex said, "I have so much to tell you."

"You're all right," Justine said, feeling the weight of worry lift from her heart. Then she asked, "Wait a minute. You're a full Kinemat?"

"Sort of," Alex said. "It's a long story."

Justine shook her head in wonder, even though no one could see her. "You're going to have to give me the condensed version. We have another problem. Moments before you arrived, Chow Yin was engaged in battle with a Kulsat warship, and he managed to wound it enough that it retreated."

The general came back on the radio. "Are we expecting it to return with reinforcements?"

"No, General, it's much worse: The Kulsat armada has at least a hundred-thousand warships. They are now aware of Sol System, and their standard response will be to send an invasion fleet there and destroy everything and everyone they consider a threat. I'm afraid they are not open to negotiation. How many Kinemats do we have?"

"Counting Alex and you," the general said, "Four."

Four? Justine wondered.

She could hear the apprehension in his voice when the general asked, "Do we have any allies who will intervene?"

"The situation is dire," Justine said. "The Kulsat are the dominating force in the galaxy. The Collection of Worlds cannot stand up to them. And even if they could, they hold to an ancient law which prevents them from interfering. I'm afraid we're on our own, General."

"We're almost to you, Justine. We'll secure the enemy ship and transfer the prisoners."

"Don't forget the Kinemet," she said. "There are several kilotons here."

"Right. Then we can go into a thorough debriefing."

∞

Alex and Michael were waiting in a large conference room just off the bridge, and Justine could barely contain her emotions. It had been less than two months since she'd seen them, but it felt like a lifetime.

Standing up and throwing his arms around Justine, Alex said, "You gave us all a scare. We thought the worst."

"I'm alive," she said, and gave him a wide smile. "I'm so glad all of you are all right."

"Thanks to Ah Tabai and Aliah," Alex said, and then formally introduced everyone to each other. Aliah excused herself to contact Naila aboard the *Fainne* and give them an update.

Justine shook hands with the Gliesan of Mayan descent. "I've been spending quite a bit of time with Yoatl."

Ah Tabai raised his brows and formed a guilty smile. "I'm sure he'll have a few choice words for me when I get back."

Justine narrowed her eyes at Alex. She could sense the change in him. "You have to tell me how you managed to complete the Kinemetic conversion. It's not something anyone else in the Collection has been able to do."

"You won't believe it," Alex said, smiling.

"Try me." Then Justine said, "Better yet, start from the beginning."

They all sat down at the conference table.

Alex told his story, beginning from the moment Justine had been abducted by the Kulsat mining ship. He updated her on the political upheaval in Sol System, Chow Yin's Emperorship, and the research into rediscovering Klaus's process.

Michael took over the story then, explaining about the ancient tale of Yaxche's friend, Patli. When she heard this, Justine quickly filled them in on what she knew about it, confirming that it had happened as it was told to them.

"It was touch and go," Michael said after describing his research on the alien body they found, and how the Grace's DNA was infused with molecules of altered Kinemet.

"While they brought me into space quickly enough to stop

me from dying, we got word to a double-agent in Chow Yin's organization—he managed to inject Alex with Kinemet before a conversion trial. Of course," he said, glancing at Ah Tabai, "apparently that wasn't the actual reason Alex entered the state of Grace."

Justine put her hand on Alex. "However it happened, I'm glad you are altered. According to what I learned, those who fail the conversion process have a shorter life expectancy. You don't have to worry about that, now. Quite the opposite, in fact."

Alex said, "I have many questions for you. Like how you survived the Kulsat ship."

Justine let out a humorless laugh, and she told them what had happened to her, about the Kulsat and how Red Spot saved her from Three Crescents. Then she described her rescue by Naila and Fairamai, the journey to Gliese, and the events leading up to her residency and political appointment as Envoy of Sol System.

Partway through her story, General Gates entered the room. He'd been busy overseeing the transfer of prisoners from Chow Yin's ship, and directing his crew to effect repairs. He sat at the conference table and listened in.

"Political envoy, huh?" the general said when Justine finished. "It's too bad you can't use your influence to rouse the Collection."

"I got the process started, but it could take a while before they give Sol System 'Emerged' status."

"So what do we do, just sit here while our solar system is destroyed?" he asked, his tone more exasperated than accusatory.

"Maybe not." All through Alex's story, Justine had a nagging thought in the back of her mind. To Alex, she said, "Red Spot's advice might still stand. She said we could make the Kulsat surrender to us if we found the final component first."

"How?" Alex asked.

Justine gave him a quizzical look. "Are you up for an experiment?"

"Sure. What are you thinking?"

"Back when we were chased out of Sol System—by Chow Yin, apparently—he launched a torpedo with weaponized Kinemet. I was able to ignite it before it reached us."

Alex nodded. "I did that earlier, when Chow Yin tried to destroy Qin Station." His face grew dark. "I couldn't stop his second attack, however."

"I wonder if you, having the full powers of the Grace, have something more than that, concerning the Kinemet."

"You want me to blow up every Kulsat ship with Kinemet on it?" Alex asked, his face pale. "Even if I could, I don't think I would."

"No," Justine said, shaking her head. "But there's something about the way Red Spot talked about the Grace that led me to believe they had an ability that inspired even more awe."

"More than setting off a Kinemetic explosion a thousand-times more powerful than any atomic bomb?" Michael asked.

Justine turned to the general. "Do you have a small quantity of Kinemet we could use?"

He nodded and spoke into his communicator.

While they waited, Justine described the techniques she had learned from Red Spot: how to hide her photonic essence while in a state of light, and how to resist being quantized. To test it out, Alex quantized himself, and a moment later, Justine was unable to sense his presence. A few moments later, he reappeared in physical form. She tried to quantize him, and couldn't.

"Very interesting," Alex said. "I can see how these techniques came in handy, letting you get close to Chow Yin."

"I think there might be an extension of these techniques that only someone who is fused with Kinemet can perform."

"How do you mean?" Alex asked, and looked up as a lieutenant entered the room with a container holding a milligram of Kinemet.

"If someone threatens you with force, a natural reaction is to either defend yourself or go on the offensive. However, if you know someone has the power to take your power away, render you useless, you can neither defend yourself, nor fight. Perhaps this is what the Kulsat fear the most, being at the complete mercy of every other race in the galaxy."

"What do you want me to do?"

"Alex," Justine said, "I'm not sure how you would go about it, but can you try to nullify the radiation from that sample?"

"Nullify?"

The general cleared his throat. "That gram of Kinemet represents a considerable amount of money."

"It'll be worth it," Justine said, then turned to Alex. "If you can make Kinemet inert, you might be able to disable any Kulsat ship."

"I'll try," Alex said, and focused his concentration on the Kinemet. Justine kept her attention on it as well, and cried out in delight when she sensed the radiation in the sample dissipate completely.

Ah Tabai, who had remained quiet through the reunion, gasped. "You did it. You are, indeed, one of the Grace. The first in a millennium."

"So we can disable their ships?" the general asked, giving Ah Tabai an uncertain glance out of the corner of his eye.

"Yes." When she noticed the general frowning, Justine asked, "What's wrong? This is good news."

"We have one ship going up against how many, a hundred thousand?" the general said. "Even with this ability, Alex can only do so much. The Kulsat will swarm him. We don't have the time to convert enough Kinemats to give the Kulsat pause, at least not before they obliterate us."

"I might have an idea," Alex said. He turned to Justine. "You mentioned earlier that the Collection had tried to take the fight to the Kulsat home world once before."

Ah Tabai answered. "Yes. We all know the story. Their entire armada returned within a short time and destroyed the invading force."

Justine squinted at Alex. "If we were able to lure them all back to their home system, you really think you'll be able to nullify their ships as they enter Kulsat space?"

"Like the Battle of Thermopylae?" Michael asked, and turned to Alex. "As the general said, there's only one of you, and a hundred-thousand of them. No matter how fast you can nullify the Kinemet on their ships, all it takes is one conventional missile, and they've won."

"And the general is right," Alex said. "A hundred-thousand ships is a lot. There's no way I can nullify all of them."

"I don't think you have to," Justine said. "Once word reaches their leaders that one of the Grace is disabling their armada, they will surrender in order to preserve what they have. Why do you think they were subservient to the Grace for so long?"

"Now, wait a minute." The general gave them all a hard stare. "I can't authorize this kind of action. We need to return and transmit an update to my superiors—we only had a mandate to follow Chow Yin and apprehend him. And we've done that.

"Any further action needs to be sanctioned. We don't have the right to make unilateral decisions concerning the fate of Sol

System, let alone the galaxy. I can't just let you 'invade' another solar system. Not to mention that we have to bring Chow Yin back to Earth for trial—everyone there needs to know he is in custody."

"General," Justine said, "there is every possibility that Sol System could be under siege at this very moment. I hate to sound cliché, but these are desperate times. Correct me if I'm wrong, but the ranking officer in any theater of operations has the authority to determine their individual force's plan of action should he not have the opportunity to receive orders from their superiors. The Kulsat invasion is impending, if not already underway. We need to take those desperate measures to give Sol System a fighting chance."

"Well..." the general said finally, "it *will* draw them away from attacking Sol, temporarily at least. That might give someone time to get back to Sol with this information to create more advanced Kinemats like Alex." He cocked his head. "You realize that it's a suicide mission."

"If you can get Chow Yin's ship patched up," Alex said, obviously making an effort to keep his voice steady, "I'll do it."

Justine said, "I'll go with him."

The general shook his head. "No. First of all, Chow Yin's ship would require nine months in dry dock. Secondly, we can't afford to sacrifice both of you. Besides, you're already established in the Collection of Worlds' political sphere. If we get through this, we're going to need you in that capacity."

"With all due respect, General," Justine said, "I don't think the entire Kulsat armada will return to their home world because of one broken-down Earth ship with a single Kinemat on board."

"And you think they will feel more threatened with two?"

"No, they won't," Ah Tabai said. Everyone in the room turned to stare at him when he added, "But they might take notice if their home world is being invaded by twenty-thousand ships."

"Twenty-thousand?" Michael asked.

"Yes. That is approximately how many Sentinels there are in the galaxy." He glanced at Aliah, who nodded her agreement. "Our ships are small, but we have experience out-flying the Kulsat battle-cruisers. I will send word out to everyone."

Justine gave him a long look. "What about the ancient law? The Collection would never condone this action."

Ah Tabai smiled. "We are not going to interfere in the evolution of Sol System. Our purpose is to protect the galaxy from the Kulsat." He looked at Alex. "And to follow the rule of the Grace."

Taking a deep breath, Justine looked at the general. "Do you have a better plan?"

Slowly shaking his head, the general said, "No."

"All right, then." Justine stood up. "What are we waiting for? Let's get this war party started."

43

USSF Warship *Liberty*:
Centauri System :

Assuring them the repairs required before they could be underway to Gliese would be quick, General Gates left Alex, Michael, Justine, Ah Tabai and Aliah in the conference room with a final admonition.

"You realize that I'm giving you a lot of leeway here. I fully expect a thorough briefing at some point."

Michael nodded to him. "You have my word. Once this crisis is behind us, we'll ensure you have all the information you need, General."

Once the officer was gone, Alex turned to Ah Tabai, and gestured to Michael. "I'm not sure what's happening to him. He was exposed to a Kinemetic blast."

Michael quickly explained what had happened with the alien body on Earth. When prompted, he outlined the story Patli had told him.

"We are all under great stress when we are within the gravity well of a planet," Ah Tabai explained. "The Xtôti—the species of being whom, until now, were the only race to ascend to the Grace—were much more sensitive. They had technology far beyond anything we've been able to achieve. They could manipulate the Aetherock a hundred ways, making it a thousand times more powerful than anything we have. One of the side effects of this was the altered Aetherock's extreme sensitivity to sunlight and fire. The radiation from the altered Aetherock is what affected those villagers so many hundreds of years ago, and what is affecting you now, Michael."

"So how do we heal him?" Alex asked.

"We don't." When everyone gave him a puzzled look, he said, "We merely complete the process. He must undertake the conversion. If it is successful, then he will become an Aetherbeing, like the rest of us."

Alex asked, "Could that have been a solution for me all along?"

Ah Tabai shrugged. "Yesterday, I would have said yes. Now, however, I am not certain. You are Grace, after all. There is an unknown factor remaining in your case. Perhaps your initial exposure on the asteroid when you were a child was unique, in some way. Once we are past this crisis, we can explore your condition in greater depth."

Michael cleared his throat. "The Grace thought it better not to share the technology." He gave Alex a stern look. "Maybe you should think long and hard before going down that path."

Ah Tabai immediately bowed. "Of course, the decision will be entirely up to the Grace. As Galactic Law prohibits us from sharing technology until a system has Emerged, I expect the Grace will follow the same philosophy, and withhold knowledge until we have met a greater standard."

Alex, looking uncomfortable with the notion of all that responsibility, gestured to Michael. "So, all we have to do is prime some Kinemet and expose him to it after it activates?"

Michael cocked his head. "I hope you have a conversion chamber nearby … Chow Yin blew up our only one."

"We have a facility at our aerie in Gliese," Ah Tabai said, "but that won't be necessary this time."

"It won't?" Michael asked, glancing back and forth between Ah Tabai and Aliah, who made an odd ruffling motion with her neck feathers.

Pointing to Alex, Ah Tabai said, "In addition to all the techniques shared by Aetherbeings, the Grace has always had the ability to initiate the Aether process themselves."

"What?" Alex asked. "How?"

"Do you know how to quantize people?" Ah Tabai asked.

Nodding, Alex said, "It was something that just kind of occurred to me. I did that to get everyone to Pluto."

"Unlike other Aetherbeings, you have altered Aetherock in your molecules. You do not require a conversion chamber. Perhaps, if you think about it, the Aether process will come naturally to you."

Michael stood up and faced Alex. "If you think you can help me…"

Getting to his feet, Alex squared off in front of Michael and seemed to be considering him for a very long time. Then, just when Michael thought the answer would elude his young friend, Alex's face lit up.

"Of course!" he said, and quantized Michael.

Unlike the previous times Michael had been rendered into a photonic state, this time he retained complete awareness of his surroundings. He was a floating cloud of light. The sensation was beyond anything he'd ever experienced or imagined before in his life.

Like a child who just discovered how fun it was to splash in a puddle of mud, Michael pushed his essence around the conference room. He reached out with his senses and saw the three stars in the Centauri System. Though there were no planetary bodies, there were millions of large asteroids scattered throughout the system. He, somehow, was able to sense their exact location in relation to where he was.

Like a powerful lighthouse, the star beacon glowed bright beside him; and, to a lesser degree, he could detect thousands of other beacons scattered throughout the galaxy.

The ship itself was a living thing to him, thrumming with electricity, and Michael could feel the electrons pulsing like veins and arteries. Instinctively, he knew he could reach out with his senses and manipulate that electricity, if he chose.

So, he thought, *this is what it feels like? I never want to stop!*

But, there was much more to do.

With a thought, he returned himself to physical form.

Justine glanced at Ah Tabai. "Do you think this will be enough proof that we are Emerged? We need to practice some of our techniques."

The Sentinel nodded. "As far as I am concerned, Sol is an Emerged system. Certainly, it will be ratified. It is a minor breach of protocol, but the techniques may be necessary to prevent you from harming yourselves or others."

Over the next few minutes, Ah Tabai gave Alex and Michael a crash course in being a Kinemat—or, Aetherbeing, as they called it. The Kulsat called them Risen. Michael wondered if every species in the galaxy had different names for the same thing.

Michael learned how to quantize inanimate objects without Kinemet; how to hide his photonic signature; how to resist being quantized, and the theory behind using the star beacons.

Just as they were finishing the lessons, General Gates entered.

"All systems are operational—it's not pretty, but it will do." He looked at each of them in turn, his gaze lingering a little longer on Aliah. "Have we all caught each other up to speed so far?"

"We're ready," Justine said, and then addressed all of them in the room. "There are quite a few people I can't wait for you to meet."

44

Any alien ship that appeared unexpectedly in Gliesan space had a matter of seconds before the patrol ships guarding the star beacon would attack them.

Naila and Fairamai would have already reported the details of the battle between the Kulsat and Chow Yin's forces, and that Alex and the other Solans were on their way, but Ah Tabai said it was better to follow protocol. The moment the *Liberty* entered Gliese space, Ah Tabai transmitted his identity through the communications system, as well as who he'd brought with him.

Moments later, the return message came through from Commander Analock. The translator on the ship was not yet programmed with the Gliesan language, so Ah Tabai let them know what the reply was.

"We acknowledge our Solan neighbors. Welcome to Gliese System. Please remain at your current position and refrain from additional broadcast until we update central command."

To Ah Tabai, General Gates asked, "What can we expect?"

"The majority of Gliesan government responses are dictated by a rigorous set of laws and protocols," Ah Tabai said. "As with many Emerged systems, we consider ourselves under a constant state of siege. Though no Kulsat ship has invaded our system in over a hundred years, no one knows what might prompt them to take notice and launch a surprise attack; it's happened before. Our protocols are in place to give our system advance warning in that event. Once central command is made aware that we are not hostiles, we'll be formally invited to visit to Skanse Aerie, which is our main diplomatic hub."

"It's an incredible station," Justine said. "You'll no doubt be astounded by the representatives of the different star systems." She smiled at Michael. "If you thought international politics were difficult to navigate, interstellar politics not only deal with different languages and cultures, but different biology. The ambassador from Mebsuta System is physiologically similar to a sea anemone; his mouth is also his anus, and they do not consider public defecation to be socially unacceptable. It can sometimes be unsettling for other cultures, like ours, to interact with his species."

"I imagine so," Michael said, his eyes wide.

The general interrupted. "How long will it take their commander to respond?"

"Very soon," Ah Tabai said. "But it will take us a little time to fly there. Once we are cleared, I will contact the Committee of Sentinels and begin to organize them."

Looking back and forth between Michael and Justine, the general said, "If they're anything like our military, this mobilization could take a bit of time. What if the Kulsat attacks Sol before we organize?"

Justine nodded at the question. "From my experience, the Kulsat are a highly structured hierarchal society. Their report will have to go up their chain of command. Once their leaders make their decision, then they will begin preparations and invade our system *en masse.*"

Impatiently, the general asked, "And how long do you think that will take?"

Ah Tabai answered, "Historically, anywhere from one of your days to a month, depending on how much resistance they expect from the target system. Considering your criminal, Chow Yin, was able to defeat their patrol ship, they will consider Sol a high threat. They will mobilize as quickly as they can, but they will also utilize the bulk of their armada. The Kulsat believe in overkill."

Michael asked, "What if the Committee of Sentinels doesn't approve of our plan? Also," he added, "what if the governments of the Collection decide to forbid the action?"

With a reassuring smile, Ah Tabai replied, "The governments only have authority over their own systems. They can set policy for Sentinel protocol while in their systems, but the Galactic Law set by the Grace supersedes local governments. When we are in a neighboring jurisdiction, we must obey local laws. When we are in an unregulated region of space, such as the Centauri System, we need only to follow Galactic Law. I am confident, once the Committee learns of the return of the Grace—Alex—they will be enthusiastic. For the past millennium, we have strived for a way to eliminate the Kulsat menace."

Their conversation was interrupted when Commander Analock opened a communication channel with them. Ah Tabai translated:

"On behalf of the Collection of Worlds, the Gliesan Parliament extends you, General Gates, official welcome to our system. During your stay, you will not undertake to acquire our Aether technology, and you will give your oath that you will uphold all Gliesan and Galactic Laws. As your system is not recognized as Emerged, you will be granted limited access to our station and restricted from venturing outside the station-star beacon corridor. As commander of your ship, you must accept responsibility for the actions of your crew and passengers while in our system. Do you agree to these terms?"

Nodding to Ah Tabai to translate, the general said, "I do so agree."

∞

The *Liberty* wasn't nearly as fast as the *Fainne,* and the trip to Skanse Aerie took almost three hours.

In the meantime, Justine spoke to Alex and Michael at length about everything she'd read on the Kulsat, their history, and their solar system.

By the time they reached the station, Ah Tabai informed them that he'd sent word to the Committee of Sentinels, and that they'd approved the plan. With one of the Grace on their side, everyone believed history had come to a turning point.

Though most systems in the Collection had numerous Kinemats, few of them chose to join the Sentinels. Many systems did not have any representative Sentinels; uncommonly, Gliese system had four. With their membership spread out among the twenty-thousand or so Emerged systems in the galaxy, it would take some time to get the message to everyone.

The plan was to have all the Sentinels converge in Gliese, where the Grace was, and then jump to Kulsat in small waves—the only way to get into an Emerged system guarded by Aetherbeings.

The attack would take place in twelve hours.

∞

On Aerie Station, Ambassador Yoatl was at the dock to

greet the new arrivals from Sol System.

"Envoy Justine," he said. "You should not have given me such a scare." His words were tinged with remonstration, but he smiled through them. "I'm glad you are unharmed."

General Gates said, "We have a number of prisoners on board. Is it possible that we can transfer custody of them to the station while we make repairs and prepare for the incursion to Kulsat?"

"Of course," Yoatl said. "I will make arrangements. I'm sure you'll find our holding facilities more than adequate." He spoke into his collar communicator in a series of whistles and chirps. When he finished, he glanced at Justine. "Speaking of which, Red Spot has been asking after you. Once she learned that you were back in Gliese with one of the Grace, she requested a meeting with both of you."

Justine nodded. "I was hoping to see her, anyway." She turned to Alex. "Unless you need some rest, did you want to go now?"

"Absolutely."

Michael said, "If it's all the same, I was wondering if I could have some time with Ambassador Yoatl." When Justine raised an eyebrow at him, he added, "Whether we're successful in stopping the Kulsat or not, we will need to join the galactic community. I'm sure there will be a lot of protocols and procedures to becoming a member of the Collection of Worlds."

"That is a fact," Yoatl said. "It is a long, complicated process. There is much to learn." He nodded approvingly at Michael. "I will bring you to the offices of the Gliesan Councilor. That will be the best place to start."

"I know the way to the holding facility," Justine said.

General Gates looked up as a tall, imposing Gliesan approached. Military men seemed to recognize other soldiers automatically, and the general saluted.

"I'm Commander Analock," the Gliesan said, the translation coming out from his collar translator a fraction of a second later. "I am at your disposal, General." The two officers headed off to organize repairs and the transfer of Chow Yin and the other prisoners.

Yoatl pointed to the opposite end of the docking bay, at an awaiting shuttle. "It will be quicker to fly to the Councilor's offices from here. He has a private dock where we can land."

"We'll catch up soon," Justine said to Michael and Yoatl, and motioning for Alex to follow, she led him out of the docking bay and to the holding area where Red Spot waited. All the while, she gave him a running commentary of the workings of the station.

∞

Though she'd described the Kulsat in detail to Alex, she still saw his look of amazement when Red Spot swam up to the computer console to greet them.

"Justine," she said. "You are continuous."

With a smile, Justine replied, "Yes, thank you. How are you?"

"I continue as well." A moment later, she said, "The Gliesans informed us of the return of the Grace." It was difficult to tell if Red Spot was looking at her or at Alex.

Justine gestured to her young friend. "This is Alex Manez. He is the first of the Solans to attempt the Rising, and he has become one of the Grace."

Red Spot waved three of her tentacles in a rippling motion. "It is my honor to be in your presence, Your Grace."

"Please, call me Alex."

"It is not permitted to be so familiar, Your Grace."

Justine caught Alex's puzzled expression. She said to the Kulsat, "Now that the Grace have returned, we hope your Consortium will end their conflict with the rest of the galaxy. We have made plans to journey to your system and make your people aware of the Grace."

"That will never happen," Red Spot said, and Justine paled, not sure if there was trouble with the translation.

"What do you mean? You said they would surrender if we found the final component."

Red Spot said, "No, Justine. I said the only way to stop them is to find the final component. The Risen will not surrender. It does not matter if the Grace has returned. We are all well-schooled in our history and our people's enslavement by the Grace."

"Enslavement?"

"How else could it be described? We had to obey the Grace, or they would take away our ability to travel beyond our solar system."

"But," Justine said slowly, "how, then, do we stop the Kulsat?"

"I will explain." Red Spot typed on the console for a few more moments. "Until we attempt to receive the Gift, we Kulsat are slaves. To us, it will make little difference who are our masters; the Grace, or the Risen. The Risen, however, will never relinquish their status. They will die first. Finding the final component, and bringing about the return of the Grace *is* the only way to stop the Risen. Alex Manez must destroy all Kulsat Risen. Only then will the non-Risen once again swear fealty to the Grace, and begin to rebuild our society."

The pallor that came over Alex's face at the statement spoke volumes. Justine was aghast at the notion. It was tantamount to genocide. Even if he agreed to such a horrible undertaking, the obstacles just became insurmountable. Disabling hundreds or thousands of ships was one thing. Seeking out and killing hundreds of thousands—perhaps even millions—of Risen was an impossible task. Discounting the moral implications of such an action, doing so would take a lifetime.

"No," Alex said. "I won't do it. There has to be another way."

"Over the past millennium, the Risen have become completely consumed by their power. They will never stop."

Alex turned to Justine. His face reddened with rage and horror. "We need to stop the invasion. Even if I were insane enough to go through with this, there's no way I can do it by myself. Maybe if there were hundreds of us with the power of the Grace—" He shook his head. "No, it's unthinkable. If I had the knowledge to convert someone to the Grace, I wouldn't if I knew they were going to do this."

Taking a deep breath, Justine nodded. "Neither would I. It's monstrous."

While the two were talking, Red Spot continued typing. Her words came out. "There is only one way to stop the Kulsat without destroying the Risen. It is an enormous risk to us, but it is possible."

Both Alex and Justine said, "How?" at the same time.

"I will only tell you once we are in Kulsat System." When neither of the humans responded immediately, she typed again. "You must return me and my comrades to our home. This is not negotiable."

"Red Spot," Justine said, her mind racing to figure out if the Kulsat had planned this from the beginning, or whether she was playing them now, "how can we know if you are … practicing deception?"

"I will not betray my world," Red Spot said through the translator. "Neither will I betray the Grace, nor the galaxy. The only way to stop the threat of the Risen is to save Kulsat from them. Only the Grace can achieve this. For the sake of the trillions of my people who are at the mercy of the few million Risen, you must help us."

"Save Kulsat?" Justine asked. "How?"

"I will only give my knowledge to the Grace, and only once we are in Kulsat System."

Red Spot typed again. "Your Grace, will you save us?"

45

Skanse Aerie :
Gliese System :

"There's no way," General Gates said when Alex and Justine approached him and explained what Red Spot had told them.

The two found the general in the Gliesan councilor's suite. Michael and Yoatl were also there.

The general's face grew a deep shade of crimson as he spoke. "Not only are we already so far beyond my mandate that I'm probably going to be court-martialed when we get back home—if I'm lucky—but even if I had any inclination to follow through on this mission now—which would be sure sign I've had some kind of psychotic breakdown—I can't imagine the Council of Sentinels would go on what's tantamount to a suicide mission." He took a deep breath when he finished his rant, his eyes flicking back and forth between the two.

"It's not a suicide mission," Justine said, but her next words were cut off when the general raised a forestalling hand.

"First you tell me that, no matter what we do, the Kulsat won't surrender. Then you say there is some kind of secret method to stop the Kulsat—by saving them!" He shook his head in disbelief. "But the only one who knows how is one of the Kulsat prisoners, who won't tell us how unless we bring her with us." Giving Justine an exasperated look, he asked, "And you don't find anything suspicious about that?"

After the general gave Councilor Ijallanna a pleading look, the tall Gliesan ruffled his dark-gray neck feathers and said, "Officially, our government has no say in whether you undertake this action—Sentinel business is not in our purview. However, if the Sentinels are on board with this, I'm certain I can convince our security council to hand custody of our Kulsat guests to you, General Gates. After all, we have taken precautions against giving them access to any vital information on our system."

At the general's incredulous look, the councilor said, "Perhaps we should invite the Sentinels into this discussion." He strode to his computer console and spoke a few commands into it.

Within moments, the monitor flared to life. Ah Tabai stood in the frame, with Aliah, Naila, and Fairamai in the background.

"Councilor Ijallanna," Ah Tabai said. "I was just about to let you and the others know. Word has come back from the Sentinel Council. Every available Sentinel will be ready to go to Kulsat System within six hours."

"There seems to be a significant hitch in the plan, Sentinel Ah Tabai. I will let the Grace explain."

Alex took a step closer to the monitor and said, "We have information that the incursion may not convince the Kulsat Risen to surrender. Red Spot indicates that they are so power-mad, they will most likely fight to the death. There's an alternative, but we don't have all the facts. Instead of an offensive, we require the Sentinels to provide a distraction. We need to bait all Risen in the galaxy to return to Kulsat, at which point Red Spot will reveal how to stop them permanently. She won't tell us how until we are in the system, however."

Ah Tabai frowned. "Do you believe she's telling the truth?"

Alex, shooting a quick look at Justine, who nodded, said, "It might be our only option."

Taking a moment to confer with the three other Sentinels, Ah Tabai returned to the screen. "We'll need to get confirmation from the Council, but we all follow the law of the Grace. I see no reason not to follow you, Your Grace."

The general let out a deep sigh. Justine and Alex looked at him.

He gave a terse shake of his head. "I must be as crazy as the rest of you." Addressing the Councilor, he asked, "Is there any way your people can assist us in building a grapple to secure the Kulsat's shuttle to our ship?"

∞

Five hours later, Alex stood on the bridge of the *Liberty*, along with the general and his staff as they went through a final systems check. They, and the twenty-thousand sentinel ships, were in formation around the Gliesan star beacon.

Red Spot and the ninety other Kulsat were already aboard their shuttle, which was firmly secured to the *Liberty* with an electromagnetic grapple. A direct communications line was set up between the shuttle and Alex's station on the bridge. When he'd reminded Red Spot about a quantum pilot's limitation of how many beings they could quantize, the Kulsat leader had assured Alex that they were all more than willing to take that chance.

While Michael stayed on Aerie Skanse—he did not have any practical experience either as a Kinemat or as a pilot—Justine had insisted on doing her part.

"I've been training for this all my life," she'd said. "I've studied the Sentinel ships. I can fly one. You need every able body." When the general and the Council of Sentinels approved her participation, Justine hadn't been able to hide the elation from her face. Alex knew, from previous conversations, she'd never believed she would ever pilot a spacecraft again, and—he kept the dark thought to himself—this might be the last time she ever did.

Though they'd gone over the plan several times, the general reiterated it for both Alex's and Red Spot's benefit. "We'll go through the star beacon into Kulsat space last. Once we arrive, we won't directly engage the Kulsat. We'll get out of the thick of the battle, and hang back until we're certain the bulk of the Kulsat Risen ships have returned to the system.

"Alex, you will nullify the quantum drive of any enemy ship that comes close to us, and we'll retreat out of their line of fire. Once the bulk of the Kulsat armada is in the system, and Red Spot lets you know whatever it is you're supposed to do to save the Kulsat, you do it. Then we'll get the hell out of there." He shook his head in bewilderment as if he couldn't believe he was going along with the plan.

A moment later, he continued, his voice taking on a hard edge. "Red Spot, I expect you to hold up your end of the bargain."

A mechanical voice came through the bridge speakers. "I do not practice deception," Red Spot said. "Expect several waves of Kulsat. The Sentinels will meet their initial defense patrol, but they will not provide much resistance—they will alert our home planet, and then they will exit the system to call for reinforcements.

"The largest force will come from within the system. The Sentinels must hold them off for as long as possible to allow those who are outside the system to return." According to consensus, that would take anywhere up to a quarter of an hour.

The problem would come when the off-system Kulsat ships returned. The Sentinels would be trapped between two armadas.

The general asked, "And how long will it take Alex to ... do whatever it is you want him to do?"

"It will not take long," Red Spot's translated voice said through the speakers. "Before Alex saves us, you must ensure you have released our shuttle, and all non-Kulsat have exited the system. Only then will I share the knowledge with you."

Alex could hear a very low growl come from the general, and though he could sympathize with the sentiment, he trusted in Justine's judgment. Red Spot had risked everything to save her—an alien—and had given no indication that she would betray them.

"How long until the operation begins, General?" Alex asked, more to distract the officer than anything else.

The general was in constant contact with the Sentinel squadron commanders through his upgraded communications console. There were five-hundred squadrons in total. From the instant the first wave of Sentinel ships went through to the last wave, it would take nearly a quarter of an hour. The *Liberty*, with Alex as the quantum pilot, would launch a minute later. The entire time, the Sentinels would be under heavy fire. Alex didn't want to think about the potential casualties.

"If I read these monitors correctly," the general said, scanning the screens, "the first wave will quantize in thirty minutes."

"Which squadron is Justine in?"

"The last," the general said. "She told me she plans on joining the Sentinels once this is all over. For some reason, flying billions of kilometers through the vast blankness of space is more appealing to her than a cushy political assignment."

A moment later, he said, "I'm getting an alert on the screens."

"What is it?"

The general raised his head and gave Alex a hard look. "The Sentinels have a tracking sensor aimed at Sol System's star beacon. They say it's activating. The Kulsat are invading us right now."

A cold bead of sweat rolled down Alex's spine. "How many of them?"

"No idea. Could be hundreds, for all I know. The Sentinel commander is giving the word to launch against Kulsat now. He hopes the Kulsat patrol will send out the alert to their armada to return before they get too far into our system to turn back in time."

The general asked, "Are you ready for this? The first wave is engaging ... now. We're up in about fifteen minutes."

"That's too long," Alex said.

"What?"

"We need to get to Sol System right now." Alex wasn't about to stand around and wait while an armada of genocidal Kulsat Risen were on their way to Earth. He knew, even if their leaders sent a messenger to recall them, they would be too far into the system to turn around. Earth was wide open to their attack.

Before the general could say another word of protest, Alex quantized all the passengers on the *Liberty*, and all the Kulsat on the mining shuttle.

A moment later, he quantized the ship itself, and headed for the Gliesan star beacon, setting a course for *Dis Pater*.

The instant before he reached the star beacon, he was still in photonic space—an elemental being within the physical universe.

The next instant...

46

Unknown:

Welcome home, Alex.

It was the haunting voice that had been calling to him for nearly two decades, and he struggled to understand it.

Though he'd been in a photonic state a number of times, before the tragic experiment on Qin Station that had completed his transformation, he'd never been 'aware' while quantized.

Since Qin Station, he'd initiated the change in himself several times—and marveled in the awareness he had while in that state of being.

He'd never traveled using the star beacons as the quantum pilot, however. Both times, from Sol to Centauri, and then from Centauri to Gliese, Ah Tabai had been in control. When another Kinemat quantized someone, it was the only time that being would not retain awareness in the photonic state.

Alex wasn't sure what he had expected. Indeed, his thoughts had been so preoccupied with getting to Sol System that he hadn't fully anticipated what would happen. After all, everything the other Kinemats had told him was that, once they reached the star beacon, there was no consciousness during transit to the destination until after they arrived in the new system.

As far as anyone knew, the journey between beacons was

instantaneous.

Now, Alex knew different.

For him, the journey was simultaneously immediate, and of an infinite duration.

Though the physical universe contained vast stretches of emptiness, there was always a faint signature of electromagnetic radiation in all parts of space, however immeasurable it was to technological sensors.

The star beacons were not portals to another dimension, as Alice Yin had theorized.

Alex recalled the description Ah Tabai had given him before: "Outside light, the star beacons occupy the same space." Without proper perspective, that was the only rational explanation for how the star beacons existed.

His mind struggled to understand the reality, and it seemed to take eons for him to realize the truth.

The star beacons did not occupy the same space, because the place it touched did not have light, or space, or time.

The monumental artifact they called *Dis Pater* was nothing more than a physical construct, built with altered Kinemet, surrounding the star beacon.

The star beacon was an anomaly—something of a fracture in the fabric of the universe. It was the absence of the universe.

Somehow, Alex guessed, the Xtôti had not been content to travel throughout the galaxy at the speed of light. After all, it would take over fifty-thousand years to get from one edge of the Milky Way to the other. The physicists at Quantum Resources had theorized that there were countless ways to prime Kinemet, and create powerful results from the alteration.

The Grace had experimented with this a million years ago. Instinctively, he realized that one of these experiments had caused their sun to supernova. Dimly, he wondered if that reaction had caused their metamorphosis from Kinemats to the Grace...

Was it possible the Xtôti, like Alex, had no idea how they'd evolved past Kinemats and become the Grace? If they had, they would have created more Grace and not have died out. They would have continued expanding throughout the Milky Way and, possibly, ventured to neighboring galaxies.

Was Alex, truly, the last of the Grace?

If so, it was up to him to rediscover the process and repopulate the galaxy with more Grace. But how? Was there some kind of similarity between that and what had happened to Alex on Macklin's Rock?

He recalled that the first readout from the security receptacle had indicated something was coming at them at light speeds. Could that cosmic event have, indeed, happened at the same time his parents had drilled into the asteroid and exposed the deposit of raw Kinemet? Whatever had happened, it must have had something to do with the Sun itself, Alex guessed. Perhaps it had been the same kind of unexpected solar event during an experiment that had inadvertently caused the supernova of Xtôti's sun.

If the Grace had never figured it out, then how was Alex going to?

The thought came to him then: even if he could figure out how to raise someone to the state of Grace, should he? Perhaps the galaxy wasn't ready for that. Maybe there were some secrets that should be kept a mystery.

But he would have to think about it another time. After all, according to what Justine had told him, he might have an abundance of that commodity to meditate on the topic.

Right now, he needed to understand the nature of that null-space between star beacons.

The story Justine had related to him on the history of the

Grace indicated that it was after the Xtôti sun's supernova that they'd begun their outward expansion through the galaxy, creating the system of star beacons to connect individual solar systems.

As Grace, they'd figured out how to tear holes in the universe, and 'sew' the tears back together with 'threads' of altered Kinemet—which were metaphysically connected to each other, as if in a state of quantum superposition.

Traveling through the star beacons was, in actuality, traveling through rips in the universe.

The monuments themselves were incredible feats of advanced technology designed to monitor and house the 'threads'. They also had the power to shield the location of the star beacons for populated solar systems.

Kinemet was a quantum element. Using it and entering the photonic state, Alex was aware of others who were also in that state, and could sense the Kinemet in quantum drives.

He imagined, if he tried, he could also sense raw deposits of Kinemet. In a way, all Kinemet throughout the universe was connected, entangled on a metaphysical level. And the hub of those connections was in that tear in the universe; it was the center of everything.

At the same time, that existence between star beacons was the purest state of Kinemet. Alex, and all those who had achieved the state of Grace, was a creature of that element. It was fundamental to their DNA. It was such a powerful concentration of pure Kinemet, it was the closest thing to 'home' there could be for someone like Alex.

Aside from those who'd died by mishap, this is where the majority of the Grace had gone. A million years of life was more than enough time for any sentient being to exist. Alex couldn't imagine it. One-by-one, they must have made a decision to take that final voyage to the null-space outside the universe, and remain there.

Instinctively, Alex knew he could stay in that place between star beacons for eternity, and be perfectly content for the rest of his metaphysical existence. It *was* home.

But ... there was something more important for him to do than remaining there, and his conscience would not let him stay.

Sol System was in danger.

He was the only one who could save it.

47

USSF Warship *Liberty*:
Sol System :

...**he was back** in a physical state, on the *Liberty*.

"What the hell do you think you're doing, young man?" General Gates asked in a growl, though he was quickly distracted when the connection to the Sentinel fleet was lost. His communications array went silent. His second-in-command tapped a few haptic symbols on his own console, and the main casement on the bridge lit up with their current coordinates: they were in orbit around Pluto.

Ignoring the general's question, Alex quantized himself, though not to avoid reprimand from the officers. Instead, he used his photonic senses to cast out through the solar system, looking for signatures of the Kulsat Risen.

When he found them, a wave of trepidation coursed through him.

During the planning phase of their military action, the Sentinels speculated that the Kulsat would send anywhere between a dozen and a few hundred of their warships to Sol System.

Alex detected well over ten-thousand Risen, all in a photonic state racing at near-light speeds toward Neptune.

A moment later, his astonishment at the sheer number of

them passed when he wondered why they would be heading to Sol System's outermost major planet. There wasn't an occupied outpost there, only a few monitoring stations orbiting the ice giant.

Then he realized the Kulsat wouldn't know which of the planets were populated with Solans, and which were barren of life. They would have to fly from planet to planet until they found Earth, where they would begin to look for the final component, wreaking destruction on any humans who got in their way.

Elated, Alex returned to his physical form on the bridge of the *Liberty*, and informed the general that there were over ten-thousand Kulsat ships heading for Neptune.

"Its orbit is very close to Pluto's right now," he said matter-of-factly. "It's only about two-hundred million kilometers away. The quantum drive can get us there in about twelve minutes."

"What?" the general asked. "The ten-thousand Kulsat are heading for Neptune?" He seemed to realize he was just repeating Alex. "What does that mean?"

"They don't know Earth is our primary world. They need to drop out of photonic space to check each planet on their way in. I would imagine they'd take a bit of time to scan each one before heading for the next. We need to follow after them."

"And just what do you imagine we can do if we get there before they leave? One ship against ten thousand?" He spoke the number in a hoarse voice.

"We're going to send them a warning."

"A warning?" the general asked, obviously not understanding Alex's intent.

"Not from us," he said, "from Red Spot. We'll get her to alert them that the Sentinels have taken advantage of the situation and are attacking their home world."

"Ah," the general said with a light nod.

Alex opened a communications line with Red Spot and outlined his plan. The Kulsat agreed to help.

She added, "Once we have delivered the message, we must leave before they scan your ship and decide that we practice a deception."

"Understood," Alex said. "The moment we arrive in Neptunian space, you must be ready to broadcast the warning."

Red Spot replied. "Understood, Your Grace."

Alex gave General Gates a questioning look, and when he got a nod of assent, he immediately quantized the crew and ship, and flew toward the Kulsat armada.

48

Patrol Ship :
Gliese System :

Justine couldn't believe what had happened. No one expected Alex to take off to Sol System like that. The entire communications network of Sentinels was swarmed with everyone trying to figure out what was going on and what to do.

Without Alex, there was no point going to Kulsat System. They would be outnumbered five to one, and each of the Kulsat warships was heavily armed, whereas the majority of the Sentinel ships were two-person scout ships. It would be a slaughter.

Justine sat in the pilot's chair of the small vessel the Gliesan Councilor had loaned her. Though it was not designed to Sentinel standards, it had enough Kinemetic armor to absorb one or two mining laser shots. She knew her role in the invasion wasn't so much for direct combat, but to monitor Alex on the *Liberty*.

She had failed that mission even before she started.

A communications alert came through her console, and she recognized the caller's identification. It was Councilor Ijallanna. When she opened the channel, she saw Yoatl and Michael in the casement frame.

"Envoy Turner," the councilor said. "What happened?"

"I'm sorry, Councilor. When Alex heard that the Kulsat had invaded Sol System, he went after them."

"By himself? What does he hope to accomplish?"

"I'm not certain, Sir." Justine addressed Michael. "Do you think he'll try to take them all on himself? That would be suicide."

In the background, Michael looked gravely concerned. "There's only one way to find out. Someone has to go there and see what's happening."

Yoatl said, "Sol System has not been ratified as Emerged. No one is officially permitted to travel there."

Ah Tabai and Aliah had gone against protocol to take Michael, Alex, Kenny and Yaxche back there. They had only done so because they did not believe they would be detected by the Solans. Justine had learned that the Committee of Sentinels were going to launch an investigation into their actions, and they could possible expel the two from the organization for what they'd done.

Now, with practically every Sentinel in the galaxy gathered in one place, none of them would break protocol without explicit orders from their leaders. That kind of political decision would not be made unilaterally.

It was up to Justine. She wasn't a Sentinel, and the only thing stopping her was her parole to the Gliesan government.

"Councilor Ijallanna…" she said.

"Of course," he replied. "You are released from your bond. Go. Find out what's happening and return here immediately. We need to know."

Before the councilor had finished speaking, Justine quantized herself and her vessel, focusing her consciousness on the star beacon, and initiating a connection directly to Sol System.

∞

The journey from Gliese to Sol System was instantaneous, and when Justine materialized in her home system after months of being away, she felt a kind of elation in returning.

Just as quickly, the feeling left her. The space around Pluto was barren of any ships, conventional or quantum. In physical form, she could only push her *sight* out a hundred-and-fifty kilometers, but in a photonic state, she could extend her senses to detect other Kinemetic signatures throughout the solar system, provided they weren't hiding themselves.

When she quantized herself and sent her senses out, she gasped when she detected a mass of Kinemetic beings—the Kulsat!—heading directly for her.

They were coming from the direction of Neptune.

Swallowing her panic, she realized that Alex must have managed to get their attention somehow. Focusing, she saw that there was one signature ahead of the pack by a narrow margin. It had to be Alex.

They were only half a minute of travel time from the star beacon. Justine's initial impulse was to launch herself through first and return to Gliese with the news, but she willed herself to wait.

Sure enough, she detected the star beacon activating, and with the ship's sensors, saw that it was connecting with the Kulsat System. As she guessed, Alex was leading them back there.

There was one big problem with that, she knew, and felt the iron grip of panic. If Alex led them to Kulsat, he would be there by himself, caught between the thousands of pursuers and the tens of thousands of warships in the system. He would be on his own, and would not last long without help from the Sentinels.

With the star beacon activated, Justine was helpless to do anything until Alex and the Kulsat had passed through to the other solar system.

The moment they were gone, Justine activated the star beacon once more, and went through it back to Gliese.

∞

Moments after arriving, she blasted the news out for everyone to hear.

"Alex managed to lead the Kulsat back to their home system. He's there alone. We need to mobilize immediately."

Hundreds of voices flooded the communications system until the Sentinel commander sent out a squelch, silencing the chatter.

Once he had everyone's attention, he sent out the order. "Prepare to launch for the Kulsat system. First arrivals, once you are there, find Alex's signature and move in to protect him. Everyone else, be prepared for heavy fire. Ready? Launch."

Justine, barely able to get her breath, intended to go in with the first wave—damn the protocol—but the moment she quantized with the first few hundred Sentinels and oriented to the star beacon, she realized there was something wrong.

The star beacon would not activate for the Kulsat System.

After repeated attempts, all she could do was return to physical space.

Through her communications console, she heard the commander issue a statement. "Sentinels, somehow the Kulsat have completely blocked their star beacon. We are not able to penetrate it."

Justine's senses swam with the implications.

Alex was trapped in the Kulsat System with no hope of rescue.

49

USSF Warship *Liberty*:
Kulsat System:

Everything seemed to happen at once.

Upon entering the Kulsat System, Alex and the *Liberty* returned to physical space.

The patrol ships guarding the star beacon detected their presence and began to lock their weapons on the intruder.

Alex knew that he only had seconds before the Solan ship was blasted out of existence, and he was on the verge of quantizing the ship again with the intention of traveling deeper into enemy territory, but his communications console streamed a message from Red Spot.

General Gates, obviously realizing where they were, was shouting at him, but his words were lost on Alex.

The message. The secret that Red Spot knew, which no one else seemed to know. There it was on his readout, but for the life of him, Alex could not understand its meaning.

"The Kulsat did not fear the Grace only because of their ability to nullify the Gift. The Kulsat feared the Grace because they could dismantle the star beacons."

In the span of a moment, Alex's mind made several connections.

The transformation into a Kinemat extended the natural

lifespan of the affected being by a factor of two or three.

The Kulsat's natural life expectancy was about two or three years, and a Risen's average lifespan was five to six years.

The Kulsat System was on the farthest tip of one of the spiral arms of the Milky Way, eighty-seven light-years from the nearest system.

Without a star beacon, it would take a Kulsat ship generations to travel from their home system to their nearest neighbor.

The Kulsat System had no natural deposits of Kinemet. The Risen would hoard whatever Kinemet they had.

The Kulsat Risen had become self-serving, egomaniacal beings since the disappearance of the Grace. Perhaps in the future, they might evolve and be willing to make that kind of sacrifice to reconnect with the galaxy, but it was unlikely to happen for centuries.

If Alex nullified the Kulsat star beacon, he would cut them off from the rest of the galaxy, and end their threat.

At the same time, that would insulate the Kulsat from the other species of the galaxy, protecting them from any possible retribution—at least for the next century or so.

He would save the galaxy from the Kulsat, and save the Kulsat from the rest of the galaxy.

Given their nature, it was unlikely the Risen would squander any Kinemet to create more Risen. Logic and foresight rarely entered into the reasoning of power-mad beings.

"Release my ship, as you promised," came the follow-up message from Red Spot.

With how strong a personality Red Spot had, and with her exposure to other cultures, it was possible that she might become a force for revolution in the Kulsat System. If she were able to get her story out, perhaps more of the native Kulsat would rebel against the Risen. For the first time in a millennium, their culture would have a new purpose. Perhaps in a few hundred—or thousand—years, the Kulsat might mature enough as a society to be ready to rejoin the galaxy.

All these thoughts occurred to Alex in the span of a few seconds.

He didn't release Red Spot right then, however. In the midst of the Kulsat patrols, she would be in danger. Also, he needed to be certain the armada had returned to Kulsat space.

"The lead ship is firing—" General Gates began to say, but Alex quantized the ship, and pushed the *Liberty*'s quantum engines to fly at light speed for the duration of one second.

They were over three-hundred-thousand kilometers away from the star beacon when Alex returned the ship to physical space. He reached out to his console and disconnected Red Spot's shuttle from the *Liberty*.

General Gates was red-faced. It was obvious he was not used to being at the mercy of someone else's decisions, especially one who still looked like a teenager. "You will tell me, this instant, what is going on," he ordered.

Alex, making certain Red Spot's shuttle was on its way safe and sound, said, "I'm really sorry to do this to you and your crew, General, but I have no other choice."

For the last time, Alex quantized the *Liberty*. Very soon, he sensed the arrival of the Kulsat armada. Aside from any possible stragglers—mining ships in unpopulated solar systems—the vast majority of Kulsat Risen were here.

Alex focused on the star beacon.

This time, he did not do it with the intention of flying the quantum ship through it to another system.

This time, he pulled at the Kinemetic 'thread' connecting the Kulsat star beacon with the galactic network. He knew, instinctively, he could not have done that outside of the Kulsat System.

Without that 'thread', the tear in the fabric of the universe repaired itself.

The Kulsat star beacon did not exist anymore.

Alex, along with the *Liberty*, was trapped within the Kulsat system.

50

January 2197

My name is Rosalia Chiquita Hernandez, and I am the first of
my village to celebrate my one-hundredth birthday. It is a
milestone, by the standards of any human culture. Of course,
the Kinemats of Sol will live two- or three-hundred years, they
tell me. In the same breath, they also tell me that those who
have become Star Travelers are something beyond human, and
something less than gods.

My birthday is bittersweet, to me. It is also the anniversary
of my grandfather's death. Yaxche, who never liked his Spanish
name, passed away when I turned twenty. Though it has been
so long since then, I remember him and his legacy every day.
He passed the care of the Song of the Stars to me, and bade
me guard the ancient scroll. I have grandchildren and great-
grandchildren. Juan, the gentlest of them, wishes to carry on
the tradition when I pass on to Mitnal. That will be soon, I
suspect. But not yet.

I have had a very full life, and often I reflect back on my
one-hundred years.

After the Emperor's defeat on Qin Station, the coalition of nations retook the solar system within a matter of days. While the alliance that had formed for that task might have dissolved over time, the return of Major Justine Turner and Ambassador Michael Sanderson caused an interplanetary stir; they brought alien emissaries from Gliese to Sol System.

While stories of the Kulsat threat—and the destruction they could have brought—both thrilled and frightened people everywhere, it was the offer to become a member of the Galactic Collection that prompted Sol System to revolutionize its political system, since the Collection would only recognize a single centralized government from each member system.

The United Earth Corporate was disbanded, and the Solan Synergy was created. Country corporations and planetary subsidiaries were replaced with democratic cooperatives, which recognized the authority of the Synergy.

Kinemetic technology was advanced with cooperation from the Collection. With cheap space travel and access to the solar system's resources, there was a population explosion on the other planets and moons of Sol System. Even the poorer regions of Earth prospered, not just economically, but in matters of health and wellness.

It was the beginning of the Fifth World, an era of prosperity and human progress.

Every year, on my birthday, thousands of people from all over the solar system—and even a few from other species in the galaxy—make the pilgrimage to my village. Kinemats and Sentinels, who cannot bear the gravity of the planet, are present in holoform, servo-assistants projecting their images and recording the sights and sounds to send back to them in orbit around Earth.

We host a daylong celebration in honor of my grandfather and his friends, Sentinel Justine Turner and Ambassador

Michael Sanderson, who have both attended every year. We honor the fallen heroes, George Markowitz, Kenny Harriman, and all the soldiers who fought and died in the years up until the Emergence.

In the afternoon, I tell the tale of Subo Ak and the Dying God, taught to me by the wise Patli, who had no heirs.

At sunset, I recite the Song of the Stars, which was taught to me by my grandfather, in honor of the Lost Grace, Alex Manez, and the brave crew of the *Liberty*, who sacrificed themselves by leading the Kulsat armada away from Sol, and thereby saving our solar system.

This year, however, before I am able to begin the Song of the Stars, Ambassador Michael Sanderson asks to speak to the crowd before the final ceremony begins.

He stands before them, and there is much emotion in his wizened face.

"Friends, citizens of the Solan Synergy, Kinemats and Sentinels. A few minutes ago, I received word that the star beacon in Heraiea, the closest system to Kulsat, had activated, the signal originating from Kulsat System."

When he says this, there is a collective gasp from those gathered together. For decades, we were told how unlikely it was for the Kulsat Risen to attempt to cross such a vast distance. Stories of the Kulsat had endured, however, and they were considered to be the bogeymen of the galaxy.

Ambassador Sanderson holds up both of his hands to quell the crowd. "It was not the Kulsat who arrived, however. It was a century-old warship." He paused for dramatic effect. "The *Liberty* and its entire crew have returned to us, alive and healthy after eighty-seven years."

His last words were drowned out by the resounding cheer from the crowd. It was only once he had their attention again that the ambassador spoke.

"His Grace, Alex Manez, is among them.

"He is coming home."

METAMORPHOSIS

...the end of *The Interstellar Age*

About the Author :

Valmore Daniels has lived on the coasts of the Atlantic, Pacific, and Arctic Oceans, and dozens of points in between.

An insatiable thirst for new experiences has led him to work in several fields, including legal research, elderly care, oil & gas administration, web design, government service, human resources, and retail business management.

His enthusiasm for travel is only surpassed by his passion for telling tall tales.

Visit ValmoreDaniels.com